HARVEST

Chris Carrell

HARVEST

A NOVEL

CHRISTINE CARRELL

NUGGET STREAM PRESS

Nugget Stream Press
730 Highgate
Dunedin 9010
New Zealand
nuggetstreampress@gmail.com

First published 2017

Copyright © Christine Carrell 2017

All rights reserved. Without limiting the rights under copyright reserved above, no part of this publication may be reproduced, stored in or introduced into a retrieval system, or transmitted, in any form or by any means (electronic, mechanical, photocopying, recording or otherwise) without the prior written permission of both the copyright owner and the publisher of this book.

The moral right of the author has been asserted.

ISBN 978-0-473-41065-0

Cover photo © picture_lia / Adobe Stock
Back cover photo © Christine Carrell

Edited by Geoff Walker
Designed by Smartwork Creative, www.smartworkcreative.co.nz
Printed by Your Books, Wellington

For Jean and Colin

PROLOGUE

1931

MARY CURSED THE WEATHER, her lack of money and her aching arthritic hands. And particularly those men in Dunedin, who sat in offices and messed up everyone's lives with their rules, keeping their own hands clean. Too clean. Not real men at all.

She turned to the blank paper and dipped her pen into the ink bottle.

Manuka Creek

Dear Sir,

I notice by form received yesterday that applicants for occupation of Sections 9 and 33 must appear at 10am Wed 11th. As we have no train service on that day could the day of examination be altered till Thursday 12th and the hour extended till 11 or 11.30am, or failing altering day could the time of examination on Wed be extended till 11 or 11.30am to suit bus service.

"Examination," she snorted to her absent audience, stabbing the nib into the blotter. The bureaucrats went over the same ground every time the half-yearly rental came up, knowing full well there was no money. Certainly not twenty-one shillings.

She might lose the land this time.

Dunedin overwhelmed Mary. She couldn't abide the gothic Victorian edifices, shouting out the security of wealthy merchants and bankers, rich from gold discovered within ten miles of her own land – she could see water races and tunnels from the top of her hill. Leases, even on freehold land, gave no protection from miners.

Years ago her own brother had been lured away by a sluicing team. Thin and miserable, he'd turned up later with a sorry tale of his friend dying in a flooded stream. No tent could battle the cold, even with the aid of the whisky. She could have done with his help but he couldn't settle to farming. Before long he vanished again. Useless git, Mary thought to herself. But she missed him.

If she couldn't pay the lease, the Crown would take back the land and give it to whomever won the ballot. Her only hope was that no one else could pay.

Does the ballot take place on November 11th? Could you advise if there is a Land Office at either Milton or Lawrence where applicants can be examined? It is very unlikely there will be any other applicants as we hold both leasehold and freehold surrounding this block.

Surely no one in this district would take it from her. There was only cousin Neil, with more land than she had. He wouldn't – would he?

You will understand the desire for alteration of time or date is to avoid going to Dunedin the day before.

They ought to know by now she had no money for a hotel. She could stay with her sisters, but she wasn't about to tell them that. Cheaper, but bound to load her with criticisms and arguments to give up the farming. If they'd found her a man they might have done something useful. Too late now. It was the land itself her heart was attached to.

She read it over. Clear as a heifer on heat.

Yours very respectfully
Mary McLeod

She licked down the envelope and addressed it to the Commissioner of Crown Lands, the office where a pile of letters recorded her father's struggle, until his recent death.

His pipe still sat in the Toby jug on the mantelpiece. She couldn't bring herself to shift his chair from the fire; it was angled to drape wet clothes over. Several copies of the *Bruce Herald* occupied the seat, a week out of date, passed on by cousin Neil. Useful for lighting the fire; no use for reading beyond lamb prices and sale notices. Too full of everyone else's misery. The Railway Workshops putting men off. Unemployed taken to work camps, living in frozen tents.

Her father, Alexander, hadn't let them push him off this land either. The leases were his for forty years. In 1915, the crown land ranger reported that the land was stocked and partly fenced when they chased him for arrears, and that Alexander was "in comfortable circumstances".

Comfortable in comparison with swagmen maybe, or men leaving the gold tailings penniless.

So Mary's father had a lease (in fact three), a family of thirteen, meat on the hoof and vegetables in his wife's garden. It wasn't his fault his sons had been called up in 1916, to spill their blood at Passchendaele.

It wasn't his fault, he used to tell Mary, that he couldn't dig holes for fenceposts anymore, and that stock wandered off to better pastures, cousin Neil's usually. It wasn't his fault they had no electricity. Or that the washtub was cracked. Or that he had missed the sale for his sheep because young Tom had gone off to work for the neighbours who could pay him something. "What could I do?" she heard so often, believing it mostly. It wasn't his fault, he explained less convincingly, that his oats rotted in cold wet ground when he planted it against Neil's advice. Neil, the lucky bugger, injured early in the war. Shipped off to England to recuperate. Not like their boys.

But why hadn't her father transferred the lease to her before he died, owing money for meat, manure, rent, rates and goods from two stock companies? Let alone his own funeral. The Public Trust declared him bankrupt. And this block was back in the public arena. Anybody could apply. Anyone.

Mary's very bones ached with the demands of this land. Like an old marriage, she felt its seasons. It governed her moods, from the brooding haze of winter to the uplifting sparkle of sun on spiders' webs. One evening last spring she had watched a duck coaxing her young onto the pond for the first time. It was so still you could hear the ripples being drawn on the surface of the water.

Chances of a husband had slipped away. She knew Margaret Campbell hadn't approved when her son set off to the gum trees where they had "accidentally" met.

Her most vivid memory was of late summer 1915.

Geordie, too young for war, sat beside her under the tree where sheltering sheep had worn the grass away. He had loosened his boots and lain his jacket down behind her. They compared ways to skin rabbits without ruining the pelt. He told tales of riding calves bareback; she told, daringly through her fingers, of the goldminers skinny dipping in Nugget Stream.

And then he lurched towards her, lips protruding.

With a push strong enough to get a horse moving, she shoved him off. He tumbled, losing his boots, over and over until he came to rest against a snow tussock.

By then Mary was off, leaping through the bracken, over Nugget Stream, arms flailing for balance as she stepped lightly across the bog, frightening the scattering sheep on the hillside. She flopped down, puffed, where he couldn't see her.

Her heart was racing. She felt so – so alive. She imagined his face coming towards her. A handsome face in its own way: green eyes, a quick grin, a forehead sun-browned and dusty.

She'd watched him at stooking time, fast and accurate at tossing sheaves. Once a girl brought him a basket of food at dinnertime and they'd wandered off together into the trees.

Oh, why had she pushed him away?

Since her father's death she had worked with neighbouring farmers whenever they asked. She needed them more than they needed her, but some men tired before she did at tailing time, lifting heavy lambs onto the block to sear off their tails with the hot iron.

She was better off without a man. She had no intention of changing her dress, her hair or her habits for anyone.

Now, years later, all she had was her father's cousin Neil a mile and a half away. When the hand pump jammed and she couldn't get water, Neil's lad, Robert, could run errands if only his mother Alice wasn't so protective.

Even her sisters wouldn't get her off this land. They had gone to the city for men of their own. She'd told them to accept it: if 18,000 New Zealand soldiers had died in Europe, 18,000 women would never find husbands. Three remained spinsters. Bessie settled for one of the 40,000 injured. She came up on the bus sometimes with baskets of baking and beef. An orange once.

Bessie could help with the traps. Her arms were strong from cooking at the Seacliff Asylum. Mary couldn't set traps or prise them open with her warped fingers any more, but she had to show she could do something. Anything to avoid begging help from sour grapes Neil again.

She could almost taste rabbit stew.

She pushed the pen and ink back into the kitchen drawer with the shotgun cartridges and her rabbit-skinning knife. With her father's woollen trousers over her skirt, she went out to chop some macrocarpa for the fire.

In the morning she would take the horse down to the Manuka Post Office.

PART ONE

PART ONE

I

AT THE PRECISE MOMENT Mary slid off her horse, letter delivered, seven-year-old Rose sped into her Havelock North yard hundreds of miles north, dropping her bicycle and running towards the orchard. Could either the ageing solitary woman or the fresh-faced child predict that their paths would cross, one to become an irritant to the other, one a godsend, holding the resolution to an otherwise insurmountable problem? Would Rose's passage through life be in her own hands, subject to her inherited chances or to the upheavals of history beyond her control, or be determined by God himself?

"Rose! That won't do at all," came her mother's voice. Rose could never beat her. "Put your bike in the shed and come inside." Couldn't she be outside or in the packing shed? Mother had her in training. Preserves, jams, pickles. Everything a woman needed to know. But she wouldn't be a woman for ages and ages.

In the kitchen she stopped. In her chair – *her* chair! – sat one of those dirty bent men who trudged from house to house with lumpy sacks. Elbows on the table, he stared at her as he shovelled food into his mouth. Without chewing. Not that he had teeth.

Mother came out from the pantry, wiping her hands on her apron and whisked Rose outside. "Hush, hush. He's a very hungry man who hasn't eaten properly for days. Daddy's finding some work for him, so you'll be … "

"But Mother, he's sitting in my chair."

"Listen to me, young lady. No one, but no one, is more important than anyone else. And yours is a perfectly good chair to share."

Parents, grandparents, aunts were always giving her advice: above all, be frugal and make the most of it. Someone is always worse off than you.

No one likes sulkers or show-offs. Grandma Grant.

Always be on your mettle. Character is shaped by how you respond when life tosses you something unexpected. Aunty Grace.

Adults always let you know you weren't up to scratch, but you must never, never say the same about them.

Around her father, Rose hadn't a care in the world. As she wriggled onto his knee, she pointed to his open Fruitgrowers Federation magazine. "What's that?"

"That, my girl, is how to graft trees. If we put a slice from this tree with a good brain," he pointed, "into a growing tree with a poor brain, we can get better fruit."

Nothing on the page looked like a brain at all. "How does the poor brain tree know what to do with the clever piece?"

"You bandage it on until the tree thinks it belongs there. We'll try it."

"Can we play lexicon after dinner?"

Her father hummed deep in his throat. "Rosie Posie, if we want this orchard to thrive, I've a lot to learn. So that you," he said, poking her stomach, "get the best education there is." He closed the book. "Working on the land can be a disaster if you don't know what you're doing. Our first place was a disaster. We had to walk away."

"Don't you take the blame for the Resettlement Office," Mother interjected. "No amount of study could help you farm sheep where the topsoil barely covers the clay."

"Land has to be your friend, your partner. If you're in the right place, you grow to love it," Daddy said, stroking her nose. "Your mother's a maths teacher, but she's learnt about soil. And here, the soil's just right for trees."

"Watch out, children. Hot jars, burning hot," Mother shouted on Saturday morning. "When they're cool we'll make peach spirals inside." At the start of the season it had been a novelty, competing for who could fill the most jars to Mother's exacting standards, while she told stories.

"Dad wants me on the tractor, loading boxes," John said, halfway out the door.

"The horse needs grass," Andrew shouted, and followed.

"Can't I go outside too?" Rose appealed.

"In this family we have to rely on each other, my dear. Right now, there is no more important helper than you. Come on, Rose, nobody likes a sulk. Look on the bright side: you'll be glad of this in the winter. So many people are worse off than us."

At the end of the season Rose stood in the pantry in her mother's arms. "If you squint your eyes nearly shut," she said, tilting her head back into her mother's stomach, "the colours sparkle like stained glass."

Mother laughed. "It's beautiful. And you've been a great help. Just the late plums to go now."

Rose biked three miles to school alone. If Andrew had started at five, Mother would have taken them by horse and buggy, but in his words, "Me and my friends aren't going to school till we're six, cos of the Depression." Mother said everyone had to tighten their belts, even the teachers with their five per cent wage cut.

Why would anyone want to stay home from school? John too. Mother was hardly ever angry, but before Christmas, she had thumped boiled cabbage onto the plates. "I told that teacher, no child of mine gets promoted to high school at ten. It's unnatural. If he won't teach John for another year, I'll do it myself." Rose wanted to be a teacher. Teachers knew everything.

Daddy tried to interrupt. "Flo, not in front of the chil … "

"We'll show the inspector. There'll be mathematics, English literature and French in the mornings – your father can teach you engineering and biology in the afternoons."

※

While Rose packed her schoolbag, down south Mary rubbed a patch in the dirty kitchen window with the envelope she'd just opened. What was that noise? She was feeling exceptionally pleased with herself. The leaseholds were hers again; no one had contested the ballot.

The muffled swooshing came again. Noooo! "Get off me cabbages!" she yelled through the window, finding a strong voice not yet used that day. She raced out in her socks, bellowing at the cow. "Get outa m' garden, you stupid damned animal. Look at the bloody mess you're making."

Daisy looked up in slow motion, half a cabbage hanging from her foamy mouth. Mary rushed at her. Daisy rolled her neck away and loped towards the hole she had made in the manuka-brush fence, her hooves shredding the silverbeet.

In the north, Rose pumped her bike pedals as fast as she could, past the forge with the pony shoes over the door, past the buttercups, up over the little bridge, and wheee down the other side, legs stretched forward off the pedals, watching for orchard trucks with wooden boxes of summer fruit bound for Wellington. February the third, 1931, was about to become memorable for far more than the day the cow ate the vegetables.

A horse and buggy trotted past, just like the one her mother drove to her relief-teaching job, when their crop had been wiped out by disease and Daddy had had to take a part-time job in Hastings with the Fruitgrowers Federation. "Even in a good season we haven't enough trees yet for an economic orchard," he'd explained. Then a car came with the job. They hadn't expected a car for years.

Why was there always a head wind in the morning and again on her way home? Daddy had tried to tell her something about heat differentials and offshore breezes. Then he had shrugged. "Just push into the wind, Rose," he said. "You'll grow strong muscles. It's character building."

Push into the wind? Day after day?

Tired legs. Tired everything. Her marble bag slapped against her leg. Today she would win her favourite marble back from Jennifer Martin. She would.

Jennifer skipped into the bike shed as she arrived. "Hey, Rose. Bring your marbles?"

They stood on the line in the dry soil. Jennifer bowled. Just a cats-eye, not the one she wanted back. Her marble rolled past the hole but was still closer than Jennifer's. Her turn. Into the hole. Rose turned and took aim at her opponent. Glass clicked on glass.

"That's not fair," Jennifer wailed.

She went back to the line for the next throw. Her stinker. It sprang out of her fingers like quicksilver.

Jennifer rolled her next marble. Yes! The blue swirly glass one, so beautiful it was magic. She had to get it back. Had to.

Over near the flagpole, boys were battling a rugby ball. Just as she rolled her marble, their ball shot out and bounced haphazardly across the dirt. "Get out of our game," Rose yelled, hands on hips. Boys piled in as the bell rang for the start of school.

At the edge of the grass Rose saw the swirly blue along with her stinker. She picked them up. Jennifer's outstretched hand thrust into her chest. Head down, she handed back the desire of her life.

※

Across the classroom Rose checked the clock as they chanted the four times table. How many minutes till playtime? Mr Scully's voice rang out. "Rose Grant. You're on mail duty. Come and see me when the bell rings."

Her heart sank. "Yes, Mr Scully."

Rose sorted mail into the staff pigeonholes. She'd hardly finished her milk when the bell rang and classes lined up. She loved drill as long as she wasn't too close to that boy in standard six who was always having to "fall out" for not keeping time.

Elbows straight.

Left, right, left ... Suddenly Rose felt herself swaying. Mr Scully opened his mouth but no words came. Her body staggered to the right. Across the playground, the wall of the school curved left. Miss Dunbar yelled, "Lie down, lie down." A huge growling came from deep in the earth. Everywhere there was thumping, tearing, shrieking, crashing.

Rose dug her fingernails into the soil, her whole body shaking. Stay still, still. Hold onto the grass. Nothing she could see made sense. Trees smashed down behind, beside her. The sky filled with leaves and dust. Someone grabbed her. Everyone was wriggling towards Miss Dunbar, who had armfuls of children. The ground rolled beneath, and rolled again, her head tossing like a paper boat on the sea. She tumbled into Geoffrey Taylor and felt his leg tangle in her skirt. Mr Scully curled up with his arms over his head. She felt sick. Someone was crying – was it her? Screams. Another chimney crashed to the ground. Clouds of dust rolled towards them.

Then the school shrank, pouring itself into the ground like lumpy icing – was she dreaming? The school, her school, had ... disappeared into a pile of bricks.

And then she shut her eyes so tightly that she couldn't see anything and hoped it would all go away.

2

DESPITE THE HEAT, the sweltering heat, Florence had jam to make. Damson plums, the last fruit of the season. But first, it was John's second day of home schooling.

"Trace the map in as much detail as you can. Yes, I know New Zealand's fiords and peninsulas don't make it easy. Do your best." Andrew lay on the dining-room floor making a clothes peg track for his wooden cars.

In the kitchen, she shifted the jam pan directly over the firebox to hurry it along and went to get the empty jars from the pantry. Smudge followed her. All at once the cat's hair stood straight up, then fffttt, she shot out between Florence's legs. Puzzled, Florence peered into the passage after her. Wallop! Her shoulder slammed suddenly against the wall. And again. What was happening? She leaned against the wall but it too was moving. Jars fell from her arms and shattered at her feet as she battled to stay upright. A confusion of noise roared outside and in, the whole house shuddering, clattering.

She glanced back towards the noise coming from pantry. Jars of feijoas, peaches, nectarines, pickled strawberries, were crashing to the floor, becoming an oozing mass of fruit and glass splinters.

The boys, I must get to the boys, she thought, lurching along the wall towards the dining-room door. At the kitchen, she clutched the door frame. In an instant, she saw the jam pan slide across the stove and thud to the floor sending plum jam up the wall to the ceiling. The kettle spilled into the hissing fire where the pan had been over the firebox. In the next thunderous moment, she was thrust back, coughing with dust. The chimney had collapsed, bricks filling the room.

She floundered into the dining room as the heavy brass clock flew off the mantelpiece towards Andrew's head.

She froze.

John gripped the table, his mouth agape. Fractured wood and clock parts disintegrated across the floor. Andrew rubbed his ear. Florence took him in her arms, panting as the shaking stopped. John clamped himself to her back. Her hands ran over them both, as if her brain couldn't be certain that they were both still here, both still alive.

※

In this heat, Lawrie would far rather be in the orchard with his shirt-sleeves rolled up than in this stuffy office. But the job gave him a view of the orchard industry across the whole province and a sense of service supporting other young families, who loved the outdoor life as he did.

He filled his fountain pen to write the concluding paragraph of his report. Suddenly his chair wobbled, lurched. Everything tipped off the desk. His telephone crashed to the floor.

"What's happening! Ahhhh!" the secretaries screamed, grabbing their desks. The building jolted, rocked, rolled on and on. "Get out. Outside," the girls cried and headed for the front door.

"Not that way. Don't go out there!" Lawrie yelled. "The balcony's unstable. Go out the back way." He gathered papers from the floor and followed. In a cloud of dust the heavy balcony thudded to the ground, exactly where the girls would have been. As he lurched across the road to his car, the building collapsed behind him.

※

Back on Georges Road the room shook again, undulating this time. Florence hustled the boys under the dining-room table and clutched them to her, clenching her eyes shut until it eased off. Andrew started to sob. "Shhh. Shhh. It's over now. Stay here. I'll ring Daddy."

She crawled out and across the wooden floor to the far side of the room, stretching up onto her knees to turn the handle round for the operator.

"Are you there?" she shouted into the handpiece. Nothing. She turned the handle again. "Hello? Hello? Why won't anyone answer? Answer me!"

※

Rose squashed into the back seat of Mr Jackson's car with other children from Georges Road. Joyce wouldn't stop crying. Mr Jackson gripped the steering wheel, telling her to stop that caterwauling or how could he concentrate. The street didn't look right at all. Bits of wall poked from lumpy piles of bricks. Where was Mr Jo's smithy with the huge bellows and the pony horseshoes all in a row?

The straight road was cracked and twisting. Mr Jackson kept jumping out to heave branches and rocks aside. Slower and slower they moved, through puddles of water spurting from broken drains.

A man waved them to a stop. "You can't go any further, matey, there's trees blocking the road."

"I just want to go home," Rose sniffed. She needed the lav. She wanted Mother.

Mr Jackson turned the car around, the lines down the side of his neck getting redder. "Get out of the blasted way, you ignorant bloody imbecile," he yelled.

Suddenly there was a familiar car coming the other way. "Stop. It's Daddy." Rose pressed her hands against the window. Out of the car and into his arms. He squeezed her so tightly her arms hurt. "Thank God, thank God," he said, over and over.

Rose heaved the passenger door of her father's car open and wriggled into the front seat. She pulled the door shut. Safe. Safe at last.

Her father opened the door again.

"Rose, hop back into the other car. Please."

"No, I'm coming with you."

"Sorry, love, I want you to go home with the Jacksons. I have to check on Grandma."

Rose slunk deeper into the seat, gripping the edge of the leather. He would NOT make her get out. Her father stared down at her and seemed to change his mind. "Right. Thanks, George. Best of luck."

Mr Jackson shook his head and drove off.

❋

Andrew and John rushed their father as they pulled up. Mother stumbled towards the car, her arms outstretched. "Oh, praise God, you're safe," she wailed, searching the back seat. "Rose? Where's Rose?" She clutched the neckline of her dress, screwing and unscrewing the fabric. "It's brick, that school, it wouldn't withstand such a ... " Rose froze to the seat.

"Shush, my love, she's ... " Rose slammed the car door. "Rose. Don't go up those steps. Stop!" Her father dashed to the bottom of the steps, grabbed her hand and picked her up forcefully.

"Come over here. Sit down all of you." He gathered the children into his arms. "There's bound to be damage."

Rose followed her father's gaze up the concrete steps, up the white painted walls where all the windows were flung open off their catches, along the ridgeline of the roof to a big gash ... where was the chimney? Above the boys' new bedroom, the roofing iron was twisted like screwed-up paper. The walls had parted company at the corner.

"No one's to go into the house. Promise?" He eyed the children. Andrew and John nodded. "Rose?"

"Can't I just get China Doll?" she pleaded.

"Not till I get back. Sorry Florence, but Mother ... I have to go." He began stepping away.

"We'll come with you ... "

"No, no. There's chaos everywhere. I don't want the children. She may be – heaven knows. Flo? Are you listening to me?"

❦

As Rose stood at the edge of the road she could smell smoke. She'd never seen so many people outside. "Have you heard? Six people died in our grocery store," Mrs Sullivan told Mother.

How could they die?

"Jimmy Brickle says there's people with smashed arms and legs."

"That's enough, John," Mother interrupted. "We don't need the details."

"Look." Everyone turned towards Napier. The city was on fire. A huge cloud of smoke billowed towards the hills.

"It's the Masonic Hotel. My cousin's just come from there. It's spreading."

"That whole block is wooden ... "

"There'll be no water to fight it."

❦

Mother seemed calmer now, even as she clutched them through another aftershock. "Are you hungry?" she asked as it subsided. "There's cold mutton in the outside safe. Do you have your pocket knife, John?"

"I'll get plums," said Rose.

"Where's the billy?" asked Mother. "John, you're the boy scout. You could make a fire in the corner of the garden. With the chimney bricks."

The camping billy was in the garden shed next to the Thermette and the camping plates. Mother kept one foot on the doorstep and leaned in, passing them out to Rose across the jumble of tools on the floor.

They huddled together on the mattresses and bedding Daddy had hauled through open windows. Rose felt safe in her new bed as stars peeked through fading red-streaked cloud and the heat of the day sagged. Mother had reached in for China Doll and Andrew's teddy bear. Rose just wanted to be close, close enough to touch everyone. She was frightened of what might happen if she went to sleep. And she wanted to listen.

"I tried to call you. Round and round and round I turned that handle, angry with the operator for not being there. Poor thing, probably under a table or worse."

"I would have been in the car by then. The one day I park on the other side of the street, we get away with a coating of dust." He chuckled.

Silence.

"I don't know how long I sat there," her father murmured.

"What a miracle," Mother said slowly, "the kettle spilling water into the fire, seconds before the chimney collapsed through the ceiling. Without that water, we might have lost the whole house." She began sobbing. "How will we get through winter? There's not a jar left."

Rose stared at the grey silhouette of her father rocking her mother, smoothing her unpinned hair. Andrew had fallen asleep.

Silence. Then a cry in the darkness. A motorbike revving. Silence again.

"My school fell down," Rose said quietly into the darkening sky.

"Oh Rosebud. Rosebud," said her father, stretching over Mother to pull her towards them.

Rose fought to stay awake but her eyes were heavy. Her parents whispered. Anxious words rose and fell with widening spaces between. "All I wanted was to know you were safe," Mother was saying. "And your mother. Your poor mother on her own."

"Shhh."

"I don't know how long I sat in the car – I just couldn't focus. Should I go to you first, capable you? Or Rose, or Mother? In the end, the rubble dictated – I had to go the long way."

"And you found me," said Rose, alert again.

"Yes, Rosie Posie. I found you." He stretched his arm across to hold her hand.

"Stop itching me," John said.

"I'm not." Rose hadn't realised she was rubbing her toes up and down his leg. She just liked feeling him there.

"Your mother will have to live with us," Mother said sleepily.

"And sleep under the stars?" Daddy's voice. Silence. "I can still hear her feeble voice: 'Lawrie, Lawrie is that you?'"

John tittered.

"She was in bed with her shoes on. I hadn't noticed how thin she's become, but those arms reaching out from the blankets … She didn't want me to leave. Where could I take her? Luckily I caught her neighbour."

Mother started to cry again. "All my crockery," she sobbed. "The cups in the china cabinet were rattling fit to shake the pattern off. Grandmother's Royal Albert." She blew her nose. "I doubt anything's survived."

They were silent for a moment. A wail in the distance pierced the night air.

"Well, we all have," her father said.

※

In the morning, her father dragged two small tents from the shed. He hammered the pegs in hard. A really strong aftershock could still collapse them so they weren't to tie the door. The boys were to sleep in one, Mother and Rose in the other. He would sleep on a child's camping palliasse in the shed. With the door open. They would all have to use the outside dunny again.

"If that building inspector's not here soon, I'm going in," announced her father. "Come on children, what can we find to dig with?"

That afternoon, Daddy entered the uncertified house. His footsteps measured out the rooms and back again. He came out and fetched the wheelbarrow. She heard scratchy sounds of shovelling, load after load. Broken glass and preserved fruit slurped into the new orchard rubbish hole. It smelled worse than the rubbish heap at the canning factory.

He hooked up a wireless aerial outside. He didn't let them listen at first. But neighbours cycling around the cracks in the road told the stories anyway: Napier burnt to the ground, bodies dragged from rubble. The death toll over a hundred. Over two hundred.

Two hundred and sixty-four.

"Where is everyone going?" Rose asked as dozens of cars drove south with overloaded luggage racks at the rear and bundles strapped to the roofs. "They're going to find work, Pumpkin. And a safe house," her father said, putting his arm around her shoulders. "Napier will be very empty without them."

"Hey, there's Jennifer. In that car. With the suitcase on top. She still has my marble."

"And you still have your mother," he said quietly, squeezing her hand.

❧

"Good news," her father called from the front door a week later. "We're back in." Andrew roared inside past the building inspector, bouncing noisily on his bed. But Rose crept up the steps, staring at the ceiling. What if ... ? Everywhere was messy. The smell was worse than the neighbour's pigsty, only sweeter. Smudge had disappeared. Where was she?

"Stay out of the kitchen with bare feet," Mother warned. "There'll be glass." But it was hot, far too hot for shoes.

Rose couldn't feel safe inside. Mother and Daddy carried their beds onto the wide verandahs where China Doll could see the stars. "You can sleep out here," Mother said, "in your own beds. There's nothing to fall down."

In the daytime Rose watched her parents move away for Private Conversations. Sometimes Daddy had his arms around her mother. Sometimes they sat back on their hands, talking to the air. Once they stood talking with their chins and necks stretched forward and their arms waving.

Mother called her for a talk in the bedroom.

"What's the matter?" asked Andrew later, poking his head gingerly around Rose's bedroom door. Under his arm was a wooden box. Rose curled up on her bed, hugging her knees.

"I have to go to Grandma's," she muttered, without lifting her head.

"Grandma's? Why?"

"Cos I've got no school left."

"Are you going on the train?" His face lit up as he stepped into her room, across the invisible boundary, which like everything else had been broken by the quake.

Rose shut her eyes. Who cared if five thousand other school children had to go to Palmerston North too? It just wasn't fair. There was no bright side. Maybe someone was worse off than her. But if this was one of the unexpected things life tosses at you sometimes, she felt deep down that she had every reason to sulk.

"Cheer up, Rose. It's only for a little while." Andrew sounded just like his father. "I could have your room when you're gone."

"No you could not. I'll be back. Soon, in the holidays." Andrew was holding the box very, very carefully. "What's in there?"

"It's Erb. My hedgehog." Andrew had been very upset when Erb had got his head stuck in a condensed milk tin, until someone pulled it off with a picking bag.

"Does Mother know he's inside?"

Andrew shook his head. "Don't tell."

"Only if you promise to keep out of my room."

PART TWO

PART TWO

3

1939

RUSSIAN TANKS HAD BEEN POISED along the Polish border for weeks. In Britain, gas masks hung ready. And now the unthinkable: Germany had invaded Poland.

"He'll be on in a minute." Rose's father leaned towards the crackly wireless.

"We've had peace for scarcely twenty years," her mother sighed. This Sunday night, September 3, New Zealand declared war on Germany, simultaneously with Britain.

The voice of Michael Savage, ill with cancer, filled the room.

Both with gratitude to the past, and with confidence in the future, we arrange ourselves without fear beside Britain.

Where she goes, we go.

Where she stands, we stand.

Mother reached to grip her father's hand.

None of us has any hatred for the German people. The true enemy is Nazism, a militant and insatiable paganism. To destroy it but not the great nation which it has so cruelly cheated is the task of those who have taken up arms against Nazism.

Her father's eyes narrowed in concentration.

The war on which we are entering may be a long one, demanding from us heavy and continuous sacrifice of hearts and wills to a common destiny.

They stood silently for the National Anthem. "God Save the King" seemed far less rousing than it did at the pictures. "God save the lot of us," said her father and slipped out the back door.

"I hope it goes on for ages," Andrew said.

"Why would anyone think that?" Rose asked.

"Because then I'll be old enough to fly a Hawker Nimrod or that new Fairey Fox and blow up the Heinkels and drop bombs on Hitler and ... "

"Andrew. You're fourteen. Do you think this war will last four years?"

"At least it's on the other side of the world," Rose said.

Her mother gazed vacantly into the air. "I thought that once too."

※

Yet it was exciting. Boys were lining up at the army recruitment office. Girls were leaving school to sew uniforms for the troops. In the school cadets, Andrew marched with enthusiasm and energy in anticipation of going far away and getting rid of the Hun for good. As school sergeant major the previous year, John had been enthusiastic about team spirit and discipline and patriotism. Perhaps he'd already signed up in Wellington.

Somehow normal life continued. Bikes got punctures, a cousin had a baby, fruit trees bent under summer fruit and Mother said Rose was far too young to go the pictures alone with a boy.

"We've just passed ten thousand cases, Flo," Lawrie said, bouncing into the kitchen at the end of January. "What a dilemma, my dear – how shall we use such unexpected wealth?"

"Pay off the debt," Florence said.

"Get a new tractor, Dad," said Andrew.

Later her father leaned on the verandah rail and gazed over the neighbour's land. Suddenly he thumped his fist on the ledge. "I've got it. We'll buy this land they're selling, for apples and nectarines. But just through the fence, here?" He puffed out his chest. "A grass tennis court."

"A tennis court?" Rose sprang up from playing draughts on the wooden verandah floor. What was her father thinking? How could relaxation and fun matter more than money in a bank account?

This moment crystallised her understanding of her father. It made sense of the illustrated scroll she'd found in the bottom drawer of the scotch chest, written in elaborate calligraphy, partly in Maori, partly English, signed by name or thumbprint of every member of the Maori Contingent on the *Westmoreland*, their ship home at the end of the Great War. Mother said it was a rare honour, awarded for his active care and compassion as a YMCA officer. At the time, Rose had been more captivated by the fact that some adults couldn't write.

"How can you build a tennis court? Back to the books, eh Dad?" John teased.

"Of course," he laughed. "Consult the experts, then call on you." John may be home now for university holidays, but he could be called up at any time despite being rejected for having only one eye. He had taken it hard. They'd promised to find him a non-combative role. But when?

In the new year, Sundays remained as they had ever been, war or no war. Five squeezed into the car for church, windows lowered in the sultry January air. Inside the church, Rose sat with her mother fanning herself with her hymn book. Andrew unbuckled his sandals to put his feet on the cool floor. As choirmaster, her father stood in front of the choir stalls, Sunday suit buttoned, hand raised.

What a friend we have in Jesus
All our sins and griefs to bear.
What a privilege to carry
Everything to God in prayer.

John sat apart, where Lydia could slip in beside him. Girls liked John. He'd been popular in Bible Class skits. Lydia always had gruesome hospital stories for Rose when she came to Friday tea and Sunday tennis. And what a tennis player!

Rose had good friends here, but no one to make her heart sing. On the table under the trees plates of food arrived as bikes gathered against the shed. "Hey, Rose. Will you team up with George?" As long as Enid partnered Harry, she could watch him without anyone noticing. Stretched to full height, he served in a fluid, hair-tossing powerful arc, his shirt untucked, momentarily baring a triangle of naked skin. Harry showed no emotion. Nor, she thought, did she.

Sundays: church, Bible Class, tennis. Inseparable.

The signs of war were growing more difficult to ignore. But today was warm and carefree, love lingering in the shadows.

※

She woke in a sweat, a fierce pain in her groin tossing her out of bed and into her parents' bedroom.

"Rose? What is it?"

"I need a doctor."

For the next two weeks Rose lay in hospital recovering from

appendicitis. Missing matriculation exams filled her with dread. Passing was her gateway to Wellington.

"They won't make me do the whole year again, will they?" Enid, Harry and George shrugged. Harry did impressions of the senior mistress reading the exam rules. "Stop making me laugh," pleaded Rose, clutching her wound. "Go and post these for me. At least I can write to my new penfriends."

"But you can't. Penfriends aren't allowed in case of encoded messages. They could be enemy agents."

"What's all this ruckus?" demanded the ward sister. "Off the bed, young man. See the sign? Two visitors per patient. You, out." With a swish of her veil, she edged Harry towards the door. Not Harry, she wanted to shout.

Rose couldn't bear to do the year again. There had to be another way.

A month later the letter arrived. Brown, official, leaning against the salt and pepper. She sped through the words. "It's, it's that new aegrotat pass! I've got University Entrance." What luck! The first year national aegrotats had been awarded.

※

Twelve months later, at the end of 1941, more than 750 men were lost when the *Neptune* sank, mainly men from the New Zealand Division of the Royal Navy on a mission to intercept a German convoy supplying troops and equipment to Rommel's Afrika Korps in Libya. Five Napier boys died, two friends of John's. In the silent house Rose thought of Harry. Not on this ship. But where was he?

After prize-giving, Rose biked home with a leather-bound copy of *Mansfield Park* and applause for her efforts as head girl ringing in her ears. She sat on the verandah and kicked off her school shoes. "It's funny how you can get fond of a gym frock after five years," she said, "even one with darns. Let's have a bonfire and say goodbye to school clothes forever."

Rose caught a puzzling glance between her parents.

"Come and sit down," her father said. "We need to talk." Mother had an ominous look.

"My dear, your mother and I ... we don't think ... we won't be able to get you to university next year."

Not go? Rose could not take in the words.

"It's easier to recover from appendicitis than a hailstorm. Even one of just a few minutes."

What were they talking about?

"We got two hundred cases of fruit away this whole year," her mother said.

Rose knew it was low, but two hundred! How had they kept it from her?

"But I have to go! I have to!" An image appeared: friends laughing at her from the windows of the departing Wellington train.

"Two years ago we had over ten thousand cases. That's how we managed the tennis court," her mother said, pushing her hands through her hair.

Rose leaped to her feet. "Who cares about a tennis court! I need to get to university. It's not fair." She strode off to her bedroom. Why hadn't they saved the money?

A tapping sounded on her door. "Rose, can we talk? There may be a better solution than you think." More tapping. Rose flung the door wide and hurled herself back onto the bed. Mother walked to the window.

"It's not just the money. Lecturers are signing up. Student numbers are down. They're cutting courses. We want you to get there – you'll do well."

Rose snorted. "Not if I can't get started … "

"That's the plan, getting you started. We found out today that enough teachers will still be here to help you with stage one papers from Victoria University College, in English, French and Latin. Possibly history."

Rose opened her eyes. "At school?"

"I know it won't be the same, but it's not doing the upper sixth again."

Outside the window her father attacked the lawn with the rotary mower.

"You had three years at university," Rose said glumly.

"Only one. I did papers in my upper sixth too, at Wanganui Girls. Then the scholarship meant I could stay and finish three more. One year in Wellington."

Her fingers straightened the books on the shelf. "You'll get there. I promise." She leaned over to kiss Rose on the forehead. "And by the way, the tennis court cost a few gallons of petrol. People turned up with tools and time to use them."

There was no choice. The wind was full at her face again. Rose lifted one arm behind her, around her mother's shoulder, in the most fragile of caresses.

※

Resigned, Rose launched back into an additional year of school life. Andrew, as tall as her father, was still too young to be called up but John was expecting a military role, possibly on Norfolk Island, despite having only one functioning eye.

"Did you hear those women enjoying themselves in the shed today?" her mother said. "When the men come home, they'll want their jobs back." She slid another tray of biscuits into the oven. "Never underestimate how important being a homemaker is, but there is more … "

More? What could be more than sharing day and night with the man you loved? But not yet. In Rose's mind she was already in the city, finding her own way, not her mother's.

The last days before she left home in January drew her into a new awareness, a separating of herself from everything familiar. She stored the images hungrily, an assurance of permanence against the uncertainty of change. She had never noticed the shabbiness of the paint in the porch or the carpet square in the sitting room. She was newly alert to the significance of objects – the empty cup offered with raised eyebrow, her mother's gesture of readjusting the hair pins around her wound plaits at the nape of her neck, signalling satisfactory completion of one task as she refreshed her mind for the next. And the automatic stiffening of her own back as she said the Grace before dinner, an echo of her grandmother's training: "Never lean against the back of the chair. A girl needs to develop backbone without the aid of the furniture."

On the last night, ready for the train, her father took her by the elbows. His voice dropped, the tone intimate but stern. "God go with you, my girl." He squeezed her arms into her sides. "I want you to promise me one thing." He narrowed his eyes. "Stay away from alcohol."

Rose leaned back, puzzled. Most people she knew didn't drink alcohol. Who had money for it anyway? But her father was not to be taken lightly.

"Of course, Daddy. I promise."

"Let no alcohol pass these lips," he said, tapping her bottom lip with his forefinger, "and have nothing to do with any young man who would persuade you otherwise."

4

ROSE STOOD OPPOSITE KIRKCALDIE & STAINS, gazing into the canyon of tall buildings. How different she felt from her last visit in the summer of 1932, when the family came here during their Wanganui holiday. It had been too soon after the earthquake, even a year later. Those narrow buildings could crash into the crowd in a quake, they agreed in fright. And the chimneys. Just waiting to fall, sending crowds in panic along every street.

Father had held her hand tightly, as if he too needed reassurance she realised now. Mother had taken charge, coaxing them up the four flights of stairs to the smart restaurant her friend had chosen for lunch. John took everything in his stride but Rose and Andrew could not leave Wellington quickly enough.

Today sun sparkled on the glass; this was her new world.

"Not like Hastings, is it?" said Margaret, squeezing her arm. "Come on, I'll show you my favourite places." A friend from many Bible Class camps, Margaret had beaten her to Wellington by a year. They wove down Lambton Quay, dodging dark-suited men and elegantly hatted women.

According to her mother's friend in Hawke's Bay, their boarding house in Central Terrace was "a safe establishment for girls". It wasn't what Rose expected: dour Mrs Worchester, her belligerent son Albert and one-legged Uncle Jeremy. So much noise for so few people, and such tiny rooms.

Two beds. One desk.

"One of us must have no intention of working," Rose said.

"Should we roster?" laughed Margaret.

Rose had every intention of working, perhaps in the university library. They strung up a line for wet stockings and pinned photographs of Mario Lanza, Cary Grant and Fred Astaire to the walls. Margaret was about to add Peter Fraser.

"Why the Prime Minister?" Rose asked.

Margaret heaved a sigh. "Because, my dear girl, he's our only hope."

"Michael Joseph Savage did great work when we were struggling, but primary producers don't need so much government control." She could hear her mother's words.

Margaret looked sadly at Peter Fraser's portrait. "He's not bad looking behind the glasses." She tossed it onto the wardrobe shelf. "Jim gave it to me, but perhaps we should be free of politicians."

※

The first week was exhilarating, yet she felt diminished, lost in corridors, in conversations, in a world others appeared to navigate with ease. Her body had arrived but something of herself lagged behind. Within the month, lines of Keats' "Endymion" crept into the rhythm of her daily climb up the steps to the university:

Where through some sucking pool I will be hurled
With rapture to the other side of the world!
O, I am full of gladness! Sisters three,
I bow full hearted to your old decree!

Captivated by the language, she decorated the margins of her exercise books with quips from her lecturer, who tended to rebuff Keats' passion with the cynicism everyone imagined was his own jaded life. He would stretch back in his chair, toss back the long flop of his grey-streaked hair as he cupped his manicured hands behind his head and peer over his round framed spectacles. "Beware the poet, my ladies – he means not what he says. Let 'Gather ye rosebuds while ye may' forewarn you."

"That man is going far too far," her classmate Beatrice said as they pushed into the corridor. "We shouldn't have to put up with his constant innuendo."

Rose laughed. "When I decide on a man, he'll be unlike him in every way."

※

At dinner, Mrs Worchester's chatter filled the room. "I hope you appreciate your steak. 2/6 a pound that cost." Rose chewed vigorously to control her giggles. More often it was tripe. Rose would never make anyone eat tripe, especially a future husband, no matter how little money they had. You would never find your way to a man's heart with tripe.

One afternoon Rose and Beatrice became stuck in the corridor beside the Socialist Unity Party noticeboard. A familiar figure appeared before them: Teddy, round smiling face, untidy fair curls, the same much-darned jersey. "Ladies, you're just the intelligent people we need. Lend us your ears," he pleaded, squeezing his hands together deferentially, "just for one meeting. This government's destroying democracy, Rose. They've taken our presses and banned us from printing pamphlets. We can't even advertise in the newspapers, just like the pacifists."

Teddy leaned on her shoulder. "It's Christianity really, fighting for the powerless underdog. Just an hour this evening."

Beatrice looked bemusedly at Rose over her glasses, took them off and began cleaning them with her handkerchief.

"Oh Teddy," Rose said slowly. The corridor started to clear. "Sorry." They moved away. "Really Bea, who'd trust them after the European Communists signed those useless non-aggression treaties?" They came into the main foyer. "Teddy used to be part of our Bible Class. Then he joined the Catholics. I think he's even tried Buddhism."

Beatrice clutched her arm. "Come tramping on Saturday?"

※

Forty students gathered on the beach alongside a settled sea at Island Bay. "I brought Margaret," Rose said to Beatrice. "I wanted you to meet somewhere warmer than our room."

"Warm? Feel my hands!"

"Come on everyone," called Roger, the leader. Around the headland they climbed, across high ridges with an exhilarating wind whipping Cook Strait into a thunderous swell at their backs. How insignificant they were against this immense landscape. Physics and geology and art students, bonded by wind and cliffs and awe.

Perched on clumps of long grass and fallen logs, they ate sandwiches to an argument about whether the Prime Minister could lift his eyes from saving the poor to lead a country through rebuilding after the war. "God save us," exclaimed an older man.

"God? How could anyone believe in a God who allows thousands to die in war?" Roger began as they rose to move on. "Especially if your lot believe they came as gifts from God. What kind of gift is free will if so many people slaughter each other?"

"So Christians should rely on atheists to keep Nazis from taking over the world?" asked Margaret.

"Hear, hear," said Beatrice. Was Bea supporting sacrificing atheists or that they would be more militarily effective? She seemed to like Margaret.

They stopped to watch fishing boats lurching towards port, clouds of seagulls swirling behind. Rose lined Margaret and Bea up for a photograph in her box Brownie, then raced up the track after Roger while the less fit puffed behind.

"We're supposed to be exercising our minds, right?" Roger said. "Look at all the banned books – sorry, none of us can be trusted to *know* what's on the list – our censorship's tighter than England's. My politics class is even banned from reading the *Communist Manifesto*."

A friend slung an arm around him. "Aren't you comforted that the PM's protecting you from anything that would undermine the war effort? Think of the end game: Hitler gone, peace in the valleys. It won't happen without sacrifice."

Roger shrugged him off. The track narrowed, zigzagging around bluffs above a high tide. Someone started singing. *Speed bonnie boat like a bird on the wing ...*

Over the sea to Skye ... the girls joined in. Rose looped arms with her friends, as the fading light danced gold on the harbour and the ferry tied up at the wharf.

※

In the middle of the night, something made them sit bolt upright. Earthquake. Concrete cracked. Water pipes shattered. Rose rolled under her bed with Margaret, her heart racing, her whole body shaking with childhood memories. Frightened wails came from Albert in the room below and Jeremy above.

Then silence. Waiting.

"Nothing like the Hawke's Bay," Rose said boldly, edging out from the squeeze of suitcases.

The chimney was down. "What are we to do?" Mrs W exclaimed at breakfast. "There's a gaping hole in the roof, my husband gone, a useless brother … "

"I'll go up, Mrs Worchester," Margaret offered. Mrs W rolled her body out of the chair to smother her in a hug. "What needs to be done?" Margaret asked, releasing herself.

"Fix something temporary over the hole?" suggested Rose.

In the basement they found pieces of floor covering. Margaret insisted on overalls before climbing the ladder.

"A bit to your right, girlie," called Jeremy, peering upwards. "More yet."

Rose passed up the hammer and nails. "There's some tails," Margaret called down. "No, they've scurried off. Probably gone to your room, Jeremy."

He scuttled away.

※

Please don't let the university be damaged, Rose prayed as she climbed the steps. Crowds of anxious faces scanned the grand entrance. "We're all here," she exclaimed with relief to her Latin classmates. "No lectures today then?"

"Carpe diem!" Patrick and Barry shouted together.

"Oh, fiat justitia ruat caelum. So the heavens are falling." Josh leaned back, arms wide. "Let justice be done. Nunc est bibendum. Who's coming for a drink?"

"Alea iacta est," laughed Rose. "And if the die is cast. I'm off to find my friends."

Eventually the university was declared safe, but not Margaret's Teachers' College. "The university's so overcrowded," Margaret complained as they walked home late from the library. "How much longer will college students have to wait for their own space?"

"Cocoa?" Rose stepped through the front door. Jeremy jumped up from the table, something behind his back, his chest rising and falling rapidly.

"What are you doing?" Rose asked. Margaret thrust out her hand. Sheepishly he handed over a pile of pages.

"That's Auntie Nora's writing. Isn't this your brother, Margaret?"

Silence.

"Shall we call the police?"

"No. Please. Please don't," Jeremy simpered, cowering behind the chair. "I only wanted some … "

"You sneaky scumbag. Where's the rest of our mail?" Rose demanded.

Jeremy pointed to a flour bag under the table.

It was the last straw. Too close to exams to move, they decided to hang on, but Rose soon found Fairview, the Salvation Army hostel off the Church Street steps, cheap and central. As they signed in, Margaret nudged her and pointed to the house rules in the foyer.

No slacks.

No smoking.

No dancing.

"Rose, Margaret," the matron said, "you're more sensible than most of our secretarial trainees. I am giving you a comfortable room, one everyone would like, and the key," she leaned back to take it from a hook, "to the lavatory."

The lavatory? Such an honour? She dared not look Margaret in the eye.

"The rules are clear. Once we lock up for the night, girls may borrow it. But only for the lavatory. See that they come back inside, or report them immediately." She waggled a finger at them. "It is not the key to the city after dark."

※

As 1943 began, the harbour was battleship grey with ships. "I've never seen so many," said Evelyn from the university. "At least twenty, but I can't separate the rigging,"

"You're not allowed to take photographs of naval ships," said Bea. "But I won't be the only Tauranga student breaking the law. People outside Wellington have no idea, the Censorship Board's so tough."

"You'll be in trouble if you're caught," Evelyn said.

"They don't check domestic mail."

"They do," Rose said. "Mr Holland sent a letter packet from the South Island to his secretary at Parliament. It got stamped 'Opened and Passed by Censor in New Zealand'. He's utterly outraged."

"I don't know whether to tell you this." Evelyn beckoned her friends closer.

"What?" Rose and Bea said at once.

"You know the prisoner of war camp near Featherston, with seven to eight hundred Japanese?" Rose didn't know. "My uncle, he's connected to the jute mill, he said over forty Japanese were killed in a riot recently. And one guard. But the newspaper and radio weren't allowed to report it."

In her cousins' town? And never in the news?

Subdued, they cut across the grass towards the harbour. "Apparently we have sixty thousand men now in the Middle East and the Pacific. And a few women. That's almost this whole city."

"My father says the war could have been over much sooner with American help. They shouldn't have waited to be attacked," Evelyn said.

"How many lives would have been saved if it had ended after one year rather than two?" asked Rose.

"So you think it's about to end now? Rose, you're so optimistic."

※

None of her friends would admit their deepest fear: that love might pass them by. Rose thought it was just her at first, as classmates, friends, brothers sailed away. But she caught it in the eyes of her friends, fighting a deeply unpatriotic dread of being the one girl too many for the men who returned or remained behind. What sort of life would it be without a man to support her? The unspoken spectre of spinsterhood was too familiar in women at church and her own aunts, remnants of the last war. Dignified but lonely women, spending long evenings crocheting, surviving in shared housing, buried in shared graves, limited by lack of money to take much part in life beyond their own homes. She felt weighed down at the thought. All those skimping, loveless, lonely years stretching ahead. It mustn't be her.

"Have you heard about Jennifer?" asked Evelyn. "She got married to Trevor at the Registry Office last Friday. Didn't even tell her parents."

"But she's only just met him," said Pansy. "Last month. At the Bop Hop."

"Is she pregnant?" Bea asked, scanning the faces.

"Not Jennifer. Anyway, where could they ... "

"It's wartime, Rose. There's always somewhere."

❋

When the "liberty" trains brought American soldiers into the city from their Paekakariki army base, the streets became a river of green as marines flowed into hotels, milk bars, movie theatres. Rose avoided going into town by herself.

Soldiers were always sidling up: "Like some cigarettes?" "Chocolate?" "Wanna date?"

Over their milkshakes they watched as Americans flooded into the Tip Top Milk Bar. Even the raucous skinny ones sounded like movie stars. A group of black men tumbled into the next booth. Coal black. One man's palms were pink as he held his mug to his mouth. And the lips. She had never seen such lips – like plasticine sculpted to his face.

She turned away as he caught her eye.

"Hey Missy? Wanna ice cream?"

She shook her head. "No thanks."

The marines were leaning into their booth now. "What y'all doin'? Wanna join us?" Then they left.

Over the weeks, the soldiers became bolder. Marines were seen drunk all hours of the day. One afternoon Rose was edged into a doorway. An arm slid down her back, squeezing her buttocks, pulling her pelvis into him. Rose pushed his leering face away, hitting him with her satchel. His mate lumbered in. "Hey, Charlie, you're already in trouble with the sarg. Lemme have a go." Rose forced her way under his arm and escaped into the crowd, shaken.

❋

"We should be doing more than food parcels at church, Margaret." She did want to believe Americans were worth supporting. "Where could we help without being harassed? Red Cross headquarters? Americans go there to relax. We wouldn't have to converse with them from the kitchen."

"Good idea," Margaret said.

"What's that official-looking folder on your bed?"

Margaret jumped around. "Nothing. It's ... "

"Are you hiding something?"

Margaret chewed her lip and took a deep breath. "It's my other war effort."

"Eh?" Rose wriggled around to face her.

"Promise not to say a word?"

"Promise."

"There's this problem with enemy aliens. Like the two thousand Germans here. And Latvians, Czechs, Italians, Poles, Russians. Everyone gets mail – but not in English. For all we know they could be sending information about troop movements."

"So you … ?"

Margaret hesitated. "The prof thinks my Russian's competent enough. It's awful for them – they can't go back. They get hardly any news of their families."

"Do they need someone to translate French?" Rose asked half-heartedly.

"Don't think so. It's easier to find translators."

Ah, the relief.

※

Rose could see Margaret's eyelashes moving in the filtered light of the net curtain one Saturday morning.

"You awake?"

"Mmmmm."

"Why don't we go to Oriental Bay today? The military police are always at the pavilion, so we shouldn't be harassed." She pulled back the curtain. "It's so long since I had a swim."

The wind was gentle off the harbour. Under the trees, a gaggle of Americans pushed a young marine into the girls' path. Rose and Margaret crossed the road. The marines called more passionately, "Hiya honey. Over here, Babes, come on, don't you want it from a real man?" But quickly their attention switched to other girls perhaps attracted by the marines' laden pockets, the chocolate, the nylons.

"Have you heard about Betsie?" Margaret said softly as they pulled up their woollen swimsuits. Rose shook her head. "Pregnant. To Clive," she whispered. "Black … Clive."

"No. She'll have to marry him."

"She wants to marry him, Jim said, but her parents have thrown her out. His leave's finished – she won't see him for months. If ever." Margaret looked around in case anyone was listening and whispered as quietly as she could. "Should have had an abortion, her father said."

Rose stared at her, mystified.

"Jim's flatmate, he's a doctor at the hospital, he said girls are coming in every day following messy back-street abortions. I overheard them talking so they had to tell me."

"But why?" Rose asked as they walked out onto the women's section of the beach.

"Some girls take what they can, before the man vanishes, before there are too few men. Can't avoid getting pregnant. If parents kick them out like Betsie, they've nowhere to live." Margaret pulled her towel around her shoulders. "Some try to get rid of it."

"What did you mean by 'messy' abortions?"

Margaret shrugged. "I don't know exactly. There are women making money doing abortions at home. A couple of girls died last week. It's terribly hush-hush. You won't tell anyone."

"Why don't they wait till they're married like the rest of us?" Rose stretched out on her towel to warm up, but a chill had seeped through her. Children made and destroyed. What had happened to love? Why was this war getting into the very fibre of what mattered?

She waded into the water. Stretching her arms into a fast crawl, she demanded her body take her away. Back and forth, back and forth across the bay, the sleek caress of water reshaping around her, cleansing and refreshing her mind. Aware of the strength and vulnerability of her femaleness, she turned back to shore.

Alone in her room that night she held back the curtain, puzzled by the noise outside. In the darkness, two shadowy figures swirled towards the steps, their image caught between trees. The Empire Ballroom poster was no longer on the brick wall but in tattered pieces blowing along the gutters. She pushed up the sash window a few inches. Laughter and giggling floated with the figures across the street, into the shadows and out. A brief waltz between doorways, slurred singing, another couple calling as they twirled out of sight to their own dance, an American accent, and then more urgent sounds, him, her. Silence. Then him, deeper. Her, higher and uncertain, laughter gone now, a more serious tone, pleading, smothered.

Rose shut the window, cutting herself off from the Wellington that part of her envied but did not want to know. She slipped back into bed, clutching the blankets to her throat, heart beating. Eyes wide.

5

"I can't go to St John's tonight, Margaret. I have to finish this translation."

"Please come. Molly needs us."

"And I need to pass."

Margaret crossed her arms and cocked her head to one side.

Rose stared back. Then closed her book. "All right, you win. But only if we speak French all the way," she laughed, rising from her chair.

"Il y a une autre raison d'aller à l'église ce soir … "

"You want to see if Jim's back yet."

An hour and a half later, with Purcell's "Trumpet Voluntary" echoing through the church, Rose, Margaret and Molly descended the polished wooden staircase from the crowded women's side of the balcony. On Sunday evenings the church was full, but with fewer men by the week. Molly was subdued tonight, her first time back after her sister's fiancé had been shot down over Belgium.

"I'd hate to be on the wrong side of Reverend Paterson," Rose said. "That wagging finger was pointing directly at me."

"You? I was wondering whose dress I could borrow for the graduation ball," said Margaret, "while he was beseeching us to 'beware the sins of Vanity and Pride' ", this intoned in an ecclesiastical manner.

"You are the least vain person I know." Rose looped her arm through Margaret's. Vanity was selfish, self-centred. But Pride? Such an ambiguous sin. Wasn't it right to feel pride in our troops? And for parents to be proud of their children's achievements?

They huddled into their coats in Dixon Street, so dark tonight without street lights because of the blackout. Cars were blinkered, windows screened. In the supper room someone waited by the light switches until the velvet drapes were closed.

If they were quick she could get back to her French.

No one played the piano tonight out of respect for the men on today's long honours list. Across the room Mattie was making a fuss of some New Zealand men in khaki.

A single woman in her forties, Mattie had befriended Rose on her first night, regaling her with stories of the battles she had been having as a single woman clothes designer, to secure a loan. Banks demanded the loan guarantee of a man, even if the woman's business was far more promising. Despite this, Mattie believed "opportunities are right in front of our eyes as never before".

"Ah, Rose, Molly," Mattie said, striding across the room. "I want you to meet a young man who's far from home. This is Robert McLeod, my – what are we Robert? – my Aunt Marion's stepson. What does that make us?"

"More than close enough," he laughed. "Cousins roughly. Are you all from Wellington?"

Rose suddenly lost the ability to carry on a conversation. Margaret introduced them. "And what are you doing in the army?"

"I'm at Trentham."

"That's quite a distance to come to church."

He chuckled. "Mattie asked me to stay a day or two. I'm on leave."

"So you have two more days of leave?" Rose's asked casually, her voice several tones higher than usual.

"Time's up, worst luck. Back tonight. We're waiting for a ship. I'm catching the train in half an hour." Rose tried to maintain a blank face.

"Are you from the north?"

"Far from it. I live on a sheep farm south of Dunedin, well away from the city. In the hills," Robert replied with a grin.

A sheep farm. Mattie drew out the bare essentials of his life as an only child, his lack of a mother, the recent remarriage of his father to Mattie's aunt and his interest in photography, which gave him something to do on leave.

Molly knew about film. "I queued for hours the last time Kodak had film. We've almost stopped taking photographs of each other."

Mattie called them over for tea but Robert and Rose lingered. He was the most handsome man she'd ever met. Her eyes wandered over his fair curls, which stopped abruptly at the army-defined line high above his ears. He had an appealing sense of being at ease.

"Are you involved in a Bible Class?" she asked.

"I was a leader last year. I wanted to get to the national conference but … "

They had skimmed over trains, horses, bicycles, before Mattie interrupted. "We must go, Robert. I don't like driving in the rain, especially in the blackout. Rose, why don't you come for tea next Friday? Bring Margaret. Robert'll probably get leave again and the house could do with some livening up. I'm not much fun on a Friday night."

Suddenly they were out on the street, the wind at their backs, the night a chaos of city sounds and scurrying women, heads bent to the weather. Rose matched her stride with Margaret's and lifted her face to the rain as they stepped into the darkness.

6

Rose struggled with her Milton essay that week. "Paradise Lost". Paradise highly unlikely, when happiness could dissolve into a ship heading for the clouds of war. Her Friday morning lecture took forever. Back in her digs by two o'clock, she found a note from Margaret. "Sorry. Can't make it tonight. Enjoy yourself." Her kind, cunning friend.

She took the tram to Kilbirnie and got off one stop early, hoping the walk would settle her nerves. Mattie opened the door dressed in a ruffled cream blouse and a rich-blue tailored skirt.

"Come in, come in. My, you are looking attractive tonight."

"Thank you."

Mattie hung up Rose's coat. "Robert's just arrived. Come and entertain him while I finish dinner." Rose took a deep breath and smoothed the front of her dress. She checked the buckle at her waist, the handkerchief in her sleeve and followed Mattie.

"Here she is, Robert. Go through, Rose. I've left some macaroons on the sideboard," she added. "Help yourself to the lemon drink."

Robert came forward to greet her, a picture of well-polished buttons and pressed khaki, his cap folded under an epaulette. The top button of his uniform was undone and his face glowed with a welcoming smile. Everything she remembered from Sunday.

His steady grey eyes embraced her.

"So Margaret couldn't come?"

"No, she's – actually she didn't explain." And was unlikely to. "What have you been doing this week? Or is that for army ears only?"

"No. But it's rather dull. Eating, sleeping – briefly," he chuckled. "Room inspections, drill, marching for miles. Twenty miles usually. Seen more than enough of the Akatarawa Valley. I could dig you a slit trench, or scrub your cooking dixies." Rose laughed. He hadn't mentioned the things her brothers bragged about – the bayonet charges, the gun practice. "Morse code's more my sort of thing. I'm getting faster. Do you know it?"

"Just the rings on the party line at home," she laughed. "Do you have a party line?"

"We don't have a telephone."

"Our number's A– short, long. And I know SOS of course."

Robert tapped on the arm of his chair and raised his eyebrows in question.

"I should ... " But she couldn't identify the pattern as a whole.

"It's R.O.S.E!"

"Looks like I won't be taking your job then," she laughed.

Dinner was cheerful and intimate at the small round table. Rose helped Mattie carry in the lamb and vegetables, and carry out the empty dishes from the apple and rhubarb pie. Robert sat back and rested his hands on the table. Pauses in the conversation became more comfortable. They swapped family stories, though Rose realised later he had said little of his. Robert had left school at fourteen but he knew poets she studied – Robert Browning, Matthew Arnold. And he was particularly fond of Tennyson.

"You're not a Robbie Burns man then, like your father," Mattie laughed. "Aunt Marion gave him a book of Wordsworth, but she hasn't got him to open it yet. Too English for his tastes."

As Mattie slipped back to the kitchen, Robert leaned towards Rose. "Will you write to me?"

"Yes. Of course. If you like." She didn't want to sound too enthusiastic, to fall into indecent haste. And yet ... "Where can I write to?"

He took out a military-issue notebook. His lean, tanned fingers curled around the pencil as he wrote his army number and the address for the armed forces. He pressed the page into her hand. As he lingered, his face so close, all her senses were alert to him, the heat of his fingers, the indent left in her palm.

Then he pulled back. "God only knows when I'll be back. Or when we embark. It was to be tomorrow but keeps changing." He tilted his head to one side. "I have leave again on Monday. Would you like to meet somewhere?"

Mattie appeared around the door. "Robert, I've just noticed the time. Don't let Rose miss the last tram. Would you be a dear and walk her to the stop? It's so dark without the street lights." She moved around them collecting plates. "You'll have to listen for the tram – they're not easy to see with their headlights screened."

❧

Monday and Tuesday and Wednesday. Three days of missed Flaubert and Augustine's *Confessions*. Rose met the train at ten, searching amongst the khaki for his walk, his wave, excited yet alarmed at her increasing eagerness to see him.

The city was hers to show. They took the cable car to the view of the harbour, the university playing fields and her route to lectures. As clouds drooped heavily over the hills on Tuesday, she suggested they take a train. Anywhere. Plimmerton? He had a free pass. Trains were warm, intimate, her mind hypnotised by his hip against hers as they rocked around the bends, separated only by layers of cotton and wool.

Back in the city she avoided places her friends might be, not wanting anyone to break this magical feeling, or remind her of where she should be.

"I want to take you somewhere special," she said on Wednesday. "You'll have to trust me." Outside the photographer's studio on Lambton Quay he was keener than she had expected.

"It's not what I guessed, but it's a very good idea," he agreed, removing his uniform cap and smoothing down his hair. If only she could smooth it for him, twisting her fingers into the curls.

And not let him go.

"I thought your family should have a proper photo of you," she said, back in control of herself. "My present." And a large chunk of her allowance.

He looked at her cautiously. "What about you?"

"No need to take my photograph till graduation. Mother puts all our beach camping holiday snaps into albums, but they're nothing like this."

"I meant would you like a copy? To keep. While I'm away." It was a larger question than she wanted to answer. How could she respond without adding to its weight?

"Yes," she said. "I would." His face glowed. Embarrassed, Rose turned towards the glass window and caught him, like her, looking at the reflection of a happy couple sharing a light-hearted moment.

His turn with the photographer. "Smile, Robert," she called from the dark corner. His eyes met hers. The bulb flashed.

On Willis Street, they came to the church where they had met last Sunday. "Shall we go in?" Rose asked. Beside him in the empty church, her thoughts floated unformed, not a prayer but an inner listening voice.

"Did you sign the visitor's book on Sunday?" she asked, holding the pen. Now he would be here permanently.

She left with a sense of peace. Yet dreading tomorrow.

"Will this do us?" asked Robert in Willis Street, scanning the menu of the Empire Café in the window.

Robert settled for oysters. And questions. Had she been to the latest Lucille Ball picture? The Bolshoi Ballet? "What do you think of Sidney Holland's chances in the election?" he asked.

"Rising. Everyone says Peter Fraser's lost support. He's taken austerity measures far too far – our rations are stricter than Britain's." She took another mouthful. "Did you vote last time?"

"I'll be twenty-one in a few days," he answered.

"At the rate they're putting off the elections, you could be back first."

The waitress came with cups of tea. As he turned, his knee stroked hers under the table. "Sorry," he said softly, with no sound of regret. She pulled her leg away, crumpling her napkin. She couldn't afford to be caught off guard.

And had she met any Americans?

A week ago she would have said far too many far too crudely and that she hoped never to meet any more. The street riot should have warned everyone to keep well away. But then she had met a friend of Molly's youngest sister. Possibly more than a friend. Not a drinker, not living for the moment with girls, frustrated with the way the other marines were behaving.

"I've had enough to do with Americans to last a lifetime," she said.

Soon they were off again, along the Quay, admiring crepe dresses in the window. Next door, the cake shop display was patriotic with lamingtons of red and white and almost blue. His breath made a smudge on the window next to hers. "See the tree tomato tart?" she said.

"There, behind the chocolate whorls. Reminds me of summer Sundays at home."

And of Harry, mouth full of tart, tennis racquet in hand. Harry would be back. She was trying not to think of Robert's chances.

"Come on, there'll be something in here you'll like," she called, leading him into a cornucopia of sea chests and Japanese parasols, furs and Victorian furniture. In one corner, two yellow canaries sang in an elaborate three-tiered cage. "Listen," said Robert. They stood together in the cluttered aisle and met each other's eyes. In an instant they left the shop. Rose wanted him to take her hand and lead her away, to where bellbirds and pigeons and tui and blackbirds were alive and free.

In the thin winter sun, they climbed up to the twisted trunks and wide canopies of the pohutukawa along the edge of the cemetery. Robert spread his jacket on the mown grass. They rested back on their elbows, careful not to touch. Vehicles rushed nearby. "I wish ... " he began, but didn't continue.

There was everything to say and nothing. Rose felt her heart swell, her restraint dissolving. How could the world be so cruel?

"It's not fair, is it?" Robert said.

"Nothing is fair."

"I mean, you'll have a photograph of me, but I don't have one of you."

She laughed and reached for her satchel. "Here. Margaret and me. At the McKenzies' last month." She tore the photograph and pushed one half back into her satchel pocket. "Molly caught us eating in the kitchen before the guests arrived." He held it tenderly in both hands.

A pair of tui landed above them, the fragile branch sagging as they gorged themselves on berries. "Now that's where birds ought to be," said Robert, patting the photograph in his breast pocket. One bird hopped higher into the sunlight and sang with pure and glorious notes. Rose rolled onto her stomach and watched the tui's throat shape the sounds. This was her moment. Just a moment, but the image she would hold onto.

And when Robert's fingers intertwined with hers, she lifted her head to his kiss.

7

July 1943

ROBERT STEPPED OFF THE TRAIN into a scene he could never have imagined, as if on stage before hundreds of waving, cheering people. He adjusted his new lemon squeezer and fell into line next to Bert. Six thousand men marched towards the *Nieuw Amsterdam* towering above, past the brass band playing "Land of Hope and Glory", buoyed by the roar of the crowd and the sea of flags.

Rose was here, somewhere, not likely at the front with the pushy women, but – there! On the promised apple box. Reinvigorated, he marched automatically now, across the wharf and into the gaping hole of the ship, squeezing his kitbag and rifle along companionways and through hatches, his eyes adjusting to the low light, unable to see beyond the neck of the man in front. With a hundred other men in his mess room, Robert peered at the numbers on the bunks hanging by chains from the roof, three rows high with only two feet of vertical space between. Rows and rows of narrow bunks on pipe frames. Acres of canvas, inches of breathing space.

Robert found his berth on the top row. He heaved his kitbag and sleeping roll up over the backs of other men, jostling between elbows. Scrabbling for anything solid to hold onto, he swung up like a monkey, lost his balance and tipped himself onto the middle bunk.

"Gerroff, idiot," came from a hump of khaki as he leaned his weight away again, turned into a horizontal position and slid into the upper bunk, his face inches from a maze of pipes. At least no bulky body sagged above him. There were no portholes here below the waterline but there was a light above the neighbouring bunk; he would be able to read and write letters.

Gear stowed, he found his friends Ken and Merv. They moved more easily now through the passageways onto the deck where the band continued to play against a swelling roar. He had to find Rose. Why hadn't he planned something, like another soldier nearby sending Morse code to his girlfriend with a mirror and she replying with hers? There was Rose, holding her arms above her head, a corner of her coat in each hand, swaying in every direction, clearly not able to spot him in five or six levels of men. He opened his tunic and wriggled it up, swaying from side to side in time with her.

Suddenly Rose dropped the coat and waved at him frantically, both arms at full stretch. For a moment he wanted to leap across, push through the crowds to her. But all at once the gangway was pulled up. His wave froze, fingers bent in mid-air until the music drew him into a fragile singing of "Auld Lang Syne", blending with the voices of soldiers and friends, lovers and children, parents, brothers and sisters, workmates. The dark water between ship and shore widened with the long blast of the ship's whistle. With an enormous roar of excitement, they pulled into Wellington Harbour.

Later, on deck in the winter wind for lifeboat drill, Bert and Merv made bets on whether there was enough capacity in the lifeboats. The threat of German submarines felt too real. Robert looked down at the water. Even if he had learnt to swim, how could anyone survive that cauldron?

They lurched into a steady southerly. The ship creaked and groaned in unpredictable motion. Surge and drop. Rise and tilt. The noise in the close quarters was far beyond barracks. Already the acrid stench of seasickness was becoming nauseating. If only he could open windows and stop his stomach heaving. The roll and thrust of the ocean currents was unrelenting, swelling up and over the deck.

In the narrow aisle below, three men pushed a burly Waikato soldier up against the bulkhead, and forced whisky down his throat. It was his twenty-first birthday. No one must know it was Robert's too.

In the morning as he shaved without lather in saltwater, rumours of secret additions to their company abounded. "Reckon we had to find shelter in Akaroa. Pretty rough on the way down," Ken said between strokes. "She's steadier now."

"I reckon Scotty's right – we picked up some high-rank Germans." Robert winced at the salt stinging his chin. He half-believed his own version of the story. "We're taking them back home. Top secret."

"Why don't we do them in right now then? Save us the trouble later," Bert sneered.

"Didn't say they were soldiers. Prob'ly women," Robert said.

"Women eh? Could do with a few on board," Merv laughed and gyrated his hips.

On deck for physical training, Robert couldn't recognise the land. Usually he knew every ridge and river valley here. Suddenly, lifting and falling in the water ahead, was Green Island, off the Dunedin coast. And the distant hills of home. He thought of his father, his horse, his dog. What impact would Aunt Marion make before he returned? At least she would take care of his father. He rubbed his fingers over the pocket with Rose's photograph, her image already imprinted on his mind as the ship turned to the ocean.

※

Rose squirmed as Margaret sat down on her bed. All her friend's gentle coaxing had not lifted her spirits. "Look here, my dear friend. Robert's doing his duty. You're not going to lie here and waste a perfectly good brain." She shook Rose's shoulder. "Are you listening? This country needs good teachers."

Rose opened her eyes. "Get up, finish your degree and your teacher's certificate, in Auckland." Margaret sighed. "You might as well be useful until he comes home."

Margaret had never been so direct. Rose propped herself up on her elbow. As if lifting three times her own weight, she swung her feet to the floor.

"See you at dinner," said Margaret, patting her shoulder. She took her satchel off the chair and closed the door behind her.

Rose had to find a way to get on with life. She stood up, rubbing her eyes. A flock of waxeyes rose into a blue sky. She stepped slowly away from the window, opened a drawer and pulled out her underwear.

Nothing had prepared her for this numbness.

8

UNDER THE ELABORATE HIGH CEILING of the university library, Rose spread her books in her own pool of light. This long table, the cathedral-like hush, had been her favourite place to study, but by October she was sick of it, impatient to be home to summer and nectarines. Anything but books. Everything she studied now seemed connected to war, exploring the depths of depravity humans were capable of inflicting on each other.

The day came at last. Outside the examination room, raised voices echoed down the corridor. "How could Teddy refuse? All our brothers have gone," Pansy was saying.

"And our boyfriends," added another.

"What if everyone refused?"

A ridiculous idea. They turned to face Carrie, their classmate who rarely expressed an opinon.

"Do you want to be overrun by Japs or Jerries?" Bea spat out each word. "Teddy deserves to be locked up."

"You mean Teddy from the Socialist Union?" Rose asked.

Pansy nodded. "His wife's had cow dung thrown at her windows, and he's not even there. She has to live with it, not him. And she's got a new baby."

"Is he locked up?" asked Rose, horrified.

"No one's sure. Imagine having a conscientious objector in the family," Bea said.

"Bea! This is Teddy. He's funny and kind. Fanatical about everything, but harmless," Rose said, her voice rising. "Can't we get him out?"

"You wouldn't even be allowed to see him. With the mood out there he's probably in the safest place," said Pansy.

"If more men refused to fight, not because they were scared, Bea, but because they deeply believed it was wrong, peace would have a chance." Carrie was moving closer to Beatrice. "Peace could save us from shiploads of wounded coming home."

"You'd have all our men become conscientious objectors, because of some selfish, cowardly, idealistic nonsense that if everyone said no to this war, there would be none." Beatrice threw her hands in the air. "Let's sit back and ignore every principle of justice while millions of innocent people are overrun by the Nazis. After all, invading someone's territory and incarcerating all your outcasts, murdering and raping and looting isn't that bad."

Clapping burst out around them. "Go Bea."

Suddenly the invigilator opened the door. "Single file, please. Fill the seats on the far side first."

Rose hung back until there were only two left in the corridor. Carrie was walking away. "Carrie, don't go. You have to sit the exam." She followed her down the corridor. "Do it for George." Carrie stopped. Rose put her arms around her. "For George."

"I don't want them to see me cry." She wiped her sleeve across her eyes. "He was screaming pretty bad last night. It's the nightmares. He was discharged a month ago but we don't know what to do. I couldn't get him out of the bedclothes this morning."

"If you get qualified, you'll be much more useful to him. You've worked so hard – it's only three hours. Come on. Please, Carrie."

Had Robert thought of refusing to go? What would she have thought of him? Of course they would never have met.

We have to be in this together. We simply must win.

※

Three hours later she handed in her paper, hugged Carrie and headed to the waterfront to meet her brother.

"Had a ball," Andrew roared, as they ate their sandwiches on the grass. "Nothing better than taking a propeller apart and feel it working again. And the dances. Those Christchurch girls know how to look after us."

"Anyone special?"

"Might be. Might not." He took another bite. "No one would believe me about the Americans here. All they talked about was the government taking advantage of new laws to hide everything. I brought you something."

He extracted a crumpled piece of newspaper from his pocket. "A poem – for the poetry lover. No, hands off." He stretched his palm towards her to keep her at a distance. "It has to be delivered in proper Canterbury private school vow-els." He cleared his throat.

If you've news of our Munitions, keep it dark,
Ships or planes or troop positions, keep it dark,
Lives are lost through conversation
Here's a tip for the duration –
When you've private information,
Keep it dark.

Rose laughed. "It's a spoof, Andrew! They're poking fun."

"It's from the *Ellesmere Guardian*. So there. You may be right. It shows you can get damned terrible poetry published if it tows the party line." He bowled the screwed-up poem overarm into a rubbish bin. "What about these?" He threw her a paper bag.

"Raspberry drops. Where did you … ?"

"Keep it dark." He propped himself onto one elbow.

"Good blokes down south. No nonsense. Do anything for you." He brushed grass off his clothes, clearly impatient to get moving. Should she tell him about Robert?

"You home over summer?" Andrew asked, as they wandered along the path.

"Of course. Orchard work's Essential now. I'm looking forward to getting colour on my pasty skin. You?"

"Home tomorrow, check up on the old man while I can." He turned to look at her directly. "I can't wait to join the great escape. There's a whole world out there, though joining the Navy to fly a plane sounds daft, doesn't it?"

Rose laughed. "Trust you to choose something loud, fast and dangerous."

She was pleased for him, but did other girls feel this lethargy, this feeling of being left behind from something momentous?

They came to the intersection of their paths.

"So, it's the end of Wellington for you," Andrew said, more quietly.

Rose nodded. "One more exam and I'm on the Napier Express home."

She held him in a long hug, newly aware of his fully grown frame, her chin on his chest. Then she leaned back and thumped him. "Go and find your adventure, little brother."

She strode a few steps down the path then stopped and ran back, tears tumbling down her face. "You come back. Do you hear?"

❦

Rose poked her suitcase into the luggage rack. Across the corridor, four cadets struggled to find space for their long legs amongst their luggage. What had Robert written?

In civilian life you are appraising a person by his clothes and occupation; in the army we're all in khaki so it's personality and general conduct. We will all return as shrewd judges of character, men and women!

Still, uniform did make men attractive. Rose opened the window, kicking herself for not booking early in a non-smoker, though Andrew had said with all the troops it didn't make much difference. In her handbag were two of Robert's letters from Cairo, eight weeks en route, with blacked-out names, stamped, inspected. She had smoothed them, caressed them, squeezed them between Cicero and Dante. Almost learned them by heart.

This train was nothing like the overcrowded army trucks Robert had been confined in, flies in his eyes, his mouth. Only sandhills to look at. And the disappointing Sphinx, sitting low in a hollow, not a commanding towering figure at all. The locals he called Gyppos – "beggars, thieves and scallywags", always rushing the soldiers, trying to sell them mirrors and combs, even newly hatched chickens. What would a soldier do with chickens?

Perhaps they had left Maadi for Italy already.

For her, fresh air and fruit. It might even feel like normality though she could scarcely remember life before the war.

9

"DOING ANYTHING ON SUNDAY, ROSE?" Hadley surprised her in the Auckland Teachers College locker bay.

"Nothing notable," she replied, stowing her history notes.

"Would you like to come for a jaunt? Family's getting the old boat out, taking her over to Motutapu and out into the Gulf."

"I'd love to." She jiggled like a girl much younger than her twenty-one years. "I haven't been on a boat since I was seven, in Napier before the earthquake with Uncle Dick. It's hard to believe we sailed where the airport is now. Anyone else coming?"

"No, just you."

What a surprise. She had danced with him a couple of times at the Capping Ball back in July. Being tall, she had to take the man's role for most of the evening with men so scarce. What a relief to fall into his arms – the normality of it. Someone had mentioned that his father was a big wig in the city, something to do with the harbour.

❀

Hadley picked her up in his father's Wolseley. She saw him leap over the low picket gate and bound up to the front door of the Greenlane boarding house. By the time she landed in the hallway, Hadley had been scanned from head to toe.

"Mrs Bateman, this is Hadley Farrington. From my college class. Hadley, Mrs Bateman." Rose ushered him quickly out the front door.

The city sparkled in the fresh morning. Across the shimmering sea, Rangitoto Island rested its elbows on the water. This was something new, something full of possibility.

They pulled into the gravel drive in Herne Bay. "You live here?" she asked. The view. The house. Two storeys, leadlight windows and detailed curlicues around the eaves where bougainvillea tumbled across gables and turrets. An arm waved from an upstairs window and disappeared.

Almost immediately Hadley's mother glided across the gravel in a floral dress, a cardigan draped around her shoulders, her hair elegantly coiffured. She looked ten years younger than Rose's mother and quite unlikely, Rose reflected, to be found up an orchard ladder.

"How lovely that you could come." She held out her hand. Rose hesitated, then shook it. In her world, handshaking was only for men.

"It's kind of you to include me, Mrs Farrington."

"We always enjoy the company of Hadley's girlfriends." Girlfriend? She gulped. And not the first – nor probably the last. Had he overheard? Hadley emerged from the shrubbery stroking a white Persian cat. He was quite handsome with his floppy dark hair, warm brown eyes and ready smile, she thought. A clever impersonator of Gene Kelly. But a *boyfriend*?

Soon they were slicing through the waves of the Waitemata Harbour. Hadley and Mr Farrington unfurled sails, fitted pieces of wood into slots and looped ropes around knobs. The breeze ruffled her hair.

Could Robert be somewhere in Italy with an Italian girl in a boat, sailing to an island?

Watching the newsreel at the pictures she couldn't bear to think of Robert in Monte Cassino, that shelled skeleton of a town under the eye of the enemy in the monastery above. By now they'd be somewhere north, in the mountains in freezing winter conditions.

Why hadn't the Farrington brothers gone to war? Poor eyesight? Flat feet?

The sails filled with wind, strong and steady. The city hugged the coastline, rising over the cliffs of the northern shore. Andrew would love this, she thought. He should have a boat.

Somehow the day drifted on, the sea, the wind, the birds, cocooning the four of them in a world far from the realities of college classrooms, Mrs Bateman's or her normal church-going Sundays.

Guilt was fleeting.

Hadley was attentive, not only to her but to "Mummy", carrying baskets up the beach, checking she was comfortable on the rugs where they spread out egg sandwiches, cold beef and cheese. Cake even, with a bottle of French white wine, cooled in a rock pool. Mrs Farrington dispensed the food, Mr Farrington the wine. "A glass for you Rose?"

Her father's words felt long ago now; it was time to decide for herself. "Thank you." She would taste it. But how much? Watch Mrs Farrington.

Mr Farrington toasted the day, the city, the Teachers College. How sweet the wine was, all sunshine and freshness. Something tingled in her body. She set the glass down too fast, spilling wine into the sand.

By five o'clock they were once again in the Wolseley. She wasn't ready for this day to end and agreed quickly when Hadley suggested a drive around the coast. "Don't sit so far away," he said, patting the seat beside him. She slid across the polished leather to where his hand could find hers as they drove the wide bends of the bays.

At the front door, Hadley turned from placing her basket on the doorstep. He put one arm around her waist, the other firmly at her back. In the low light from the street he kissed her. All the sounds of the sea, the wind in the sails, the salt in the air and the sun filled her senses once more.

"Good night," she whispered, and slid inside with a flicker of her fingers. She leaned against the front door as it closed.

Kissing on the first date! Not really the first; it was just that other people were usually there. She scooped up her mail and tripped lightly upstairs. Stretched out on the bed, she grinned at the ceiling, feeling the gentle rock and sway of the boat, the car, his arms enwrapping her.

Eventually she looked at her mail. An airgraph from Robert. Her heart thumped. She put it to the bottom of the pile. One from John. Coming home. Two other armed forces letters. Friends of Andrew's.

Robert's airgraph barely filled the palm of her hand. She opened the flap.

Dear Rose

I suppose I could start "My Dear Rose" as you feel that to me now since we have shared so much in our letters. But I will save that for when we can meet face to face again. Luckily I have kept your photograph in my pocket all this time. If I had posted it on a wall it would be worn out from all the moving. I wish we were not so far apart.

Rose read the paragraph again and squeezed the letter tightly to her chest. What could he say more than this? He was alive, and he cared for her.

I have not been able to write to you lately as I have been in the military hospital in B ... for the past four weeks. I missed the last days of Cassino by being stretchered out with blood poisoning from a hand injury. I am to rejoin the forces in about a week. The meals here are the best imaginable but the local music has done as much for my recovery. I have been to two symphonies and an opera in the last week.

Surely the Germans will give up soon, so clearly are they beaten. We all hope to be home later this year.

Alive and well, Rose thought with relief. Yet he sounded weary and listless.

Was he ready for the next battle?

10

"Palmerston North," Rose said with relief. "Where are you posted? Open it."

"Whangarei."

Hadley sat back, dispirited. From the whole of New Zealand, all forty-five secondary teachers trained in Auckland. They could be sent anywhere for their last practicum.

But five hundred miles apart!

※

"You're a very different girl from the lost little one who arrived after the earthquake," Auntie Nora said once she'd settled in. "Your grandmother and I managed to convince you that the world was safe again – now look at it. From your letters, you have a few friends in the forces."

"Bible Class friends from Wellington, Cousin Eddie, they look forward to mail." She tried to sound casual. "And Robert. I met him at St John's. He's from a farm down south." She couldn't control her change of tone. Her aunt raised her eyebrows. "I don't know him very well either."

Auntie Nora was knitting socks for soldiers. In the warmth of the sitting room Rose couldn't concentrate to prepare lessons against clatter and chatter. "Is there enough wool for another pair?"

Grandma Grant had died the previous year but in her work basket were two skeins of 4-ply grey, sock needles and a tatting shuttle. "Look what I've found." Rose sat on the floor with an unfinished tatted edging. Grandma hadn't thrown it away. The memory returned: crinkly black taffeta, the warm smell of talcum powder, sitting under her arm as the shuttle flew and lace appeared. And Grandma encouraging her small fingers into making this strip, the loops far more orderly than she remembered.

"I could make this longer, to edge a cloth, or a neckline."

"Or a wedding dress?" smiled Nora. Rose laughed and shook her head. Why was she so focused on marriage?

※

"Rose, I've something to show you," Auntie Nora called from her bedroom one evening. A polished wooden box squatted on short feet, with an art deco design on the side. Rose lifted the lid. Inside was a removable wooden tray above a space large enough for blankets.

"It's magnificent."

"I want you to have it. For your linens. You need to be prepared."

"Prepared? But this is precious."

"Once, if Eddie had come back."

The penny dropped. Auntie Nora was afraid for her, afraid that Rose would face the same fate. Too few able, fit young men for all the girls who needed them.

"You're young and attractive. And who are those Whangarei letters from?"

"Auntie Nora! It's private. Oh, all right. I was going to tell you about Hadley."

※

Hadley. The window into a social Auckland lifestyle which felt not entirely real. He seemed to be both showing her off and relying on her for some kind of protection.

"Had enough of that teaching business yet, young Hadley?" friends of his father would ask. "Ready to join us in the city?"

"Teaching's a vitally worthwhile profession," Rose would interrupt, diverting attention.

Any enthusiasm Hadley had ever felt for teaching had vanished. "I'm not cut out to be a teacher," he said, tossing down his practicum report. Alongside "High level of subject knowledge in physics and mathematics", was the damning statement: "Lacks a presence in the classroom. Has difficulty maintaining discipline." She, on the other hand, had warm supportive relationships with her students, and they were sorry to see her leave.

Rose liked Hadley's father, but she couldn't work his mother out. What did she do? Certainly not cook, or garden, or clean the house, or work anywhere else. But she was out every day with a full diary. Was that what Hadley would expect of a wife?

His father's factory had expanded from making sails to sewing every canvas article the forces needed. Gas-mask bags, ground sheets, ammo bags, tents, strapping. Essential war manufacturing. Hadley claimed to have no interest in work of any sort. She cared enough to see he had to break the impasse. Soon.

"Teachers' College kept the olds happy," he said.

Rose listened quietly, leaning on her elbows in the milk bar after the others had left.

"If you're after adventure, why haven't you signed up?" There, she'd said it.

"I can't go." He shrugged his shoulders. "Heart condition."

"Seriously?"

"Might be." There was a glint in his eye. "Thought I might find a job near you."

She sat with her mouth open. "You'll be manpowered if you don't teach."

"Never." He shook his head.

What was he planning?

❦

Mrs Bateman handed her two airgraphs. "When exactly are you leaving, Rose? My daughter and her little boy need the room, with her husband taken prisoner. It could be permanent."

In her room she flicked the first airgraph open with her fruit knife. Robert had her parcel, her first-ever socks, and loved *that your hands had made every stitch*. And the gloves fitted. The last pair had given up the ghost after winter.

The whole Sigs team had shared her fruit cake during slow travel on shelled roads, sleeping on the floor of an old charcoal dump with her Robert Browning for comfort. Her own saggy springs and lumpy mattress suddenly seemed luxurious.

She tore open the second, dated the same day, only three weeks before. The padre had bought him a camera in Rome so he'd been taking pictures of grazing valleys and castle remains. What's this? *I've decided to apply to be an official war photographer again.* Wouldn't that take him closer to the front line? Oh Rob!

Arthur and Les got a dozen eggs for a 2lb tin of marmalade and 5 for a small tin of cheese, a better rate than bargaining cigarette rations.

Hungry. Always hungry. And hunkered down for winter, some not wearing proper uniform, even turning up to parade without regulation boots.

The boss arrived, looking the worse for drink. He cancelled rifles for parade and isn't following routine orders coming through Signals. We marched out of sight for a procedure talk before the vino was consumed in a very erratic discussion though not without amusement. I was about the only perfectly sober person!

Affectionately,

Robert

Rose scanned the letter for the personal bits, the heartfelt comment, the morsel for her eyes only. Nothing but a picture of a surprisingly static life. What's happening to our army?

What's happening to us?

※

"The orchard's too much for your father now," her mother said over the dishes. "At sixty-seven he's not a young man." Her mother look tired too. No wonder they were selling.

"John might have taken over," her mother continued, "but he wants to study science. So that's that, really." She heaved a sigh.

How could she let it all go so pragmatically when Rose herself felt heavy hearted? This was the only home she'd had ever known.

"There's something else, I'm afraid," said Mother, hooking her apron over the back of a chair. "Harry."

"Not ... " Her legs felt unsteady.

Her mother nodded slowly. "In Florence. Germans in retreat and still firing."

Rose pressed her hand over her mouth as her mother gathered her into her arms. "We were all fond of Harry," she said as Rose began to sob, "especially you." Her mother's hand stroked her back.

Later Rose sat on the front steps and stared at the tennis court. Was it such a short time ago that she'd followed every shift in his body, the soft look in his eyes? Harry had been a certainty in her life since they had first paddled in the waves together and planted acorns in the sand. She had assumed he would be here whenever she decided to come back.

He was supposed to be here. Here. Right here. Alive. Bloody alive.

※

Two days before Rose left to begin her teaching career, Hadley came to stay for the weekend with two friends, tenting on the front lawn. Hadley didn't have a position yet. Rose suspected he hadn't applied. She wasn't sure what she felt about him as they played doubles against his friends.

"Good bloke, that Hadley," John said.

"Good bloke, your Hadley," Andrew panted after beating him in a race around the orchard.

Rose caught her mother watching from the kitchen window as they set off for a swim.

They sat close on the riverbank, laughing and tossing sticks into the water. Rose felt relaxed in his company. Yet something was missing.

"Last one in the water's a sissy," she called, leaping up. She dived long and shallow, shutting her eyes to the sun and floating on her back downstream under the willows. Suddenly he was beneath her, lifting her out of the water, rubbing his wet nose on hers. Kissing her.

Electricity rushed up her body. His legs wrapped around her. Only water separated skin from skin, a thin veil of fabric over her nakedness, an unfamiliar hardness against her leg.

She ducked him, laughed, raced away, long strokes carrying her under the bridge, near families she knew. On the riverbank, she towelled herself down. He followed, bare feet cautious on the gravel, shaking his hair and growling like a lion. She tossed him a towel.

He came to church with them on Sunday morning, checking his watch through the sermon, unsettled in the prayers, but fully at ease afterwards with her old friends. Her mind strayed to Robert's last letter, with the padre trying to get men to a service.

Religion is still a necessary element in life. If a man can't acknowledge the Love of God then he has no anchor & no vision. Under war's conditions, men get really browned off and religion becomes a subject for foolish argument yielding nothing.

She had read his words so often; his thinking matched her own.

It's just simply a matter of comparing one who is clearly a Christian with one of the opposite order and seeing that it's faith that outshines and confounds the critics. I have declined in my fervour perhaps, but my faith I have always.

❦

Sunday evening came. Alongside her mother on the verandah, Rose waved as the car pulled away.

"Happy, Rose?" her mother asked.

"Of course, Mother. Isn't he … isn't he marvellous?" Rose said. Her mother gazed at her with a faraway look.

11

ROBERT LAY ON THE STRAW MATTRESS sharpening his pencil. What could he tell Rose about two weeks of exhaustion and hunger, being knocked flat by diarrhoea, over and over? Almost as bad as Cassino.

But nothing could be as bad as Cassino. Like rats in a rubble maze. Cold. Fearful. Bert, his sergeant, beside him at the Cassino railway station one minute, the next blown to smithereens. Robert had to shut his eyes and toss a blanket over what remained. Weeks later the image still haunted him.

How could he expect Rose to understand? He must shield her from it. He flicked over the pages of his diary for something safe to tell her.

9 April. The big day. Btys arrived at positions, taking up ready laid lines of communication. After lunch heavy bombers bombed the enemy rear echelons not far behind the front lines. They came 20 at a time dropping thousands of 20 pounders, 700 planes. Fighter planes followed them around, dive-bombers next took over, huge distant dust and smoke clouds rose to view.

Robert expelled a long breath. You had no choice – finish the job. Not what Rose should hear.

10 April. Night duty. Sigs very busy. 500 prisoners taken, every half hour a group passed our casa. Wireless people flat out all morning. Medium bombers were active all afternoon besides incessant strafing and dive-bombing.

Sun 15. Slept till 1130. On exchange 1pm to 5pm. The blossom is out, sweet fragrance in the air, miles of orchards, pears, vines, apples. It's all lovely away from the traffic and dusty roads. B Ech are camping in the orchards under canvas.

Ahh. An orchard. Sap rising. He skipped over the enemy dead, lying exposed in slit trenches, the Italians eating horse flesh. But the father in the adjacent casa, an engineer from Bologna, an organist and opera conductor? He could tell her about the music, the rich defiant singing.

25 April Wed. No sleep. The Ities hadn't settled even by 2am when I went on duty. Summer issue made today. A great crowd of refugees stayed last night, the room very hot and uncomfortable.

He turned the page. Crossing the River Po by moonlight had been a weird mixture of furious noise and yet also flowing silence, a huddle of insignificant men exposed on a pontoon, intensely aware of their utter helplessness. Ack-ack might be the last thing they ever heard.

He shut his eyes.

Turned the page.

Opened his eyes – and chuckled.

Thursday 26th April. AWOL! Word came about 9am to pack up, so we had everything ready by 10am. Waited two hours. I took a chance to photograph the Po so went 1 1/2 miles along to the stopbank and returned to 51B corner to find them gone. I hitchhiked along brigade route following our signs. Walked, rode on a motorbike, on a lorry step and eventually got them mid-afternoon. Got a rip from the Sergeant but everything is OK & the risk worthwhile.

His one small triumph, glittering like a gemstone in the mire. Would Rose laugh about taking such risk for a photograph and a momentary escape?

27 Friday. Heavy rain so no dust and fresh clean air. Yesterday the regiment was well spread out. The various batteries hadn't a clue where the rest of the show was, so swift was the advance. Artillery fired by wireless so Sigs very busy!

Six hours of concentration to keep the firing away from their own men. Recognise voices, change of plan, change of plug, keep up, keep up. Catch the shouted co-ordinates and commands.

And now hundreds, thousands, of Partisans with enemy rifles and grenades under their coats needed to be disarmed, and smartly.

He smoothed the airgraph and began.

Dear Rose,

It is very picturesque here on the river terrain, which is a welcome change after the flats …

12

ROSE LAY ON HER STOMACH and shifted the writing paper into the evening sunlight.

Dear Robert,

I hope you are safe and not too far from coming home. Thank you for the photograph of the River Po.

After more than a year, it was like writing to a ghost she couldn't quite grasp any more. Laughter floated through the window, the girls next door biking off for the night shift at the engineering factory now that women were allowed to work at night.

We've decided to put on Pygmalion at the end of the term. Many of the girls are suffering from family tragedies so I hope it can occupy their minds for a while. One of my French students will be Eliza Doolittle. Her brother is serving in France.

Sometimes, when all heads were down working, she strolled between the rows to the back of the room and just gazed at the girls, loving them (not that she would admit it), wanting for them the best of life – even little Jenny the sniffer and Geraldine the sullen one. A classroom was much like Robert's company: all-comers from the refined to the plain uncouth. It still surprised her, the way they obeyed her directions. Who was she to have such an influence in their lives? In one term they had taught her to think of herself as an adult. She didn't always want to.

I saw the newsreel of the Sangro River battle and realise how much you can't tell me in your letters. Surely you're on the home stretch now. All we can do is to make this a country worth coming home to.

Yours sincer

No, too unfriendly. She wrote over the letters: *affectionately,*
Rose

She was fed up with war. She lay back on her bed, her eyes roaming across the shelves of hat boxes, vases and stacks of photograph albums packed into this tiny boxroom. Her coat and two dresses hung from the door. If she leaned over the end of her narrow stretcher, she could find the rest of her clothes in her suitcase.

In one motion she rolled off and grabbed her coat – "Just posting a letter, Auntie. Back soon" – and dashed out the door to visit a friend with a decent spare room.

※

A standing ovation. Flowers and tears. And yet despite *Pygmalion's* huge success on the night, everyone was talking more about the imminent end to the war. Across Europe the Germans had capitulated, except in Trieste where they still refused to surrender to General Tito. He had claimed the Italian port of Trieste for Yugoslavia, seeing an opportunity to push further into Italy to the river Isonzo.

Rose hugged herself with exhausted pleasure. Holidays. She stretched out her hand to feel for the paper Auntie Nora had dropped onto her bed. Two glorious hours until the drama team clean-up.

Trieste was in the headlines again. Where Robert was. After celebrating victory in Venice, arriving there was a shock for the New Zealand troops. The border war was far from over. Thousands of anti-Fascists were rioting against the Germans in the streets. Skirmishes broke out daily between well-armed Italian and Yugoslavian partisans, Fascist and anti-Fascist.

And a grim discovery: a concentration camp with a crematorium on Italian soil. Thousands of Jews, Slavs and Italian anti-Fascists had perished here.

※

As the clock chimed ten, Rose slotted her bicycle into the empty staff cycle stand. Her footsteps echoed in the corridor on her way to the hall. In the wings she picked up the lavender stalks Pamela had tossed over everyone after curtain call.

"Miss?" Pamela stood at the bottom of the stage steps, a shadow of the girl who had commanded this room last night.

"I saw your bike. Oh Miss, Miss." Tears streamed down her face as she rushed up the steps. "Alfie, my brother Alfie. Oh Miss, he's … the war's supposed to be over. He di … while I was … Alfie's dead!" Rose reached out her arms and the girl fell towards her.

On the train a day later Rose read the letter that had arrived as she rushed out the door.

Tuesday 29 April 1945

Dear Rose,

Your letter came through a few days ago full of Christmas and summer camping.

Three months for my letter to arrive? And a month for Robert's. The time warp was confusing, distancing them; her war was over, but not his.

I walked up behind our casa with Demelia, who is nine or ten, and her mama, to inspect their thirteen new lambs. A very different breed, but they smell real enough.

It was a domestic picture of waiting, the army dispersed around village casas. And Venice, an edgy mix of celebration and wary nervousness.

Hundreds and thousands of cheering people waved to us. I hung to the back of the truck and smacked as many hands as met mine. No time for gondolas in Venice. Rebels were everywhere with looted guns.

We slept in a large storehouse with rifles ready.

"Tickets please. Tickets please." Rose held hers up and kept reading. He was moving again, north to Trieste.

Two cooks' trucks got lost but luckily we traded a cake of lifebuoy and a packet of cigarettes for six eggs. Two Battery blokes lent us a primus and pannikin, so we managed poached eggs on toast.

In the evening I went along to the local hall where there was a huge crowd at a dance, about 30 girls, a piano and an accordion.

Of course there'd be girls. She felt a stab of jealousy. There had always been girls.

"Don't look so serious, love. Here, have one of these. It's all over, you know."

An old woman dropped a rose onto her lap.

But it isn't over. Robert's not here.

"It's a victoryyy," the woman called down the aisle, showering rose petals over the passengers.

I found my thrill-ll, three men sang in the corner. Others joined in. *On Blueberry Hill …*

When I found you …

"What's this song got to do with anything?" someone called.

"Who cares?" *My dream came true.*

A young woman burst into tears and rushed out of the carriage.

❦

Molly fought against the crowd on the railway station, elegant in her dark-rose two-piece costume and high heels. "Rose, you look fabulous. I do like the permanent wave. Here, let me take your bag. Isn't it exciting?"

Outside the station, people rushed in every direction, linking arms and singing "Land of Hope and Glory", "It's a Long Way to Tipperary". Anything joyful, anything loud.

In the street the crowd poured into Parliament grounds. Street vendors called: "Union Ja-acks! Whistles! Victory ca-aps!" Church bells rang. In Stout Street, office workers threw streamers from high windows.

"Mother wanted me to pick up some bread – look at the queue. No more bread for two days and the shops will be shut. I hope you didn't want to go shopping."

"I can't afford to. Will we see Margaret today?"

"We're meeting at the Tip Top – it probably won't have any food, mind. You may have to be satisfied with conversation."

"Ridiculous!" said Margaret as she took her coat off. "I've just heard that the police have been asked to control 'irresponsible' parents who let their children use rattles and streamers and whistles *today*, because the official celebration is *tomorrow*. Decorum is hugely overrated." She slid into the booth.

"We must restrain ourselves," Rose laughed. "No extended peals of laughter, no ringing out any good news till seven tomorrow, after every bell and siren in the city."

Margaret leaned forward. "You're sounding more alive than I expected after your first term."

Rose screwed up her face. "And you are clearly weighed down by love, and all those little children, and not getting away from Wellington."

"Nonsense. Wouldn't be anywhere else. So, what's keeping you awake at night? Come on. Spill. I've only got till three."

※

From Molly's house she watched the lights come on and people pouring down the street below.

"Mother's taken food down to the Carillion. There'll be bells on the hour from seven am until late. They've been practising 'The Ash Grove', 'Men of Harlech', even the Russian anthem, would you believe. And your favourite, 'Londonderry Air'." Rose groaned. "All over the world bell-ringers will be playing a new 'Victory Rhapsody'. Simultaneously." She shovelled coal into the firebox. "Mother's trying not to think too much about the lost ones."

"How's she coping, your Meg?"

Molly sighed. "Just."

Rose unfolded the newspaper across the dining table and turned past the advertising to page four. Prague still not freed, the war against Japan continuing. Germans hiding out in basements and forests.

"Here's the headline for today:

First Steps of Peace. The armies of liberation have completed their first task but before the work of restoration is completed other armies must follow ...

Haven't we had enough of armies?

... armies whose weapons are not planes, tanks, and guns, but food and clothing and all the necessaries of life. Already we have had heartrending pictures of the devastation and desolation ..."

Her voice faded away She sagged in the chair.

"Why can't they let us rejoice in the streets for one day? What about our fifty thousand men still in Europe, surely they'll be safe now?"

"Shortbread?"

"Thanks." She read on.

As a country that has escaped the physical impact of war and whose people have suffered little privation, New Zealand must take a big share in the work of relief in Europe. It is not only a question of giving what we can spare but of going without ourselves.

"As if we would turn our backs on Britain. Or Europe." Rose folded the newspaper. "That's really taken the fizz off. What are we up to tomorrow?"

After the Governor-General's speech and the parade there were thousands of people in uniform everywhere – Red Cross, pipe bands, brass bands, horses, Air Force, WAAFS, military. Rose squeezed against Margaret as they shuffled through the gates of the Basin Reserve.

"Over that side, under the trees. Not as much wind in that corner," Jim said.

"Well, I have the rug and I think we should be closer," Molly began, but Rose didn't catch the rest. Just ahead of them was a man's head she recognised. Tidy ears, hardly showing through thick dark hair. Or was it? He turned around.

"Rose." In two steps she was beside him.

"Hadley. I didn't expect ... "

"I thought I'd find you here." He took her by the elbows and kissed her cheek. Molly gave her a nudge in the back. "Oh, meet my friends: Molly, Margaret, Jim. Hadley's – a friend from Auckland, from Teachers' College." His eyebrow twitched.

"And this is Natalie, my cousin. What a bonus, discovering you so soon."

"And being here for all this," said Rose, in search of breathing space. Her voice had risen, blood rushing to her face and her brain. "Like to join us?"

"I have to meet my parents off the train in a while. If I can get through the crowds. They're coming for Natalie's wedding. Sit here, Rose." He laid his sports coat on the grass beside the rug where the others were jostling for space. "Come this side Natalie? Room for me in the middle. Squeeze up." He put one arm around each woman and pulled them towards him.

Her pulse rate was hardly settling. Here he was, arm around her, their thighs thrust together. Between socks and trousers his legs were dark tanned.

Crowds were settling around them. "Now, I don't want to hear anything about teaching," Hadley said, "but tell me about you."

Rose laughed. How could she possibly separate the two? "I'm loving it. You don't notice the long hours if you're enjoying yourself. It beats

T-Coll hands down." What else was there beyond teaching? Boarding problems, church? "I've made some new friends, teachers of course," she laughed, "and joined a tennis club, and there's my cousin's farm on Sundays. And you?"

The loud speakers squealed. "Back with the olds since last month," Hadley shouted over the noise. "Officially temporary. Amongst constant changes at the factory – supply problems and staff heading off – I seem to have the knack of finding raw materials at the right price. We're Essential to the war effort, Rose. I reckon Dad can't do without me. Who would have thought I'd cave in to a steady desk job? I spend a lot of time with friends out on the boat though – wasn't cut out for working all day."

Friends, on the boat? Who? Rose wondered. She turned her head to look at him. He pecked her on the cheek. "Your eyes are bluer than ever." The blue hat always brought out her eyes. "Let me look at your hands. No scratches? No arguments with ladders or pruners or trees?"

❦

"Where have you been hiding him, Rose? He's gorgeous."

She chuckled. "Yes."

"Come on. You can't stop there," Margaret demanded.

"I did tell you. I wrote about sailing and everything I did in Auckland. That was Hadley."

"And the 'friends' you had home in the summer?"

"Hadley too."

"He's pretty keen on you."

❦

Life goes on more placidly now at Aurisina, Rose read, shivering on the boarding-house verandah in thin sunlight filtered through winter trees.

Sometimes it's hard to fill in time but the ERS field library has come. I'm reading Dante, a marvellous script, the language so concise. Earlier I spent a long time washing a yellow atabrine stain out of my trousers. We have to use this malaria concoction, with all the mosquitoes.

What a domestic scene, she mused, imagining his fingers stained yellow-brown, like a smoker's. His fingers ... she remembered them pressing his address into her hand. And stroking her hair, lifting her head, kissing her in the gardens.

I have my official card at last as the unit photographer. Last night was a Beethoven symphony concert in Trieste. You would have enjoyed the warm evening drive home along the sea coast and cliffs with the sea lit up by lights of the fishing fleet.

But not his version of trouble in Trieste – being moved out of town, across a causeway. A grubby town. A dance after the YMCA song service. Moved again, to Santa Croce.

But after breakfast in the school we were taken back here, our original position! The woman of the house was cold and morose as she had scrubbed out our dust and wasn't wanting us back!

The NZ troops and tanks and leaders are proud of our part in the June 12 negotiation which achieved a German garrison surrender. Stability has arrived.

And a four-day trip to Milan and Lake Como.

Some of the bridges are still out, but we had three nights in the open air sleeping beside the truck. One night we went to the orchestra at La Scala and the next to "The Barber of Seville". The third was at the church army club and dance.

Another dance, Rose mused.

The Kiwi concert party attracts big crowds of Ities to the railway station. What brings the house down is when one of the men dresses as a woman. 28 Bty put on a dance with decent music and a good crowd of girls afterwards, though we can't get far with the language.

She paused and looked out at the trees. Was this the whole truth?

Aunt Marion reports that Dad is struggling with the farm work. She cannot do more with all the young men gone. Everyone is frustrated at not getting home. Even the CO can't promise when a ship will be available. Some blokes are really off the rails with the vino.

I long to see you.

Fondest regards,

Robert

13

September 1945

"Wouldja look at that," Blinky exclaimed at the crowded Lyttelton wharf.

"Look at it? I can smell it," said Robert.

"Got a girl waiting for you?"

"Maybe."

"Don't rush it, Sarg said. But hey, we're home. And home's where girls speak our language."

"Who cares about language? I'll take Italian women any time," scoffed Olsen.

"You'd take any woman any time."

Shouts and whistles filled the air.

"We did it, boyo."

"Hey watch me shoulder. Bone's jus' mended."

"Stand back. Stand back. Let the stretcher through."

Home, yet not home. Two nights in barracks and a train trip to go.

❧

A surge of emotion rushed into the carriage as the train pulled into the Dunedin Railway Station. The men had been sombre for most of the journey, a mix of tired excitement and anxiety at meeting wives they'd longed for and children they hardly knew. Beside Robert, Arthur sat still, tears streaming down his face. He knew Arthur's mother had died in his absence and his fiancée had changed her mind and married someone else. Yet he'd spoken with longing for home.

How could any of them explain what they were feeling? Robert certainly couldn't. He was twenty-three, ready to get stuck into life, sick of filling in time, sick of reading in the Sigs truck these last months, with almost no duties to perform. Others had played two-up the whole voyage, gambled anything, even bet their five pounds disembarkment money on which hour they would dock in New Zealand.

That had been the army all over: ninety per cent boredom, ten per cent sheer hell.

He would never discuss the hell. All he wanted was to be free of the army, free of marching, of duty lists, of ranks, of having to conform. His life was his own business. He couldn't wait to get to work on the farm with his father until the farm was his. And he would make an effort to accept Aunt Marion.

And yet without the army, he would never have seen Egypt or Italy. Or sweltered down the Red Sea, or smelled the ports of Aden and Colombo. Or wandered through Hobart.

Home was all he wanted. With Rose.

Why did everything feel so uncertain?

"Best of luck, Arthur," Robert said as they shook hands. "Look me up when you're ready for a break from city life."

Arthur ducked under the bunting and disappeared into a crowd of flags and children on shoulders, accompanied by a pipe band. Men hobbled from the train into the arms of their families. At the windows, women in their Sunday best hats and coats craned their necks over each other to peer into the carriages. One woman pressed her platform entry card against the window, pointing to a soldier's name. Robert shook his head and indicated the next carriage.

The whistle blew. Two more stops to go.

❋

It was weeks before Robert was sleeping normally again. Neighbours called in most days. Some hadn't made it back. "They'll have to sell up with both sons gone. The old man's heart's broken. No chance of a grandson farming now."

At the district welcome he had sat politely through the politician's address. He'd heard more than enough talk of heroism, had more than enough parades and marching. His father heaved himself from bed later than he remembered. Aunt Marion milked the cow and cut foot rot from limping animals. You had to give it to her, thought Robert, this was not what she expected when she married my father.

At first Robert often leaned on the fencepost at the top of the hill staring into the distance, staggered by the poor state of the pastures, of everything. In Italy, bomb craters, ruined stone fences and dwellings littered the landscape. Here, so far from battle, fences were in disrepair or non-existent with no wire available because implements of war had demanded the metals.

Aunt Marion reminded him the dogs needed to be fed. Two were his own, but they knew his father, not him. He had to snap out of it. He had a life to build and a girl to win. Over time he coaxed the dogs to take meat from his hand, to chase him around the yard. He would go inside less heavy hearted.

"Here, finish off the apple dumpling," Aunt Marion said. "Body and soul, Robert, body and soul." He must get ploughing with the horse team or it would be too late to sow the oats. Surely then he could find a break from farm pressures to travel north to Rose. He had his free rail pass and his soldier gratuity. Meanwhile, he could write to her, write and write. The stack of her letters had grown too. There was less restraint in them now that he was home. More than that, she wanted to come south, to see the place he spoke of "with such commitment and affection". Surely her words must echo her feelings for him. But letters were far from enough.

One Sunday he biked six miles to see his friend Keith and his new wife Maud on the family farm now that Keith's parents had moved out. Three years before they had biked to the pyramids in Egypt, before their separate wars through Italy. But they weren't here to talk of war. Farming would be the life all right: interesting, absorbing, remunerative in time.

"Good piece of land," Robert said, as they rested at the highest point. "If you can get your meat on a ship to Britain, prices are rising, they tell me."

"Fences are going in soon along this ridge." Keith pointed down the slope. "With crop rotation we should double the sheep numbers in five years, thanks to the rehab loan. Have you sent away for yours?"

"Last week. Shouldn't be long."

"You need a wife, Robert. You'd better get on to that too."

"Don't you worry, my friend. Don't you worry."

※

One night a gunshot pierced the stillness. He leaped up to grab his boots and uniform trousers. Then he stopped, recognising his father's step in the kitchen, setting his rifle down, fumbling in the knife tray, heading back out to skin a possum for the dogs.

He curled up, imagining Rose beside him in the darkness as his heart settled. What if her interest had cooled? Or had she found someone else?

He wanted her here in the wind and the rain. Here in the perfect mornings.

He must ask his father today. No. This time he would *tell* him.

14

Rose opened the front door. "Hadley!"

"Don't look so shocked! Aren't you going to ask me in?" He thrust a huge bouquet into her arms, picked her up and whirled her around.

"Put me down, Hadley. Put me down," she laughed.

"Why? Is your aunt here?"

"No, she's at the office. I don't live here now. I've brought her birthday present. Put me down."

He placed her gently on the Axminster carpet.

"Rose. I've missed you."

"She'll be here any second. Come into the sitting room. We never have bought flowers – these are beautiful."

She'd not seen him for three months. She fussed over the flowers, chattering away about her aunt's love of her garden – and had he heard that Sal and Monty had a new baby?

She felt his hand at her elbow.

"Rose," he said softly. She pulled away and indicated a chair. Looking at him now, his eyes were steadier than they'd been over the summer. He had his more confident voice back. His clothes, as always, were casually impressive. And that smile.

Running his hand over his well-tamed dark hair he studied her, one elbow on the chair. "Just look at you. Phenomenal. Teaching must agree with you. Palmerston North must agree with you." He leaned back and spread the arms wide. "Even funny old Nora must agree with you."

"Don't insult my aunt."

"Never."

She shook her head at him. "Let's go for a walk." Perhaps the exercise would calm her. And avoid having to explain him to her aunt. She wanted to feel back in control.

Wrapped in winter coats and scarves they drifted towards the riverbank, through remnants of autumn leaves, past the hollow sounds of hammering on a building site. They stood quietly on a bridge and looked into the flowing water, comparing notes about who had died overseas.

"Let's go to the band rotunda," Hadley said, clapping his gloves together.

He strode off quickly. She scurried after him until they fell into step.

"I'm going to work for my father," he said as they climbed the steps. "He's come up with an offer I can't refuse. I have to admit it's time I settled down."

"Marvellous," she said. "You get on so well together. I'm glad you have – you're sounding so keen."

For a moment he looked serious. "I won't be working with him exactly. I'll be managing the production plant." He chuckled. "I can come and go as I wish. Salary's not bad. And there's a house when I'm ready." Rose gulped.

He held her gaze and paused, rubbing his hands together, waiting for her response. Rose knew she had been presented with prospects.

"You're getting your life together at last."

"Ha. You're sounding like my mother. Now there's one woman I'll have to keep away from the house – she'll take over the whole redecoration given half a chance."

A Scots terrier bounded on stubby legs to the top of the rotunda steps. He cocked his head and looked back and forth from Hadley to Rose, as if affronted by their presence. A woman appeared with a lead.

Rose felt the cold creeping up through her shoes.

She jumped up. "It's too cold to sit still. Let's keep moving." She felt exhilarated, unsettled, flattered by the future he had dangled in front of her. But was she captivated enough by the man himself?

15

SHE MET HIM OFF THE TRAIN FROM WELLINGTON, clutching her hat against the wind with one hand, her cotton skirt with the other, searching the crowds on the Palmerston North platform, eyes heavy from restless nights, from excitement, then from the fear surging through her tossing brain. Would she recognise him, love him in the flesh? Or he love her?

He scanned the waiting crowd, dismissing children and old people, confident of a warm welcome.

And there she was.

There he was.

They fell into each other's arms, feeling the solidity, so different from the flimsy pages that had been all they had had of each other. Not letting go, each leaned back to examine the other. He saw the wide sparkling eyes, her flawless skin, her glowing face offering him everything he had imagined. She saw the curls, thick and fair, no hint of army haircut now, his rugged, gentle handsomeness, certainty in his eyes. Yet there was a chiselling, a refining of the man in her photograph. A more knowing gaze.

He touched her cheek. "My dear Rose." They kissed for the weeks and months they had waited. As if it should never end, this moment in the diminishing crowd, with the whistle and smoke and hiss of doors closing and metal forcing motion, sun shimmering white on the picket fences.

At the Soldiers' Club after the walk from the railway station, Robert slung his kitbag against the desk. He took the key and began to usher Rose up the stairway.

"Excuse me, young man. No women upstairs. You may talk in the lounge here." The manageress pointed to a collection of chairs within earshot of the front desk. "Or outside on the verandah." Rose blushed. Surely after three years they could be alone.

Robert took her by the elbow and whispered into her ear. "Silly old bird. I'll drop this off and be right back." He kissed her forehead and turned to go. "Don't go away," he called back, as if she were an apparition he didn't quite believe in, and galloped noisily up the stairs. Over her reading glasses the woman stared sourly after him.

In the square near the Chief Post Office they found a sunny bench. He took her hand. Neither would let go. They spoke of Wellington landladies, the farm, her parents' move.

"They haven't finished building the house yet, so they're still in the caravan," said Rose. "I can visit them, but it's not home, not our orchard. Dad's planted more trees – he can't help himself."

"That's what I want to do, plant trees. In Italy the countryside is festooned with trees, following the rivers and contours of the hills. I want to do that on the farm." Rose felt his enthusiasm.

"It's different at home with Aunt Marion in the driver's seat," Robert said slowly. "She keeps Dad moving, but he's aged." They watched a pair of tui in the flax, curling their beaks into the flowerheads. "Somehow all her food tastes exactly the same. And she's been making me eat more of it. Come on, let's go to the Greek café."

They sat opposite each other in a corner booth, saying little. Under the table his knee sought hers and she responded, laughing, swaying his knee sideways, bone on bone. Then, refreshed, they set off to walk the mile to Auntie Nora's, where her brothers were joining them for dinner. Their first meeting. After Robert's long train trip and a night on the Lyttleton ferry, he looked exhausted.

❦

The mantel clock struck ten as they left after dinner. "Your brothers are different, aren't they? Andrew seems pretty relaxed, but John, he's watching out for you."

"You know older brothers."

"I don't."

"And if you had one?"

"He'd be telling me not to let you escape." He pulled her under the spreading elm away from the street light.

"When can I see you tomorrow?" he asked minutes later.

Rose promised to meet him under the Post Office tower at nine. She wanted to show him her school and Victoria Esplanade.

At the end of the third day they sat on a bench in the rose gardens, "Damask Perpetual" cascading around them, eating each other's cream horns. "Hey, you've ice-creamed my chin." Rose laughed and reached for a handful of rose petals to shower over him. In a moment they were competing for petals, shaking the fading flowers, stuffing them down each other's necks.

"I give in." Rose flopped back on the bench.

Robert got down on one knee. Rose leaned towards him, yes, yes.

"Rose. Would you ... will you marry me?"

"Robert. That's wonderful!" But suddenly Hadley leaped to her mind. She gasped. "I ... believe me, I want to say yes," she panted the whispered words, "but I, I can't tell you yet." Before her eyes he crumpled like a deflating balloon.

She covered her face and burst into tears.

"What's the matter?"

She shook her head. "It's just, it's just ... nothing. It's such a big decision." She sniffed and clutched Robert's hand to her chest. "I need to think, all my family's in the North Island. But ... I do love you, Robert."

A wood pigeon swooped low beside them. Startled, she jumped up. "I'm so happy you've asked me. Promise I won't keep you waiting long."

"Just say yes."

"Come on, it's a long way back for dinner."

Robert plucked a rose from the tumbling plant and stuck it in her hair.

"Beware fair maid, you'll not escape me,

For I shall ask again till ye do take me."

❦

Later that night Rose opened the door at her aunt's. John? Still here?

"Evening." He swung his legs off the sofa. "I wanted to catch you alone."

"Nothing serious I hope."

"Catch your breath – you're looking flushed."

A big-brother talk. She sat down.

"Hadley, and you, and Robert. What's going on?"

"What do you mean?"

John raised his eyebrows.

"I'm still working it out, big brother, but it's my business."

He leaned forward. "Rose – you can't keep stringing Hadley along for ever. I bumped into him last week in town. That man has a huge future," he said, with an open-hand gesture. "He's a good chap. Affable, few vices. You'd never have to work. He dropped a hint about being around long term."

He lowered his voice. "He has asked you to marry him, hasn't he?"

"Perhaps."

"Then why you haven't agreed yet is beyond me."

Rose looked at him in silence.

"Look. Robert clearly has serious intentions. He's a pleasant enough chap, hung on your every word last night. Coming here from way down in the cold south can't be easy. He has some very traditional ideas about farming. Hardly scientific. His education's been … "

"John, that's enough." Rose jumped to her feet. "You've just been more helpful than you realise." She took him by the elbow and guided him towards the door. "I promise I'll tell you of any decisions as soon as I make them. Love to Lydia. Good night." She gave his shoulder a firm nudge and shut the door behind him.

In her room, she sat at the desk. Paper. Pen and ink. Envelope. Everything at hand but the words.

Yet there really was no option at all.

16

THE LIGHT FROM THE ROSE WINDOW streamed across the altar. Beside her, Robert played nervously with his cuffs. Robert. Her Robert.

Put on then, as God's chosen ones, holy and beloved, compassion, kindness, lowliness, meekness, and patience, forbearing and forgiving one another. The minister's words washed over her. *And above all these put on love, which binds everything together in perfect harmony.*

Rose turned to face Robert for the vows, his voice firm with concentration. Then it was her turn.

I, Rose Dorothy Grant, take you, Robert McAra McLeod, to be my husband. Before God and these witnesses, I will be your loving and faithful wife; in plenty and in want, in joy and in sorrow, in sickness and in health; as long as we both shall live.

Robert lifted her veil over the coronet of white roses and kissed her. "Kiss her again," a voice called. Someone hissed her into silence.

Hands entwined, they turned to the congregation, the twenty-seven official guests, parishioners, school colleagues, neighbours. And her fourth form girls, up to something, bunching closer together.

A cloud of confetti burst over them.

❦

"So, Robert, you've really taken on my sister," John said, pumping his hand. "Good luck with her."

"Less cheek, big brother," Rose laughed, but his tone had been warm, respectful even.

A puff of wind lifted her veil across the porch and up, up towards the climbing roses. "Careful, it can billow out to ten feet," her mother said, stretching to help Molly gather it in. "Her grandmother wore this veil. In 1885. Don't let it catch on the roses."

Minutes later the wedding party stood in front of a painted Grecian orchard in the photographer's studio. "Remember, Robert," laughed Molly. "No standing to attention or 'at ease' either. You're not in the army now."

❦

"Such a shame your family aren't with us today, Robert," Rose's mother said over the roast lamb at Uncle Jack's farmhouse.

"Come and visit," Robert said. "Stay as long as you like."

"You're safe for now," her father chuckled. "We've a house to finish. Caravan living palls in the winter."

Not even Robert had offered any reasonable explanation for his family's absence. Couldn't a neighbour have looked after a cow and dogs and horses for their only son's wedding? Perhaps it was the travel. It can't have been money. Not money.

In the borrowed Vauxhall was a bundle of petrol vouchers, hoarded by three families. What a gift. A week of guesthouses and the sandy beaches of Gisborne and Opotiki enfolded them in the glow of new ardour. By the time they returned the car to Tauranga, they knew the irresistible texture of each other's skin and in their entwined sleep the nature of unconditional love.

PART THREE

PART THREE

17

March 1947

THE TRAIN CREPT TOWARD THE STATION, hissing steam as it settled at the platform.

"There they are," Robert pointed.

"Where?" asked Rose.

"That's Aunt Marion in the blue hat. Helping Dad up from the bench. Come on."

Robert slung her carry bag over his shoulder. His breath caressed the back of her neck as he guided her towards the door.

"You hold the bag, I am going to hold you." Twisting their bodies through the narrow door, he lifted her onto the rear platform and down the narrow steps.

"Dear me. What an arrival," Aunt Marion quivered with conviviality. "You're looking fresh for such a long journey. Welcome, welcome. Rose my dear, call me Aunt Marion, everybody does."

Robert's father clapped him on the shoulder and shook his hand vigorously. "Guid to have ye back, son." He bent towards Rose with a wide rugged smile and lifted his hat. "Welcome to ye, bonnie lass. 'Tis a greet pleasure to have ye in the family. Ye've painted a smile on tha' young man's face, ye have."

They left her glory box and bicycle at the station to collect later. Robert heaved one suitcase onto the roof and tossed the rope back and forth to his father to secure it. Neil lashed the other to the rear luggage rack before Aunt Marion climbed into the driver's seat. Robert stowed his kitbag inside. Rose rested her head on his shoulder until she felt Aunt Marion's eyes in the mirror.

Two train journeys and a restless night on the ferry forgotten, she wanted to take in everything. Pale-gold wheat and oats stretched across the Tokomairiro Plain. On the low hills, sheep grazed in the most vivid green pasture she had ever seen.

Soon the road sliced through rocky cliffs, climbing through the narrow twists of the Manuka Gorge. With a surge of revs, the car turned up a steep gravel road. Now the highway was far below and the ridges flattened across a wide panorama towards the west. On first impression, the plateau was a uniform curve towards the distant mountains, but as they drove across the ridges, she could see where it was fractured by deep gullies, so unlike the landscape she knew.

"Did the letter come?" Robert shouted over the chugging motor and the rattle of gravel beneath.

"Nae. Wheels turnin' slowly as ever," Neil answered.

A collie dog rushed down a drive and barked alongside the moving vehicle. Rose pressed her forehead to the window. Black and white hair pounded so close she was certain Aunt Marion would hit him. "Go away, silly dog. Robert! We'll kill him." Robert leaned over her, unconcerned.

The dog fell away. "Always stops at the boundary." Robert opened his hands in a don't-ask-me-why gesture. They stared out the back window as the dog stood in the middle of the road, his head still flicking with barks.

A dark figure crossed the road in the distance and slid through a hole in a high macrocarpa hedge.

"Who was that?" she asked.

"Just Mary," Robert said dismissively. Over the next rise he pointed out their oats. "Heavy crop, Dad. Looks ready. Tomorrow, do you think?"

"Aye. Guess it'll wait till then."

Honeymoon over.

"Here we are, Rose," said Aunt Marion, pulling in at the roadside. Dogs barked. To her surprise, Aunt Marion gave her handbag to Neil and hefted a sack of flour into her arms. Neil walked ahead between two solid upright wooden pillars framing a wrought-iron gate, and along the straight gravel path to the front door. Rose hung back to take a first look at her new home.

The house nestled comfortably in the dip between two small hills, an elegant family house sheltered from winds east and west but targeted, she would find, by the prevailing southerlies that funnelled up the gully behind. A wide verandah extended across the front and wrapped around to the sunny north-west. Above the front verandah, the twin-gabled roof supported four double chimneys. Towards the rear, a thin streak of smoke rose. Two black cats leaped off a pile of sacks and disappeared into the grass.

Robert put down the suitcases. "Well, what do you think?"

"It's bigger than I expected."

"Then welcome to your home." He picked her up again. "Hold tight." Through the front door he carried her into the first room off the passage. He pushed the door shut. "I hope you'll be happy here for ever, Mrs McLeod."

"As long as you're here with me, husband," Rose echoed, rubbing his nose with hers, the word still foreign. Suddenly she pulled back and looked at him intently. "It's only just occurred to me," she whispered. "Your father and Aunt Marion. They're married, aren't they?"

"Yes, of course," he whispered back.

Rose laughed. "I knew they shared the house, but you call her …"

"I call her Aunt Marion because I spent a lot of time with her five nieces. Too late to change now, just because she's taken up with my father."

How odd. Would it change anything? She nestled back into the familiar smell of him. For a moment there was only him and her, alone.

"Cup of tea you two?" Aunt Marion's voice called down the passage.

They pulled away. "*Aunt* Marion!" Rose laughed quietly.

Suitcases to untie, tea, dogs to visit, clothes to unpack, presents to unwrap.

❦

She peered through waking eyelashes at the blue rose wallpaper, aware of her own breathing in the strange quietness. She turned to Robert. Not there. What was the time? She leaped out and pulled the crocheted circle on the grey blind cord. It sprang up with a snap, twisting the cord out of reach.

Aunt Marion was coming in the garden gate, carrying a metal bucket that swung heavily. Rose moved away from the window, pulled on her clothes and ran a brush quickly through her hair. "Good morning," she greeted Aunt Marion at the back door.

"So you're up. Pass me the white jugs, will you? They're under the kitchen window. I'll show you where we keep the milk." Rose followed her along the worn track behind the house, pushing aside elderberry branches heavy with fruit.

"Watch your head." Under the rainwater tankstand, sun never warmed the grey concrete walls. Aunt Marion manoeuvred awkwardly around Rose in the tiny space and heaved the milk bucket onto the bench. She lifted the muslin from a basin and pressed the crusty surface with her finger. "This one's firm enough. We'll make butter later."

※

Back in the kitchen, Aunt Marion stoked the coal range into life and shifted the porridge pot. The men were coming through the back door. Rose moved forward, then hesitated. How should she greet Robert in front of his father?

Robert gave her a casual hug. He looked different. Handsome in anything, he suited this farmer uniform much better than khaki. She remembered last night's words. How he still couldn't believe he had found an intelligent, beautiful, practical woman he loved more than he'd ever imagined. Here in his house. "Will you still be here for breakfast?" he had whispered. Well, here she was.

"'Tis a right bonnie mornin'." Neil broke into her thoughts. "Horses fed and ready. By my reck'nin' the oats'll be dry enough in an hour."

"According to his fingertips," said Robert, rubbing his fingers together.

"Aye, should keep us busy till twilight." She wanted to be busy too, to fit in, to be useful. Above everything, to make Robert happy.

※

What would she do once she had cleared the table? Aunt Marion decided for her. "Go and see what they're up to. Enjoy the sunshine."

Six draft horses were harnessed to the reaper and binder. Neil clambered onto the metal seat. "Hey up," he called across their backs. They moved in powerful unison from the first step of the lead horse. Robert explained how they were yoked by height and weight, to maximise the strength of the more passive followers and challenge Goliath out front.

No wind today, just the rhythmic creaking of harness, wood and metal, and Neil's indecipherable commands fading as the team lumbered slowly down the paddock and out of sight, Robert now on the back step. She picked her way along the edge of the paddock, where the wire fence disappeared into the ground. Thin wooden fenceposts were broken in places. Soon they appeared again on the upward slope, Neil's voice raised, urging the team, their heads bent low with effort.

Bundles of oats fell from the binder to the ground in a patterned swathe, ripe heads in one direction, cut ends to the other. Robert stepped off. "How much of this country is yours?" Rose asked.

He pointed out each boundary, naming the six family owners beyond, from the steep northern tussock, to roads west and south, and a row of sheltering pine trees just visible over a ridge, where the land softened and fell away towards the coast. "And Mary, over this hill."

Her family's ten-acre orchard would be a speck on a hillside here.

"What are those level ditches around the hills?"

"Water races. They're all over goldmining country."

"Goldmining? Here?"

"A couple of Chinese miners were still living past Nugget Stream when I was young. See that cart track following the hawthorn hedge? Cobb and Co coaches drove into the Waitahuna Goldfields from there – it's only three miles away."

"Someone must have found gold if that creek's called Nugget Stream," Rose said.

"Your turn, m'lad," Neil waved on his next round. While Robert drove the horses, Neil leaned against a post, leaving Rose free to wander.

A cloud of seagulls glided on the air currents. Rose followed their flight, shading her eyes. Higher up, a larger brown bird hovered, its jagged wings gliding. Suddenly the seagulls scattered as the large bird dived to the ground just yards in front of her. Talons stretched forward, the bird snatched something from the fallen oats and lifted, small legs dangling from its beak.

Alarmed, Rose tripped over the clods of earth in her clumsy boots and fell back into the long grass at the edge of the paddock. Somewhere above her, the bird disappeared. Robert's father was moving towards her at a remarkably agile speed.

"Ye all right, lassie?"

She pointed to the innocent sky where the seagulls had resumed their waiting game. "Did you see that big bird dive?"

"The falcon? Aye, clever bird. Sees a field moose from near a mile off. Have tae admire 'em." This man clearly had no sympathy for a small creature. "Thar's one moose we'll not see in the hoose." Rose laughed tentatively.

Robert stopped the horses. "Could you bring the water bucket please, Rose?" he called. "It's there, in the grass."

"Whoa, girl." A shout and a whinny came from the roadside.

Robert looked up. "Uncle Adam and Andy. Be warned. He's not one to mince words."

"So you've still got the strength to do some work, me lad," Uncle Adam roared with laughter at Robert. Rose blushed and tried to hide behind him.

"I can see the lassie blushing, Robert. Ye'll have to look after her better than tha'." He flung his leg over and jumped down from the tall mare, looping the reins over a post. "Enjoying yerself, Rose?"

"I love it here. Thank you," she answered cautiously. Compared with the more retiring Neil, his older brother had a loud presence in the stillness.

Aunt Marion arrived with a basket and the tea billy. Tea, scones and jam. Fruitcake. How could so much food disappear at one morning tea?

The conversation turned to harvest yields and moisture problems. "You won't want to bother yourself with that," Aunt Marion said, getting to her feet. "Shall we head back to start dinner?"

The kitchen smelled of coal smoke and boiled mutton. Rose peeled a large pot of potatoes and went to find silverbeet in the back garden. Two rabbits leaped from the carrots and bounded over the single-wire fence.

"They're a plague," Aunt Marion said, stirring the stew. "We can't have them eating our winter vegetables. Worse still, they eat the new grass before the sheep have a chance. Rabbit stew would be a fine change from mutton. Did you eat rabbit in the Hawke's Bay?"

"Not that I remember."

"First time for everything," Aunt Marion said, rubbing her hands down her apron. A trace of a smirk crossed her face, or did Rose imagine it? "Right, now for the pudding."

She felt as if she were back in her childhood, given discrete tasks to humour her, tasks the cook could easily have done more quickly. One too many women in this kitchen.

"Does the coal range keep a constant heat?" asked Rose, as Aunt Marion rattled another shovel of coal into the firebox.

"This beastie?" Aunt Marion shuddered and shook her head. "Goes out in the middle of cooking dinner if you're not careful. I clean out the soot tray before six each morning, or it chokes. And ashes out twice a day in winter. The damper knob has to be just *here*. It's supposed to keep going through the night but it hardly ever does." She paused. "I've a mind to get you a better stove before we quit this house."

Was that a promise or a throwaway good intention? Robert will depend on me to operate this, she thought. Aunt Marion will not be here for long.

"Rose, lass." A voice boomed from the door. Adam. "Robert is bringin' ye doon for tea on Wednesday to meet my Lucy. I'll be awa' back now or she'll have me liver on a plate. Gidday to ye both." The door shut firmly behind him.

"Aunt Marion? I really would like a bath, if possible, after our travels. Is that…?"

"Of course, my dear. We'll set you up in the washhouse."

18

Rose leaned her head against the damp bricks of the washhouse and closed her eyes, lathering soap over her arms, her shoulders, her breasts. Steam rose from the copper beside her. Was this how Cathy took a bath in *Wuthering Heights*, once Nellie Dean had cajoled her into taking her clothes off?

Curled forward on her knees, she swirled her hair in the water. Back and forth, like seaweed in the ocean tide. How delicious this bath was, this crude tin vessel and a mix of swirling steam and wood smoke, with paltry light diffused through the frosted glass window.

Nothing like her bath in Wellington. Margaret and Rose, pushing through their bedroom door, laden with towels, talcum powder and clothes, shoving each other down the passage.

"I have to be first. I'm dirtier."

"No you're not."

"But Jim's coming."

"Robert's only here for two days."

Margaret had relented. "Only if I can wear your stockings."

Her best stockings. Her only stockings without darns.

"Deal."

And what a bath, she now realised in her cramped tin tub. Even lying full stretch, head tilted back into the water, her feet had barely touched the end. Enamelled for sliding up and down – until there came a knocking at the door and Mrs W demanding, "That's enough water my girl. Can't you see the notice on the wall?"

If she closed her eyes she couldn't see it, but she knew the words: *Residents will observe the limit of three inches of water in the bath at all times.*

※

Rose felt her energy sag after the heat of the bath. She wrapped her hair in a towel turban and took her book, *A Tree Grows in Brooklyn*, outside to the verandah step. In the distance, the men's voices coaxed the horses around the hillside.

She felt oddly removed from her surroundings, as if she had happened upon this place in a dream. Nothing was familiar, everything felt ephemeral. She flicked water from her hair onto the concrete. Drops appeared, evaporated. Like herself, of little substance here.

The house up close was far from the elegant residence she had first assumed. The paint, where there was paint, was often cracked and peeling. Rusty green streaks ran down the walls from leaks in the roofing iron. Odd pieces of wood covered holes where weatherboard had rotted.

Along the edge of the verandah facing the road was a muddled profusion of late-summer flowerings in the only flower bed. A rusty garden fork suggested someone's good intentions.

How would Aunt Marion react if she started work on the garden?

This would all be hers. It *was* hers. As soon as Robert got his government rehabilitation loan as a returned soldier, they could buy the farm and Neil and Aunt Marion would have money to buy elsewhere.

But not before. Robert had made it sound as if all he had to do was send in the forms.

She wished she had talked to her friends about what it might be like sharing a house. Not that it was uncommon after the war. Although she'd known Aunt Marion would be here, she'd imagined bursting into the kitchen, rearranging everything her own way, shifting furniture from room to room and spreading the treasures from her glory box.

How selfish and greedy, she admonished herself. Not everyone has the good fortune to marry into a farm with a four-bedroomed house, two each, fully furnished.

Not everyone has to share it with another woman.

And no one else has Robert.

She ran her eyes under the verandah roof. A tatty bird's nest sagged from one corner. Among the spider's webs she found seven.

"Rose? We should get that butter made." Rose leaped to her feet. "We'll take some to Waitahuna when we collect the mail. Like to come?"

"Yes, please. What birds nest here?"

"Och, starlings. Grubby birds. Never get rid of them so I've stopped bothering. They've every right to be here. You'll hear them making quite a racket in the spring. Quite a racket."

Rose followed Aunt Marion to the scullery. Back home Mother had given up on their cow after the earthquake. Butter from a neighbour was exchanged for fruit.

Aunt Marion skimmed the crusty layer off three basins and slithered the clotted cream into the drum-shaped churn. "All you have to do is turn the handle, like this," said Aunt Marion, forcing the handle around. "It won't become butter if it's too cold. Or too hot. Sixty degrees is ideal."

Aunt Marion's arm was slowing.

"Could I try?" After five minutes Rose's arm ached. She changed arms. Her back ached. But Aunt Marion mustn't guess. Fifteen minutes passed until they heard the sloshy liquid thicken. "Oh my. That's quick," Aunt Marion said, taking the butter pats off a hook. "Beginner's luck?"

※

Rose followed Aunt Marion through the red door of the Post Office. "Lorraine, meet Robert's new wife, Rose." The women exchanged greetings. "Lorraine's from up the Gully," Aunt Marion explained, pointing through the wall. "Near the remains of the gold sluicing."

Lorraine took a pile of mail from a pigeonhole.

"One for Robert." The two McLeod wives reached for the brown envelope. Aunt Marion held it long enough to discern its origins, then took her hand away with a laugh. "Nothing from Invercargill for you, sorry Mrs McLeod, but there's this, from Gore. And Rose is in luck. Wellington." Rose perked up.

"You're a North Islander aren't you?" asked Lorraine.

"Yes, Havelock North. Have you been there?"

"Me?" the postmistress laughed. "I've been to Balclutha that way," she pointed over Rose's head, "and Alexandra inland. Dunedin twice. Don't know anyone who's been to the North Island. Except you, Mrs McLeod," she nodded to Aunt Marion. "Your sister's away for the day, if you're looking for her."

They stepped into the sunlight. "The whole township'll know about you before the day's out," Aunt Marion said quietly.

What on earth would Lorraine tell anyone? They'd hardly exchanged a word.

"Let's see what Tid has to say." Aunt Marion waved a letter. "Neil's sister. Mathilda." She held the letter between them. "They're coming for two days next month. Look: '*I have a surprise for the young couple.*' " Aunt Marion raised her eyebrows. "You'll like her. She's warm-hearted. Like Adam without the voice." She tucked the letter into her handbag. "I'll leave the butter in my sister's safe around the back." She walked off towards the three small wooden houses opposite the Post Office.

"Had you known Robert's father long, before you married?" Rose asked on the way home.

"Dear me, I can't remember not knowing Neil. Of course he was sixteen years ahead. Our fathers used to help each other on their farms; we all belonged to the same church. I remember Neil telling us he was marrying Alice. Middle of the other war, 1916. They lived in the married quarters at Featherston before he left." She coaxed the car into third gear. "Alice was a lovely woman. Very tragic, the cancer."

"Robert hasn't talked about her."

Aunt Marion pulled up beside a wooden box at the base of the hill. "Come the right moment, he will. Neil never spoke of Robert being at the war either. It would have been the end of the McLeod family if we'd lost Robert, with Adam having daughters. Neil's a changed man since you arrived. It's not only Robert you've made happy." She climbed out.

"That letter for Robert," Aunt Marion said, setting three bare loaves on Rose's knee, "should be the approval for his Rehabilitation Loan. With that they can get started on the fences. Then we can run more sheep. And cattle."

Her voice rose over the noisy engine. "You and I must make changes to the house while everyone wants to please you." Surely it was the other way around – but to Rose this insight clearly carried a warning: act now, before it wears off. "It won't occur to them to improve the house they already know how to live in. You may think the long-drop lavatory's a crude affair, but the end of the shed's a huge improvement on the little hut down the gully when I arrived. And the washhouse with the copper was even further down, near the spring."

Rose swallowed. Her family and everyone she knew had flush

lavatories. But imagine dashing down the gravel path in the dark of winter. Or carrying chamber pots into the trees each morning.

※

Rose ran towards the oats paddock, letter in hand. She stopped on the stubble. Nothing but paradise ducks honking. Three horses turned to stare at her.

"Hello there, Missus," Andy shouted as his horse drew closer. "They're at Mary's getting a cattle beast out of the bog."

"How long will they be?"

"Half an hour," he said, shrugging his shoulders. "If they're lucky. Mary's got them fixing a gate. Canny woman, that Mary. She'll let them away before dark, no doubt," he laughed and trotted off.

Inside, she opened Margaret's letter. The baby was keeping her up much of the night. Picnics, parties, translations. Jim was looking for paid work while he finished his PhD. Rose folded it under the pillow. Her faraway friends must come to visit, to see how well this life suited her.

In the kitchen Aunt Marion scraped the remains of the stew into a pie. Rose ironed her travel-crumpled dresses. She liked the simple rhythms of ironing, the warm odour of heated fabric and the smoothness under her hand.

"When will they be in for tea?" she asked, wanting Robert to be here, or she there, wherever he was.

"The weather's holding, so probably not till dark."

As she hung her dresses in the bedroom, her eye caught Robert's letter on their mantelpiece. What if the letter did not … ?

※

Across the yard was a wattle and daub cottage. She had heard of these, made with straw and earth. A crumbling sod chimney anchored the building at one end. Rose stepped up to the weathered grey door and tried the brass knob which wobbled but stayed firmly shut. A calico curtain hung haphazardly over the side window. Pieces of worn leather harness were scattered across the wooden floor.

Aunt Marion appeared. "I'll set some traps for those rabbits in the garden. The chook food's in here." She shouldered the door and heaved it open. "Can't let the hens get in." She plunged a metal dipper into a sack of wheat. "But they need a bit more than they get just scratching in the yard."

She scattered grain inside the hen run where the floor was thick and springy with dry bird droppings, deeper under the perching rails. Instantly twenty hens charged like darts from far-off bushes, wings tucked, beaks forward. Rose twisted in alarm as feathers brushed her ankles.

"You'll know every one of these before long. Including the clucky madame in the nesting box." Far too intimate for Rose. Too close to giving them names.

"We're lucky," Aunt Marion said. "Not one stoat in the six years I've been here."

"Stoats?" asked Rose uncertainly.

"They come to steal eggs but they attack hens around the throat. Once they get a taste for blood, the poor chooks become so stunned with fright they almost line up. Dear me. It's gruesome for the poor birds. Rose?"

"I'm sorry. I don't cope very well with blood." She leaned against the door.

"Blood. That's one thing you *will* have to get used to."

※

Neil kicked his boots off at the back door. "Aye, lang day. The lad's tending the horses. He could do wi' a lantern if ye've a mind to."

Rose took one from the shelf. At the stables Robert was brushing down Goliath. "What have you been up to?" He bent to brush the hind leg.

"Finding my way around. Getting to know Aunt Marion. She's being very helpful."

"Don't let her boss you about."

"No chance," Rose said without conviction. "We'll manage. It's not for long." She put her hand out to the horse, which blinked his dark eyes and ignored her. "I wish I had his long eyelashes," she said.

Robert reached through the door for a half-filled sack and poured oats into the feeding trough. "These stables are better than when I first came home, but look at this harness. So stiff it wore a bruise on his neck today." He nudged the horse's head around and patted him on the rump. Goliath plodded out. "Two more to do, and this floor. Dad hasn't mucked out since I left for the wedding."

"This looks like something I could do."

Robert paused, the shovel mid-air. He heaved the load out onto the dung heap. "It's not a job for … "

"Nonsense. Give me something to wear and forget it. Then you," she said and kissed him, "can be inside earlier at night."

※

Rose turned down the flame of the bedroom lamp. With a start, she glimpsed the forgotten letter. She would give it to him the minute he came in. His chair scraped in the kitchen. She rolled onto his pillow, warming his side of the bed – and promptly fell asleep.

"Rose." A loud whisper woke her. "Put your shoes on. I want to show you something. Bring the eiderdown." Rose opened her mouth to object. "Shhh."

Darkness engulfed them. They crept through the front door, sharing the eiderdown, stumbling like escaping school children. The freshness of the night tingled her bare legs. "Where are you taking me?"

"Not far." They found the gravel path, the gate, the road under their shoes. He steered her up the hill and felt around for the broken posts into the paddock.

At the fenceline, they tumbled into the long grass. He kissed her fleetingly and grabbed her hand to pull her up. She looked beyond him and gasped.

The sky was deep indigo, with pastel tints of yellow and pink near the horizon. As their eyes adjusted, more stars appeared, one by one, and at once into thousands. She stood slowly, intoxicated by the clarity, the wonder of it. Robert loosened himself from the eiderdown. Separately they rotated in a slow waltz, to take in the whole dome of the sky, the Milky Way, the Southern Cross and a supporting cast of millions.

She drew him back into the warmth of her wrap and nestled against a stook as the harvest moon rose over the hills, a mere arm's length away. A benign grey luminosity flowed over the landscape. Stooks poked above the horizon, a field of resting witches' brooms. Seedheads over her head sparkled moist and capricious.

I want to be part of this, Rose said to herself. Not just part, but essential to it. I need to be strong enough for anything Robert wants of me.

Robert wrapped himself around her more closely. "I was expecting the moon, but I hadn't counted on the stars as well."

19

"Any news?" asked Aunt Marion, looking from Rose to Robert as she dolloped porridge onto their plates.

Rose gasped. "There's a letter, a government letter."

Robert was already out of his chair. "Where?"

"On our mantelpiece. Excuse me," she said, snatching her serviette from her lap.

"He'll be back with it." Aunt Marion's tone was unquestionable. Rose sat down.

Spoons clattered. Neil slurped his tea. Rose could bear it no longer. "Excuse me, I must see."

In their sitting room, Robert sat slumped in a chair, papers across his knee. He looked up, a distressed, blank face. "What is it?"

He pushed the papers towards her. *Application is declined ... state of fences ... stock in poor health ... ratio of developed land to undeveloped gorse-filled gullies ... most significant is size of property ... insufficient acreage for an economic unit ... cannot attract development funding.*

Rose knelt down and gathered him into her arms. He leaned stiffly against her shoulder. "I can't get a tractor. We can't even get started."

※

In the kitchen the men stood at the window. Neil stared at the page, one hand on Robert's shoulder.

"Come and finish your breakfast, Neil," Aunt Marion said. Robert came to the table, but Neil took his tobacco down from the rack. Robert spooned cream onto his lukewarm porridge.

Aunt Marion tried to coax Neil into eating. "Damn it, woman. Leave me be."

Rose recoiled. Robert's eyes widened.

Aunt Marion thrust her hand out for the letter. "Isn't this acreage before the last survey? What about the leasehold block? Gorse-filled gullies. We can get out there with matches. Burn them clean. What nonsense this is. There are four of us now."

"Enough, Marion. We don't want Rose to be saddled with men's problems. Come on, lad. Work to be done." He emptied his barely smoked pipe into the fire, the air tense. Aunt Marion grated soap vigorously into the sink. Abruptly she stopped.

"It's hard for us to leave it to the men, but that's how it works here. They won't interfere in the house, we let them have their way in the fields. There'll be enough for you to worry about before long. Now, is that oven hot enough?"

※

In gumboots and Robert's overalls, a scarf over her hair, Rose shovelled dung until the stable was so clean she had to stop herself chipping into the packed earth floor. On a cluttered shelf she found tins, horseshoes, metal implements. She sniffed the liquid in an unlabelled jar. Whooh. Something darkly soothing with eucalyptus. Another tin. She prized the lid off and stuck a finger into the pungent emulsion. This must be saddle grease. If Robert showed her which harness he wanted supple, she could do this too.

At morning tea, the stooks had lost the magic of last night. Across the paddock, a woman heaved a sheaf against three others. A young man looked up, spoke to the woman and increased his pace. Four more sheaves secured the stook. They dropped their tools and wandered over, heads down, arms swinging.

Robert and his father strode over the brow of the hill. No sign of tension now. Out here it was as if the letter had never arrived.

※

Robert gestured to the woman. "Mary, this is my wife, Rose. Rose, Mary."

Mary nodded. "Hello," she said and grinned, showing a gap in her teeth. Her hair was tied in a loosening knot, dark once but coarse and greying, escaping tendrils covering her eyes as she leaned forward. She wore working boots like the men, hers tied with twine several times around the ankle.

"And this is Jim. Mary's nephew." Robert pointed his cup at a young man about her own age, sitting a little apart. Jim acknowledged her with a nod.

"You look like an expert at stooking, Mary. Is it difficult?"

Mary shrugged and sat next to Jim.

They looked at the sky. Cumulus was building to the south. Left lying, the whole crop would rot if it rained.

"More tea?" Mary thrust her cup towards the billy, her hand ingrained with soil, scratched by the grain stalks.

"Would you like sugar?" asked Rose.

Mary spooned one, two, three, four teaspoons of sugar into her mug. She tossed the spoon with perfect accuracy into the basket from a distance and wandered away.

Robert's eyes met Rose's and the two grinned at each other.

"I'd like to try that," said Rose.

"Teaspoon quoits?"

"No, silly. Stooking."

"Really?" replied Robert in surprise. "Come on – I'll show you." He pulled her up. "It's easy. Poke the curve of the fork into the sheaf like this. Pull your arm back, and flick it up as you swing forward – there. Got it?"

Rose took the pitchfork and dug it into a sheaf. The tynes stuck in the ground.

"Let the curve carry the weight." Next time she managed to lift it, but she couldn't find the balance and fell over to the sound of clapping from across the paddock.

"I'll get one up yet," Rose declared, drawing the fork back. With Robert's help, she lifted the sheaf against the stook, almost where it belonged.

"It's so awkward. How does Mary do this all day? She's over twice my age."

"She's very strong." He dropped his voice. "But maybe not in the head."

"Robert. Don't be so unkind."

※

Mary unfolded her sacking bag. That Rose, with her pale eyes and pretty face and tidy hair, she thought. Too weak for stooking, still so slow at the end of the day, even if she'd almost got the knack of it. What use will she be on the farm? She had an air about her, Mary mused. Not 'airs' exactly, but she wasn't like anyone else around here.

She squeezed under the barbed wire to collect cones from Neil's pine trees. No one would see her. They'd all gone inside.

But voices were coming. Robert, laughing. He never used to laugh. And her. Coming into the hay shed.

Mary hid under low branches until they'd finished giggling and grunting and came out covered in straw, pulling each other along, swinging out, and back. Out and back.

Cones forgotten, she crumpled up the empty sack and scurried home, her pulse racing.

✺

"Surely they understand that lack of fences and the state of the stock are the very reason we need the loan," Aunt Marion said after the Grace at the evening meal. "I've an idea." Robert and Neil lowered their heads and began eating. "Neil, why don't you get William – his brother-in-law, Rose, a lawyer politician from Alexandra – he could speak to someone in the ministry. Will and Betty would do anything for Robert."

Neil pulled himself straight in his chair. "We'll none o'tha' nonsense," he said fiercely. "We'll look after ourselves, thank ye. Family finances stay reet here." He beat his bone-handled spoon on the table. "In ... this ... hoose."

With no pleasure Rose ate the unfamiliar barley broth. It made her feel like a child again, swallowing obediently for the good of her health. Somehow it fitted the occasion.

✺

As Robert slept, Rose slung her arm over his chest, trying to relax with his breathing. He'd explained what they meant by "an economic unit" but she couldn't get him to talk of their prospects. Everyone had closed down the discussion, drawing it inward. Were they protecting her from worry? Or knowledge? She could only take Aunt Marion's advice: leave it to the men. What could she offer anyway?

She had hardly fallen asleep when Robert gripped her arm. "Someone's outside," he said in a low voice. "I think I heard voices in the bushes." A horse whinnied near the front gate. All at once came the sound of men in a war dance – a trumpet, saucepans and rhythmic caterwauling. Robert groaned into his pillow. "Oh no."

Rose sat up in alarm. "What is it?"

"We're being tin-canned. Quick, get decent."

"Why?"

"It's, it's a local custom – for newlyweds. For us."

Rose felt more puzzled than grateful as she leaped out. Robert knocked the matches onto the floor as he tried to light the lamp, but by then she had most of her clothes on from the pile on the chair.

"Get up young McLeods," they chanted. Dogs barked. Stones cascaded down the iron roof. Noise everywhere, pot-lid cymbals, spoons drumming on saucepans. "Ten, nine, eight ... "

The sound of bottles clinking came from outside her window.

"This isn't a drinking house, man," she heard someone say fiercely. "Stow 'em here. Pick 'em up later."

Rose joined the crowd, taking Robert's arm, not yet over the shock. Aunt Marion came from her bedroom with plates of food.

"You knew," Rose exclaimed.

"It's been under the bed. I had to stop Neil taking a bite."

Men brought butterfly cakes and sponge kisses from wives who'd stayed home with children. One couple laughed scornfully. "Better for our nippers not to know we've left the house." Rose moved among them, collecting best wishes, batting off warnings of it all wearing off. Jimmy rippled his fingers down the piano and lead everyone in singing "For They Are Jolly Good Fellows".

"What about a bit of Bing Crosby, Jimmy. Do y'know 'Don't fence me in'?"

A roar of approval.

Oh, give me land, lots of land under starry skies above, sang Jimmy.

Don't fence me in, everyone joined in.

"Are you related to any of these? Rose asked Robert at the end of the verse.

"Half the room. Distantly. She's my cousin. The rest have been around all my life." So everyone in this room knew him better than she did.

I want to ride to the ridge where the west commences
And gaze at the moon till I lose my senses ...

"Most of us are related to each other somehow," said a man with a moustache and shaggy eyebrows.

I found my thrill, on Blueberry Hill. Everyone swayed.

Between songs she tried to match names to farms. A community of cousins and in-laws. It wouldn't pay to speak ill of anyone.

"Neil, Neil. What's the one you sang at New Year? The one about gathering folks into the warm heart o' the family. Mighty suitable for the occasion. Do ye know it, Jimmy?" The pianist shook his head.

"Never mind." Neil dropped his head, stared at his feet and swallowed. Then his head lifted. A rich baritone filled the room.

Call the ewes tae the knowes,
Call them where the heather blows,
Call them where the burnie rowes
My bonnie dearie.

By the fourth verse Rose was humming along with the chorus, imagining the young lovers amongst the hills of Scotland.

"Robert, where's that fiddle of yours?" someone called. "Give us a jig before supper."

"I'm too rusty," Robert objected. Rose felt for him. They mustn't push him.

"Nonsense. Most of us are tone deaf anyway."

Reluctantly Robert took the violin, passed from hand to hand from the top of the piano. A careful tune-up, a few bars of a slow strathspey, and the "Eightsome Reel" burst from the violin. Robert was confident in tune, rhythm and pace. Pitch mattered less as the clapping increased. His fingers danced on the strings. How absorbed he was, how inwardly focused.

A couple sprang to their feet and twirled around the wooden floor. Robert inclined his head to the instrument, his smiling eyes fixed on Rose. Her man. Centre of attention. Not so much a solo performance, but his music drawing everyone together.

Nothing in their days in Wellington, not three years of letters nor three weeks of marriage had ever hinted he could play like this.

Eventually "Auld Lang Syne" faded and everyone stumbled out. Aunt Marion looked at Rose. "Was it worth it?"

"Great fun. I feel caught up by this community." She stacked a pile of plates next to the sink. "Thank you so much for your part in it. I had no idea." She stepped towards Aunt Marion to hug her.

But the older woman turned away. "Indeed, a real tonic after this morning's news."

For a few hours, the contents of the letter had evaporated from her mind. But now she felt them returning with a thud.

※

Mary looked at Adam's account for dipping her two hundred and fifty sheep. Why did people keep asking her for money she couldn't possibly pay? Of course they had to be dipped. Or suffer skin-creeping diseases, like lice and ticks and blowflies. After her father had died, dipping was one job too many, so she ignored it until she found some of them standing dead still in the paddock, mangy, wasting away, without the will to live.

The next year she drove them a mile or so to Neil's dip which her father had shared, pushing each sheep under the pungent liquid with the dipping plunger. But when her sheep wandered off onto Neil's pasture, taking two days to separate from his, Neil was so angry, waving his crook at her, that she would have agreed to anything. Adam had come up with this arrangement.

She sat down on the tree stump. There had to be another way. She could repay Adam with labour. A day's work at tailing or stooking. But his daughters and neighbours usually turned up for Adam.

Across in the paddock her ewes were resting, some under the yellow flowering gorse hedge she'd planted when Neil kept complaining about her sheep wandering onto the road, a menace to horses and his new wife Aunt Marion's new-fangled car. Her sheep were too docile to be a menace to anyone, barely reacting to her as she picked up her thistle slasher and wandered into the paddock. Two hundred and fifty of them, she thought proudly. She began to count: five, ten, thirty-five under the macrocarpas. Fifty-seven on the grassy slope, ninety along the gorse hedge, sixty-three down by the pond. Where were the last five? She laboured up the slope, slashing at thistles. Four more. Two hundred and forty nine?

Then she counted them again. Two hundred and fifty. As it should be.

But it had given her an idea.

20

AUNT LUCY USHERED THEM from the low-ceilinged kitchen into the sitting room. Rose had expected to be quizzed about university life and her lack of experience with sheep, but with Aunt Lucy there seemed no need to justify her right to be there – no need to reassure her that she would learn everything. Here nothing was at stake except family and neighbourly relations.

Away from the horses, Adam was charming, in a well-pressed shirt and a change of braces for the occasion. He was older than Rose had realised.

The room struggled to be warm enough. Even on this mild evening, the thick stone walls absorbed heat for their own sake rather than offering it back into the room. The simplicity of these spaces, however, conveyed a sense of sufficient elegance belied by the exterior of the cottage. Scrim covered the walls of the hallway, hidden behind beautiful wallpapers and heavy drapes in both the sitting room and the tiny bedroom where Rose had left her coat. Soon, soon, Rose would have a whole house to put her mark on.

"This is Katy, our Karitane nurse," said Aunt Lucy, lifting a photograph from the piano. "She married a farmer near Clinton. And this is Alena, our hairdresser. And Miriam, almost finished her nursing training." A smile exactly like her mother's. "The others aren't home often, but I do hope you'll be friends."

Rose could do with a friend. No one in this whole province, in this whole island, could be called a friend. Except Robert.

"Ye've met Mary, have ye Rose? Och, there's a canny one." Adam lit his pipe. "Tried to put one across me, she did." The smoke drew satisfactorily. "Ye see, I dip her sheep."

"Adam spent all day, mustering," Aunt Lucy broke in, "dipping, droving them back just before dusk."

"She pays me, that's the arrangement, so I drop the account in her mailbox."

"And she claims he didn't return two of her sheep. She crossed out the total and wrote 'minus two sheep not returned' – which meant she owed him nothing."

"Dinna cover the cost."

Robert laughed. "She leaves us her shopping list in the mailbox, but with never enough money. But you'll do it again next year, won't you Uncle?" he added with a grin.

"Och, lad, why would I do that with ye at hand?"

※

"So we'll see you at church on Sunday?" Rose asked as they prepared to leave.

"Ye'll see me at funerals and christenings, Rose, and may there be many of the latter." Adam chuckled. "Robert, lad, dinna give up on the loan. Ye'll have one before long."

Robert muttered something indecipherable.

Adam kept moving towards the gate. Was he simply saying he was on their side? Or involved in some way?

"Pity we didn't manage a son, eh Lucy?" he'd said over dessert.

"Tut now, Adam. You've three wonderful daughters."

"Narry a sign of any farming lads after the last two. Aye, there's a good livin' on this property for a younger man." Rose imagined Adam and Neil, smoke curling under their hats, one with a son in need of land, the other with more than he could manage. Was she missing some nuances of finance and favours?

※

"All right, you win," Rose puffed as she stepped off her bike. She could beat Robert on the flat, but the hill stretched muscles she hadn't used since Te Mata Peak. Robert leaned over his bicycle handles, his shoulders heaving.

"See that gully?" Robert pointed below them. "Did I tell you I had a car once?"

"You had a car?"

"A Model T. I bought it from a farmer before call-up. Dad was distracted by Aunt Marion – I must have been eighteen. Twelve pounds ten shillings, I paid. More than two years' wages."

"So where is it now?"

"I parked it right here one afternoon, put the handbrake on and called in to see Winston." His face fell. "When I came out, the belly thing was down there, upside down on the other bank."

"No." Rose started to laugh, quietly at first.

Robert stared disconsolately into the gully. Three sheep stared back up.

"I'd left her idling cos she was so hard to crank – the vibrations must have released the handbrake."

Her laughter swelled with the improbable image.

"Everything except the windscreen was twisted and smashed."

"Oh Robert," she laughed uncontrollably. "I can just see the wreck, you standing here."

"I got the horse to pull it over the creek. Took weeks to get it off Winston's land." He turned to her. "It wasn't funny." But despite himself he started to chuckle.

Then he laughed aloud. "Just as well I kept my bike," he said. "Hey, Uncle Adam didn't offer me a whisky tonight. Maybe Dad talked to him about that too. You're having an influence."

"Rubbish."

"Come here, Mrs McLeod." Robert held his bike steady with one hand and kissed her, his free hand under her coat drawing her closer. Oh, how she wanted him, all of him, now.

He pulled away suddenly. "Race you home."

21

SUNDAY. TWO O'CLOCK. There was quiet reverence as the minister climbed the steps to the pulpit, dwarfed by the plastered shell shape of the preaching space. Sixty, seventy people of all ages sat on solid pews in this chilly Oamaru stone building, a church unfussed by cushions, unadorned, in keeping with the Scots distaste for decoration. The plain wooden panelling drew her eye to the splendid wooden ceiling above. Women sat attentively in their Sunday-best hats, frocks and cardigans, children with clean knees and freshly polished shoes, older men in suits with waistcoats and pocket watches. She ought to have worn something warmer.

Aunt Marion, on the organ, pumped out the introit.

All people that on earth do dwell, her voice led the singing,

Sing to the Lord with cheerful voice.

Neil took a little longer than anyone else with each line and remained seated.

"Today we welcome Mrs McLeod, Robert's wife," began the minister. "We are most grateful that she has offered her talents to the adult Bible Class, along with Robert." Robert's friend Keith and his wife Maud turned and smiled as a murmur of welcome enfolded her. No clapping in church, of course. The familiar service swept her along and the sermon drew her into preparation for Easter.

From clear leadlight windows, sunlight streamed across the backs of the family in the front row and caught the black marble memorial board, where a scroll was engraved "To the Glory of God" in gold letters above a list of local men lost in the Great War. Neil's brother Andrew. And two more McLeods. Other young men she had known who had not returned sauntered through her mind.

But there's so much to praise God for, she thought.

And a great need of His strength.

This place feels more like home than home does.

She had expected the farmers in ties and tweed at the picnic ground the following Saturday afternoon – the tartan rugs spread under the oak trees, the sandwiches, the cream sponges and the flasks of tea. But she hadn't expected that this community gathering was in her honour, with gifts: shortbread, linen handkerchiefs, cup and saucer sets, strawberry jam, knitted gloves and crochet-edged tray clothes. A teapot.

"Come on, Rose. It's the three-legged race," Robert called, pulling her up from the rug where women had gathered. They tied themselves together at the ankle and tried jogging. Rose couldn't follow him at all.

"Think of me as the lead horse of a team," he said. "When I say 'go', it's the outside leg first."

"No more practising, you two. Come and make fools of yourselves in the real race," called a voice. But they had clicked. Youth, love or considerate opponents, they beat everyone to the finish line.

"I haven't done that since varsity days," Rose said as she flung herself next to a plump baby and tickled him under the chin. A long wail followed him to his mother's arms. What had she done? Babies were a mystery.

"Varsity? What's that?" asked the young woman beside her.

"Just slang, for university," Rose replied, puzzled.

"Did you go to university?" another asked.

"For a couple of years before I went teaching," Rose said.

"You must be very clever." Rose could think of nothing in reply.

"I've never met anyone who's been to university before," said the baby's mother. Shouts came from across the grass. "Patricia, your Colin's in the river."

"He'll be all right. Just wants to show off." Patricia sat down again, her neck stretched just high enough to observe her son. "Left school at fourteen myself. Got a job at the draper's."

The others had similar stories: work at the woollen mills, the post office, secretary to the stock agent, helping her mother till she got married. Rose felt isolated by an education she'd never had to defend. She didn't want to be separated from the warm female companionship, defined by their common youthfulness and the area of the rugs.

"I learnt a lot there, but I wish I knew how to make my stove go all night so that I don't get up to a stone-cold house."

With some relief, Rose found them take her lead. For ten minutes they compared stoves and ways to combat the cold.

"Wait till you have children. Then you'll know you're alive, day and night. Hardly time for your husband."

"No energy to fight off your husband, you mean."

"Cynthia!" they objected in unison, roaring with laughter.

Spots of rain appeared on her stockinged legs. Thunder rolled around the valley and everyone scattered. "See you at the meeting on Tuesday, Rose?" called Ness, a young woman she had just met.

"I hope so," said Rose as she clambered over the stile, laden with gifts.

22

"'Tis A CRITICAL HARVEST, Rose, this oats," Neil explained as she poured water into the horses' trough. "Canna get quality pastures and profit from sheep without plentiful food for the horses." Neil was energetic today, the unprecedented number of sacks lifting his spirits. "There's more than they're needin'. We've cash in this barn."

"With a tractor," Robert called from high on the stack, "we could sell it all. A tractor doesn't need oats, or a rest. Ploughing would be much speedier." He looked down at Rose for support, but her mind had drifted to the distressing memory of the orchard horse being led off to the tall brick building with the high chimney.

Neil's face clouded. "Och, lad. Ye'll take many years' wages for a tractor with the horsepower o' this team, for a few handfuls of oats and a rubdown." He heaved a sack against the wall. Robert had been shifting four sacks to every one of his father's, but leaned against the door as Neil finished the job.

"Last one? Will ye bring the rams to the yard afore they go oot, lad. Rose, you'll be wanted in the hoose, no doubt." Something not for her eyes? Rose lifted her eyebrows to her husband above her and stepped outside.

How different the countryside looked today as they walked across Bill's Hill to check for cast sheep, alert to the sombre southerly muscling in from the coast. Hills blended into each other with no shadow of definition. Behind them to the east, pale-grey sea lay indistinguishable from pale-grey sky, the horizon a mere construct of the mind. The dogs dived into the gully after rabbits.

She pulled her woollen hat over her ears. As long as they didn't loiter in the autumn wind she was warm enough, with a heavy coat over her skirt and thick stockings. "Robert," Rose began. "What will happen to us if we don't get that loan?"

Robert tucked her arm tightly under his.

"The worst thing? The four of us struggle on with no chance of improvement. Worse than that? Starting somewhere else. Cheaper land, more isolated. Or turn our backs on farming altogether." He kicked a dry sheep turd. "That will never happen."

"How?"

"Dad has plans." He walked with his head down. She couldn't decide if he had no confidence in those plans, or disagreed with them, or had no say. Could he be trying to protect her?

"Can't you do anything?"

"We already are. It's complicated."

"It's my worry too. I need to understand it."

Robert sighed and stood still. "Firstly, the titles are a mess. Dad's mother, Grandma Catherine, put some sections under one title when she was living with Uncle Will in Alexandra. But others are still separate, going back to Dad's grandfather. The solicitor's tidying it up. Anyway, we've a new plan. All it needs is the stock company's approval."

"You're hopeful?"

He took her arm and began walking again. "Five hundred ewes aren't enough. We've fifty acres in grass or oats or swedes. But look at all the useless land. Hundreds of acres. The maddening thing is that a loan would get them productive. They don't lend on imagination, just on what they see – only fifty acres cultivated."

Out here, the situation was self-evident. Across the rolling hills, the cultivated tops oozed to the crest of each ridge, like green icing poured over buns, before the land fell away into a confusion of broom, briar, elderberry and manuka. Steep unworkable gullies. Other ridges grew only matagouri and tussock.

"Those ridges are Mary's. If I got my hands on them, we could run three, four hundred more sheep. Her father's sheep roamed everywhere. He was more interested in the drink than in the fences. Tried his hand at blacksmithing for a while. That's where our gear in the smithy came from. See the lumpy land, running up from that kanuka scrub? Big Stones and Big Holes we call them – wrecked by goldmining. Imagine all that in pasture. Right after lambing that's where we'll be. Two-horse teams, clearing rock. We'll show the assessor it'll work."

"You've no intention of leaving this land, have you?"

"Never."

"Then neither will I. We'll have to work out how I can help."

❋

As she swung the egg basket through the gateway, Rose hummed "Jesu, Joy of Man's Desiring". Stepping between piles of hen poop she lost the rhythm. Such a smelly mess so close to the house. There must be a better way.

What was that slow creaking? The rhythmical sound drew her behind the sod cottage.

Inches from her eyes, the hooves of a sheep swayed. She lifted her gaze to the gaping cavity of the carcass and the chains binding the naked hind legs, which were hooked over a bar between branches of the macrocarpa tree, metal grinding on metal in the wind.

The head was missing. Blood dripped from the neck stump, splashing into a pool on the ground. Dripping, dripping ...

She came to in the darkness of Neil's worsted jacket, his arm looming across her body, his close tobacco breath checking hers.

"Och, lassie." He pulled back awkwardly as she regained consciousness. "What's come over ye?"

Rose jolted alert. Instantly she remembered why she had fainted. She shut her eyes again, attempting to deny the image. "It's that ... "

"Ye canna have yer meat without ye kill it. Come on, up with ye. Keep yerself to the fowls for noo." He steadied her as she recovered her balance and bundled a fresh sheepskin into her arms. "Here, take this to Aunt Marion. She'll be making a rug for your room."

How could she ever be a farmer's wife if she fainted every time blood appeared?

At the kitchen door Aunt Marion hooted with laughter. "Did you hurt yourself?" Rose shook her head. "No? Come on then, this needs attention right away."

She spread the skin wool side down on the verandah concrete. "He patted you on the cheek?" Rose nodded.

Pulling small pieces of flesh away, Aunt Marion scraped the pelt with the knife from her apron pocket, separating sinews and muscle fibre from the hide. She sat back and looked at Rose, bemused. "Neil was down on his knees, leaning over you?" Rose nodded.

Aunt Marion warned of the danger of cutting holes in the new pelt and showed Rose how to trim the edges with shearing blades. Satisfied that no extra matter remained, she rubbed layer upon layer of salt into the folds and ridges, until it seemed an inch thick.

"That's it. A week in this cool corner and we can begin the tanning." She laughed again. "Just wait till I get that man. He claims to be so stiff he can't bend to fill a coal bucket."

23

JUST AFTER THREE O'CLOCK some weeks later, a car rumbled down the road. And a second car? Rose hadn't put out enough cups. Robert was already welcoming his cousin, who turned towards Rose as she approached, her blue eyes sparkling. From her ruddy complexion Rose could tell she was an outdoors woman, with classic taste in clothes: the stylish coat, the tweed costume and the fine leather shoes.

"Meet Margie, my cousin. And here's George, her husband," Robert said. The driver of the second car shook her hand enthusiastically.

"And Mathilda, Neil's sister," Aunt Marion announced as Mathilda adjusted her black hat, shook out her full skirt and emerged from her daughter's passenger seat.

"Ahh, lass, we meet at last. Ye often had a mention in his letters. Poor Robert, worrying about ye with those Americans in Wellington ... "

Rose laughed.

"Perhaps we can make amends for not sharing your wedding day – so impossible to leave the farm for time to travel such a distance – if you would do us the honour of accepting ..." – her arm traced the length of the car – "... our wedding present."

What? Had she understood? Aunt Marion covered her face. Robert looked dumbfounded. This couldn't be true.

"Before she married, Margie drove me everywhere off the farm," Mathilda explained. "Once George moved in, his car came with him. We share it now, since my cottage is so close to the new farmhouse. The Hillman is simply superfluous."

A superfluous car?

"Dear nephew, it's yours." She held the keys aloft. "Why don't ye take Rose for a drive?" She put the keys behind her back. "If ye promise me the car stays on the road, mmm?"

Robert looked sheepish. "Promise, Aunt."

She dropped the keys dramatically into his disbelieving hands. "Tea?" she said, with a laugh, taking Aunt Marion by the elbow. Neil followed through the gate, still shaking his head.

Rose ran her hand over the high curve of the mudguards, the door handles, the grill. "This is such a beautiful car."

"If you need to crank her," said George, "hold the handle side on like this and stand back, well back. Otherwise you'll get it in the shins from the kick-back when she catches."

Rose peered at the leather seats and the travelling rug in the back seat.

The motor caught. "Get in, get in," urged Margie.

Their own Hillman Minx. Rose stroked the upholstery. Robert tested the foot pedals. At the top of Mary's Hill, they stopped in the gateway. From this high point the air was clear through to the mountains today, the spiky peaks of the Remarkables white against the distant mountain ranges, softened by hazy blues and violets.

"Imagine having a house here," Rose sighed.

Twisting past the steering wheel, Robert took her in his arms. "You've just confirmed my favourite site."

"It's spectacular."

"You'd need to be resilient to build here. It's darned exposed to the wind."

"We'll always be resilient."

"You'd need wind breaks first. Conifers and blue gums around the head of the gully. Rhododendrons near the house, anything your heart desires." He drummed his fingers on the steering wheel.

She could almost see it. Their own house.

※

"Keep it to yourself but George knows someone who's after horses," Robert said under his breath as the men headed for the stables. Rose gulped. Was Robert about to challenge his father? Perhaps he needed Neil and Aunt Marion to move on just as much as she did.

"Shall we go for a walk? The duck pond?" Margie suggested.

"Good idea. I've not been there yet."

"Don't rush back. Dinner's all done," Aunt Marion said. They pulled on oilskin coats and gumboots.

Rose walked backwards across the road, scarcely believing that the black car would still be there when they returned.

"When I was a child, I loved being here in the holidays," Margie laughed. "We'd get so dirty, finding bird's eggs and tadpoles. Robert's mother, Alice – Aunty Pal, everyone called her – she'd wash us down in that tin bath."

I would have wanted you here for Robert too, thought Rose. Lively and affable.

"And she sang, always, even while she picked barley stalks out of my hair." Margie stopped and pointed into the distance. "There's the pond. Oh, look."

A pair of white geese took to the air, rising unsteadily in the fickle wind, flying eastward overhead. "What did you do if it was wet?" Rose asked as the honking faded.

"We wrote stories. And poetry. Robert's idea, the poetry. I wasn't much good at it. He wrote lots. And his mother let us help with the bread making."

How close had they been? Did he ever write poems to Margie like her own treasured love-filled lyrics? Don't be absurd, she said to herself, they were children. Nevertheless, she couldn't extinguish the feeling.

"Robert and I both had adoring mothers, but no siblings. We both lost a parent. My father died suddenly. But Robert's mother was sick for ages." Margie lowered her voice. "Robert wouldn't talk about it. My mother stayed here when she was dying. Afterwards she and Uncle Neil could manage only two or three days in the same house." She paused and bit her lip. "Then Uncle Neil wouldn't let anyone come."

That big house. Cold, lifeless.

"His mother's family took Robert to Oamaru to his spinster aunts, but he wasn't happy."

They walked in single file around the sheep track at the head of the gully. Rose pointed to the clay bank. "Look at all the rabbit holes."

"Oh dear." Margie shook her head. "You know how Robert hates killing anything."

She didn't know. She knew nothing compared with this woman who knew his every childhood secret. Was Margie unaware of making her feel inadequate, or was she doing it – surely not – deliberately?

Downhill their steps quickened. "Bessie kept house for them for a year or two. Uncle Neil's cousin, Mary's sister. You've met Mary?"

"At the stooking."

"Bessie's different. Capable and warm-hearted."

Mary's sister cared for Robert? No wonder Neil was so charitable towards Mary. She was still collecting the payback.

"Robert was fond of Bessie. There was another housekeeper before Aunt Marion came." Margie laughed. "Robert thinks of her as the last housekeeper – he'd never admit his father and Aunt Marion were a real love match. He was off on army training when they were courting."

At the bog they held onto each other, laughing as they wobbled from clump to clump across the oozing black ink. "Luckily Robert's very focused on the future," Rose said, wiping her boots on clumps of clean grass.

Rose frowned. How could she reclaim Robert, to find something Margie didn't know? "He doesn't want to talk about the war. He's not even keen on Aunt Marion's memorial plans."

"He's always been optimistic," Margie said. "He once told me in a letter that 'an optimist is often as wrong as a pessimist but is far happier'."

Rose fought her jealousy over the trail of intimate contact. Margie cared about him. They had to be on the same side. She squeezed between the wires of the fence and held them apart for Margie. "He sees swathes of trees across all this, Italian style." Rose stretched her arm out confidently to the hills. "And he wants everything mechanised."

They walked companionably towards the house. A particular passage from one of his letters floated into her mind, how he'd wanted to tour New Zealand and "breathe in my own country". At least he had satisfied some of that during their honeymoon. Over and over she had read about his desire "to absorb the essence of everywhere which is New Zealand, to understand the variety of my fellow countrymen, met in foreign fields in unaccustomed times". Like her breathing in everything here: the land, people past and present, their expectations and limitations.

Their obligations.

24

"Why don't you take a day off before winter," Aunt Marion said. "Take the car for a decent run. You've got plenty of petrol coupons."

Robert held his fork in mid-air. Days off were unheard of. Apart from Sundays. "Why?" he asked, bemused.

"Because, dear boy, your wife needs your attention."

Rose hadn't asked for more attention, though Robert had been working the horse team from dawn till dusk. "Where could we go?"

"Alexandra, perhaps, to Aunty Betty's," Robert said slowly. "She's Dad's sister. I recuperated there for a few months after time in hospital with double pneumonia. Which I caught at the Waiwera army camp. Very dry climate, Alexandra."

"And it worked?" Rose asked.

"Eventually. Aunty Betty's a bit of a socialite, but she spends her days looking after the poor and needy." He laughed. "That was me at nineteen. Or we could go south … "

Aunt Marion looked perplexed.

"Alexandra. That's inland, isn't it?" Rose said. "I haven't been further than Lawrence that way. Is it in the mountains?"

Aunt Marion let out a satisfied sigh.

❦

"Stay a week," Aunty Betty's telegram said. Robert agreed to one night.

The morning hinted at frost but the day was clear as they chugged through the young poplar trees of Lawrence, disturbing the swirling carpet of yellow leaves. Robert pulled in at the garage to check the tyres.

Rose looked in the draper's shop window. Baby wear. Pinks and blues, ribbons and laces. White wool and knitting patterns. Beautiful smiling, clean babies. Robert was at her elbow. "Babies, Mrs McLeod? Very pretty." He was suddenly still. "That shawl, I've seen it before."

"What?"

"Nothing. It's just," he said hesitantly, "like one Mother kept. I once had a brother, for a few hours. Before me. I was never allowed to touch that shawl."

"You almost had a brother? Your poor mother."

※

Before long the hills seemed to close in, with no apparent way through. They followed a horse and trap across the Beaumont bridge, her first view of the Clutha River, magnificent, ice blue-green, churning and rushing below.

Suddenly the barrier of the Beaumont Hill loomed before them.

Robert changed gear. Would this car make it to the top?

What a relief to pull over where others had their bonnets up, steam billowing from boiling radiators. "Come on. Let's climb the rocks while she cools." Robert held out his hand. "There must be an even better view."

They took photos of each other: Robert triumphant on a huge rocky outcrop; Rose crouching in a cave; Robert peering into the engine impersonating a mechanic; Rose in sultry starlet pose, elbows on the car, balancing on one foot.

Relaxed and excited now, they reached the orchards along the river valley. "Apples! Please stop." She checked the familiar boxes – cox's orange, red delicious – and poked her nose into the packing shed. Ahhh, the aroma. Back in the car they crunched apples all the way to Roxburgh where they found a grassy bank overlooking the river. Above them, the tired brown of parched hills and the shock of a cobalt sky.

"There'll be a dam here soon," said Robert as he stretched out on the tartan rug with his mutton sandwiches. "Italians and Yugoslavs are coming to build it. Not enough technical know-how in New Zealand."

"It's so brown above the river. Your sheep wouldn't do well here."

"But look at the colour in the water. See how the shadows never stay still." He pointed to the craggy rocks and the swirling water below. "It's the ultimate contest. Water is dynamic; it wears down the rock. Rock's immobile, defying summer heat and freezing winters and the unrelenting sandpaper effect of the water." He fiddled with the settings on his camera. "Water appears to be benign. But it's a demon with charm. Water always wins."

He looped the strap of his camera around his neck and clambered down the bank to the edge of the river.

Rose stood above him shading her eyes, watching him jump nimbly from rock to rock. He crouched to line up the shot, leaning lower, lower. He straightened and leaped to the next rock. She lifted her face to the sun.

The river rushed towards him, pouring in ever-changing curves over huge rocks, smooth and black-wet. He aimed his camera towards the yellow willows in the distance. Turning to move again, he looked up and waved. Suddenly he lost momentum mid-stride, teetered on one foot, slipped and landed hard, legs in the water.

Rose leaped off the rug with a gasp.

She knew he couldn't swim, couldn't fight a current like this. If he was pulled in, she could never save him. She looked around. No one. What should she do?

He held his camera high at full stretch, searching for a fingerhold with his other hand. In slow motion, he heaved his upper body across the rock. His head sagged. He pulled forward again, water draining from his torso and lay still, panting.

"Wait," Rose screamed. She floundered through the long grass as he heaved himself forward again, lunge after lunge, still clasping the camera, making no headway against the pull of the current. Slowly he dragged one sodden leg after the other onto the rock. She was halfway down the bank before he drew himself onto his knees. Sagging, he seemed to lose all energy.

And then his head rose. He waved. Slowly he stood up. Eyes fixed on his feet, he came across the rocks and clambered up towards her.

"Saved," he shouted, waving the camera above his head, his trousers hanging dark and heavy. At the top he held it out to her. "Closer to losing this here than through the whole of the Italian campaign."

"You're safe, thank God you're safe." Rose wrapped her arms around his wet body and tried to calm her breathing. "If you'd been caught in the current – all I could see was you disappearing. You're not bulletproof." Too late she realised it was a bad word for a soldier. "I thought I was going to lose you," she said quietly, arms folded tightly across her chest.

"Must have looked worse from this angle. Sorry. Come here." He wrapped her in his arms, neither caring about the wetness seeping into her clothes.

"Probably looks deceptively passive from the rocks," she murmured into his beating heart. "You did say that river's a demon with charm."

She pulled away. "We'll have to wring your trousers out." Robert looked up the slope to the road. "Don't worry, no one's here. And we're married. Take them off." The relief of laughter. She wiped away tears as he hopped from one leg to the other.

They squeezed out his trousers between them. "I didn't pack you a spare pair of trousers."

"I own one pair of dress trousers. These."

Soon the rocky heights opened into the vast basin of the two river valleys, the Manuherikia stretching north and the Clutha to the west, with Alexandra at the junction. Robert pulled over and pointed out the mountain ranges.

"I'm glad Aunt Marion talked you into coming here," Rose said.

"She did?"

"She was up to something."

Robert tipped his head back and laughed. "Aunt Marion wants Uncle Will to use his political influence to get us the loan. Dad doesn't want a favour he can't repay. She needs to keep out of it." He drummed his fingers on the steering wheel.

※

They turned into a side street and stopped. Swathes of roses draped tiredly over the arched entranceway. A wandering gravel path drew them into a luxurious garden.

From beyond the walnut trees came a flailing noise. "Bother."

"Aunty?"

"Is that you, Robert? At last, there's a man about when you need one. Take hold of the other end, will you? This netting keeps springing back. Hardly worth the trouble. Not enough strawberries to satisfy anyone. Just a moment. It's caught in my hair."

A strand of thick hair came away from her carefully pinned thatch.

"Careful, the other end's caught on the raspberry canes." Her glasses on a cord around her neck tangled with the floral brooch that fastened her silk blouse. Carelessly, she stomped across the garden in leather boots several sizes too large. Men's overalls covered her legs, the sleeves tied around her waist.

"Thank you," she said, dusting soil from her hands. "I noticed this ugly corner when we had the National Party ladies here for afternoon tea. I've been so caught up trying to get care for my poor babies that I couldn't do anything until today. My, Robert, what's happened to your trousers?"

She didn't wait for an answer but stepped through the azaleas onto the path. "Hello. You must be Rose."

❧

"Och, Mother never settled to brown hills and rocks," Aunty Betty said over tea. "She insisted on being buried at Waitahuna, near her green hills. It wasn't just to be with Father."

"Had she always lived there?"

"No, no. Her own father was surgeon to a Scottish regiment, then a GP, in Perthshire. When he died, Grandmother took the unmarried ones to Adelaide. Mother was eleven. Do you know your grandmother's secret, Robert? She was signed on as a domestic servant. Perhaps it gave her a free passage."

"But she travelled on to New Zealand. Did she come alone?"

"With her twin brother James and her mother. She'd be a nurse of twenty by then. I'd forgotten – people used to turn up at home with blood-soaked bandages. She'd lie them on the kitchen table."

"She set broken bones?"

"Possibly. Mostly cuts, I expect, from saws and knives and horse kicks. We were never allowed to look. There was whisky in a high cupboard for anyone she had to stitch up. Probably Adam got his first taste when she wasn't looking."

❧

"You're isolated in the country in an emergency," Aunty Betty said to Rose as they strolled around the terraced garden. "You must know your first aid. Accidents can be just a frisky horse or a swollen stream away."

Rose could see her point. How could she, a strong swimmer, have been prepared for Robert being swept away? No one's life had ever depended on her before.

"Nowadays babies usually survive, but there are still far too many poor malnourished creatures." They gazed through a gap in the hills where the river turned a bend. "Mother would have been at Doctor's Point during the Depression, handing out the broth. Many families lived there in miserably cold caves and stone huts." She sighed. "You have to get involved in politics if you want real change."

Robert's hand appeared around her waist. "Where does that path go to, Aunty, on the other side of the river?" Rose smiled to herself. He was clearly getting restless.

"Why don't you find out for yourselves?"

❧

"You're back," Aunt Marion called. "Did you talk to Uncle Will?"

"Rose will tell you," Robert said, carrying the suitcase up the passage.

"It was lovely. Craggy rocks and the brown hills are surprisingly beautiful. Aunty Betty is astonishing. We talked about nutrition, irrigation schemes, Wellington politics."

"See you at tea time." Robert patted Rose on the shoulder. "Don't tell her about the river."

"Never."

Aunt Marion appeared again at her bedroom door. "So he didn't talk to Uncle Will?"

"Uncle Will? He was in Wellington." Without a word, Aunt Marion turned away.

❧

"Neil and I are visiting my niece for a few days," Aunt Marion said that evening. "We'll be back on Saturday afternoon to play the organ on Sunday. Are you sure you can manage?"

"Of course. And if I can't, I do have Robert."

Aunt Marion paused before replying. "Yes. You do."

25

IT WAS A MILD DAY, a June breeze rising from the gully, the sun weak but persistent. Despite it being winter it was a good day for washing. Aunt Marion usually got the copper started, but today Rose fed twigs and kindling onto the burning paper. She filled the metal bucket from the outside tap, back and forth, for both the copper and the rinsing tub.

She had never used a copper before. In Havelock North there had been an electric washing machine as long as she could remember, and everywhere else she'd lived as well.

She had to prove herself today. To Aunt Marion. To Neil. But especially to Robert. Keeping house was only commonsense. And staying alert. Coal on the kitchen fire, don't let it go out. Check the water in the copper – not even warm. More wood. Back to the kitchen. Mix the scones. Dishes.

She stood with her hands in the warm sink and allowed herself to drift.

Robert's fingers ran up the nape of her neck and through her hair. "We're alone, alone in our house at last. Mmmm, your neck smells of – of woodsmoke."

"Have you come to help, by any chance? Washing, drying? Your choice."

He undid her apron and led her by the hand to the bed she had not yet made.

❋

Clouds of steam billowed as they came back to the washhouse. Laughing and flapping towels at each other, they cleared the air enough to find Aunt Marion's homemade soap. Rose grated it into the water and dunked the sheets with the manuka pole. They stood for a moment to admire their success, adult and pragmatic.

Robert went for more wood. Rose stirred the cauldron, imagining Macbeth's witches muttering love spells into the vapours. Steam dampened her hair, her dress, her shoes. Round and round, *Cruisin' down the river, on a Sunday afternoon.*

Back in the kitchen she checked the other fire, mixed and cut a batch of scones then slid the tray into what seemed to be a hot oven, judging by the heat on her face.

"I'm off now on the horse." Robert waved through the window.

Rose fed the sheets through the hand wringer into the rinsing tub. If she was quick, she'd have time to read the newspaper. Being so far from Wellington hadn't taken away her desire to be informed. She needed to catch up on Mother's hobby-horse: the government's adoption of the Statute of Westminster. Although the Dominions had been given official independence in 1931, New Zealand had never taken it up. At last the country could now be fully independent, without the colonial shackles of the past.

The cold rinsing water chilled her arms as she stirred the sheets in the tub and fed them back through the wringer, forcing the handle around, squeezing out the water. They dropped into the wicker basket like flattened cardboard.

She'd done it. Linen, long johns and bloomers flapped on the line. A good day for midday dinner on the verandah: mutton chops, mashed potatoes and silverbeet. Pear and rice pudding for dessert. She went inside for a tablecloth from her glory box to cover the crates.

※

Rain in the night fused with dreams of cars and slamming doors. She woke unrested. Robert had promised Aunt Marion he would milk the cow again today. Everything must be perfect when they came home.

The kitchen was Arctic cold, the coal range completely dead. Why now? She'd kept it alight for three nights.

Shivering in her nightgown and slippers, she opened the soot trap at the back of the stove. A puff of wind blew down the chimney, wafting sticky black powder into her hair, her face, before she could block it with the coal scuttle.

Suddenly Robert's arms were around her waist. "My lovely Rose," he laughed. He dipped his finger into the soot and ran it down her nose. He'd pay for that. She dipped three fingers, wiped them across his cheek and darted away. He dipped again and chased her around the table, behind the chair. Whooping with laughter, they dived from stove to table, dodging the parry and thrust of blackened fingers.

Someone coughed. Robert's father stood in the doorway, stroking his stubbled face. "Mornin'." With slow dignity, he carried his chamber pot outside.

Rose and Robert exploded with laughter.

Neil returned. "Aunt Marion's still not feeling well. We came back in the night. She'll be in bed awhile. Dinna let me interrupt," he chuckled.

26

AUNT MARION LOOKED UP from stirring the porridge. "Good sleep for everyone? Won't be so quiet once we've bairns in the house." Couldn't Aunt Marion *think* it rather than saying it aloud? Robert just assumed children would turn up. *When* exactly, was in the hands of God. He laughed off baby jokes; but she felt their bite.

Last night she'd been reading the *Free Lance* from Margaret, showing her Pahiatua pupils in Polish costume as a guard of honour at her wedding. Right next to the photograph was an official advice notice: women were to book their maternity hospital as soon as they were married. Really. And yesterday the Prime Minister emphasized the moral duty of women to have children. "The family is not only the centre of the loving home but the heart of the nation's rebuilding."

Marry for love; discover you're responsible for the nation's future. A month ago she would have wholeheartedly endorsed his thinking, but now – now a slither of anxiety had crept in. Childless women were swept aside like collateral damage.

What if something was wrong with her? Had this occurred to Robert? Being here with him was all she could wish for, and she was certain he felt the same way. For now.

Since living here, she'd realised how essential children were to family farms. Land wove a binding around the heart, strengthening as it passed down the generations, a far more visceral contract than the paper of title deeds passing between strangers. Robert was inseparable from the three generations before him, bound as firmly to the land as they were to each other.

Yesterday Robert had shown her the crumbling remains of another cob cottage. "Can you credit it? Fourteen children." No government edicts about booking into hospital for this wife.

"My brother John played Benedict in *Much Ado About Nothing*," Rose laughed. "I can still see him shouting 'The world must be peopled!' in his squeaky fourteen-year-old voice. We had no idea why Mother and Father were laughing."

She stepped over the flagstone. Last night she had tried not to move so blood didn't leak from her cloth pad. Into her fourth month of marriage, she was not peopling anywhere.

"Dad built a cottage like this once," Robert said, kicking at a lump of clay. "Three blokes had government tents out on the hill. Once a week they'd ride past to collect their twenty shillings a week subsidy and come home at night loaded with flour sacks and tins. Mother would drag them in for a meal." He gazed up at the hills. "Imagine it: tents in winter."

"Why were they there?"

"Official government goldminers. If they found anything, they had to declare it and pay the government ten per cent. A couple of them stayed on and found a nugget. I can still feel the weight of it in my hand." He stepped out of the crumbling remains. "Dad took pity on them and built a cottage. He knew how to diamond-cut the sods and taper the blocks for the chimney."

"Do you know how?"

"I suppose I do."

※

"So you have the last land valuation?"

Rose pushed the paper across the table to the Rehabilitation Officer.

Mr Brown's lips twitched as he read the page. "And the stock valuations?"

Robert pointed. "That page."

Everyone waited. Four hundred and fifty lambs last season; over five hundred ewes. He tapped his pencil on the numbers and grunted. His finger ran down the list of rams, hoggets, two-tooths, wethers. At dipping, nine hundred and forty-two sheep. What was he seeing?

"Good." Mr Brown leaned back, his arms embracing a generous acreage of torso. "Stock condition's improved – a credit to you. You've increased pasture, though it's still on the low side. So," he said, pushing his chair back, "I'll be putting in my recommendation."

"Hallelujah." Rose clutched Robert's arm. Neil slapped the table. Who could doubt them now?

"Once you have the backing of your stock company, it will be up to State Services."

❦

Winter slowed the work on the farm. Men rose with the later dawn, fed the dogs, broke the ice on water troughs, harnessed the horses and carted hay into sheep paddocks. Rose wrapped herself in Robert's army greatcoat and tossed bales from the wagon.

In his diary, Robert kept a tally of his hours and wages. "Just thirty hours this week. It'll be double that in the spring," he promised.

He wrote the new minimum wage for farm workers on a scrap of paper – £5/5/- a week – followed by a trail of multiplication. At least it wasn't the female rate of £3/3/-, thought Rose. "Looks like we'll have some money this month," Robert said. "We don't owe anyone, do we?"

❦

Winter was the season for dancing. Robert bought a gramophone. In their sitting room they pushed back the rugs and furniture. He placed the needle delicately on the record and sang along with Frank Sinatra and the Tommy Dorsey band. *I'll be seeing you in all the old familiar places* ... He whirled Rose around in the tiny space, their feet a tangle.

... that this heart of mine embraces, all day through ... She leaned back in his arms and swayed, moving hardly at all. *I'll find you in the morning sun and when the night is new, I'll be looking at the moon, but I'll be seeing you.*

"Take it away, Mr Trombone Player." Robert moved to the swing. "What dances did they do in Hawke's Bay?"

"I've forgotten anything I ever knew."

"The Maxina? Gay Gordons? Foxtrot?"

"Probably."

He dropped his arms, puzzled.

The gramophone wound down to a deep drawl. "Our church didn't approve of dancing. I never missed it, truly, there were so many other things to do."

"Can I turn you into a bad girl then and get you dancing?" He took her hands. "Let yourself go, just feel the music. Here everyone goes to the dances – Catholics, Presbyterians, Anglicans."

No, it wasn't that. She just didn't feel the music the way Robert did. Perhaps it was only practice. "Can I wind up the gramophone?"

"Come closer to me." Robert drew her into his chest, his lips on her forehead.

"You'll stand on my feet."

"No I won't. I'm as light as a dancing dog."

"You, my handsome one, are more like a shaggy lion tiptoeing through long grass before leaping on its prey."

"And biting them in the neck like this." Someone blew their nose in the room next door.

"Shhh. Control yourself."

"Only if you'll dance closer."

※

Saturday night. A hand reached for Rose's egg sandwiches at the doorway to the clattering kitchen. The hall was already half full. What a sight, what a transformation. Looping crepe-paper streamers decorated the wooden walls and the high ceiling. Bunches of balloons hung from every corner. Lights covered with pink and orange cellophane cast a glow across excited faces. On the stage the red velvet curtain was held back by heavy gold cord with tassels. Large tubs, covered with gold fabric, held small trees, one on either side of the stage. A deck of lights turned the stage into a magical cave of musicians.

Around the edges of the hall the wooden forms were almost full of suited older men, and women in fur stoles and long white gloves laughing, chatting, waving to others on the opposite side. Near the doorway, single men in jacket and tie, white shirts and braces, hair trimmed and slicked down snatched glances at the young women in the far corner where they were admiring each other's swishing skirts and fancy hair decorations. That would have been me last year, Rose thought.

Robert had already been swallowed up. "Miriam. You're back." A young woman with dark brown eyes and hair, olive skin, wide friendly face pushed through the crowd.

"And you look a bit better than last time I saw you, up to your knees in mud."

"Under new scrubbing rules. Have you met Rose?"

"Rose, I'm so pleased you're here." Miriam. Adam's second daughter.

The nurse. "You must have been to lots of dances. You'll be teaching us a few steps."

"Not at all. I've needed coaching."

"You could have a worse teacher. Have you settled in?"

On the stage a saxophone squealed through a run of semitones. Snatches of songs came from the squeezebox; a lean man with dark curls tumbling over his forehead plucked the string of the tea chest, straining to hear. On the piano, a grey-haired woman limbered up.

"Cyril. Been busy with the dusting powder?"

"Floor's smooth as a baby's bottom, Robert, me boy. You'll glide straight to heaven."

Suddenly the band found a common purpose and launched into "If You Knew Suzy."

"Come on, Rose. Oh," Robert said, bowing deeply, "I almost forgot. May I have the pleasure of this dance?"

"I do hope it's a pleasure, sir."

Robert's movements embraced the slippery floor, the tilt of his head echoing the rise and fall of the phrases. She placed her feet cautiously, concentrating on the two-step, trusting his arms to steer them through moments when her feet became disembodied from her brain. Gradually their bodies merged into each other, relaxing into new rhythms. She shut her eyes momentarily in the turn.

The tune ended. Robert pressed his forehead to hers. "Congratulations. You're officially a dancer." She flushed unexpectedly at the pleasure of it.

The Military Two-step. A quickstep.

And now the Gay Gordons. Rose could follow the simple pattern. But changing partners! Being held by men with clammy hands and insecure footing. Across the moving circle, Robert was not only dancing, but laughing and bending in conversation to each new woman.

The music ended. Everybody clapped.

"The next dance is the Ladies' Choice," came the announcement. "The waltz."

Robert, you are mine.

Too soon they called the last dance. A young man rushed past, dropping something into her hand. "Not yet," said Robert. "Auld Lang Syne", hands held in a circle, a surge of singing and swinging arms, swaying and crossed arms.

And at last streamers tossed across the hall, entwining each other.

❧

As June became July, Rose sat at Aunt Marion's treadle sewing machine altering her skirt for the next dance. Outside, in the barest hint of heat from winter sun, Robert and Neil planned their afternoon. Normally Rose didn't mind the sweet smell of Erinmore tobacco drifting through the back door with their conversation, but today it was making her queasy.

"We need to face the National Mortgage, son," Neil said slowly.

"Do we have the new stock valuation?"

"Arrived today. I'll ring 'em from Hughie's." The nearest telephone was two miles' walk away. "It's set to be rainin' Friday – see if we can get to it then. Pass me my coat, will ye."

"Time we got our own telephone, Dad," Robert said.

Rose threaded the needle. Imagine having their own telephone. She'd be able to speak to her parents without driving to a Post Office where you had to shout to be heard and the charges rose rapidly after three minutes.

With luck, the silence meant agreement.

Or his pipe had gone out.

Suddenly Robert was bending over her. "Do you want to come to Dunedin on Friday? We could go to the pictures. *Citizen Kane*'s on. Orson Welles."

❧

They pulled over near the the Exchange. "Good luck," Rose said, squeezing Robert's hands. She watched Neil and Robert cross the street and disappear into the imposing entrance to the National Mortgage.

Dunedin was alive with the bustle of cars, clanging trams, businessmen in suits and hats, shoppers in their best clothes. She knew no one in this whole city, but loneliness didn't stand a chance. She had money of her own and time to spend it.

Aunt Marion had dropped her in the Octagon, pointing out the corner tearooms where they would meet later. She wandered through the DIC, past cots and elaborate Hyde Park prams, angled so that you couldn't resist rocking the handles. Past fur coats, into the fabric department. Rolls of viyella for baby gowns. She fingered tweeds and taffeta but couldn't make up her mind.

Outside again she passed the bronze Robbie Burns statue and turned north into George Street. Ah, the dresses in Penrose's window and the sophisticated high heels of the women behind the counters. There – the fabric she wanted, for three ration coupons and a ten-shilling note from Robert. With a whoosh, vacuum pipes carried the metal capsule with her money across the ceiling and whooshed back again with the change.

Arthur Barnett's felt like Kirkcaldies, with lofty ceilings and aisles disappearing into the distance. The floorwalker directed her to the tearooms. She lifted her tray high over highchairs and prams and headed with her fish pie for a corner table. Babies were everywhere. Suddenly she felt naked without a child, and very alone. The pie was turning her stomach, or perhaps it was the motion of the car.

She pushed her plate away.

Back in the store she was drawn to rows of strappy Italian-style shoes. So frivolous, so tempting, the shiny blue with the white stitching. Could she justify more than one pair of dancing shoes? If she'd been twenty. But she was twenty-four and needed brown leather lace-up brogues. And nylons. She bought two pairs. "You're lucky," said the assistant. "There'll be a rush in the morning. These are our first for months."

※

Aunt Marion was settling into an alcove when Rose arrived but there was no sign of their husbands. They ordered a pot of tea, custard squares and Eccles cakes. Rose made a hole in the brown paper wrapper to show Aunt Marion the curtain material for their bedroom and woollen fabric for a skirt. "How did you get on?"

"The Otago Centennial Committee," said Aunt Marion, "was unanimously in support of unveiling the miners' monument on Anniversary Day. Waitahuna will get attention at last."

She stretched against the window to watch the pigeons outside, Aunt Marion in the same blue hat as the day they met, the same scotch thistle hatpin. How well they knew each other now. Rose admired her in so many ways, especially her broad interests – from gin traps to Oscar Wilde, John A. Lee and Soviet politics. And her endless drive for the community.

Has she changed or have I become more tolerant, she wondered. Aunt Marion had stopped hanging rabbit skins along the front fence, but wasn't likely to stop using coal dust for toothpaste. And she did seem to appreciate Rose's efforts to fit into the rhythm of farm life. Despite twenty-five years' difference in age they could manage, as long as there were walls between them.

Though please not for long.

Robert and Neil arrived in buoyant mood. "How did it go?" Rose asked.

"Very well. Dinner at McDiarmid's Beau Monde along Princes Street and back to sign the documents."

"Bravo," Aunt Marion cheered. Heads turned as she gave Neil's cheeks a double smack.

Robert slid onto the bench beside Rose. "That's as long as they … "

"Dinna settle yerself, lad," Neil scowled, cutting him short. "We must set off affore dark. Roads'll be frosty. Och, Aunt Marion, we had tea and cakes at the company."

※

They woke to silence. No movement. No sound, but an absence of sound more arresting than the normal quiet of morning. Something deeper, denying even the smallest vibration of gate swinging, bird flying, grass bending.

Rose snapped up the blind.

"Snow! Robert, it's snowed. Come and look." She dragged him out of bed to the new vista beyond the white piles curving up the corners of the window. The loaded trees, the immaculate smoothness of the lawn, the delicately poised inch of snow on the washing line. She marvelled at the disguised garden shrubs, the bird tracks already across the lawn, the sheer magic of it. A hare sat, grey against the whiteness, his erect stature extended by tall alert ears. He moved suddenly, leaping, bounding across the lawn and into the shrubbery, leaving exaggerated paw marks and puffs of white dust with each bound.

Robert saw all this but she could see that his mind was turning to the threat to his ewes, in lamb and vulnerable in heavy winter fleeces if they hadn't found shelter. He needed to get hay out after oats for the horses. The dray needed to be loaded. And a shovel in case a sheep was caught in a drift or the dray got stuck. He would need his father too. And extra coal to heave nearer to the back door. At least there was enough kerosene for the lamps.

Rose hugged into his warmth, ignoring the cold seeping from bare boards into bare feet. Fragments of fluffed ice separated from the greyness above, floated and swirled past the window, a mass of something pure pouring down over the whole of creation. Robert caught her excitement. Together they watched, enchanted in the moment.

❧

After the snow's eventual disappearance the tired grass gave in to the cold and lay patient in the soil. Water froze in the pipes, for two days not running at all.

Tonight had a new intensity, as she stretched a sock heel over the wooden mending mushroom. Robert sat beside her, writing his diary. Occasionally she looked over his shoulder. "Wages £17. Polly has infected foot. Two ewes lost in Stewart's bog."

Through the wall Aunt Marion was practising hymns for Sunday, the rhythm of notes unsynchronised with the pumping of foot pedals.

Robert began tapping his pen nib on the paper. "When I was young, there was always music in this house," he said with a faraway look. "Always. Mother had a few pupils. She didn't play like Aunt Marion. She, she *felt* the music. Mozart, or Schubert mostly, or Scots songs, they just tumbled from her body. You'd be drawn in, until the music absorbed you too." He turned away and screwed the top onto the pen. She mustn't interrupt.

"Now Aunt Marion," he cocked his thumb in her direction, "she urges you into the hymns – see, my father's fallen into line." Neil's voice was adding the words. "He can't resist singing along after a few bars. She's not concerned about dynamics. Well," he said with resignation, "the organ leads the congregation, after all." He stood to place the ink bottle back on the shelf.

"Not like my mother's piano."

Rose snipped off the yarn. Here in the flickering light sat the man who loved her, who was tender and attentive. Intelligent and enduring. And he still hadn't got over losing his mother. It's true, she thought, love bears all things, believes all things. And hopes all things.

She pushed aside her sewing. She had something to tell him.

Her waiting was over. She'd not bled for over a month.

27

"WE'VE FIXED THE DATE," Aunt Marion said, thumping her papers onto the table beside Rose's sewing. "Make sure your baby isn't born on March the twentieth. Everyone who matters will be at Waitahuna Gully. You simply must be at the unveiling."

Rose raised her eyes. "It'll be close." The year 1948 would be unforgettable, Otago Centennial or not.

"Keep yer head still, lad," Neil said, snapping the shearing blades in the air.

Aunt Marion pulled out her hatpin. "I still can't credit that hundred thousand ounces of gold came from this area in one year."

"Including gold from our land?" Rose asked.

"Only folks to make money're the merchants," Neil said. "Take a look at Princes Street. Tha's where the gold went."

"Not too much, Dad. You're making a mighty pile on the floor."

"There'll be enough left to keep the wind oot." Rose eyed the scattered clippings around Robert's feet. Just as well his hair curled. Blunt cuts would merge eventually.

"Mary pulled down your father's goldmining hut, didn't she Neil? According to her, it was a danger to sheep, but what she was after was twenty pounds for the tin. They had a real barney." Aunt Marion laughed. "Neil swore it was the last time she'd put one across him." Robert smiled at her under his father's elbows.

"Up ye get, lad. My turn noo. Short as you like." He rasped the file across the blades, tested the sharpness with his thumb and handed the shears to Robert.

For a moment they could hear the clock ticking over the clacking shears. And a distant thump.

Aunt Marion cocked her head. "What's that noise?"

The chug of a mechanical hole digger sounded close.

"Power poles, for the electricity," Robert said. "Must have reached the top of the hill."

"Oh Rose, we'll have all the mod cons before long," Aunt Marion said.

"Light. That's all ye need," growled Neil.

"And a refrigerator," Aunt Marion said.

"A wireless," declared Robert, flicking hair off his father's shoulders. Had he heard her at all? "It'll keep you company in the evenings, Dad, when Aunt Marion's out at her meetings."

They'd all forgotten the most essential thing. "I hope there'll be a washing machine, once the baby arrives."

"Och, the electricity'll turn ye all to greed. Best pray for a guid lambin'."

"Yes, Dad, and we know the cheque won't come till January. Anyway, no one knows when the poles will carry power."

⁂

Winter was overtaken by a wet spring. From the south, cloud built up over Mt Stuart, rain overflowing the feeding troughs and creek beds. In the house, everyone stepped around a billy and a bucket where the roof leaked.

And then it cleared.

Relieved to get out of the house, Rose walked across the paddocks with Robert in a fresh September breeze. Just a few yards ahead a sheep waddled away, swinging something extra at her rear, slick with the birth sack. Robert's stride changed. He moved smoothly, low like an albatross readying for take-off in a stiff wind. To the right, to the left, he guided the wary ewe into the junction of two fences and tackled her to the ground.

Rose hadn't moved, barely aware of her shallow breathing. Robert knelt astride the sheep. His hand pushed and twisted at her rear end. "Steady, steady old girl. Nearly there." Rose's feet carried her forward as Robert eased a colourless slimy creature onto the grass, all sticks of legs and staring eyes. Not white or frisky or familiar. Her first newborn lamb.

She felt amazed, elated, contained with Robert in this moment, her squeamishness gone.

Keeping light pressure on the ewe's flank, Robert rubbed the lamb's belly as the afterbirth followed. With a shudder the lamb wobbled itself upright. The ewe turned her head and bleated. Robert squeezed her teat, squirting milk onto the lamb's face. In a few shaky steps, the lamb found her udder.

"It looks so fragile," Rose said, as Robert lifted it closer to suckle. "Will it live?"

"She'll be all right." Robert wiped his hands on the grass and stepped back.

She hadn't thought of Robert being so intimately involved with his sheep. So instinctive and decisive and respectful of his animal.

"When we have daughters, we'll lock 'em in the house during lambing. Might scare 'em," Robert said. And I am unscareable? thought Rose.

Robert reached for her hand. She pulled hers away, at the thought of where his had just been. Puzzlement darkened his face. "Oh, don't worry, I'll scrub later. Come on, there might be more."

Rose looked him directly in the eye and shrugged.

Hand in hand they bounded down the slope.

❧

At the end of November, Rose felt the baby quicken, filling her life with new purpose. She had been trying to ignore the fear that their hold on the land could disintegrate. It didn't pay to think too far ahead.

"Reckon the lad should be enterin' the Agriculture Cup, Marion. 'Tis a right picture, that paddock. Narry a patch where seed's run out, or a horse stepped frae the line," Neil said over dinner.

"If you say so, Dad," Robert smiled, basking in his father's rare praise. "Rose and I are off as soon as we've planted the last row of potatoes." He paused to eat. "If the film reels are at the Post Office we'll check them through at Keith's, ready for Friday night. I'm still amazed eighty people turned up when we screened 'Moses and the Red Sea'."

❧

The films hadn't arrived. But a letter had. A long brown envelope. Robert ripped it open. "No. They can't. NO," Robert roared, clutching his eyes as if to deny the words on the paper. "Is this what they mean by helping soldiers get started again?"

Rose stood helplessly as Robert stomped on the letter and ground it into the gravel. "Damnation! The stupid ... idiotic ... brainless ... fools."

He picked up the remains of the letter and threw it high over the hawthorn hedge. Rose didn't need to read it. Nor did the postmistress at the window.

"Don't talk to me. Just don't talk to me." They drove home in silence. There was nothing to say. And so much to discuss.

※

He spent a long time feeding the dogs that night. From the bedroom window, his lantern appeared in short flashes between the trees, behind the stables, moving towards the rise in the road, from where she knew he could see the whole farm.

He rushed inside, flinging the bedroom door open and landing on his stomach on the bed beside her. "I've had an idea. I'll talk to Mary directly. Her land is our best solution. Forget the government and the rehab loan. I'd talk to the stock company about fencing."

Rose sat up. "That's capital. And she likes you."

He moved closer, his eyes wide. "Dad asked her once and she said no, but the woman must be sixty. Maybe more."

"Would she listen to me?" asked Rose. "I could appeal to her for our family."

"I think you scare her. She's not a mother. And she won't have Dad once they've moved."

"But she will have you."

"And I will have you and all our babies to look after." He rolled away onto his pillow, his right arm wrapped across his face. "Urggh. I need more land."

※

"You know, I've never seen Mary smile," Rose said, more to herself than to Aunt Marion.

"How often have you seen her?"

"Hardly at all. It's almost as if she disappears when I'm there."

"She's not had the happiest of lives, our Mary. She might not manage a conversation but she could teach you a lot about living a simple life. Neil called Alexander, her father, his most useless cousin. Once that man got the leases he just let the tussock and wild Irishman grow. He was more interested in his brother's blacksmith's business over in Clydevale. Even more interested in the public house next door."

"I wanted to appeal to her myself."

Aunt Marion lifted the clean porridge pot out of the enamel basin. "I think you need to leave this to Robert. With Mary, man to man will be the best chance." She handed the pot to Rose to dry. "Are you up to the meeting this afternoon? The speaker's from the mission field in China."

China? Why not. She could do with someone else's predicaments to think about.

❧

Fifteen women, six preschoolers. A good turn-out. All the windows were open to the heat. The election began. Someone nominated her – for president. "Pardon? I'm just new. I don't know how to run the branch."

Rows of eyes turned to her. "But you've been to university," her neighbour whispered. "You can do it."

"Is there something else I could do?"

Five minutes later she was the secretary.

Rose heard the mission talk through a mix of self-doubt and pleasure at having her first role outside home. Snatches of the speaker's words caught her attention. China, the new battleground of poverty; a dispirited people in desperate need of hope. Missionaries could not turn their backs, though the Chinese state could deny their visas at a whim.

Even in this township, so far from where the speaker laboured, this tiny group of women could knit and sew and fill mission boxes with pennies for China. She snatched up the pamphlets. Now she had a project of her own.

❧

Robert was sitting on the back doorstep when they got home.

"What's wrong?" asked Rose.

"Mary. No go." Robert looked up at her. "She turned up here just after you drove off with a scythe to sharpen on the grinder. It seemed a good moment." Rose squeezed in beside him. " 'Sell my land?' she said. 'Never. This is my place. I'm not selling.' She walked off talking to herself. She even forgot to warn me I'd have to buy a new scythe if I ruined her blade."

Rose rested her head on his shoulder.

28

Beyond the heat of summer, the March sun rose sluggishly. Rose had lost the ability to focus on anything beyond her own body. She felt the days merging into an endless haze of increasing heaviness. Would this child ever leave and let her rediscover the girl beneath?

Aunt Marion handed Rose the sheets to peg to the line, saving her from bending to the basket. "As soon as our Member of Parliament cuts the ribbon, the school chi … "

"Arrrgh!" Rose dropped the sheet and clutched her belly. Then she puffed out and straightened herself.

Aunt Marion bundled up the sheet. They looked at each other. "Is this my time?" asked Rose, searching Aunt Marion's bewildered face.

"Neil!" Aunt Marion shouted. "Neil!" He appeared at the back door. "Get Robert. I think the baby's coming." A clanging beat rang out as Neil hit the rusted disk hanging from the stable roof.

Rose felt a hot wetness run down her legs and into her new shoes. Her body had been overtaken by a force so alien, so disintegrating of thought and reason. Dreading the twelve-mile journey ahead on the narrow winding road, she gripped the corner of the shed as another contraction took over.

*

Push, push, push. Gas. Stirrups. Forceps. Gas. Oblivion.

When Rose floundered her way back, a baby was crying on the far side of the room.

"Here you are, Mrs McLeod. A beautiful baby girl."

She nestled the baby under her chin, the sweet newborn odour filling her senses as she skimmed her fingers over the delicate skin. "Where's Robert?"

"He'll be here in a jiffy. He's been phoning from his aunt's every half hour." The nurse lowered her voice. "It's past visiting hour but we'll let him in. Sister's just gone home."

Rose wiped wet tendrils of hair from her face. Every pore of her body seemed to ooze moisture. She'd never thought of herself as a mammal, but now her entire being seemed whale-like, dedicated only to procreation. There seemed no space for anything beyond exhaustion and euphoric emotion.

She wrapped her arms across the baby and shut her eyes, lost in the wonder of this moment. She would never let her go.

Except that the nurse had rules. Rest for the baby – in the nursery.

The door flung open. Robert rushed in, hat askew, sports coat flapping. "Rose, Rose," he said, stroking her forehead. "Ah, my love, you're all right?" She nodded. "And we have a little girl?" His cheek rested on hers. "Where is she?"

The doctor appeared, his hand thrust forward in a handshake.

"Congratulations, Robert, a healthy wee girl. Come and meet her."

Rose propped herself up. If she could pull the curtain back a little, she could see down the corridor where the men stood pointing through the nursery window. The doctor left. Robert suddenly stepped away from the nurse who was wagging a finger at him. Then he was beside her, easing the baby between them.

"Look at her wrinkled face! And her fingers … " He had unfolded the tight wrapping. "You can see through them, like blades of new oats."

"Five minutes," the nurse tossed over her shoulder.

Robert stroked the baby's face with the edge of his hand and kissed her forehead.

Half an hour vanished. The nurse took the baby back to the nursery.

"Shall I leave you to sleep?"

"I'm longing to sleep but not for you to leave."

Robert looked at his watch. "Bother, I promised Aunt Marion I'd get to the celebration. Since we missed the unveiling." Rose had completely forgotten. "I can tell everyone the good news." He picked up his hat and strode out the door. It slammed again and he reappeared. "Missed you already." She lifted herself to make space for his arms around her and shut her tired eyes.

He came most evenings. "Please be home soon. It's desolate without you." The matron's starched veil quivered more vigorously each time she escorted him out, always the last to leave after the bell.

When he couldn't come she felt as desolate as he did. Especially on the third and fourth days, down in the dumps, her body a formless, flabby mess, an overwhelming feeling that this baby, sucking endlessly at her engorged breasts, would walk out of her life as suddenly as she'd entered it. Yesterday she'd felt on top of the world. Today she'd slipped into a chasm. Why? She daren't ask anyone. New mothers were supposed to be joyful.

On the fifth day she was allowed to bath her. Rose undid the clothes until Frances looked more helpless than a newborn lamb.

What was she supposed to do now? Under the nurse's eye, she held Frances' head over the warm water and bathed her hair, her eyes, her ears, every crease under her chin. How slippery this noisy little body was, so difficult to grip.

Frances quietened in the water, her eyes flickering.

"I did it, Frances," she whispered in her ear as she sat back in bed to feed her.

❦

Aunt Marion and Neil turned up on the sixth day. They peered through the glass, not allowed to handle her until they were home. Aunt Marion cooed at the dark hair and tiny ears.

"Och, she's a reet bonnie lass," Neil grinned. "Takes after her mother."

"She's a McLeod, you'll see. Likes her sleep." Aunt Marion laughed. "And you? Getting up and about again?"

Aunt Marion was full of the afterglow of the centenary weekend, floating on a wave of congratulations for her organisation. She left Rose a copy of the booklet.

Would skim-reading be enough? So, two hundred people had lived in the wide gully during 1860. By 1864 there were four thousand. Twenty hotels, a bakery, bootmakers, saddler, blacksmiths, saloons, a school. Miners lived close together under canvas or makeshift caves in the hillsides.

Rose lay back and closed her eyes. All she had noticed was that there were half a dozen houses, eroded clay cliffs and some swampy sheep paddocks.

Frances, what a relief you weren't born until now.

After two weeks they were home.

Through autumn and into the shortening days of winter, Rose spent many night hours in the wicker chair, feeling the baby merge into her own body as her tiredness held her in a near-sleep trance, her only awareness the rhythmic sucking and the rushing release in her breasts. If she kept to the Plunket regimen of three-hourly feeds, all would be well.

With Robert, she marvelled at Frances' gurgling over the next months, her laughter, her hand clapping, her sitting up, her ready affection. And eventually her sleeping through the night.

29

AFTER THE FIRST FLUSH of neighbourly visitors, life had become settled, too settled. Could she entice old friends to lift her spirits in this enclosed space? She must act as if this were her home too, decide who to invite, expect Aunt Marion to adapt. No boiled mutton with visitors, please, the steamy smell throughout the house. And no tripe, onions or not. Or barley broth. Roast hogget? Yes. And could we time the washing to avoid visitors ducking under the ceiling rack in the kitchen?

In the spring Molly arrived, showering Rose with chocolates and baby clothes. She filled the house with stories of Wellington life and of her sister in America with her officer husband, who had turned out to be quite the gentleman.

Was that Wellington life only three years ago? In quiet moments, Molly's face looked drawn. If her Eddie had survived Monte Cassino, it might have been her baby they chased around the floor.

After two wet days, the clouds rolled away. "I'm walking the cow along the road. Like to come?" Robert asked her.

"Who would have believed this?" Molly laughed, looking down the oilskin coat to Rose's gumboots.

"Pretend you're a farm girl. Go." Rose pushed them out the door.

※

A while later the front gate squealed again. Rose looked up from writing to her mother as Molly rushed past and up the passage. Robert grinned around the kitchen door. "Bit of trouble with the cow. Didn't want to co-operate. If we don't watch out, we'll have no milk."

Rose grimaced. "You did tell Molly why you were taking her, didn't you?"

Robert stared at her. "I thought you had. No wonder she kept her distance. Daisy was more excited about the long grass than Bertrand, swaggering and snorting. She turned on her haunches."

"No sense of duty," Rose laughed. "Molly'll get over it. She's with your father choosing duets for the eisteddfod. I hope you haven't put her off coming back."

❧

Rose hadn't seen her younger brother since the wedding. Andrew joked over the phone about John's description of her living in harrowing circumstances after a recent flying visit. "As if you can't cope, Sis. Big brother exaggeration?"

"Come and see for yourself." He would come from Christchurch on the Christmas Day train. She could get a chicken from Andy Dixon for Christmas dinner. As long as Aunt Marion plucked it.

"You could do with a concrete path around the house, Robert," Andrew said on Christmas afternoon. After two days there was one, barely set before she hugged him goodbye.

Two weeks later, Enid, her old school friend from Hawke's Bay, lay with Rose in the long grass mimicking their teachers, giggling wildly at their teenage lives, remembering Rose's father telling them off for raking boy's names into the fine soil as they helped prepare the new tennis court.

"Marvellous change from office life, thanks," said Enid's husband after three days.

❧

"Thank goodness that's over," said Aunt Marion.

"What?" Rose asked, puzzled.

"Those two. So loud. Your friends need to get up early and go to bed before midnight. All those card games and laughter through the wall. Draping their wet socks over Neil's tobacco. And what was he doing all that time in the lavatory? For heaven's sake, Rose, I don't know how you . . "

"They're my friends. You didn't have to be here."

What had she said? She wanted the words back. But Molly, Andrew and Enid understood her as no one here did, even if their visits revealed a need for friends who shared her new life too.

She lifted a dripping Frances out of the tin bath. It had been so much simpler when she'd fitted into the kitchen sink. On the back doorstep she brushed Frances' wet hair into curls.

Aunt Marion squeezed in beside her. "Neil and I've been thinking. It's time for us to leave you to it. The house will be very full with the next babe." Rose bristled. No one knew yet. "My sister suggests we join her in the township." Frances wriggled from her lap and ran unsteadily down the path.

This was the last thing she expected. "That house is tiny."

"We wouldn't need to take money out of the farm to buy one."

Rose could barely control her smile. But Aunt Marion and Neil without a home of their own? This wasn't the solution. "There's no hurry for you to move yet." Rose couldn't quite believe the words were coming from her own mouth. "Truly. We have room. You've lots to do here. I can look after you if you get sick again, and you can look after Frances."

"I know, I know." Aunt Marion patted her hand. "But this must be your home, not ours. Another year of good prices might persuade the company that the farm could service a loan." She rubbed the side of her face. "Perhaps we can leave it a little longer. Somehow we will be elsewhere before another child arrives."

"Thank you." Rose whispered the words without conviction as Aunt Marion went inside. She didn't regret her words at all, it felt almost as if she had a right.

❋

Robert finished harrowing the last of the turnip block. The women were visiting a new baby and his father was mending a gate. He took the lid off his dinner plate, warm at the back of the stove. Mashed potatoes, mutton stew and his favourite, cauliflower. He turned the *Bruce Herald* to the stock sales.

Someone was knocking at the back door.

Mary stood on the doormat, looking at the handle. "Robert." She breathed slowly, hands thrust into her pockets. "I will sell."

"What?"

"I will sell my land. To you." She raised her head and grinned.

"All of it?" Robert replied, overcome. Of course it would be all of it. "Why?" Oh, don't ask her why in case she changes her mind.

"Jim's gettin' married. Goin' south."

Ahhh, Robert thought. She can't manage without Jim. "What are you going to do?"

Her face and shoulders sagged. "Move." She pulled her jacket closer around her shoulders. "To Elsie. Or Kitty. Or Jane." Her team of single sisters sounded more wounding than promising. She took a few steps away and turned back.

"You want my land?"

Robert shook himself. "Yes, Mary. Yes. Yes. I do. We both do." He stepped outside in his socks and held out his hand. "I'll work hard on it, promise." A look, an understanding passed between them. A rare moment in a handshake.

Such a simple act, the handshake. Security for another hundred years.

Perhaps.

30

"There. The door shuts and there's room for the milk."

Rose stopped scrubbing the butcher's boards, wiped her hands down her apron and opened the fridge doors. "You fitted every piece in?" Aunt Marion's fridge packing was quite unlike her usual casual approach to domestic order.

"Everything." The older woman stood with hands on hips. "There's not enough space in this kitchen for a refrigerator. Even a smaller one than this monster. Robert certainly has an eye for quality. He did well to get National Mortgage approval."

Double doors and an icebox. The motor took up the whole bottom half. "The room's the problem – far too small." Aunt Marion had read her thoughts. She tightened the leather straps around her suitcase and swung it off the table. "I'll take that food safe in the car now." Aunt Marion wouldn't have a refrigerator. Was the safe Aunt Marion's or hers? Had it been Alice's? Robert might be wanting it for the dog meat.

The move was possible now that their situation was secure. Robert had bought the stock from his father. Neil would pay rent on the leased sections and lease Robert the freehold sections 51 and 74, two hundred and forty acres, for seven years at £88 per annum, with a purchasing clause of £1700. Neil carried the mortgage on the other freehold land; Robert would pay his father rent, the only income Neil and Aunt Marion would have bar the pension.

Did things belong to people or places? Right now, ownership felt like a fluid concept, a negotiated peace for deciding on the flotsam of a hundred years.

"Give and take," Aunt Marion had said, as they'd sorted linen into two piles. As long as "give" was reciprocated, and "take" was agreed. Rose grimaced and rescued the sheets Aunty Grace had given her. She could see the ridiculous side, trotting after Aunt Marion, clawing back her own possessions. Perhaps she should let her take them all. That would eliminate the drying problem: hardly enough to go on the beds, let alone change them.

What about the kitchen table? The fire tools? Mirrors? Even the broom in her hand? Such a disadvantage not knowing each object's history. Where was Robert when she needed his opinion?

Yesterday they'd had a clipped discussion about the garden tools. "I must take the spade. The rake too," Aunt Marion announced as they picked broad beans. Frances dragged the empty coal bucket across the garden with her doll inside, clattering between the currants.

"But I use that spade almost every day. Frances – take your doll out of that filthy bucket." She strode over the comfrey to rescue the doll.

"And the bucket. I'll take the bucket." Aunt Marion's tone prevented argument.

But Rose was not willing to give in this time.

"So what will we do without a bucket? Get the coalman to dump it here – take it in shovel by shovel?" She knew she was being ridiculous but she couldn't stop. Her grip on the bucket handle tightened as the child within her kicked. She strode into the kitchen in her galoshes to set the bucket down where it belonged.

It could have been Aunt Marion's, for all she knew, or Alice may have given it to Robert before she died.

Breathe deeply. After all, it's only a bucket.

But really it wasn't at all – it was inheritance in miniature, a tangle of shared ownership, taken for granted until someone tried to untangle it.

"Two each?" suggested Aunt Marion, dismantling the spare beds.

"Of course. You'll still have visitors. What about the blankets?" Rose asked.

"They were Alice's."

Rose stepped back. Did Alice's blankets go with Neil or Robert?

"How about whatever is on the bed now stays with the bed."

"Good idea." Immediately Aunt Marion filled her arms with bedding. Rose opened the car doors and helped her stuff it into the back seat.

There would be no argument over the piano, thought Rose, running her fingertips over the wood.

❧

Robert poked his head around the back door at midday. "Hello," he grinned as she washed soil off the carrots. His face was splattered with plaster, his hair speckled in a premonition of going grey. Rose mussed his hair with a wet hand as he removed his boots. Grabbing her around the waist, he waltzed her around the laundry.

"What's got into you?" Rose asked, laughing. Frances scattered wooden pegs across the floor and demanded to be picked up. Robert pulled a feather from his pocket and tickled her outstretched fingers. She snatched the feather and ran into the kitchen.

"We'll have this house to ourselves in a fortnight. Dad and I've just finished the outside plastering. You won't recognise Mary's house when we've finished."

"How much more is there to do?"

"Spouting, a washing line, a window in the bedroom, paths – nothing much. Aunt Marion's cranked up the stove for their dinner today. Reckons she can cook chops and eggs, and toast. They're behaving like newlyweds." He tossed his overalls into the clothes basket.

"I'll walk Frances along after her sleep," she called over her shoulder. "When you're at the house this afternoon, could you look in the cupboards? Bring back anything she shouldn't have taken, yours or your mother's."

※

"Nana has to be very, very careful over these holes in the floor, little one. Here we'll have a bed just for you. And plenty of space for my sewing machine. A genuine sunroom." What a transformation. The house no longer seemed laden with Mary's troubles. "I'll have curtains before Christmas. Come and see the kitchen."

Mary's seldom-scrubbed wooden bench had been sanded back to bleached honey. New shelves hung above the sink, full of familiar tins. The carving knife in the leather pouch Neil had made hung below the shelf. Above the coal range, his pipe rested on a tin of tobacco next to a jar of Lane's Emulsion.

Cosy. Plenty of space for two.

"Watch your head," Aunt Marion warned. A brand-new bath glistened in the bathroom. "The water runs out down the paddock. It's costly to put in drains, far too costly. See this commode chair? Much easier than traipsing out to the long drop."

"Aren't you having a flushing toilet inside?"

"All in good time." Rose fell quiet. Aunt Marion was keeping a tight rein on her spending so that Rose could improve her house.

"Don't look so crestfallen. You have the growing family. Neil will be happy as long as he can see his banks and braes. He's building boxes for my ducks. Just for nesting, mind, they'll be free to wander."

※

Back home, Rose stretched. She stood in the middle of the kitchen, raising her arms wide, her fingertips lifting towards the high corners of the ceiling. She turned through the filtered afternoon light, gathering the kitchen space into her arms. Mine, she thought, all mine.

On Friday they would have dinner at Mary's. Aunt Marion's. Mary herself had vanished into South Dunedin.

"Any mail?" Robert shouted from the washhouse.

"It's on the table. No wool returns. But look at this." She pulled a letter from her apron pocket. "You know how sluggish the government has been about housekeepers for new mothers. We've got it. Women's Division has approval to run our own government-funded scheme."

"Good news."

"It's a life-changer. Women's Division of Federated Farmers get things done. This is official support for farming mothers. It's impossible to feed a new baby every three hours with ten for dinner and mountains of baking. And crutching and shearing last even longer now with higher sheep numbers."

She squeezed the folded sheets into the rack above the stove. "I hope we can find good women to employ. Housekeepers will be in demand."

※

Summer caught them by surprise. A sudden hot summer. Not humid like up north, but a stifling, savage heat. In the mornings Rose functioned normally – the Christmas cake was baking in Aunt Marion's parting gift: a new reliable Shacklock coal range with a thermostat in a little glass window.

In the bedroom she pulled down the blind against the dazzling afternoon light, kicked off her shoes and lay down. A spider on a single thread dangled from the bare light bulb and floated in the air currents. Electricity had changed everything, even opportunities for spiders. There was carpet in their first real sitting room now that they had a vacuum cleaner. And a radio for music and politics in the Queen's English.

Was she being greedy longing – oh how she longed – for a washing machine? The round white one in the magazines, with the rollers on top and the agitator to save your arms from pushing nappies around with a pole.

Experts were saying the ideal healthy family, best for the nation as a whole, was at least four or five children. The MP on the radio even suggested women who limited their families were selfish. Robert was sure this one was a son.

❧

"We'll see you and the bairn at dinnertime?" Aunt Marion called from the pantry.

"We'll be there." Any moment now there would be a rare embrace, a moment of mutual appreciation for the years of tolerance and understanding. Aunt Marion would confirm Rose's governance with her blessing and invite her to change whatever she wished.

But it wasn't to happen like that. What was she doing in there, shifting glass about?

"I'll have to come back for the others," Aunt Marion declared, coming out with a cane basket of jars. "I can't fit them all in."

Jam. She never imagined. All the jam Rose had made. Not her raspberry jam. Not the raspberry from Alexandra that she was saving for visitors.

"Aunt Marion, the raspberry jam … "

"Yes, thank you my dear – Neil's favourite."

Rose hesitated. The pulse on her neck urged her to reclaim the jam. Her jam.

Just as Rose was visualising the shelves empty, Aunt Marion smiled. "I left the cape gooseberry from your mother and the tree tomato from your aunt." Not Neil's favourites. Or hers.

Among the jam jars Rose caught sight of the hot horseradish sauce. Robert's favourite. Only Robert's.

"Ah, Aunt Marion … "

"Must rush. The plumber will be at the knowes by eight-thirty."

Aunt Marion gathered up sheets and towels tied with string and leaned over them to kiss Frances. "Come and see me every day. Oh Rose, I will so miss her."

A sharp gust of air blew back as she shut the door behind her. Was I invisible, thought Rose? Have all the words been spoken?

Or is she not really leaving?

Dear Mother and Daddy,

We finally have the house to ourselves. I have many plans for change as soon as my energy returns. Helen is lying beside me watching the light on the wall moving with the swaying trees. I have to stop Frances prodding her into opening her eyes. I think she expected an instant playmate.

Rose mimicked Helen's sucking noises. "Schurlph, schurlph, my little beauty. Aren't you just? My gorgeous girl." On the sofa lay the love of her life in his Sunday clothes, mouth open, chest rising and falling to Beethoven's Third Symphony.

Maud and Ness, my wonderful new friends, turned up with meals all week after we came home, a life-saver with fencing contractors here.

I'm sorry you couldn't make it down again now, but Daddy's health is much more important, even if he has to be tied to a chair to stop him overdoing it in the orchard.

A rhythmical rattling came from Frances' bedroom. "Robert," Rose said gently. "Frances is shaking the cot." Robert cleared his throat and threw an arm across his eyes. "Don't move," Rose said. "I'll get her myself."

After all, she shrugged, it was her role. Like every aspect of her life, duty defined it. And satisfied it. As long as husbands provided and women nurtured, family life was unbeatable; men and women complemented each other. She would make this home fit for their children and support her hard-working Robert in any way she could.

She bent to kiss him on her way out.

What more could any woman want?

PART FOUR

PART FOUR

31

HER MOTHER'S LUGGAGE was full of grapefruit, lemons, feijoas (Robert winced), Chinese gooseberries and tree tomatoes. No wonder she staggered off the plane, dropping her bag to pick up her granddaughter. Frances wriggled away.

Her father's eyebrows had become coarse, grey and unruly. "Sun protection, my dear, ideal for walking." For the next two weeks he disappeared often, piggy-backing Frances, blowing "One o'clock, two o'clock" on dandelion seed heads. He helped Robert sort wool and Rose pick plums. In the long twilight, grandmother and child marched around the lawn, chanting Christopher Robin, and *Jonathon Jo had a mouth like an O and a wheelbarrow full of surprises*. Friends now, they peered around the grain shed door – and not an inch further – to spot mice.

On their last night, Rose sat on the bed as her mother shook her coiled plaits free. She took the hairbrush. Mother relaxed against her body. "A hundred strokes, my dear. If you take on any job, do it properly," she laughed, patting her daughter's leg. She twisted around to look her in the eye. "You've really found your place here, haven't you."

"I'd better have. We've just found out there'll be another McLeod in the spring."

※

"Isn't it time we had a bath and a flushing lavatory inside?" Rose said.

Robert looked up from his tax papers. "Inside? Where?"

"Come and see." Rose heaved Helen onto her hip.

Rose strode out imagined rooms across the grass. Robert grimaced at the roof line. "We might manage it, if wool reaches a pound for a pound. Your mother was odd about the dunny, wasn't she? Don't think she liked the wetas."

It was autumn before a truckload of pipes rattled to rest under the plum tree. Plumbing had never been exciting before. But an indoor lavatory, day and night. *And* an enamel bath. Fifty-five pounds worth of agitator washing machine would be delivered tomorrow, in plenty of time for the next round of nappies.

All day muffled metallic ringing rose from under the house. "Missus?" A head poked up from the hole. "Something to show you." Could she really squeeze through the manhole? Slowly, slowly, she lurched crab-like after the builder's lantern, pushing through huhu beetle carapaces and fragile insect wings, spider webs catching her hair. This was no place for Mother.

Between the rows of piles was an older set, stumps really, supporting nothing. She ran her fingers through a dark patch where fragments of wood and stone charred the clay, the gritty remnants of fire.

"Did anyone know there was an old hut under here once?" she asked before dinner.

"Och, don't bother with the past, lassie," Neil said, filling his pipe. "Ye've enough to concern yerself wi'."

"Ask Aunt Betty." Aunt Marion was excavating garden soil from her fingernails with the vegetable knife. She had come back to dig "her" carrots.

"I reckon it'd be m' mother, Catherine, those ashes." Neil said.

Catherine died there? thought Rose horrified.

"Cooking ashes," Neil chuckled, his pipe waving in the air. "It were a shepherd's day hut, not fit for livin' in. Afore the cob cottage. Now tha', ye could live in. Did so m'self. P'raps she and m' father met there, a'courtin'."

She hadn't realised how long this family had occupied this land. So different from her parents, searching like gypsies, no roots deeper than a dozen years. Even in retirement replanting themselves in a new orchard.

❧

The plumbing took two days. At last hot water and steam spurted from the bath tap. "Look at us. Excited over hot water. Come on, we're going in." Rose stripped off and climbed into the bath, splashing and laughing with Frances and Helen.

"Aren't you supposed to be at a church manager's meeting?" Rose called through the doorway.

No answer. Forgot probably, thought Rose.

She stood next to him at the table, shaking talcum powder over

Helen's stomach. "You look tired. Your eyes are sagging." Fragments of dried thorns lodged in every crease.

"It's the vibrations. Twelve hours on the D2, ripping out those roots. Worth it when a big one comes loose and flips into the gully."

"As long as you don't go over." Progress, any progress, depended on Robert taking risks. Clearing twenty-five acres for pasture was dangerous.

"A bath's what you need," Rose purred in his ear, aware of her own softness, the smell of gardenia soap under her dressing gown, the child under her arm smelling of gardenias too.

※

"If there's more snow tonight we'll never get you to the maternity annexe," Aunt Marion said three months later. "I could stay."

Robert jumped up. "I'll top up the diesel in the tractor. We'd get to the main road on the D2 if we have to in the night."

"On the blade? You must be joking." Rose tossed her head back with laughter. "I'd be vibrated into instant labour. You could deliver the baby in the snow. Wrap it in straw, find a manger ... "

Aunt Marion stared out the window at the solid grey clouds. Smaller flakes continued to fall. "The drifts are six feet deep in places. This is the most we've ever had. Robert, why don't you drive your car down to the main road and leave it in the clear. You'd walk back in thirty minutes." She scanned the sky again. "We could get her down that far with the horse and wagon."

"Aunt Marion!" Robert and Rose exclaimed at once.

※

Baby Annabel punched through the waters on a morning when phone lines were unburdened by snow and the doctor was at his surgery. Aunt Marion settled Rose into the car with pillows and towels and waved them goodbye with her arms around Helen and Frances. "Go slowly, Robert. Slowly. You could slide off that icy road into the Gorge."

Two weeks later, blossom burst from the pear tree and starlings squeezed under the eaves, their beaks laden with straw. In the warm kitchen, Frances and Helen hovered around the baby, burrowing for fingers and toes under the coverings.

Frances twirled, singing "Annabel-le, Annabel-le". She was belle. Très belle. Perfectly shaped head, soft, perfect skin.

"Bella. Bella," copied Helen.

Rose rested her cheek against the baby's fine downy hair and breathed her delicious honey-fresh smell. Bella.

Having one baby had been a relief, a bewilderment, a novelty, the child a happy appendage transported anywhere or left with Aunt Marion, making little impact on card evenings and dances, movies and social gatherings. The second child cemented them as a family. The third shifted her perspective, her role now definitively Mother. At times their utter dependence overwhelmed her.

And dancing? A distant frivolity.

❀

The long row of cloth nappies sagged lifelessly from the washing line. Yesterday had foreshadowed summer, still and warm. Bees were active. Today grey clouds folded upon themselves from the west, more promising of drizzle than drying. "I've brought you a couple of lambs." Robert reached under the armpits of his oilskin. "Sleepy sickness got the mother."

What apparently lifeless skin covered these skeletons. The children crouched over the motionless lambs on the sack as Robert fed them milk through an eye dropper. "Look at the poor sick wee lambies, Bella," Frances murmured.

"There was another bee on Helen's bed this morning, Robert. They're even in the bassinet."

"We've lost five ewes today – it's costing us. Uncle Adam's lost twenty," he said, screwing up his face. "He suggested petrol for the bees. Think we'll try gas."

In the evening when the bees were least active, Rose taped him into his overalls, tied binder twine at his ankles and wrists, and covered his head with white curtain net. "No bee can possibly get through this," she laughed.

Robert climbed the ladder and pumped into the darkness. Later Rose peeled off the layers of clothing. Three stings. Five live bees. She pressed the blue bag firmly onto each wound.

"Busy on Thursday night?" John asked, from Wellington. "I'm coming to look at high country tussock for the DSIR. There's a bus gets to Manuka about five."

Rose met him at the main road. How relaxed he was, enthusiastic about his new work, his family. Then, "I bumped into your Hadley in Willis Street." My Hadley? Rose kept her eyes on the road, but her heart was racing. "He's setting up a factory in Island Bay, expanding already."

So his wife won't be struggling for money.

"Always knew he'd do well." John said. "Still single though. Great catch for someone." He flicked her leg with his rolled newspaper.

"Steady on. You'll have us in the ditch."

They were just inside when a pained cry came from the washhouse. Helen looked up, her face awash with tears. A squashed bee lay between her chubby fingers. On her swelling lip, a sting.

"Poor darling." Rose bundled Helen into her arms. "We thought we'd got rid of the bees."

"Bees? Where?" John's eyes lit up. "You must have missed a few. Drones protect their queen. Or perhaps the smell of honey's still in the wood. I'll smoke them out."

Within minutes he was up the ladder with a crowbar. Weatherboards cracked.

"That should do."

Robert grimaced. Grourrnnnch. Another board.

Rose tapped the window. "Steady on, not too much," she shouted. His enthusiasm was destroying their house.

Grourrnnnch. Splinters flew. Robert flung his hands in the air. "Hey!" But John had taken charge.

"Hand me the smoke gun," John said, admiring the hole. Robert obliged. His friend Keith's smoke gun. John hadn't considered the possibility of rain, but minor details never stopped her brother.

"How are we going to replace half a wall?" Robert threw his shoes across the bedroom. "Overpaid Wellington pen-pusher."

"He does have the knack of getting things done," Rose said remorsefully.

"I hope there's a good crowd again tonight," Robert said, lambing now behind them. Robert rarely missed the Scottish Country Dance Club. They depended on his record player and his Jimmy Shand record collection. "We had four sets last week. Frances, not too much water now. George's got a whale of a voice when he gets going." An unforgettable voice, part pulpit, part army, calling the steps for the walk-through.

"Frances," Rose shouted, "turn the taps off, please." Frances was whirling her arms through the steam. "Taps off, Frances. Now."

Suddenly a panicked screech came from the bathroom, a gasping, ghastly scream, which would haunt her for nights to come. Rose thrust Bella at Robert. "She's ready for bed."

In seconds, she had grabbed Helen out of a bath full of boiling water. Helen thrashed the towel away, her head back, letting forth a horrible, animal wail.

Robert stared aghast from the doorway. "There was no cold running," she yelled. "The cylinder's been boiling all evening. What do we do?" Oh why hadn't she gone to the first aid courses?

"Cool the skin," Robert called. "We have to cool the skin. Cold water." He thrust his arm through the scorching water and released the plug.

Rose lifted the squealing two-year-old back into the bath. "Shush. Shush," she shouted above the noise. "I am helping you, love. Lie back and let the nice cold water take the heat out." Rose felt anything but comforting. Helen thrashed, rubbing her scalded skin at every turn.

"Put her on the kitchen table."

"Frances, go and get Helen's pillow." Anything to distract her. The four-year-old ran off. They laid wet towels on Helen's legs, her stomach, anywhere she didn't kick them off. "Turn over, love," Rose coaxed. "We'll cool your back down. Gently, gently." Rose took the wet sponge from Robert. "How did you know about cold water?" she said over the crying.

"Italy. Burns in the war. It worked for some. If we were near a river."

She leaned close to him. "I want to ring the doctor. Should we get him up here?"

He nodded. "Give me the sponge."

Cupping her hand over one ear on the phone, she strained to hear. "Yes, some blisters on her feet. Yes. Just a minute." She lowered the mouthpiece. "Have we got Tannafax? And gauze?"

Robert looked inside a cupboard. "We have."

Spread the ointment liberally on the blisters. At least that's what she thought he said. The doctor was dubious that cold water would do any good. But if the child was making that much noise, she should recover perfectly well.

Rose slumped against the wall, her feet tripping over Robert's forgotten dancing pumps. He was already squeezing jelly from the brown tube. Intermittently Helen's body shook with triple intakes of breath and sobs.

She'd never felt so inadequate, so lacking in solutions to normal hazards of life. What next? Aunt Betty had warned her. Be prepared, more prepared than she was.

*

The unpinned metal ramp clattered to the ground. Steam hissed from the stationary train, replenished after the slow climb through the Manuka Gorge. It wafted over the hats of the stock agent and the stoker, roped in to get cattle off as quickly as possible.

Robert smiled to himself as three shorthorn heads appeared at the top of the ramp, ears pricked, alert, sniffing the air through the door of the railway wagon. He gripped Ben's collar. The dog's ears were up, his body stretched forward. "Hold on, Ben, hold on." Twenty yearling steers bought at a very good price. Feed them grass and watch the pounds pack on. They'd pay for carpet as well as fencing the new block. That should put a smile on Rose's face.

Suddenly the cattle beasts clattered into freedom, a surge of smooth shiny brown backs glistening in the October sun, their heads up, heads down, nostrils quivering. They swirled around each other in the yard. Robert stroked Ben as he counted them. "Steady, steady." A sudden movement could turn controllable cattle into chaos. The stoker gave a quick wave and disappeared into the engine. "Twenty head? No injuries?" the stock agent called.

"All here," Robert nodded as he came forward to shake hands. "Fine animals. Thanks."

"All set then. Next stop Craigellachie." Smoke billowing, steam rising, the train drew away. The whistle blasted, long and magnified in the narrow valley.

From the mass of cattle, a startled white-faced steer lowered his head at the penetrating sound, shoving his horns into the animal in front. The injured steer bellowed, twisted his body sideways and leaped onto the top rail of the yards, front legs over, back legs scrabbling at the fence. Floundering his full three-hundred weight forward, he knocked a rail off and tumbled over, making for the railway tunnel.

Not the tunnel!

Robert pushed through broom to the cliff face to cut him off, Ben barking at his heels. If the steer went in he'd be lost for days. Or slip into the gorge and kill himself. Let alone endanger the next train. Elderberry bushes cut the yards from view. He couldn't hear other cattle following.

He reached the tunnel first. The steer paused, his ears declaring his readiness to charge forward again. Robert stared back from the portal, his chest heaving, deciding on patience. In the intensity of the lengthening moment, the damp musty smell of the tunnel mixed with lingering coal smoke; drips from the coronet of mosses and ferns marked the seconds. All he had to do was turn this steer, which would head back to the herd. Release the gate. Stand back while Ben drove them out, across the main road and up the hill.

He stepped back into the tunnel across the wooden sleepers and stretched out his arms, occupying as much of the space as he could. The steer looked bemused. His tail twitched. Lifted. A steamy flow of brown plopped onto the ground. A front foot lifted. "Ben." Barking loudly, Ben guarded the tunnel, but the steer was defiant. He rushed the dog, horns low. Ben escaped into the broom. The steamy breath of the charging cattle beast brushed across Robert's hand seconds before a tremendous pressure knocked him into the earth of the tunnel wall. A hoof clipped his shin as the beast thrust past him into the darkness, rails echoing as it floundered, confused by the track and sleepers and the coarse gravel beneath its feet.

Robert lay curled in the gutter unable to breathe, to make sense of what had happened. His leg throbbed. Mentally checking every other part of his body, he lifted himself up onto the sleepers where Ben waited. He staggered up, clutching his thigh. Wetness soaked through. Blood.

He'd get on that horse and drive nineteen cattle home if it killed him.

32

THE ALARM CRASHED into her dream, saving her from an insect with enormous fingernails dragging her by the hair. Robert's reassuring hand caressed her shoulder, ran down the curves of her body, down …

She shrugged him off and rolled out of bed into her slippers. In the kitchen, she switched on the radio and blew through new kindling until the red glow burst into flames. Shivering, she rubbed a peephole in the steamed window. Sunrise was warming the crest of the hills.

Dressed now, she took Robert a cup of tea. "It's six-thirty, my dear. They'll be here in half an hour." He grunted and rolled over.

"Where's your school bag, Helen? It's not on the peg again," Rose sighed, arms full of lunches and reading books.

"Under my bed. I'll get it." Helen dashed out the door. Bella watched her mother from the daybed as Rose zigzagged around the kitchen getting a pencil for Frances, stirring the porridge, folding washing from the rack over their heads, checking Bella's temperature, taking newspaper out of their dry shoes.

"Have you heard the van, Robert?"

"Should've been here by now."

As she hurried the two girls to the car to meet the school bus, the shearer's van roared over the crest of the hill and sped through the shed gate. Dogs barked. Rose dashed back to the kitchen. "You go, I'll take her with me." She tossed a blanket around Bella's nightdress and hoisted the child under her arm.

Robert followed her out to open the kennel doors. Tip and Joe raced to the road and back, leaping on him for a fondle under the chin and the reward of a biscuit caught mid-air. Fluid with morning energy, they dashed off again, leaping over each other into the grass across the wheel tracks.

There was nothing like shearing to concentrate the mind; the whole year's finances depended on the wool clip. He'd need to bring in the next mob before midday once the dew on their fleeces had dried.

The dogs bounded onto Robert's truck deck as Rose drove back into the garage. Rose set Bella on the path remembering, for once, the doctor's warning: pregnancy didn't have to make her back ache – if she could only resist picking up children.

In the unheated bedroom she pulled back the thin curtains. Ice had made magical patterns on the glass, a thick forest of ferns arising from the wooden sash frame, with intricate woven branches reaching to the top. She tried to scratch ice from the window. It was solid. This room would grow hardy children.

Beds tidied, she checked her watch. "Come on, Bella. Your programme's on the radio." Baking must be in the oven before *Kindergarten on the Air* ended.

She stoked the firebox. Five minutes of choreographed routine later, the tray of scones slid into the oven. She held her hands above the heat for a moment. Next, afternoon tea. A date and walnut loaf and Anzac biscuits. Eight years ago shearing took half this time, half the food.

Half the flock. Half the income.

"We could be shearing by contract before long," Robert had said last week, "though by gum, they know how to charge." He paused to read again. "You wouldn't believe it. Shearers are going to want kitchen facilities and proper smoko rooms in the sheds. Just when we've built without them."

"Why would it be so expensive?" Rose asked.

"Their cooks prepare the food."

Too good to be true.

"It's the wages."

No sign of that affliction here.

"Looks like we'll have a choice. The children could still be useful if we booked for the school holidays. Contracting might suit bigger properties. I can't see us paying for it. We'll be doing our own meals for a while."

I like the "we", she thought, her heart sinking.

※

Soon the full basket of food sat on the table. Robert had said he would collect it, to save her carrying it to the shed. She wanted to rest. Just a cup of tea, a break with her feet up. She wiped wisps of hair from her face. While the woolshed was being built there had been builders, roofers, electricians, plumbers. Morning teas and midday dinners. She could have kept a housekeeper occupied for months, not just four weeks around the birth. And here it was, the grand finale: blade shearing at an end.

This baby was demanding attention already. It didn't feel like another girl.

A muffled rustle, intermittent barking. Sheep on the run, close. Rose had to keep them from turning down the side road. "Stay here, Bella." The child pressed her face against the wires of the ornamental gate as Rose scuttled across the road.

Steam rose across the whole mob. The leading sheep paused, eyeing her flapping apron, then spurted ahead, disaster averted. Robert leaned from the truck window. "Get away out, Tip. Get in behind, Joe." Two hundred ewes turned obediently into the shed yards.

Robert revved the truck forward and stopped for her to catch up.

"There was a gate open on Mary's Hill – took me longer to round them up. Can you bring the morning tea over?" He drove off banging his arm on the side of the truck to chase the stragglers.

Rose dropped her arms and stared after him. He'd promised to collect the basket himself. Suddenly she felt very, very tired.

"Mummy, Mummy. Joe's taken my biscuit." The black collie was sniffing the ground for crumbs.

At least someone appreciated her efforts. "Get in behind, Joe," Rose attempted, pointing towards the shed. The dog slithered off in the opposite direction through the long grass. "Stupid dog," Rose muttered and headed inside.

※

Soon Rose and Bella were puffing up the concrete steps of the loading bay. Rose loved being in this highly organised workplace, the men in their self-made sacking mocassins, heavy enough to cushion the pain of a sheep's hoof and thick with lanolin like the floor itself. There was something enviable but exclusive about their closeness, bent alongside each other all day.

Johnny was coming down the steps to meet her. "Give you a hand with that, eh missus?"

"Thank you."

"How's your back today?"

"It still bends. Complains though. How's yours?"

"Better for a day off yesterday. Least yours'll be over soon, eh?"

She agreed. But that was not what the doctor suggested.

Robert's voice floated up from the basement, commanding the dogs, crowding the sheep into pens.

Bella peeped between the railings at the heavily fleeced faces inches from her nose. "Baaa," she said in a whisper, breathing into their eyes. The ewes stared at her, unblinking. She jutted her chin out and dared more loudly, "Baaaaa."

"Bella, we're going," came her mother's voice.

Four more days.

Rose put the kettle on for her own tea and sat watching Bella telling her dolls why sheep had to have all their wool off and why Joe was the baddest dog in the world. She really wanted to have someone put her to bed and cook for everyone for a whole month. If only Mother had been well enough.

She would settle for just one day.

In two weeks' time she could have a housekeeper, just before the birth, too late for shearing. She should have persuaded Robert to pay for one sooner, but with the woolshed loan money was tight.

Keep calm and carry on. And ten minutes with her feet up on a kitchen chair. She could peel potatoes sitting down.

❧

At midday the clatter of boots and a knock at the door sent Bella running to the kitchen stool. "Come in," Rose called, placing gravy and mint sauce on the table. Five barefoot men in black singlets, trousers tied close at the ankle, ambled through the door. She turned up the radio to avoid awkwardness, strange men here without Robert to intercede in the conversation. Not the relaxed companionable warmth of the shed, but the heart of the family kitchen.

Rose laid out bowls of mashed potatoes, chops, vegetables. "Help yourselves." Bella watched from the corner, one leg swinging. Steamed pudding and preserved pears. Rose moved from table to sink, to stove, to cupboard. Jugs of milk. More tea.

Suddenly they were standing and thanking her. With unexpected courtesy they cleared the table, stacked the plates in the sink, and were gone.

Bella rested her head against her mother's on the pillow. "Why are your eyes shut? Mummy – move over."

"Have a good rest, sweetheart." She kissed Bella's fingers. Dishes.

*

Why do fools fall in love ... Hank Williams sang out. It was almost two o'clock. If she didn't get a rest soon, the girls would be home from school. Except she could hear Robert whistling up the path.

"We're out of twine for the bales," Robert said as she handed him his dinner. "I lent some to Graham last week. Any chance you could go to town for some tomorrow morning?" He looked at her hopefully.

Rose stood motionless, trying to control herself. Could she be angry with him for helping his neighbour out?

"What's the matter?" he asked, to her silence.

How could she tell him in a way he would understand? "Robert, if you are free to make the morning tea, and get dinner for the men at midday, and the girls to school, I will have time to get your twine."

"What about if you made morning tea now – it would be fresh enough."

Tears welled up. Her arms hung uselessly at her sides. "I can't. I can't do any more." She rushed out of the room and lay rigid on her bed.

Voices on the radio rattled through the market prices and the weather to the steady clatter of Robert finishing his meal. And doing dishes. Surely not.

He came to the bedroom doorway with the teatowel. "You're all right, aren't you?"

Rose drew in a long breath.

"Look, I know pregnant women are over-sensitive and irrational at times."

She stared at the ceiling. Then with a great heave she swung onto her elbow and eyed him fiercely. "I just need a rest, Robert. A rest. Or some help. You did have something to do with this, you know," she said, hugging her pregnant hump. "It's too much. Aunt Marion away, no housekeeper ... "

A sympathetic look crossed his face. "Right then. Sorry. Stay here. Have a rest. I have to get back to the shed and start baling – the wool's piling up. Looks good though. Finer crimp this year, heavy and clean, less gorse."

Deep breathing, Margaret had told her, when Jim finished studying in the early hours of the morning with his favourite symphony and a nightcap. It had woken both her and the baby the first five times. The deep breathing had been for getting up a full head of steam, to warn him that next time there would be shattered symphonic records to show for it.

Rose closed her eyes. The phone rang.

She dragged herself off the bed.

"Keith here. Could you give Robert a message? The projector lamp's blown. We need his spare for the film evening tonight."

Film evening? I need him to help with the girls. "We're in the middle of shearing, Keith. I don't think he'll be there by seven-thirty if he gets there at all."

"Good-oh, Rose. He won't see us stuck."

'Film projector light bulb' she wrote on the blackboard beside the telephone. She stared at it. Something wayward surged through her body, a self-preserving instinct long suppressed.

The first two words disappeared with the duster. Now he would have to work it out for himself, if he noticed at all. A satisfying sabotage. Inexplicable, but satisfying.

"Come on, young lady. Time to meet the bus."

At the shed, Robert came out for the basket. "They're practising for the Golden Shears. Young Potae's on a hundred and eighty-five already. Could do with Frances after school to give us a hand with the gates."

"Uh-huh." When she's folded the washing, perhaps.

At the main road Rose swung her legs up onto the bench seat of the Chev to wait for the school bus and shut her eyes.

"Giddyup, Daddy, giddyup." Robert was crawling around the floor with one pyjama-clad child on his back and two chasing behind, all whooping and giggling.

"Hold on tighter, we're going fast."

"Go under, come on, Daddy." The sheets she had just folded were tangled under the piano, through the chair legs.

Robert usually hated hearing them at full throttle, expecting his home to be as quiet as it was in his childhood. Any moment now he would insist they stop instantly. And if they didn't? Chances were, sleep was a long way off and tears much closer.

Rose flopped onto the cushions of the kitchen daybed and inspected her fingernails. Cracks around the nails were widening, red, inflamed. Flour in the cracks in the mornings. Swollen redness from peeling vegetables later. Irritations from soaps and washing powders. No time for splits to heal. She'd tried creams, and gloves, but the list of allergies was growing faster than the doctor's suggestions.

Her back ached from leaning over the bath, from washing too many small bodies. Robert had bought her a heat lamp. He had even become quite good at massage, when he had time. The baby within her stretched, a moment of familiar pleasure. Pregnancy was the only time her babies could demand her full attention. This one was an expert.

"Robert, just put them to bed."

"We're having too much fun, Mummy. I've got the feather. I'll tickle you, Daddy."

Feathers, she gasped. The hens. How could she forget? She heaved herself off the daybed. At the back door, she slipped into her gumboots and waddled into the cool night air.

Her fingers found the latch on the gate. She pushed past the overgrown veronica bush with her wheat ladle.

The door to the hen run was ajar, but the row of perching white hens that should have been glowing in the moonlight was missing. Scattered across the dirt floor were eleven lifeless clumps of feathers, necks oddly angled, eyes reduced to pinpricks of reflection. Blood oozed darkly into the soil. Beaks hung open. Stiff claws clutched the air.

She stood transfixed, unable to take it in. Filled with surprising compassion, a love she had developed for her hens. Why had she not heard the urgent ruckus which must have rent the night air?

The ladle clattered from her hand, wheat scattering across the dirt floor as she reached out to touch the coarse cold feathers, feathers no longer pulsing with the silent rhythm of life. Too late. She, the feeder of body and soul, the protector, had failed in the simplest of duties: she had not fed the hens. She had not shut the gate against the invader. A stoat had destroyed every one.

Clutching her distended belly, she sank sobbing to her knees, her last residual energy seeping into the soil. She slumped forward, rocking back and forth, her boots carving holes in the dirt. Tears coursed down her face into her skirts, the moonlight fading behind a cloud, merging her shape with the earth of the henhouse floor.

33

November 1955

"Look at him. Just look at him." Aunt Marion stroked the baby's dark hair as he lay in Rose's arms. "Eyelashes exactly like his father – before the stubble fire." They could laugh at it now, Robert coming inside with singed eyebrows, blunted eyelashes, smelling of burnt hair.

"This wee man is just what the family needs," Aunt Marion said. "He'll be a farmer just like his father and his grandfather. Doesn't it make you proud? Yes, little fellow, we're all so proud."

"Hae ye a name for him yet?"

"Adam. He's to be Adam." Robert said.

His father nodded slowly and smiled. "Thank ye. Thank ye."

"A strong sensible name. Bible and family in one," said Aunt Marion, putting on her coat. "Lucy will be well pleased. She still doesn't know if your Uncle Adam died from a heart attack or from falling from his horse. Ah, Rose, nothing better a woman can give her husband than a son."

Three daughters discounted so casually? Rose looked down at the fragile infant still inhaling his first breaths of family air. You've a destiny already, wee lad.

What did she want for her son? This warm bundle-child would choose his own path, her arms around him always.

❦

Rose heard the car and trailer clatter around the pear tree as she picked rusk biscuit from Adam's luxuriant dark hair six months later. "Come and see what Daddy's up to."

Bella raced ahead.

The trailer was piled high with wire frames unlike any building materials she'd seen. "What's this?"

"You'll see. We'll have our own eggs again in no time." He unloaded bundles of small squares and metal plates. "It's the latest thing in hen-houses," he shouted proudly. Metal landed on metal. "Stoat and ferret free." Crash. Bella put her hands over her ears and ran off to talk to the dogs. Rose pulled Adam's woolly hat over his ears.

"No hens in your garden and no nests in the trees."

By midday he was rubbing his hands together. "Just have to wait for the concrete slab to dry."

"Do you need a hand?" she offered.

"No. I want to surprise you."

❧

Rose shut her eyes obediently as he led her towards the tarpaulin. "There you are." Robert's voice was full of pride. She couldn't make sense of it. Wire boxes. Little cages with metal guttering, "For the eggs," Robert said. "You don't even have to reach in to collect them. Here's where the water goes – and this one's the feed trough."

Rose ran her fingers around the wires. "So each chook's in a separate cage?"

"They can't ever scratch each other."

"But they never scratched each other before. So during the day you take each one out through these little doors?

"That's the beauty of it. They don't need to go out at all. Everything's right here."

"Oh, Robert." Rose's shoulders sagged, then she strode back down the path and into the house. She plopped Adam down in the playpen and sat at the kitchen table, looking blankly at the cupboard door. How could he? Something was terribly wrong. Her hens never scratching in the dry dirt or pushing through the flax bushes? Would new hens be content, in their bird brains, with life in a wire box with regular food and water?

If only he'd asked. The more she thought about it the more agitated she became. She'd accepted not having any say about land issues, and Robert and his father visiting the lawyers without her. But the hens had always been hers. She would never, never have chosen to put her chooks in cages.

Angry now, she picked up the phone to cancel the order for twenty Rhode Island reds.

❧

"Those darn cats. Thoughtless city people dumping unwanted cats here to fend for themselves – they're just passing the buck. Must be a dozen – you can hardly get past their snarly little faces. Have the girls been feeding them porridge scraps again?"

Rose didn't answer. She thumped Robert's plate in front of him.

"What's wrong?"

She took a deep breath. "I know you expect me to be pleased with the henhouse. But you didn't ask me."

He looked puzzled. "Ask you what?"

She hung her head a moment and hissed through her teeth. "Yes, it was my fault we lost them, but they were mine. I don't make decisions for you out on the farm."

She stood at the window, her back to him. Suddenly she whirled around. "But with no consultation, you've whipped up a contraption I'd never approve of and put it bang, here, right in view of my kitchen sink – which you've never challenged the ownership of, by the way. How could you?"

"So what exactly are you not happy with?"

"Ohhh. Ohhh. Robert." She flung her arms over her head and gestured wildly, her face tense. "Birds don't belong in cages."

"Might I ask where the new hens will go tomorrow?"

"I cancelled them."

"Cancelled?" he shouted.

"Just take it down. Please. Take it down."

"I've just spent three days putting it up."

"If you'd asked me, you could have spent three days doing something useful."

"So now you're telling ME what to do? Keep your dinner." He slid the plate across the table. "I'm off to do 'something useful'. Blasted cats," she heard him yell.

Rose stared at the plate. She had a good mind to put it outside for the hungry animals to help themselves to.

❧

Rose, Eva, Maud and Ness helped each other lift their prams onto the concrete step. Bella scrambled up, jumped down, then up again. The small wooden hall echoed with children racing from end to end and twenty-nine women settling. Soon the Women's Division of Federated Farmers meeting was under way.

"New dress?" Rose asked Maud between last month's minutes and the correspondence.

"I finished it last night listening to *The Archers*," Maud whispered back.

"Tricky bias trim. You're so clever." Rose glanced along the row. Everyone had detailing on their cotton dresses that she could never attempt. Maud's sewing was meticulous. When she had turned up one afternoon, Rose had climbed onto the kitchen table, handed Maud the yard rule and commandeered her to mark the hem, promising no jokes while she had a mouthful of pins. Then Maud showed her different ways to hide the fastenings and smooth the darts.

"Thought For the Day?" Madame Chairman scanned the room.

"I have it," said Pamela, scrabbling in her bag. " 'It is better to preserve a kindly silence than to speak an uncharitable truth.' "

Kindly silence! Sharing a house with Aunt Marion had taught her the discipline of silence, and its power, but there had been nothing appealing about the silence with Robert. Grass had grown through the cage wires where they lay. There was still no plan for a new hen run.

Last month's Thought had stayed with her: 'Anger is a wind which blows out the light of reason.' Humbug. Anger could help distil the truth. It had freed her to say what she thought.

After the argument, she'd found one from last year: 'Gold is tried in the fire, friendship in need.' Now that resonated. Could her marriage be gold again? Right now it felt like beaten lead.

"General business? Mrs Robert McLeod."

"Some of us were wondering if this branch would support a Women's Division rest home in Otago," Rose said, "like the one in Canterbury, where members go to recuperate, or have a family break." An approving murmer ran around the room. Last year she'd been elected branch rep unopposed, still puzzled that no one else wanted to be where issues could lead to real change.

"Are you able to explain this further?"

"I could find out how theirs came about. And how it works."

"All those in favour of Mrs McLeod investigating this matter further …" Every hand shot up. Here she could make a suggestion and have it adopted.

A baby woke in a pram behind. Not Adam. Bella climbed onto Rose's knee. Eva's daughter climbed onto hers. They sucked their thumbs and swung their legs at each other.

"I have a request here from the Blind Society wanting help with their annual appeal," Mrs Stewart said. "Any volunteers?"

Ness put up her hand. Rose followed. Her father depended on the Blind Society.

"Thank you. And a hospital parcel will be sent to Mrs Jack – your turn with that, Mrs Barton." Everyone knew about the unspoken hysterectomy.

The president packed her notes to make way for today's speaker. The amazing new Swiss Bernina sewing machine that could embroider and zigzag, hem and darn.

Rose put her hand up again. "Would you like my report from the regional meeting?"

"Can you hold it over until next month?"

Did she have any choice? Essentials first: cook, clean, wash and sew – she'd take any help with sewing. But they needed to know. "The submission for having women on juries will be taken to Parliament, Madam Chairman, but it needs more support," she said. "I'll tell you all over afternoon tea."

"Six grains of sugar. No more. No less," Eva asserted over tea. "Don't need any more sweetening than that. Where do I sign?"

Rose lead her to the paper. "Friendship is tried in need," she thought. Was she "in need" enough to tell Eva about the cages?

Too disloyal to Robert. They would have to forgive each other.

❦

The memory of last night's frosty kiss returned the moment she awakened from a dream of being tossed into the Clutha River, sucked down through swirling leaves into holes between rocks, where debris held her suspended in constant motion. Her hair stretched into the current like giant stoat fur. The children, covered in white feathers, rotated just beyond reach, disappearing into caverns among the boulders, rising featherless, disintegrating into sparkling clouds of bone.

She stretched her legs across the bed. He wasn't there. Her neck ached. Sounds of the girls in the kitchen. School holidays.

Elbows on the pillow, she dragged herself up, dizzy. Frances tapped on the bedroom door. "Are you getting up? I've made porridge and Helen's doing toast. Bella spilled milk all over the tablecloth but we've wiped it up."

"You're the best eight-year-old there is. Where's Adam?"

"Daddy's feeding him."

"You're a treasure. I'll be up in a minute." She flung an arm over her forehead to block out the light. Her head was burning.

❧

A swarm of voices accompanied the next three days. "This might hurt a little." A prick in her arm. Sometime later, another. "No, we won't move her, the temperature's down slightly." The doctor. "Meningitis? Surely not. Why hasn't he put her into the hospital?" Aunt Marion. "If they can't dance without your record player and your records, you'd better go. Just go. I'll stay." Much whispering at the door.

"Sit up." Robert's arm was around her shoulder. "Come on. You have to drink every hour." In the distance the high chair fell over. Wails. Comforting sisters. Doors shutting, cries diminishing. Robert again with cold flannels.

She closed her eyes and willed the cold into her body. "I'm so relieved you're better. You've given us quite a scare." Robert was kissing her forehead with such tenderness. Was she supposed to be still angry? Or forgive him for something? He seemed to have forgiven her.

34

ONCE SHE HAD RECOVERED, Rose felt ready to invite her parents for a visit. Two pages later she sealed the envelope. The children had been oddly quiet for the last ten minutes. "Frances?"

No reply.

Three heads were pressed against the glass, staring out of the kitchen window. "What are you looking at?" Rose said, moving towards the window.

"Tabby's done funny poos," Bella said.

"Stupid," said Frances disdainfully. "She's had a baby. Mummy, quick, another one's coming." The cat lay oddly stretched, abdomen writhing. On the mat was a sticky, wet curled creature, eyes tight shut, ears flat against its head.

"Why doesn't it stand up, like a lamb?" Helen asked. The mother cat twisted around to lick them. "Ugh. Mummy, you didn't lick us like that when we were bornded did you?" A third kitten oozed out, blood now staining the concrete.

Under pressure, Robert had agreed to their having a family cat. A black one. Spayed. No dumped domestic cats like this tabby, "wild scavengers, screeching, whining, getting under your feet every time you go outside," he had said. "They're perfectly capable of finding their own food. The barns are full of mice and rats. Feed one city reject, you'll attract a crowd."

Rose rolled the sack and the wriggling mass of cats into an apple box and washed the stains from the back door. "Let's put all the kittens safely in the shed in case it rains or Daddy steps on them in the dark. Be careful not to touch them so that they smell right for their mother."

Robert came inside later to a rush of girls clutching his trouser legs.

"Daddy. Daddy. The wild tabby cat's had five kittens. They're in the shed," said Bella.

"Mine's the first one," Frances said.

"Mine's the black one," said Bella.

"Mine's the little tabby one like its mother," said Helen. "Adam can have the littlest one cos he's a baby." Adam was more interested in wobbling his way around the furniture.

Rose raised her eyebrows at Robert over their heads. His silence told her that the chances of any being alive tomorrow were slim. Very slim.

As soon as the children were in bed, Robert disappeared into the dark and reduced the number of kittens to two. It was to have been one, but he missed the dark one hiding in the fold of the sack.

Life began, life ended – pragmatic decisions made by farmers every day. Robert had dealt with something she condoned but could never have carried out herself. She'd colluded in silence.

How would they – she – explain the disappearance of the kittens? Could the wild mother have sneaked them away in the dark, by the scruff of the neck, one after the other?

There's a time for every treason. This was not the time for unmitigated truth.

※

"The last thing we want is women in the pulpit," Robert declared after midday dinner the next day as he sorted the mail, tossing Rose the new church magazine. "We need thinking men. Scholars. People who'll be looked up to in the community."

"Are you suggesting women are not looked up to?" Rose said, scanning the cover.

"In their own way, they can be."

"*A new day dawning for women*. What's the *Outlook* saying now?" Surely nothing to do with the recent equal pay for public sector women, not that she would ever be affected by pay rates. *Greater opportunities for women to serve*, she read.

Women as ministers?

Here it was: women could now be invited to become elders, full members of the core leadership team. Not ministers. Ministers were always men. But two writers argued that with this change, ordination was not far off.

Robert leaned across and tapped the page. "Don't you go getting mixed up with that radical lot."

"Radical is the last thing I want to be," said Rose. But you had to admire them, she thought, hefting Adam onto her hip.

"Mummy, Mummy, read me the one about James James." Bella dropped the A. A. Milne book on the sofa and scrambled up.

"*James James Morrison Morrison Weatherby George Dupree,*" Rose began, latching Adam onto her breast. She was tired, so tired. This boy was ready for weaning.

"*Du-pree,*" Bella echoed.

"*Took great …* "

"*… care of his muvver …* "

"*… though he was only …* "

"FREE!" Bella clapped her hands.

"*James James said to his mother, 'Mother,' he said, said he, 'YOU MUST …* '"

" ' *… NEVER GO DOWN TO THE END OF THE TOWN IF YOU DON'T GO DOWN WITH ME*'," Helen and Frances joined in from the kitchen.

In the last verse, Rose remembered, the mother finds her inner free spirit, puts on her golden gown and floats "quite of her own accord" to the end of the town without asking anybody. At times it seemed the most desirable wonder she could imagine. If she wasn't careful she'd turn into one of those awful radicals.

35

"How many does that make?" asked Patricia.

Rose scanned the growing pile of cheese rolls. "Five dozen. Five more to go." She laid out another row of bread slices.

"We missed you at the dance last week. The band was in good form."

"Robert wanted me to go, but Aunt Marion had the children all afternoon."

Patricia's knife paused. "Robert enjoyed himself, dancing with that new Audrey, the pretty one." She put down her knife. "Oh, whoops, he hasn't told you."

A knot tightened in her stomach. "Wasn't her husband there?"

"Oh yes. He's one of those men out at the cars half the night. You never want to dance with them when they come back in."

※

"You've been quiet tonight," Robert said as he ran water into the hand basin.

With every reason, Rose thought, leaning on the door jamb. "Was that new couple at the dance, that chap who was helping with lambing, Stewart is it? And his wife? Of course they don't go to our church ... " She tailed off, her words not quite following each other.

Robert had arrested the movement of blade over skin. "Darn," he muttered, reaching for the facecloth. "Nicked myself." He pressed the cloth to the corner of his jaw.

Enough said? Not quite enough. "Patricia said she's a good dancer." A heavy pause hung in the air between them.

He swished the razor in the water. Their eyes met. "Very good partner, she is, since I had to find someone to dance with."

Rose smarted. "That's not fair." She couldn't fight the tears. "I don't object to staying with the children. But you don't have to dance all night with the same woman."

※

Rose propped the gate against the tree and drove through. She had no plan, no ready phrases to volley towards the woman who may or may not have been taken with her husband. Or he with her. Too late to turn back. "Morning Audrey," she called around the door.

Dirty dishes cluttered the lean-to kitchen. A partly cut onion lay on the chopping board. "Audrey?"

"Be there in a minute," came a distant voice. "Sorry. Just putting some ironing away." No sign of an iron cooling.

Audrey's hair was swept across one eye, caught with a clasp of butterflies at her neck, lending her an air of fragile beauty.

"I've brought your milk billy and newspaper from the mailbox," said Rose, "and some plums. We've lots if you'd like more. I'm collecting for the Blind Foundation."

Audrey stared into the space over her shoulder.

"Are you all right?"

"I'm fine." Audrey unfroze enough to pour the milk into jugs. "I didn't sleep very well. Stomach bug." Holding her hair in place, she lifted the rinsed billy onto a shelf. "You're collecting for something?"

Her eyes were dull, her movements jerky.

"If there's anything I can help with," offered Rose.

"No need. I'll be better tomorrow. Here's five shillings. Will that do?"

Five shillings! More than generous. What was she thinking?

As she reached to put it into the collection box, Audrey's sleeve slipped up her arm, revealing a purple bruise.

"You've hurt your arm."

"Have I? I hadn't noticed. Must have hit it on something when I tripped last night, on the way out to the lavatory."

The tentative loop of conversation snapped.

"I'll let you get back to your onions then." Rose moved to the back door and turned. "Audrey ... "

"Yes, I know, Stewart was late to work again this morning. But we can let the men sort it out, can't we? See you."

The door shut.

Rose put the full collection box into the writing desk. "Robert?"

"Mmm?"

"What time did Stewart come to work today?"

"Late, that's when. He couldn't remember two instructions at once. Waste of time, that man."

"Audrey had a bruised arm."

Robert stared at her, puzzled. "Why?"

Rose swallowed. "I think it's something to do with her husband. She wasn't herself." Robert looked down at his shoes. A moment of silence. He raised his eyes to the fire.

"She probably provoked him."

Rose turned away. How could Robert suggest it was her fault? Men might have certain rights, but they certainly didn't include bruising their wives. Audrey had no family nearby, no children to soften any confrontations. Should she interfere?

❦

When Frances and Helen came home with chickenpox, Audrey slipped from her mind. For three weeks, children drooped around the house in spots and scabs. "Robert, the doctor wants us to shave Helen's hair off to treat her scalp. Will you do it?"

"I wouldn't mind looking like Yul Brynner."

"Try telling that to a seven-year-old girl."

A few days later, Robert succumbed to the pox as well. Bella dabbed calamine lotion on his back until the pink dots joined. Rose rang neighbours to finish the tailing, but she couldn't face asking Audrey's husband, even if Audrey needed him to be working. Others needed casual workers too. Hopefully he had work elsewhere.

"I'll have to go into town," Rose said, scraping the bottom of the flour bin. "It would be so much easier if you'd let me have my name on the cheques. It's 1958 and I still can't sign for my own shopping." Robert stretched out his arm, his fingers twitching for a pen.

❦

"I've just heard Audrey and her husband are leaving," Aunt Marion said on the telephone a week later.

"They've hardly arrived." Rose rested the handpiece back in its cradle. If they stayed, what help could she be? Marriage, for all its veneer of contentment, was precarious. And some women were seriously vulnerable.

Robert staggered into the sitting room and sat in his striped pyjamas on the piano stool, his shoulders sagging, his hair fluffed up like a storm cloud. He took down the long-ignored violin case from the top of the piano. With his ear bent to the instrument, he twisted the pegs to tune it. Then he slumped, head almost to his knees. Leaving the violin on the piano stool, he wobbled back to bed.

※

All morning, rally cars varoomed along the gravel road, the drivers waving to the four children beside the mailbox. But the dust. No point in washing – Rose would cut back the peonies instead. "Here comes anuvver one, Bella," shouted Adam.

"See if we can make them wave to us," said Helen.

"Pfff, you can't *make* them. They will anyway," Frances said.

"Not if we turn our backs."

"Quick. They coming."

"Helen, how will we know if we're not looking?" Bella asked.

Helen was silent. Her eyes moved to the top of the hill, awaiting a more exciting idea.

Over the hill came a black Austin sounding like a plough hitting a pile of stones. It clattered to a halt. A woman in trousers jumped out and looked underneath. "Oh bugger! The muffler's shattered. Hand me the sack, Percy." A sack was squeezed through the window. She laid it under the car and edged onto it, on her back.

"There's a hole, Percy – a big hole in the radiator." The man stepped out in an elegant hat, cravat and cream jacket. "Damnation," the woman spat. "We won't get a mile further."

"Can I help?" Rose pushed the secateurs into her apron pocket.

The woman thrust out her hand. "Cressida. How do you do?"

"Rose. Cup of tea? Something more practical?" The man – husband? employee? lover? – nodded.

"No. But I could do with a large potato and a knife, and the children's help."

Five minutes later the children sat on the verandah step in ecstasy, a mouthful of forbidden Juicy Fruit gum each. When the taste was gone there was more.

At intervals cars sped past.

The woman stretched a brave hand out for the gum and strode off, everyone following.

"Hold this, Percy." She slid back under the car with the reshaped potato. Lots of grunting later: "Gum please." Percy passed one piece at a time. "That should do it. Let's try filling it with water."

She climbed out and reached for Rose's kettle.

No water leaked from the radiator. At last the woman smiled. "You drive, Percy. We'll have time penalties anyway. I need to calm my nerves before the mountains." One hand around his neck, she pulled him towards her and planted a loud kiss on his lips. Percy smiled smugly and climbed into the driver's seat.

Something about this woman disturbed Rose in a way she had never encountered before. It wasn't only the trousers, or how she understood the workings of a car. What kind of intimate relationship did a woman have with a man that was based on ordering him about like a, well, like nothing she could think of. She couldn't think of any women in charge that she knew, except in a hairdressing salon. And sole-charge schools. And the Waitahuna Post Office.

In this house, the boundary lines were distinct.

Too distinct?

"The lady waved at us," said Adam.

"She had trousers on, like a man."

"Mummy, I like the chewing-gum lady."

"Good, but chewing gum is still not allowed in this house. Right?"

She couldn't imagine any man raising his hand to Cressida.

36

"But it's New Year's Eve." Frances swayed to keep her hula hoop rotating. "Can't we pleeease stay up till midnight?"

Helen lunged her inadequate hips back and forth. "I ... will be ... a decade ... old in ... twenty-one ... days." The hoop fell to the ground. "It's not fair. How can you keep it going?"

"As it happens, your father does have something for tonight." Rose knotted the last thread of Bella's hem. "Watch the pins." The tin teetered on the ledge of her fifth child, due in three months.

"Is it fireworks?" Frances demanded.

"It is fireworks, isn't it? Rockets," Helen said.

"Careful, don't climb on me. Possibly not rockets. You'll have to wait and see."

"Can we go to meet them?" Helen said.

"Then how would there be room for their six in the car? Don't worry, they'll be here before dark."

"Tell me their names again," said Frances.

Four sleepy children tumbled from the car as Rose hugged Lydia, her old friend and sister-in-law.

"We've made it," John said, holding her at arm's length.

"Are you Diane?" asked Frances.

She nodded.

"I can make toffee. And fudge."

"I made the fudge," Bella said.

"Fudge? Where?" The boys darted towards the gate.

"Come back here. You think the tents will put themselves up?" their father roared.

"Oh Rose, your garden." Lydia stood admiring the sweeping lawns and the twilight-soft silhouettes of rhododendrons and maples, spindleberry and camellias.

Rose squeezed Lydia's arm. "Come and see what we've done to the house."

She led Lydia into the extended kitchen on the east side and the new lounge on the west, where their first bathroom had been. "And see the farm worker's hut, past the silver birches?"

Two tents rose from the ground, fixed with Boy Scout knots and kindling stays, kitted out with army surplus stretchers. Robert had sworn he'd never sleep in one again, but despite earthquake memories, tents reminded Rose of campfires and drifting to sleep to the sound of the sea.

"So how are things going?" asked John between orders to the boys.

"Couldn't be better," Robert said. "We're getting record prices for wool. Meat's higher than ever too."

"Holyoake's certainly achieved what he wanted: peace, stability, prosperity."

"It's all those farmers in Parliament," Robert laughed. "Almost every government minister's a farmer. You need us to pay your wages."

Robert, Robert. Don't alienate him or they'll never come again, Rose thought. I want my children to know my family.

John pursed his lips and looked across to the tents. "Hey, don't tie that rope to the wire," he called. "Use the post."

"There's a whale of a lot of new land in grass here now that we've cleared the ridges. I'll show you around tomorrow. I've had contractors cut tracks around the gullies – there's access everywhere." He didn't explain how easily he'd obtained the loans.

※

"Ready for a surprise?" Robert stood on the verandah at dusk with a large paper bag. Children appeared from the bushes.

"Me, me." Adam copied the others.

"Guess." Robert held the bag high. The children stetched up trying to take it from him.

"Sherbet."

"Lolly scramble."

"You're all wrong. I'll have to put it back in the bedroom." He hugged it to his chest.

"No, Daddy, what is it?"

He pulled out three bags of sparklers.

"Hold your horses. Spread out in a line – visitors first – away from each other. Further, further."

"Two, I want two," Bella jiggled. He gave her one.

They drew the magic light across the darkness, the night hosting a festival of sparkles, their dancing limbs becoming the light itself, wave after wave as Robert lit more.

"Any left?" Rose asked. Robert held up the last four.

"Come on, Lydia." They kicked off their shoes. Two sparklers each, the women whooped their arms in slow circles over their clapping children. Rose let her head fall back, her voluptuous maternity frock billowing. The sparkling wands floated across the sky, drawing the Milky Way down, down through the horizon, into their front yard.

※

Unexpected overnight rain had wet the hay. "It has to be dry before you store it," Frances explained, "cos wet hay rots. It can even burst into flames." Six children rolled the oblong bales a quarter turn in the morning – fun, a novelty – a quarter turn in the afternoon, duty breaking into diversionary stack building and competitive gymnastics.

"Anyone for a swim?" Rose called at last. Into the Chevrolet they packed, four, five, six in the back seat, the two littlest between the adults in the front, togs on, ready for the Waitahuna River.

"Follow us," Frances called along the narrow track through the trees.

Rose and Lydia stretched out in the shade, watching lithe bodies scramble up the willow on the far side to leap with Tarzan whoops into the swimming hole. Helen blew up the lilo.

"If you could invite anyone, *anyone* to dinner, who would you invite?"

"Marlon Brando," Lydia shot out immediately, "though I'd be so overcome I couldn't speak."

"I'd rather have Cary Grant," Rose laughed. "But what about a New Zealander?"

"Yvette Williams – she's so modest about all her Olympic medals. I could easily talk to her." The children were standing about at the edge of the river.

"I'd ask Esther James."

"Who?"

"Esther walked the full length of New Zealand, long before A. H. Reed did. Everyone knows about him – no one knows about Esther. She went further: Cape Reinga to Bluff, and then right across Stewart Island."

Shouts came from the cousins, shrieks as boys tipped girls off the lilo.

"Whoops. Our girls could do with boys to play with more often," said Rose.

"You won't be saying that for long," Lydia laughed. Frances dogpaddled towards them.

"Esther had brains and stamina. She contacted manufacturers everywhere and wore their New Zealand-made clothing – even leather shoes. Business people fed her and hosted her the whole way."

"You're making her up."

"I'm not. She's a distant relative." She handed Lydia a plastic mug of homemade lemon cordial.

"Is she still alive?"

"She fought her way into architecture. It wasn't easy. Men don't like pushy women," she laughed. "At Women's Division we had a secret vote for our dinner guest. Guess who?"

Lydia shook her head.

Rose laughed and covered her eyes. "Prime Minister Holyoake. Unanimously. Me included."

"Rose. You're becoming so serious."

Frances tiptoed over the stones, pulling her towel around her shoulders. "They're splashing too much."

"You're nearly one of the grown-ups, Frances," Lydia said, moving over. "I hear you're deciding about high schools."

"Mum's hoping Otago Girls' will have a hostel next year." Her aunt looked puzzled. "It's top of the government list."

"Except it keeps getting knocked off for 'higher priorities'. " Rose heaved a sigh. "We may have to send her to Waitaki Girls. In Oamaru."

"It's too far to get home very often," Frances said. "I'm getting changed." She flicked stones out of her plastic sandals and disappeared into the bushes.

"What can you do? She'll be only twelve," Rose said, picking gravel off the rug. "District high schools will never improve if we send able pupils away. Their pupils usually leave at fifteen. But we can't gamble on our children wanting to stay on, or the school offering quality senior courses for a tiny number. Children deserve a better chance." She looked at her watch. "Time everyone was out."

Bella and Adam raced the cousins to their changing rooms amongst the heady aromas of broom and hemlock. Girls through the track to the right, boys to the left. The demarcation was sacrosanct.

※

"I'll help with the dishes," John said, picking up the tea towel. "Unlikely to be interrupted. I'm worried about you. We know 'The world must be peopled', but not by you single-handedly."

She froze. How dare he – just because his own limit was four children. She rested her stretched belly against the Formica. It was none of his business if they wanted ten. "I am perfectly happy, John," she murmured under the flop of her hair.

"You don't realise how tired you look."

Wouldn't a week with six guests make any pregnant woman tired?

John drew himself up to his full Important Public Servant stature. "I'll have to talk to him."

"You will not. Keep your voice down." She turned to face him full on. "Do you want to lose any respect he has for you?" Typical John, always believing himself wiser, more worldly. She stacked the wet plates. John snatched them away. "Anyway," she said with a grin, "you're getting quite a paunch yourself."

John was taken aback. Rose grabbed the tea towel and hit him around the ears with it. "Truce," he yelled, arms folded over his head. "I can't defend myself against a pregnant woman."

※

The next morning John bundled everyone into the car with Robert and disappeared in a cloud of dust. He had never mentioned Hadley. Not once. Rose felt an ache in her heart at their departure, as much for Lydia – such easy company, such an instinctively helpful friend – as for her brother.

Through the window Rose could see Frances and Helen, chests forward, elbows out like wings, pumping their arms back and forth. Bella copied half-heartedly, Adam with vigour. A new song? She opened the window. "I musT – I musT – I must increase my busT– I musT – I musT –" She shut it again, shaking with laughter. Cousins.

How many children did she want? She had the answer now. They would both know – deep within – when enough was enough. Like knowing, deep down, who to marry.

And there would be more to life after that, though she could not imagine what.

※

Thomas arrived on time, Good Friday: a smooth trip to the hospital in a reliable car on dry metal roads, housekeeper in place, three adoring older sisters and a four-year-old brother almost ready to give up his mother's knee. Everyone's baby. He seemed to have always been there. While Tom slept, Robert took future farmer Adam fencing, dipping, checking the wheat crop. Once the housekeeper had left, Rose could rely on Frances to roast, bake, fry or boil almost anything. Helen had mastered apple crumble and custard.

"Look at these School Certificate results." Rose said to Aunt Marion. "Private schools are all very well, but the Girls' High's way ahead. If only they had a hostel."

"That's what the state's for," Aunt Marion said, burping Tom. "Quality and equality. Such a pity you can't get it closer to home."

※

How could she be pregnant so soon after Tom? Her body barely back in shape, barely awake to Robert's desire. Wide-eyed, he laughed. "I'm still up to it, eh?" And an after-thought: "And you."

By the fifth month, still feeding Tom, she'd have to tell the children.

But one morning she woke to a sudden grabbing pain. Agony clawed at her body, bent her double on the edge of the bed. Her fists clenched, her face tightened, her thighs clutched each other.

She wrapped her nightgown across her knees. Blood. On the sheets too. She tried to stand and stretch against the pain. What was happening? Pain gripped her again, tearing pain. She staggered to the toilet.

Elbows on knees, hands pressing her skull, she sat until the pain diminished. She stood clutching the wall and stared into the toilet. Red. Red and lumpy.

Robert was at the toilet door. "Take me to the doctor. Quickly," she squealed. "Don't let the children see any blood." She clung to the edge of the washtub. "I'll get to the car. Bring towels. Dressing gown. Slippers. Let's go. Tell Frances to look after the little ones till we can call Ness. Tell her my back's playing up again. Go. Yes, I can walk."

But she couldn't get beyond the back door. Something terrifying was happening.

※

Through a daze, she recognised the maternity ward curtains and the nursing sister sitting on the end of the bed quite careless of rules.

"I'm so sorry, Rose. It would have been a little girl."

Robert stirred in his chair.

This had not been just another baby; it would have been theirs, theirs to love and laugh with, to chase through trees and watch her grow.

Dumbstruck, paralysed, she gazed at Robert, himself exhausted, gaunt. Slowly, slowly he reached out his hand. She tugged it lightly. He came towards her in slow motion and wrapped her in his arms. Tears came, her sobbing, his. One sound. One grief.

"Get me out of here, Robert," she whispered.

※

"Dad's not saying much about where I should go," Frances said as she helped Rose change the sheets. Routines helped, anything to keep busy.

"Whichever option, it will be a lot better than he had."

"What do you mean?"

"Your father didn't have a car to get him to a school bus. Rain, hail or shine, he had to catch his pony." She shook her head. "School at Manuka was hardly worth riding to when it dropped to three pupils." She tossed a bundle of linen into the doorway. "Then it became a grade zero school, not eligible for a trained teacher. They had dreadful people – one man just sat at the teacher's desk writing letters, if he bothered turning up." Frances was gaping at her. Rose decided not to mention the bullying woman with the leather belt. "No wonder he failed Proficiency."

"Dad failed? Failed primary school?"

"So would you if you'd never been taught. He sailed through when they moved him to Waitahuna School. But then – high school." She stuffed Bella's pillow into a clean white pillowcase. "Would you like to walk two miles to the main road to the bus, get to school an hour late each day and hang about waiting for a six o'clock bus home? Not to mention the final two-mile walk. He never had the chance of boarding school."

What would Robert have done with an education like her brothers'?

The season slowed. Wind from the gully sneaked through the weatherboards. On the roadside, cocksfoot bent into soggy mounds. A grey ceiling of cloud spread across her world which now shrank back into the kitchen. Robert had been gentle but was losing patience with her rejection in bed. She couldn't bear to lose another. How she longed for her mother's arms around her. February's visit was still far off.

"Wherever you end up, it's a good idea to get an education," Robert was saying to Frances as wind rattled the sitting room windows. He counted five places along the Monopoly board.

"Marylebone. That's mine. Two hundred pounds please," Bella said.

"Teaches you to think," he said, handing Bella her money. "Your mother can think. But girls shouldn't get too much education. Men don't like a woman who's too educated. Unless he's more educated than her."

"Robert, you can't seriously believe that." Rose called from ironing in the kitchen.

"What?"

"That they should limit their education to appeal to a man." Rose hung up the shirt.

"Makes sense to me. Even *you* have made more use of homemaking than university learning."

He had hit a vein. "Education's not just for a job. Educate the woman, the whole family benefits. You need a decent education to see what needs to change and how to go about it." How could she explain without diminishing Robert?

"You can learn as you go," Robert said. "I didn't need to stay at school to read Ayn Rand or Bertrand Russell or soil reports."

"Park Lane," shouted Frances. "I'm buying it."

"Urghhh," Helen and Bella wailed. "You've got Mayfair already."

"Once Frances reaches twenty she'll be interested in more than marriage, Rob. Girls today have their own careers."

"Of course," he called back. "Then they get married."

"They might marry and keep working."

"How can a woman keep working with a husband and family to look after?"

"The husband could share some of the housework."

"Now you are being ridiculous."

"Don't argue, you two," Frances said.

"Aren't we allowed to have different opinions?" Rose answered.

"People should marry someone they agree with."

"You'll be lucky, young lady, or have to stay silent for a great deal of your life."

"I'm going to find someone with the same ideas as me. We won't be like you two at all."

Robert brought his cup and saucer to the kitchen bench.

"Dad, we haven't finished the game," called Helen.

"Finish it later," Robert called back.

Frances strode to the piano. "Rondo Alla Turca" with attitude resounded through the house.

"We'll miss that playing. Perhaps she's more ready for high school than we know," Robert chuckled.

"Robert, you don't seriously ... " She couldn't frame a question. "The more education they get the better. There's no end to what they could learn." She unplugged the iron. "I think we should accept Eva's offer: Monday-to-Friday board. It's very kind of her. Just till the hostel's built."

"You're the expert. Whatever you decide."

37

"Slide of the year. Congratulations!" Rose kicked off her shoes, "I knew you'd do it." Robert sat up in bed, his diary open across the blankets. "How was the banquet?"

"Would've been better with you there."

She sighed. "You know I wanted to be. It was hardly an easy choice: photographers' banquet or your eldest daughter's first teacher interviews, with the quality of our two-teacher school up for examination."

The clock in the sitting room struck midnight.

"Which photo was it?"

"The slide of Adam."

"That's quite a cup." She folded her cardigan into a drawer. "Frances wanted to show me every part of the school, even the choir room. She's in her element there." What a relief, especially after the agony of driving away, leaving Frances standing alone on the city footpath in January, her two envious younger sisters sitting silent in the back seat. Rose hadn't expected the depth of her loss, the aching hollowness.

Days later her parents' visit had distracted Rose, especially her surprise for them: two wonderful days with her in a Queenstown motor camp cabin, despite the long journey on gravel roads. How they'd laughed at her clam-tight eyes as the bus crossed the Kawarau bridge, a hundred and forty feet above the river. She shuddered at the memory. But she would never forget leaning on the wooden rail of the *Earnslaw*, arms linked with her mother's, in wonder at the majestic snow-capped mountains scissored from ancient rock, sunlight dancing on the lake.

"The teachers were very complimentary – no one's found gaps in her country schooling." She unclipped her suspenders and peeled off her stockings. "Guess what. A college friend of mine called Martha's teaching there – three daughters and back at work. She wouldn't believe our youngest's not yet one." And there might have been another.

She hung her dress in the wardrobe

"Tell me about the banquet."

"Nothing to tell," said Robert and rolled over.

Rose lay on her back, playing over what her friend had said. Teaching. There'd be a time. The children were growing up.

All week Helen, Bella and Adam had led their reluctant pet lambs around the ram paddock with plaited binder-twine rope and Neil's horse-harness collars, in training for Pet Day. Now the animals waited in the trailer.

The doorbell rang. Strange. No one came to the front door in the morning. "Good morning, madam." The Bon Brush man removed his hat. "Lovely day. May I interest you … "

"Come in, I always need something." He followed her in, with talk of new designs in flue cleaners. With Tom on her knee, she flipped through the catalogue. "I could do with this yard broom," she interrupted, pointing to the page.

The phone rang. Short long short. "Excuse me."

"Oh Rose. Dreadful news." Aunt Marion's distant voice. A sniff? "I can hardly bear to tell you. Maud. Dear Maud." A spluttering noise as Aunt Marion blew her nose. "You knew she'd lost the baby? Now we've lost her."

"What?" Not her friend Maud. The blood drained from her face. Her knees buckled. The Bon Brush man pushed a chair under her. "No, no – surely they could have saved her?" The call ended. Dropping the handpiece to swing on its cord, she slumped onto the chair, staring at her feet.

"I'll get your husband. I saw him on the tractor."

He snapped his suitcase shut and ran.

❧

Three days later, Rose squeezed between Robert and Neil in an overflowing church, struggling to believe Maud would no longer be part of everything. Only ten days ago they had spent a relaxed afternoon doing home-permanent waves on each other's hair. Through the heavy silences came distant shouts of teenagers playing rounders with the young ones in the school grounds. This was no place for children, thought Rose.

Abide with me, fast falls the eventide, thin voices sang. Aunt Marion pumped the pedals of the organ as if she wanted it over.

Sombre-faced men carried Maud's coffin, Robert behind Keith, his lifelong friend, both survivors of Monte Cassino, leaders of Bible Class, Sunday school, the weekly film strip evenings in the new hall. Both had lost a baby. Only one had lost a wife.

After the committal, Rose tossed soil into the grave and drifted away through rows of headstones, up the slope to the older graves under the macrocarpas. One stone caught her eye. Catherine McLeod, wife of Adam, daughter of Luke McAra, surgeon to the Scottish Regiment. Robert's grandmother Catherine, who had lived in their cob cottage, the woman who saw to it that her son Neil and Alice had a large house, now hers.

The slumped stone memorial must have been impressive once. Rose scraped moss from the base with the toe of her shoe. How long did people remember anyone?

Neil appeared beside her. "A fine woman, me mither." They stood together, one with real memories, the other constructing a woman into a vacuum. "She could pull a calf from a heifer on a Saturdee and be the picture of a lady for kirk on Sundee." Neil bent to pull out a thistle. "Dinna stand no nonsense, mind."

Below them a few people still lingered near the fresh mound of earth.

How does a farming family survive without a mother?

"There was anither fine woman – Maud." He shook his head. "A different breed. Och, there's no two women alike." He stepped aside to let her pass. "Thank the Lord," he said, and roared with laughter.

Life was so fragile.

She would have to make more of hers.

38

Rose and Robert stood alongside each other, backs to the kitchen bench. Between sips of tea, he seemed to be about to say something.

"Is something bothering you?" she asked.

"Someone thought you might be useful on that church union committee."

"Who? No one's asked me."

"I didn't think you'd be interested, with so much to do here."

"Robert! How do you know what I would be interested in, apart from keeping five children organised and food flowing?" It might be six. That salty sweet taste was in her mouth again. But how could that be? The new pill, the wonder pill, seemed to be disagreeing with her, with hot flushes and rashes and vomiting. But she had to persevere. The doctor suggested it might take a few months to settle. She couldn't bear going back to diaphragms. Or abstinence. Robert would never cope with abstinence.

"We didn't finalise anything. It could come up again."

"Was that an apology? If I'm nominated, don't decline on my behalf."

She placed her empty cup on the bench. "You'd better get to that ram sale while you're still ahead. There's no comparison between my other committees and getting Methodists and Presbyterians and Anglicans and Congregationalists to co-operate." She tapped him on the chest. "Imagine being a part of that."

He looped his sports jacket off the kitchen chair.

❦

"Bella's broken my jigsaw," Adam yelled, holding up fragments of split wood.

Bella looked indignant. "I did not. Tom tipped me over."

"Outside," Rose said firmly. The dreaded damp May school holidays. "Never mind the drizzle. Boots on, coats, hats, gloves. Come back when you can behave like civilised people."

She held the door open. One, two, three, sullen heads passed under her arm. "You too, Adam." The six-year-old followed, imitating his father's stride.

"Me too," Tom said, toddling after Adam.

"Not today. Sleepy time for you."

The children were already jumping down the steps, chanting "Nine, ten, a big fat hen." They'd be at least an hour, making huts in the gully and catching cockabullies. She poured water into turpentine and methylated spirits and shook it.

How still the house was.

Window cleaning could wait. She picked up the newspaper. Elizabeth Taylor marries Eddie Fisher. Her fourth wedding. Toss one husband aside and on with the new. No negotiated peace there. Her fourth!

※

Two hours later the girls rushed into the kitchen.

"Mum, Adam smashed the baby rabbits."

"There's squashed brains."

"Yucky blood all down the post."

"The dogs swallowed them all up."

"You two, back out. Wash your hands. Helen, can tell me what happened?" She looked out the window. "Where is Adam?"

But the boy had already developed the finely honed skill of letting a breathing space separate stories and outcomes. Cause and effect. Too young for the gun hanging beside Robert's army kitbag with its number fading on the side. Old enough to understand the necessity of his father shooting rabbits, though he might wonder why he had given his neighbour permission to shoot ducks on their pond rather than do it himself.

Years before, Rose had been arrested by the movement of the luxurious growth on the hills at twilight, flowing liquidly in a light breeze. Now the same hills moved to an army of grey fur. Rabbits stripped the grass bare. Stock was hungry, thinning, weary-eyed. Hungry ewes could not breed.

Something must be done about the rabbits.

Rose could imagine Robert with Adam, encouraging the dogs to sniff out rabbits in their holes, Robert reaching in, throwing the young to the dogs. Yesterday Robert and his father were deciding if they could afford the rabbiter, who had just shot eighty-eight, ninety-two the day before. She heard them laughing over putting poison in jam. Not her jam, please. A new poison was coming, 1080. Carrots soaked it up and carrots could be dropped from an aeroplane.

The sooner the better.

Rain usually drowned young ones in their burrows, but there had been no rain. Every three months, each female could have a litter of ten, themselves ready to breed in three months. A female could head a family of 800 in a single season. Rabbits and flies – what was God thinking?

Wasn't Adam's "rabbit punch", the quick hit on the back of the head, less cruel than poison? Farm children lived with the facts of life and of death: animals nurtured and sent to slaughter. Seasons of death and renewal determined every work cycle.

❧

Six months later, Rose manoeuvred Tom's pushchair through the school gate. Bella clambered off the jungle gym. Helen was turning one end of the long rope, where girls were skipping and singing, "*Ee-vy, i-vy, o-ver*". Adam's legs appeared from a swarm of boys wrestling a rugby ball.

"I'll take him." Bella leaned her body into the push across the grass. Tom gazed up at the circle of girls.

"You didn't tell us your mother's up the duff again," a squeaky boy's voice shot across the playground. Ball forgotten, the boys stared, hands on hips, feet astride. "She's been doing it. With your father."

Rose kept walking. Seven-year-old boys making her blush?

"And he's the Sunday school teacher. Ooo, Adam." Someone pushed him. She hesitated, four teacher interviews waiting on the other side of the door.

"How do you think you got here then, eh, you stupid bugger," Adam shouted, pushing him back.

Language, Adam. She shut the voices out and stepped inside. He'd cope.

39

Rose swung her aching legs onto Helen's bed and flicked through the Hong Kong mail order catalogue full of things impossible to buy in New Zealand: padded jackets, hair-pieces, wigs, curling wands, tape recorders and headphones. Even swatches of fabric you could order from home.

Robert had turned up with dress fabric last month. Lemon and lavender, her least favourite colours. Quality fabric, but twice the price she'd ever pay. She might be having her sixth baby – seventh? Is she counted? – but her brain had not atrophied completely.

Some women would see only his good intentions. Be grateful, she told herself.

"I'm sorry I won't meet your teachers straight away."

"That's all right," Helen shrugged. She was half in the wardrobe, stretching her gym-frock box pleats in and out, wearing her knotted tie over her T-shirt, casually smug that she'd got it now, she could knot her own tie independent of her mother. Or her older sister.

Demanding or not, this baby would have to slot in, without Helen's help or the unpredictable directions of her lively mind. Three-hourly feeds were no longer in vogue. Feeding on demand sounded easier.

The bedroom smelt of new leather. "I hope you appreciate that pigskin bag – it's the best luggage in this house." Neil and Aunt Marion's 'going off to high school' present, with an undisclosed top-up added by Robert.

"It's the best present ever." Helen slipped her name card into the leather pouch.

❧

Summer holidays lingered, the last days hanging heavily. "What are we going to call the baby?" Frances asked as they podded paddock peas for the deep freeze. "We don't have a Margaret," she said. "Princess Margaret's much prettier than Elizabeth."

"If she was Elizabeth, we could call her Beth or Lizzy," Helen added.

"I don't like names you can shorten," Rose said. "Or flower names."

"Yours is a flower name," laughed Frances and Bella together.

"That was to stop my father calling me Wilhelmina. My parents couldn't agree."

"You'd be Willy. Willy for short," Bella giggled into her hands.

Tom flopped across her lap and laughed up at her. "You're not even a boy."

Rose laughed. "Peas in the bowl, Tom, not your mouth. Anyway, it could have been Mina for short. Who'd want to be called that?"

"Mrs Easton says you can tell if it's a girl or boy if you hang a special stone over your stomach and see which way it swings," Frances said.

"I've got a special stone," Adam said.

"Lie down, Mummy?" Bella stroked her arm.

"Let's get the job done first. Mmmm?"

❧

Lillian arrived on the first of February. Rose had only to turn her head to see her, the merest rise and fall measuring life in the cotton wrap. The folding windows of the maternity wing were wide open, net curtains wafting the perfume of roses inside along with the shouts of children playing softball beyond.

She swung her legs over the side of the bed, waited for her head to stop swimming and tenderly slid her fingers under the wrap. Clutching the baby, she pushed her heel on the cross bar of the bed, and lurched back onto the pillows.

"Mrs McLeod! Let me put her back. I know you want her rooming in, but you mustn't get out of bed yet. You need your rest. Do you need a bedpan while I'm here?"

"Come on Nola. Just give me an arm and I'll get to the lavatory under my own steam. I'll even wear slippers if you insist."

The nurse came close. "Don't you get me into trouble, Rose McLeod. Just three more days, then you can sashay out of bed whenever you want to. Doctor's rounds in five minutes."

On Saturday Robert brought them all in: Frances full of fifteen-year-old responsibility, Helen wanting to be first to unwrap the baby, Bella running straight to Rose for a hug, seven-year-old Adam poking at the baby's cheek for a reaction. Tom rested his chin on top of the bassinet and made faces at her. "Wake up, baby."

He lost interest. Robert lifted Tom onto the bed where he tunnelled under the bedclothes. Bella brushed her mother's hair while Frances flicked through magazines in the corner until she could get a word in about what she should cook for dinner.

Maybe the nurse was right, thought Rose, exhausted, as they left.

※

"Mmmmm. Mmmmm." The specialist clicked the lamp off and replaced his spectacles. "Get yourself dressed, Mrs McLeod." Rose tidied herself and sat in the adjacent leather chair.

"I think we have to say your uterus is ready to retire." He ran through a raft of conditions, which made her womb sound more like her enemy than the powerhouse, which had shaped her whole married life.

Hysterectomy and childbirth. Over. She felt bereft, not relieved. It hadn't been their decision after all.

※

"Mum," Helen whispered around the door. "Are you awake?" And louder, urgently. "Mum, you have to wake up." She came close to the bed.

Rose rolled over. Helen was looking distressed. "What is it?"

"It's ... " Helen took a deep breath. "I'm bleeding." She dropped her voice and pointed to her crutch. "Down there." She was panting now.

Rose propped herself up on the pillows. "It's good news. You're growing up, becoming a woman."

"What should I do?"

"Shut the door. In that drawer, there's a calico bag. It's been waiting for you."

※

Robert laid the dinner tray on the bed. "Do try to eat, my dear." He stroked the hair across her forehead, opening his mouth to speak, then closing it. Finally, "It's been hard on you, all these babies. You don't realise when you're having the fun part," he chuckled, "until you've all this to deal with."

"I did the vegetables and the pudding." Helen came in carrying Lillian. Tom waddled behind. Robert scooped him up and took him out, wailing.

Rose lifted herself to feed Lilly, less often now looking for the lost one in her face.

"Thank you, Helen. How are you feeling?"

"The bleeding's stopped. I took all that uncomfortable stuff off."

"Oh no, love. You need to keep it on for four days."

"Four days!" Helen looked horrified and slunk out of the room, rolling her eyes.

This is just the start, dear girl. Medications, probings, organs cut out.

40

Rose curled up on the sofa with Lillian while Robert took out his violin, disappearing into another world with the haunting melodies. Was he back with his mother in his childhood? Or Italy, where he spoke of picking up a fiddle on a clear night in a cobbled yard, as a mother and daughters twirled and clapped. He often opened the piano after she'd gone to bed, wandering through melodies of his own making, weaving Celtic phrases into the dreams of the sleeping children. At first she'd tried to entice him to bed, swaying to the music in her nightdress, running her fingers through his hair, but his music had to run its course, midnight or not. As winter tightened its grip, Robert discovered Deutsche Grammophon. A new LP had arrived. Tomorrow there would be Sibelius, and friends with classical tastes.

Over dinner the Dutch beekeeper told of his European childhood: his mother a flautist, grandfather a cellist, playing through the grimmest of times. Afterwards Rose sat on the window seat as the row of polished black shoes moved to Sibelius.

The beekeeper sat tidily on the sofa, his right foot tilting gently with the uplifting phrase. The vet's foot was vigorous, commanding the horns. If he'd had his way, he'd said, he would have been a conductor. His left hand subdued the violins and glided through the evocative moods of the cellos to the poignant restrained woodwind. With the drum roll, his fingers quivered, held and stilled.

Eyes snapped open. "Marvellous. Marvellous."

"Bravo." Rose had always loved the "Karelia Suite". "Tea everybody?"

She left the room to get supper. She wasn't so keen on the "Valse Triste" but this evening was a welcome change from reels and strathspeys. Robert had broad musical tastes; he'd even shown interest in buying a piano accordion. Hopefully he wasn't serious, but her opinion counted for nothing when it came to music.

What was her equivalent passion?

Aunt Marion had passions. Daring passions. Fiercely Presbyterian, she was still brave enough to order communist magazines, to ignore stereotypes and prejudices, to argue that Christians should listen to socialist ideas. Out of the blue, she wanted to travel halfway around the world to the German town of Oberammergau to see the *Passion Play*.

For Rose, life revolved around the children. It wouldn't always be so. Would it? Could distance and finances limit her for ever? Since losing the child with no name, a clinging sense of unease had settled over her.

※

Patricia, in a new blue dress and pearls, handed around the ginger gems. "Our farm girl made these too. Worth her weight in gold. Much better than a young man." I doubt if you're paying her gold, thought Rose, as she placed her jam and relish amongst recipe books and spice-set gifts for the bride's pantry.

"When there's not much happening on the farm, she can help inside. She bathed the children and babysat the night of the dance." Everyone looked amazed.

"I'd never let our lad loose on the children," Fran said. "Dave gave him the farm bike the other night. He came home late from the pub and went over the bridge. He's OK but the bike's out of action. Dave's brassed off about having to walk around the sheep."

"Time for games," announced Patricia. "Pencils everyone?"

"What does she do on her day off?" Rose asked.

"She doesn't really need one. We don't work her hard and her hut takes no time to clean." She laughed, others sharing the joke. "We took her to the ram sale on her last day off – she met a friend for a couple of hours."

"Does she have any transport?"

"Oh, she's marvellous – can drive anything. Tractor, motorbike ..."

"I mean to use on her day off?"

"Our bikes don't have a road licence."

And she will never earn enough to buy one, thought Rose. Her friend Barbara had mentioned difficulties for girls who wanted to stay in the country. It was hard to define their role, not like the land girls during the war who kept farms operating and stepped aside when the men returned. Country girls loved land and animals and expected to work on farms, but not necessarily as wives.

How would it be to have another woman knowing your property better than you did and working with your husband all day?

Later as she urged Lillian's pushchair up the hill, she could see the children digging potatoes, Robert's rotary hoe parked at the top. Sacks dotted the slope. Helen and Bella were showing Tom something, worms probably – they could be eight inches long out here. Frances shared a bucket with Adam.

A fine team. She would take them mushrooming tomorrow. Prices at the auction rooms in Dunedin were higher now that they knew to cut off the stalks. This season they'd filled a record four buckets a day. Good pocket money while it lasted.

The telephone rang as Rose walked inside. Barbara. "Rose, I'll be quick. Neville's warming up the car. We're off to a meeting about the new dam on the Waitaki, up at Benmore. Remember I spoke to you about girls working on farms?"

"That's a coincidence! I've just been hearing … " and she told Barbara about the gathering.

"Could your branch find other female farm hands locally?"

"Some of us ought to look at their living conditions," Rose said, the idea tumbling out unformed. It wasn't something that had concerned her before.

"Exactly," Barbara said. "Could we get enough material to speak about it at next conference?"

"There's an idea."

"It's tricky – WD members are probably the worst offenders. Girls work for so little and all hours. There aren't any guidelines, and no contracts. At least we wives do it for love. Well, most of us."

Rose laughed. "I haven't done anything like this before, Barbara. Remember I'm still a newcomer. I don't know the wider district."

"Fresh eyes. Exactly what we need. Stop apologising – it's a distinct benefit. What we need is a sympathetic ear, a sharp mind and a strong public speaker. You're an asset, Rose. Oh, he's tooting. Everything OK there with you?"

Rose drew in a breath to reply. "Yes, we … "

"Must rush. Talk later."

Rose hung the phone up savouring her words. She could be an asset. More than a useful committee member, a wife, a mother.

An asset.

41

ROBERT BENT OVER THE NEWSPAPER. Car advertisements.

"What are you up to, mister?" she said.

"We might go to Dunedin on Wednesday. I need to see the agent."

Surely this year the stock company wouldn't have to approve every purchase. Not that Robert took them too literally, buying cameras when he felt like it. If she had more say there'd be carpet in the boys' room and heating in the passage.

"Nothing to do with cars then?"

"What about tea with the girls, stay on for the orchestra?" he said, his arm around her hips under the broom handle. A warm flush welled up. "Want to come?"

Rose wriggled away. "I have to be here for the young ones." She swept under the children's play table again. "If you have (sweep) more money than I was aware of (sweep, knock over small chair) "what about," she pointed to the opposite page, "this advertisement. For linoleum." She waved her arm towards the floor. "Look at ours."

She kissed him where his hair was thinning on top. "Can you be around tonight? Adam could do with help on his science project."

"What do I know about science?"

"Clover and nitrogen? Lots."

He pursed his lips with an indrawn breath. "I'll be in the darkroom. I need to do the wedding prints."

"The whole evening?" Another escape from the family. Probably why he'd set up the hut in the first place. He'd become less tolerant of the crowd he'd created since they'd grown into noisy, boisterous, argumentative creatures. What to her was the normal cut and thrust of family life was to him with his single-child upbringing a cacophony of noise, every challenge to his instructions a deliberate affront to his authority.

Rose laughed inwardly thinking of Frances before the Young Farmers' Club dance. "I'm not taking you anywhere with your hair poofed up like that," Robert had said. "Make it a bit more – decent."

"Is that better?" Frances had said five minutes later, not a hair in the teased bouffant realigned.

"Let's go then." Robert jangled the car keys.

The older girls knew how to wind him up, to bait him after Sunday sermons with arguments about personal freedoms, alcohol, clothing and St Paul's narrow-minded thinking on women, teachers in particular. And more broadly: that living in communes would be better for everyone; that New Zealand had no business in conflicts overseas, in Biafra, Asia, the Middle East. She encouraged their debates. They were hardly convictions, just testing their ideas, no matter whether she agreed with them or not.

Robert often left the room.

Converting the bunkroom of the empty farm workers' hut into a darkroom had been an inspiration – no more developing films in the kitchen, Robert snapping at everyone when he couldn't feed the film perforations onto the sprockets of the development tank by feel in the lightproof bag. The acrid smell of chemicals would fill the room. No one would dare speak while he counted inversions and tapped the canister to disperse air bubbles.

Now Rose often sent Adam to the hut to remind Robert that night was moving on, hoping he might show an interest. But Adam was more interested in soil chemistry right now.

"It's not an instant process," Robert said. "Come and see."

※

She smiled at the SHOUT IF YOU WANT IN sign, but the darkroom door was open. Inside, her nose twitched. Negatives hung from wires above the yellow film boxes stacked neatly on the bench. At the other end sat the new enlarger.

"Just in time. Shut the door behind you," he said, tying on an apron. He switched on the red light.

"There's a rare sight, you in an apron," she laughed.

"Don't get used to it."

"I'd hardly recognise you in this light."

He pulled her towards him.

"Get off," she said half-heartedly.

"Just checking you had the right bloke." He turned to the bench.

"Oh, I've got the right bloke all right. What's this for?"

Ten minutes later black and white enlargements were pinned up to dry.

"So, there you are," Robert said, rubbing his hands together.

"Marvellous. You're a magician." This skill, this passion for something she didn't understand, surprised her again. "I'd better get back to the children. Adam really could do with talking over his project."

Robert crossed his arms. "Where Adam is now with chemistry is beyond me. Just leave it."

"You've got more to offer than you realise." She leaned on the door frame. She had reading to do herself. She didn't want to go to her first meeting as a church elder without knowing about the issue stirring in Dunedin, a professor of theology teaching something radical to the ministry students. "Don't be too late." In the dark, she felt around the gate for the hook and crossed the lawn towards the light in the windows, back to bedtimes and shoes to clean.

*

Robert hung up the phone after breakfast. "Mervyn Taylor wants me to photograph his daughter's wedding." He grinned. "It's only a couple of weeks away. Must be a shot gun. Have to be careful where I aim the camera."

"Robert!" she laughed.

"That's the second request this month."

"Your reputation's getting around."

"I hardly know Mervyn. I only see him at calf sales."

"I hope you're charging them properly."

Robert looked taken aback. "Why?"

"Because this ... hobby ... costs a lot."

Robert's mouth turned down at the corners. "We got a handy donation from the Fletcher wedding. Enough to cover paper and the chemicals."

"But not your car or time not working on the farm, or the paper you discard."

"I can't charge for those. It's people I know. I'm not interested in charging." He pulled on his overalls. "I'll be over with the contractor. We should get the fence finished today, though there's more rock than we expected."

"What about the equipment? The enlarger, your new hassle bratt ... "

"Hasselblad." Robert picked up his thermos of soup and plastic box of sandwiches. "Just leave me to my photography, eh?"

His money. Only his? His hobby. She could work something out for him. Something fair, not city prices, but not subsidising the community either. Growing children cost, even with two girls paying their own way now — thank heavens for bursaries. Adam had worn out his school shoes, there was a scout camp and a tramp into the Eglington Valley, sports fees, violin lessons."

She couldn't leave it all to Robert. She would put her name down for teaching at the high school.

❦

The phone rang during dinner. Short, long, short. Rose picked up the quoit by her feet and tossed it at the plastic pole. The quoit wobbled over the top – and dropped. "Score," shouted Tom in amazement. Lilly echoed him, drumming her spoon on the table.

"Shhh," hissed Adam, Bella and Robert.

"Hello. Rose speaking."

"It's Andrew, Sis."

"Andrew. How are you?"

"Bad news, I'm afraid. Mother died half an hour ago."

❦

She stood beside her dark-suited brothers at the graveside, oblivious to the fog sweeping across the cemetery. Her shoes sank into the claggy soil.

John took her elbow, drawing her away.

"Come on, Sis, time to move." Andrew coaxed her, offering an arm. No one from the south was here. She yearned for them now, Robert especially.

"I should have been here, John. I should have been more often. You've had to shoulder everything." They walked towards the cars.

"She's always had us, especially Lydia." In silence they shared his loss again – a brain tumour had won the battle three months earlier. "Lydia was like a daughter to her."

"But not a daughter. I let Mother down. Especially since she broke her hip." Tears streamed down her face. John drew her into his chest.

"Mother was well cared for and you came when you could. She was proud of you, always – she lived for your letters, and the children's. Don't fret, she really did understand."

Rose leaned against him, the brother who struggled to accept her choices in life. The brother who had learned to nurse the nurse as she faded.

In their shared grief she felt closer to him than ever before.

The previous day John, Rose and Andrew had sat around the walnut table, reliving their childhoods through photographs. Unlike the quietness of today, there had been laughter, teasing, yet a softening in the gibes, grief not only for a mother but for the happy simplicity of a distant life. The fourth chair sat empty as their father shuffled by, picking up objects to stare at, offering cups of tea minutes after the last.

She'd really gone. Gone before Rose had a chance to tell her what a triumph Frances had been as Viola in *Twelfth Night*. Next month, after the National Conference, she would have visited with news of everything she was working on, picking away at education services for rural people. Her mother would have pulled the crocheted rug close and applauded with intense and dancing eyes while her mobile tongue and pursing lips would eventually find the words to remind her that nothing was more important than the bringing up of her children. Not that she'd always approved of her methods.

But no letter would come in Tuesday's mail.

She would have to do better for her father.

42

It seemed too soon, too trivial in the wake of grief, unprepared as she was for its weight, for its draining drag, but Robert encouraged her. "Go off for the day. It's something different. Something new."

And here she was, her first interview.

"Geraldine? Geraldine Smith?"

"I'm Gerry. You must be Mrs McLeod."

"Rose." The girl was no older than Frances, but why use surnames?

Gerry put down her bucket. "Welcome to my place," she said, sweeping her arm across the pigs, the sty, the rolling green of central Southland, the morning mist lifting along the river in the distance.

"What are you working at this morning?"

Gerry tipped a bucket of greens into the trough. "I look after all these fabulous animals. I do love pigs." Her wild blonde curls bounced as she talked. "They're so friendly. Sounds silly but we understand each other. And they look after their babies so well."

She climbed into the pen to fill the water trough, pausing to pat the sow. "This old girl had nine in her last litter."

"Nine. No thanks," laughed Rose.

The pig rubbed against Gerry's overalls, her snout twitching. "You're not supposed to see this," Gerry said, offering her a handful of popcorn.

"Popcorn?"

"Yeah, I had some in my pocket one day and she wouldn't leave me alone. Genevieve's my favourite."

"Have you named them all?"

Gerry turned to the row of shelters down the slope and pointed to each in turn. "Penelope, Christina, Beatrice, Cleopatra, Elizabeth, Anastasia, Sofia ..."

"They sound like queens."

"They are. Look, they're coming out. Most of them spend all day routing under the trees. That big one, Alexandria, I have to trim her feet today. I'll take you around, then we can talk in the cottage."

"How's the winter been? Must be tough in the frosts."

"Na. Just put on more clothes. If they can cope, so can I. But they get real grumpy and depressed in winter. Rain's the worst. Especially three or four days of it."

"Seems you're enjoying this job."

"Wouldn't change it for anything."

Inside over mugs of tea Rose tried to press Gerry about her future plans.

"Have you done any training?"

"What for?" Gerry was more interested in the present.

"This is a stud farm so it's all about the breeding programme. Right?"

"Yeah, Mr Watson writes everything down. I give him a hand with the weighing."

"There's a course about breeding that could help you understand – selecting animals, different feed, I'm not sure to be honest. I know far less than you do about pigs." Rose laughed. "There's always more to know. That's the thing about education: you don't know what you don't know till you try it. You'd be surprised."

This girl was exactly what farms needed, dedicated to looking after animals since she had quit school on her sixteenth birthday. She mustn't scare her off.

"Researchers at Telford or Invermay talk to people like you about what they've found out. There are lots of courses, cadet schemes and correspondence as well as full-time study."

Gerry stared at her. "I never knew there was anything like that. Do you know any other girls working with pigs?"

"Not yet, but you'll be the first to hear. This course might get you started. You'd find out for yourself if you go." She hesitated, and leaned forward. "Would it be a problem if there were only boys?"

Gerry roared with laughter.

"You'd like the information then?"

"Too right."

※

"Honestly, she's the happiest person I've ever come across," she told Robert over midday dinner. "If all the girls are like this, it'll be more fun than I expected."

"Can I come next time?" asked Lilly.

"If it's in the holidays."

Tom ran in as the post van roared off. "One letter for Mrs Robert McLeod." Drat, thought Rose. Still 'Mrs Robert'. It's time they used her own name."

"And one for Mr R. McLeod, Manuka Creek, No 2 RD, Milton, Otago ... "

"New Zealand, the World," added Lilly.

Robert opened a small envelope, read quickly and handed it over the children's heads to Rose. From Bessie? She hadn't heard anything of Mary's sister for years.

She gave a short gasp. Mary was dead. She looked up at Robert who raised his eyebrows at her. They'd buried her two weeks ago. In the Andersons Bay cemetery. In the same single grave as her sister, Rose (Rose? She had a sister Rose?) seven years ago and her sister Abigail two years before that.

A pauper's grave. Bessie's husband had covered the costs. She hadn't left anything of any value in her tiny rented house, but they'd found a slasher under her bed. One of their boys might like it.

Rose stared at the paper. In an instant, the image of a younger Mary in the oats paddock shovelling teaspoons of sugar into her tea became another, a family of bones laying silently underground.

What did she feel? she asked herself. Detached. Yet oddly connected by her sister's name.

"And one for Miss F. McLeod."

"Give me that," Frances hissed, snatching it away. She glanced at it quickly and sat on it. A flush ran up her cheeks.

"And another fat one for Mr ... "

"Thank you, Tom," said his father. A familiar envelope. He tore it open and flicked out three thin pages covered in figures.

Rose heard the intake of breath.

"Uh-huh. Uh-huh," he grunted, mouth twisting, eyebrows mobile.

Wool returns, the raw facts of their main income. "How is it?" she asked.

Slowly Robert pushed the pages back into the envelope. "We won't starve," he replied. As they'd been warned – a lean year ahead and three children at high school.

Lilly was surreptitiously carving slices off the Chesdale cheese, hidden by the foil wrapper and the yellow box. Rose let it go. "Lillian, put that knife down," Robert ordered. Chesdale was expensive, for Robert only. There was a whole block of mild for everyone else. "And wait till your mother sits down before you start."

❧

"Good letter?" Rose said quietly to Frances over the dishes.

Frances' eyes flashed. "I suppose so."

"I'd guess it's not from a girlfriend."

"Could be." This girl wouldn't keep a secret for long. Frances turned to look at her directly, her face glowing with a new light. "No. It's not from a girlfriend." The words curled softly around each other.

"Are you going to tell me who?"

Frances turned her back. Cutlery clattered into the drawer.

"OK," she said quickly, shoulder to shoulder. "He's called John and I met him at Knox Church. We've been to the pictures a couple of times."

"Mmmm. What's he like?"

"Don't worry. I'm not going to marry him."

Rose had forgotten the letters she'd reluctantly tossed on the fire before she married Robert. Two letters. Not romantic. Just breathing warmth and life and energy. Harry, wrapped in a black ribbon.

❧

The year 1967 was becoming a disaster. Wool prices collapsing. Meat prices too. Banks calling in mortgages.

"Robert, please don't wander off. Talk to me."

He raised his eyes from his dinner.

"Please." She put her hand on his wrist but he pulled it away and took another spoonful, his tongue pushing the food around and around before he swallowed.

"Oh. You're hopeless." She hit the tea towel on the table. "I can't do anything if you won't talk to me." Dishes rattled. He poured cream over the steamed pudding and stirred it into the nectarine juice. Around, around and around.

She sat down again. "Are we in trouble?" He strode over to the desk, pulled a thick package from a drawer and flung it onto the table.

At the last page of figures, she started again. Columns, unfamiliar terms. A short list of income; a long list of loans and pages of expenditure. It made little sense, hardly surprising after years of Robert and his father lightly tossing reassuring summaries to their wives.

And now, his father living five miles away in the township, Robert was on his own. The change had been so gradual she'd hardly registered that Neil no longer offered advice. Robert had carried it all, while she had been too concerned with the children, her parents, rediscovering her own life. He needed her support, but was he ready to turn to her?

If not now, when?

What pride he would have to overcome.

What necessity.

What good use of her assistance.

❧

The school principal was keen to have her as a reliever. Hypothetically of course. Straight away. And would keep it to himself for now. Hypothetically.

There would be a right moment to talk it over with Robert, she kidded herself. He was used to her frequent absences for community organisations. If she wasn't home at critical times, the children stepped in. He never had to prepare a meal.

But teaching?

A hypothetical conversation: "Robert, if I got back into teaching, just part-time or relieving, we'd have some breathing space."

"Are you sure you can manage more? You're already pulling your weight." Other women would be envious. Teaching paid much better than spinning coloured wool or making pickles. Almost everyone was trying something.

At the present rate they'd never be able to support the children once they left school. They would have to earn their own way through university.

❦

Robert turned back from gazing out the window. "Why on earth do you want to get yourself tied up with teaching again? Isn't there enough to do here? Why can't women be content on the farm?" He had been raising his voice more often, now he was openly angry.

"It's my profession in case you'd forgotten, something I was good at before … " She stopped herself saying something she'd regret. "I want to help." She paused to get her voice back under control. "Just let me help."

"We're not destitute. We're not broke."

And you are angry, not facing realities, and terrified of what this community would say about you having a working wife.

"Dogs need a run."

❦

"Got a hundred and thirty away today," Robert said, scrubbing his hands. "Not many over-fats this season." A joke. He'd made an ironic joke. Dare she hope for a lightening of spirit?

"And how many underweights?"

"A few." She held her gaze. "Sixty-two." She gasped. So many.

"Fussy, that lamb buyer."

"No need for excuses. It's time for some honesty."

"If you want honesty, there's not enough grass to fatten them or money for more feed." The quiver in his voice resonated as he went into the bathroom. Rose leaned against the washhouse wall and closed her eyes.

❦

"Taxes have to be paid on last year's income when prices were high, but with this year's money."

"Surely you put money aside?"

"Never needed to when prices were on the rise. And we couldn't have made as much hay without the new tractor. The sheep condition through winter would be even worse than it's going to be."

There could be worse if Britain joined the European Economic Community. Protections would go, despite heart-thumping rhetoric.

"It's the low point of a cycle, they're saying."

"Nothing ever stays the same, Robert." Even us, she thought, a glimmer of hope fluttering. We're talking. Don't let it stop.

"If Britain joins the Common Market what will it do to us?" she asked.

Robert scratched his head. "Darned if I know. Sheep are the backbone of this country. All these years we've had guaranteed minimum prices – Britain's taken most of our production. We propped them up through the war and the recovery and this is what we get."

"Why don't we go to the accountant together this time?"

Robert looked affronted. "You serious?"

"If we share the load, we share the worry. Like you did with your father."

Robert chewed on the idea. "Can't see it doing much good. But if that's what you want."

In the lounge, the notes of Tom's violin wandered agonisingly up the scale. Lilly was somersaulting over the cushions on the floor.

"We'll still have concessions on loans," Robert said, "and subsidised fertilizer. Government's paying for rabbit control. That reminds me, there's a truckload of poisoned carrots on the way. A plane'll drop them on Tuesday. Have to keep the dogs tied up. If any of them eats a dead rabbit they'll be a goner."

Do you love me? she wondered as he closed the door quietly behind him. Love was not something to talk about, but something to know. The words of Shakespeare's Cordelia, the great respecter of bonds of love, bloomed in her mind.

Unhappy that I am, I cannot heave
My heart into my mouth. I love your Majesty
According to my bond; no more nor less.

Would Robert see that bond as limiting love or, as Cordelia intended, acknowledging its boundless nature?

She turned away. Suddenly Robert burst in, kissed her on the cheek and left.

※

A few days later the tractor left the yard at speed. And returned very slowly. Robert sat slumped on the deck.

"Is something wrong?" she called, walking towards the tractor. He lifted his face, crumpled and pink. On his lap was his favourite dog:

handsome, intelligent Pete, with the glowing, flowing coat, the eager eyes and rocket-like speed. Still.

"I found him on Mary's Hill. With a rabbit. Poison must have got him."

"But you tied them up."

Robert was quiet. "He was begging to be let off."

Rose stroked his coarse fur.

"It's my fault. My fault," Robert said.

"What are you going to do with him?" asked Rose after a long silence, already choosing a place under the macrocarpas.

"I'll put him down the hole. Soon." The offal hole where all dead farm creatures ended up. Surely Pete deserved better. "He's just another dead animal now."

Rose held Robert's head against her.

She wandered inside. Life and death, so precariously balanced, so interwoven with the decisions we make, planned or spontaneous.

Shortly she heard the tractor start up to take Pete for his last run.

43

NEIL AND ROBERT STOOD BACK FOR HER, but Rose took the old man's arm and supported him forward, his gnarled fingers clutching the doorway.

The last time Rose had been in this room, she'd helped Aunt Marion with the flowers on a Saturday afternoon, the table covered with chrysanthemums. Now the red velvet curtains were drawn. The wooden panels glowed beneath shelves of Bibles, brass vessels and sparkling cut-glass vases.

Five men turned from a huddle over the two-bar heater. Familiar faces. Tartan ties, tweed jackets, leather buttons buttoned.

"Dorothy would set the cups here, afore the meetin'," Neil wheezed quietly.

Rose hesitated. She was the only woman. She wanted to start on the right foot. A moment of choice. A flicker of resistance; a resignation. "You'd like me to do the same." She straightened the damp tea towel over her tray of sandwiches and went to find the cups.

They'd kept her a seat next to Robert as the gathering settled around the table.

"Gentlemen." The voices quietened for the minister. "Good to see a full muster of Elders. It's my pleasure to welcome Mrs Robert McLeod to join us as a member of Session. I trust this will be the start of long and valuable service." The men clapped dutifully.

Reverend Mackay cleared his throat. "As you know, we have a serious matter to discuss." He stared at his page as if daunted by the very thought of publicly criticising one of his own kind.

"Our most respected scholar, Professor Lloyd Geering, in charge of training every Presbyterian minister at Knox College, has been presenting his students with ideas at odds with our central beliefs concerning the resurrection of Christ and the life everlasting. He has been accused of – heresy." He paused at the weight of the word. "This has never, ever happened before in any part of our worldwide church. The exact words are 'doctrinal error and disturbing the peace and unity of the Presbyterian Church'. I expect you'll have read the articles in the *Outlook*. And the *Otago Daily Times*."

Alistair Cameron screwed the lid onto his fountain pen. "There's been a lot of talk about the Resurrection, but this is really about free speech, not criminal action. Seems to me it concerns the interpretation of the Resurrection, rather than yes it happened, no it didn't. Shouldn't we look at what he says, test the measure of it?"

Rose nodded in agreement. Most of the men were leaning back in their chairs, arms folded.

"We need experts to interpret for us in each new age," Alistair continued. "Does that make the interpreter a criminal? I say keep him out there. He's good for all of us."

"What do you mean 'criminal'?" asked Aunt Marion's brother Bob.

"That's what's at stake here, Uncle Bob: is he a criminal?" Robert said. "The church's Assembly becomes a court, with procedures: prosecution, defence, evidence, judgement." He counted the words out on his fingers. "Is he a heretic or not? That's what he's charged with."

"Used to hang people for that," interrupted the man at the far end.

"Still can if it's treason," said another. "For murder, they abolished execution in 1961, but not for treason."

"Eighty-five people have been executed in New Zealand," the first added.

"Eighty-five," exclaimed Rose in horror. Surely not. Only one woman, Minnie Dean, the baby farmer in Southland, hung at the end of last century. But eighty-four men? Frances had investigated the death penalty. She remembered now: National brought it back in 1949 'as a deterrent'. In the mid-1950s, Jack Marshall, as attorney general, endorsed the death sentences of twenty-two men. Eight of them were hanged.

Perhaps the professor was in danger.

❧

Rose stepped out into the dark, her head buzzing. Across the road, branches of the school oaks tossed and jibed like waves on the ocean. Isolated clouds scudded across the sky, the moon bright, stars alive with the vigour of the wind. Look up, look up, it demanded. God, what a storm you've created down here tonight. It must have been a lot easier when everyone believed that heaven was just past the stars, where vision turned into imagination. Surely Mother was with God, wherever He was, in whatever afterlife there was, where Father expected to join her.

She pulled her cardigan tightly around her and followed the pale colour of the concrete to the church hall and through the double doors until she could feel around for the light switch. She filled the kettle with boiling water from the zip. Ordinary movements, ordinary actions. Extraordinary night.

She'd seen these men at church for years but never listened to them talk of what they believed. Or didn't.

Holding the hot spout wrapped in a tea towel, and the handle in the other hand, she nudged at the door, trying to ease it open with her heel. Suddenly it opened wide, knocking her elbow. Hot tea splashed down the wall.

"Sorry. I thought you might need a hand." Not Robert, but Alistair Cameron, dark eyes smiling.

Rose clattered the teapot onto the bench and squatted at his feet to wipe the spill. "Bad timing, but thanks."

"It sounds like we're thinking along the same lines tonight, you and me. As we normally do."

"Perhaps." Her opinion was far from clear, even to herself.

"Most of that lot came with their minds made up. They're pragmatists, not philosophers. It's not as if they don't want change. They'd change farming practice tomorrow if the facts stacked up."

"But where are the facts here? I don't know, Alistair, but I want us to work through it more." She laughed. "It's not easy to fight tradition." Home life had taught her that. "I thought our Church Union Committee was challenging enough, trying to get Methodists and Presbyterians and Anglicans to agree on anything."

They laughed in unison. Rose put the sugar bowl and milk jug into his hands and picked up the teapot again. "But we've made progress, haven't we? Most of us don't think it's sinful to enter the doors of another's church any more. But talk about traditional differences – it's like wading through inter-family warfare."

He held the door with his foot as they stepped outside.

"Thought you'd got lost in the dark." Robert's voice came from the silhouette in the doorway.

※

Rose rested her head against the car window. It jiggled and bumped hard against the glass as Robert changed gear to drive up the hill above the village. He walked his father into the house. She waited in the car, her eyes closed.

"You got them listening tonight," Robert said, pulling the car door shut.

"I had the impression no one was listening to anyone else."

Robert laughed. "They talked more than usual."

"You didn't say much."

"I'm still thinking about it. At least we can let the dust settle and get back to something we can all understand."

"I don't want to go back." Rose stretched her legs out. "Different viewpoints wake my brain up. I'm not agreeing with the professor necessarily, but I want to understand what he's saying.

"That man will destroy his own church. We can't let him continue teaching."

Rose said nothing. Perhaps the students should be taught by someone else until the church decided.

They drove a distance in silence.

Robert heaved a sigh. "You can't toss the Resurrection aside after two thousand years – it's the whole centre of the Christian faith. Catholics, Anglicans, the lot of us. If there's no Resurrection, we're left with his life, yes – but Jesus becomes just one of thousands nailed to a cross."

44

"Mixed flatting's causing a stir in Dunedin," said Robert. "A thousand students marched on the Students' Union. Imagine – mixed flatting en masse. Isn't that boy they've expelled related to your Middlemarch friend?"

Rose tipped the fresh playdough from the pot onto Lilly's board and looked at the newspaper over his shoulder. "Not Evelyn's son. He's training for opthamology. They can't expel him – he's clever."

"Must be, to get three girls to live with him," Robert chuckled.

"Look. The university's wavering. Not everyone thinks young men and women can't live in the same house without getting up to hanky panky." But she wasn't so sure. "We were innocent at that age, weren't we?" She shaped a lump of playdough into a hippopotamus – or was it a cow – and added it to Lilly's menagerie.

"By crikey," Robert said, "there's a rumpus going on at that student health. Doctors are handing out the pill to anyone who asks, married or not. Patricia Bartlett's on the case. That Jim Baxter poem they mention," he kept his finger on the page and looked up, "have you read it?"

"That'll never be in the paper. It's pretty risqué."

"You *have* read it."

"Barbara had a copy. It's an attack on 'upstanding' citizens for denying what went on in their day. If you believe Baxter, you'd never send your children to university."

She wasn't going to admit to reading it twice. Some lines she couldn't forget:

> Hush! It is the living make us blush
> Because the young have wicked hearts
> And blood to swell their private parts.

"Baxter's the last person who'd persuade them to lift the ban. As long as students mix in other ways, I agree their bedrooms are best kept far apart. Otherwise it's like dangling whisky in front of an alcoholic."

She chuckled at a memory of ten minutes smooching in the front of Hadley's car. Daring, intimate, arousing. Forget it. "Right. Sheets for Bella's friends, though they'll hardly sleep in them with the Young Farmers' dance on Friday night and driving to Te Anau on Saturday."

"As long as it isn't my girls." Robert folded the paper.

"Did you hear Holyoake's cancelled the rugby tour, Mum?" Adam announced moments later.

"Why?" Amongst the clatter of scraping chairs, plates, cutlery, she remembered the last time South Africans had demanded New Zealand keep Maoris out of the team. Was it 1960?

"Politics have no place in sport," Robert said. "Vernon's boy's picked to go to South Africa. He'll have to stay home now. We could send a team without Maoris."

"And buy into apartheid?" Rose said. "Do you want New Zealand to run a racial selection process? There was a petition last time: 'No Maoris – No Tour'. Thousands signed. Mr Holyoake ignored it. He's switched sides, thank heavens." Had his popularity dropped?

"Don't tell me you'd vote for Norman Kirk."

"Not likely, but he is a compassionate man."

"Fair go, Mum. You think we shouldn't go?"

"Adam, I think people should be treated fairly, no matter what their skin colour, and if that means a few suffer from cancelling a tour, in the long run the principle will hold – players will be judged on their ability."

"That'll never happen," Adam muttered.

"Well there's another campaign for you." Robert said, slurping his soup.

What had happened to the stability of the fifties? Every certainty was being tipped upside down, the moral fibre fraying, young people demanding every sort of freedom. You couldn't blame everything on the Beatles and those uncouth Rolling Stones and whatever it is they're smoking.

꽃

"Have you read the letters about Professor Geering in the *Outlook*?" Rose tipped the stool up and stretched the skein of wool around the legs for an evening's wool winding.

Robert heaved a sigh. "I've heard enough on the radio in the jeep. It'll settle down, after the trial. Just let it go," he said.

"It takes a lot of thinking through."

"Look, it's all right for you university types."

"University types? This is for everyone in the church."

"You know what I mean – you like to read and read, argue, argue."

"Discuss."

"I like a bit of peace. There're other things to think about."

"Like rugby?"

"Like the breeding programme, fertiliser, fencing loans, trees to order. You enjoy 'grappling with the ideas'. You're the one with the education. Not all of us have the advantages of higher learning."

She gaped at him. Her education had never come between them before. She was so swept up with the Geering debate that she hadn't noticed him pulling back. Should she back off or argue? This was a quicksand too unpredictable. "I'm off to bed." She gathered up her lesson plan.

So what if he was right? They did approach new ideas in very different ways. He'd accepted her teaching only so that the children could go to holiday camps and take music lessons. And for a second car. But they needed a long-term financial plan. When Adam eventually took over, how could they buy a house away from the farm? She couldn't risk failure in the classroom. Robert mustn't see how nervous she was – he could scuttle it so easily.

He wasn't vindictive. Never. Just unhappy. Yet – was that all?

An ache hung heavy in her heart.

※

Room 10. Don't be timid, she told herself, as she gripped the door handle. Begin with a sense of authority. Benign authority.

Shrieks of laughter fell away as she opened the door. "Watch it," someone called from the scuffle in the corner. She pulled herself up to her full height and smiled, her heart thumping.

She waited.

The noise subsided. "Good morning. I'm Mrs McLeod. I'll be with you while your teacher's away. Have a seat everyone." Taped to the desk was a class roll. Twenty-nine pupils. Why so many empty chairs?

"Let's find out who's here. Lisa?"

"Yes, Miss." No need to correct her today.

"Christine?"

"Here, Mrs McLeod."

"Susan?"

"Yep."

"Tracey?" A hand waved.

"Peter? Peter Black?"

"He's off today, Mrs McLeod. Calving."

"Thank you Tracey. Erua?"

"Yep." She lifted her eyes at his attempt at deep gruffness.

"Bruce?"

"Here." The boy was threading a pen through holes in his jersey sleeve.

Five sick, three helping at home. Another two unexplained. Her poetry lessons had better not lead to a longer list of absences. She had prepared "The Charge of the Light Brigade" and "Tarantella", heroic rhythms with strong rhymes. Poetry wasn't easy when you didn't know the students. Character and action, she had decided. If they could read aloud, together, the reluctant readers might be drawn in.

Might be.

By mid-week their roars subsided as Sassoon's "Suicide in the Trenches" briefly sobered their nascent desire for heroism.

"It wasn't like that, Miss, was it?"

"What do you think?" At home no one spoke of either war. The last was recalled too vividly. Nothing to serve by exposing it; get on with the future, families said.

It was time for something closer to home. James K. Baxter's "Farmhand". The ease, the competency of a young man in the field – yet when *girls drifting like flowers* fired his longing for love, his social ineptitude constrained him from reaching across the dance floor.

His red sunburnt face and hairy hands
Were not made for dancing or love-making
But rather the earth wave breaking
to the plough ...

But ah in harvest watch him

Forking stooks, effortless and strong –
Or listening like a lover to the song
Clear, without fault, of a new tractor engine.

The room was quiet when she finished and then someone laughed.

"Is this about the Town Hall dance here in Milton?" Tracey asked.

"Nuh. His girls're better looking," Erua answered.

"He's like my brother and his mates," Tracey said. Baxter had it right for any country dance on a Saturday night. Not for Robert though, she reflected. When the first chord struck he'd always find someone to dance with.

Susan loitered at the end of the lesson. "Aren't you staying, Miss?" Bruce came back in, waiting for Susan,

"Mrs Hitchcock will be back on Monday."

"Can't you stay?"

A warm glow flooded her body. "I may be back, but thank you. And Bruce, if you get the chance, take dancing lessons."

Of course she'd be back. She couldn't resist the paradoxical forces of teenagers: the thrum of their vitality and passions, which could flip into apathy in a breath; their demand for individual rights, yet their need to merge with the pack; their finely honed sense of injustice, yet they were unaware of causing it; their desperate need to knock the world into their own shape; and their more secret desire to be certain of the boundaries of acceptable behaviour, if only to locate the place to strain against.

45

"Church union meeting tonight," Rose said.

"The car's still not fixed."

"Alistair Cameron's picking me up."

"He's coming all the way over? Is there no one closer?"

"No, so he offered."

Robert said nothing for a moment. "I don't know why those meetings finish so late. You weren't back till nearly midnight last time."

"There's a lot to discuss. Are you keeping tabs on me?"

Robert shrugged. "Where's the meeting?"

※

Bert dropped another shilling into the metre box. The lights came back on over the trestle tables in the bare supper room of the Methodist Hall. The two-bar heater glowed again.

"So we're agreed. Next month we look at Baptism – the wording of promises, age of candidates, how we use water, godparents or not. Remember: bring your own liturgies."

The door burst open. Robert stood there transfixed, eyes blinking at the light, peering at the eight people around the table peering back over their spectacles.

"Oh my word. What is it?" the Methodist chairman said.

Robert hesitated, like a possum caught in the headlights. "It's … " he looked at his watch, "after midnight."

"What's happened?" Rose asked.

Robert shook his head in a small jerky movement. His body relaxed. "I just came to take you home."

Rose was at once sorry for him but also furious. "Excuse me everyone, I'll just have a word with Robert outside." She hustled him into the darkness and pulled the door shut. They stood in the square of light from the window.

"You came twelve miles, and left the children, to tell me the time?" He pulled her towards the car. She shook his arm away.

"It's far too late. And one of those children is fifteen."

"If the farmers could get here by eight we'd be finished sooner. I'll be home in twenty minutes. It's no later than you in your darkroom, or your long chats after Federated Farmers."

"But I'm not there with the likes of him." Robert stabbed a finger towards the church hall.

"Him? I'm going back to collect my things. I've a good mind to go home with *him*. At least *he* behaves rationally."

All eyes were on her as she burst into the hall.

"Is everything all right?" Alistair asked.

"Yes fine. Fine." Head down she wrapped her empty plate. Notebooks. Minute book. Coat. Pen. She needed to say something to Alistair. Publicly. "Thanks for the ride, but I'm all right for getting home." She felt deeply embarrassed. Humiliated.

Desperate to regain her dignity, she lifted her head. "See you all at the Anglican church next month."

❦

For a moment Rose sat in the silence beyond words, her body rigid in the car seat.

"I've never been so humiliated in all my life," she said quietly. "How dare you come barging in like that." The words emerged sharp like static on the radio.

"Someone had to."

"Rubbish. I cannot see why any sane person needs to thunder into the night to interrupt a perfectly harmless, in fact constructive, community group."

"It may be, but I won't have him driving you home after midnight."

"What are you suggesting?"

"Exactly what I said."

"You don't want me in a car with Alistair at night? Mild-mannered gentleman Alistair? Who happens to be a good parishioner who listens to what I say?"

"That's what they all say."

" 'They all' who?"

"People who end up doing things they don't mean to."

"Oh no!" Rose punched her fist on her knee. "Stop the car."

Robert stepped on the brake. She jerked forward. The car sat silent in the middle of the gravel road.

"You might have pulled over."

"Nothing's likely to please you."

Rose breathed fiercely through her teeth.

"Why did you really come? Why?" She stretched her neck out towards him.

"Because these late evenings, you get home all excited and fizzing with ... I don't know. It's doing something to you."

"You've done something to me. How do you think I'll feel walking into the next meeting?"

Robert started the car.

"What's got into you Robert? Is it all men – or just Alistair?"

Hand on the gear lever, he turned to her. "You can't travel with Alistair on your own. It's not done. It simply isn't done." He revved the engine.

The colourless shapes of trees sailed past in the darkness. Beneath them the smallest pinpricks of light showed where sheep were watching.

"Let me out at the top of the hill," Rose said.

"Eh?"

"Just let me out. Here. I want to walk."

"It's dark."

"I'll cope."

He pulled the car over.

※

Her face in the morning mirror looked no better after cold water.

"What time's the agent coming?" she asked Robert crisply between organising clothing and transport to rugby practice and Brownies. Adam needed a haircut or Mr Donovan would be onto him again.

"Two oclock."

"So when do you need me in the yards?"

"Nine?" Robert reached into the hot water cupboard for socks. "I could do with you guarding the junction in half an hour." He was avoiding looking at her. Good. She didn't want to look at him either.

"As long as I can visit Dad later."

"Right. I'm off."

"Tom, nugget those shoes properly. They're looking scruffy."

"Awww, Mum." He slunk away in his socks.

Children to the school bus. Toss the washing into the machine. Thank God it's automatic. Muffins in the oven. Beds. Thermos.

※

They eyed each other from opposite ends of the sheep yards. She waited, picking lichen off the top rail with her fingernail.

"Ready?" Robert shouted.

She nodded and opened the gates into the central pen. Hurrying back, she coaxed the sheep forward. Robert pushed the vertical handles of the drafting gates apart so that the sheep could see the illusion of freedom in the distant grassy paddock. Momentarily Rose felt tempted to rush though and escape too.

Unsuspecting ewes drew their jittery lambs under Robert's elbow. He thrust a gate across after the ewe, turning ram lambs into the right-hand pen, ewe lambs to the left, judged in an instant by which ear carried the ear mark, one clip on the back, two on the front. He had to concentrate.

Rose kept the sheep tight, heads forward, until they reached the end of the race. The air was heavy with unexploded accusation.

"We have to talk, Robert."

"Now?"

"You can't stand me going to the Church Union committee because of Alistair."

"He's part of it."

"You mean there's someone else you don't want me there with? This is outrageous. Not to mention the irony. We're looking to build bridges to include blind traditionalists with closed minds. And I find one in my own house."

"A pack of do-gooders more like. Calm down. You're unsettling the sheep."

"Well, yes, do-gooders we probably are."

"Women!"

"Some *are* women."

"Would you just refill the pen?" He ordered Mack into the yard behind Rose. The dog slunk low and eyed the sheep, who turned obediently towards the narrow race.

Beyond Robert, bewildered lambs swirled, hungry for the reassurance of suckling, desperation in their cries increasing. Ewes bleated back, confused, unable to see through the railing. Rose steeled herself for three nights of weaning, the worst sound of the farming year.

She walked another twenty ewes and lambs towards the race. "What's the hold up?" Robert shouted.

Rose forced the gate shut. "Keep your hair on." Usually they worked companionably, enjoyably, predicting the next move. Today she resented everything.

Robert stared down the race. "I don't know what the trouble is with that Union committee," Robert called. "Meetings have gone on for years. Should've been done in half the time."

Rose let her body sag. "You can't change religious differences overnight. Thousands of people are involved, all over the country."

"Won't come to anything."

"Rubbish." She shook her head and pushed between woolly fleeces to the back of the mob.

Robert caught a lamb sneaking through with its mother. "Know what the trouble is?" he said, heaving the lamb into the ewe lambs' yard. "Not enough experienced leaders."

Rose stopped.

All at once she understood. "This isn't about Alistair, is it? It's about you. About you *not* being asked onto the committee. That night you came home all sullen – I thought you'd got over that. It's been festering. Well, that's one wound I'll not be dressing. Learn to live with it." Would he have been a better choice? He had been an Elder for years. Truth was, he hated confrontations, preferring someone else to find a solution he could agree with. Or back the status quo.

In a moment she saw it clearly. Ingrained in Robert was the truth accepted by every male in the district: men took the hard road for their families. Not only with physical work, but in soldiering, in protecting wife and children. In creating the legal framework for their livelihood, in shouldering financial burdens. And men took those same responsibilities for community assets, churches, halls, schools, showgrounds, sale yards. A woman could take any of these roles if no man was available. But deep in his psyche the man knew it was up to him – and the leader should be asked onto a committee ahead of his wife.

※

Later that afternoon Rose pulled up beside the hospital rose garden. She picked up her handbag and the page about Gerald Duffy, one of her father's choristers singing at Covent Garden. That should raise a flicker of interest.

But the matron came out before she had opened the car door. Her father.

※

So different from farewelling her mother, over a year before, in a gathering of old friends and relatives. In her father's church service, with Robert, her brothers, Neil and Aunt Marion, there was no one he'd sung with, worked with, worshipped or soldiered with. He'd been here just a few weeks in her local hospital after the stroke he'd suffered as soon as he arrived scuttled her plan of having him live at the farm. Friends and neighbours were there for Rose, never having known the sparkle in his eye, his talents, his generosity. All they knew was the shell of the man, hanging lonely as a ghost without his Florence. Now in the crematorium the coffin glided mechanically between the curtains, before his last trip north to be with her mother.

Rose felt weightless, and very, very alone.

46

NEIL PUSHED HIMSELF SLOWLY, agonisingly, up the bed, waving away her offer of help and gripped the sheets with his large, twisted, nicotine-stained hands.

Rose pulled back the curtain. Afternoon sunlight caught his grey hair in a spiked halo against the pillow. She pushed up the sash window to let fresh air into the stale room. No need to look under the bed to know that the chamber pot was back in use.

"Always guid to see the younguns after church," Neil wheezed. "Bella's a reit bonnie lass. The lads'll be after that one."

Already are, thought Rose, smiling to herself. "She's careful with the way she looks. Not that we always approve." Robert had challenged her short skirt and black eye liner before youth group last month, but on Sunday night she'd slipped out with a distant shout the moment she heard the car. Not for Neil's ears, the battles getting her off the phone. Two boys and a party line. Good looks don't guarantee an easy life.

"Did you hear Professor Geering on the radio last night?" Rose asked Aunt Marion.

"Too late for me." Aunt Marion looked weary. "Neil's back on the medicine." Winter had been tough on them both. "The new *Landfall*'s on the kitchen table for you."

Rose followed her into the kitchen.

"Yesterday Mrs Cooper told me the professor should be hung for what he's been saying."

"But she's a Catholic."

"All the more reason. The professor thinks God's the only one with an immortal soul. Catholics have the immortal soul even more ingrained – it's so hard to believe Plato came up with the concept, not the Bible. Or that Christians once believed life ended at death." Aunt Marion never ducked for cover when things got tough. She didn't need to know that Robert wouldn't discuss it any more.

"I told Mrs Cooper she should listen to the full discussion," Aunt

Marion continued, "not just the headlines. Do you know what she said? 'Take your Proddy ideas and jump in the river.' I've never been spoken to like that." She shook her head.

Rose emptied her basket onto the table. "The staff in Gray's were talking about the afterlife on Monday, would you believe? Same at the drapers."

※

Adam looked up from pushing the lawnmower as she drove in the following week, a shower of cut grass arcing behind him. Neil stood at the back door with his walking stick.

"Good to see you on your feet," she said.

"Aye. Have to keep an eye on the lad."

Rose looked from one to the other. Alike, those two and very fond of each other.

"Next time we'll tackle the holly hedge mebee. I'm thinkin' I can trust him wi' the slasher noo."

Aunt Marion peered over Neil's shoulder. "Neil's got his own personal slave there, wrapped around his finger."

"Nothing wrong wi' hard work for a lad."

"Speaking of slaves," Aunt Marion waved her finger in the air, "Professor Geering says the Bible was wrong about slaves. Had you noticed that slaves are mistreated without criticism in the Bible? Wrong about widows too, though we do hear about their injustices. Perhaps our new feminists have taken biblical inspiration, using slave terminology for women." Aunt Marion roared with laughter, flapping her apron.

"No comparison," Rose laughed, then stopped. Could this, for some, be a reality?

※

"Got to get a better picture on this television," said Robert. Rose looked up with surprise. "Don't want to miss the drama. They're saying it will take three days."

The screen had never been sharp like the ones in the shop windows in Princes Street. Here the pale double image flickered, enough to give you sore eyes after an hour. Distance from the translator, they said.

Static in the air. House in a dip. Robert could fix that. A new aerial and a long, long cord.

"Watch the picture, will you Rose? Tell me when it clears."

He took the aerial up the lawn. "No better." Across to the farm worker's hut. Rose raised her voice. "Still no good." The cord ran out near the sheep yards. "A little better," she shouted. He couldn't hear her. Louder: "It's still ghosting." He clambered onto the hut roof to tie it to the chimney, Adam holding the ladder.

The television's been on all day but the reception's bad again, she wrote to Margaret. *We've given up. It's better on the radio.*

Work didn't stop for a heresy trial – Robert listened to the radio outside, Rose in the kitchen.

The General Assembly galleries were packed with over a thousand people and hot with television lights. In the end, it was over so quickly, Professor Geering acquitted of doctrinal error and disturbing the peace of the Presbyterian church. How exciting it had been, everyone said.

"That's a relief," Robert said. "We can get back to normal."

What is normal? thought Rose.

"Mummy, come ooonn. Everyone's waiting. They've been on their best behaviour for ages." Lilly pulled her mother outside to where the little red chairs held all her silent friends. On the play table, in a circle of daisies, Lilly had laid the cups and saucers of Rose's childhood tea set. A plate of Dutch windmill biscuits sat beside a jug of orange cordial. "You're the guest of honour. Tea?"

"Thank you, my dear." Normal.

⁂

Rose tossed Coreen Brownlee's interview folder onto the passenger side of the bench seat. "I'm glad you wanted to come, but there won't be pigs this time," she said, strapping Lilly into the back seat with Cindy under her arm. "We're off to see the orchards," she sang, "the wonderful orchards of … " what rhymed with Oz? Snoz? Roz? "Because because because because be-cause … because of the wonderful things they grow, Lilly, my Lilly, flam-in-ingo." Drat, I'll have it on the brain all the way to Roxburgh.

It was twenty years since she'd spent an afternoon in an orchard, packing export apples to Britain, though she could still crack a golden delicious in half with a quick flick of the wrists.

Lilly waved a finger waggle as the owner's daughter took her away to see the new foal. It was lunch break. Rose and Coreen leaned against the crates while they ate their sandwiches, Coreen's hands stained leather-brown, her short legs swinging under the trailer deck.

"How are you managing the ladders?" Rose asked the quiet girl with the warm brown eyes and freckled face.

"No problem, once you get the hang of it. I don't let the boys borrow my ladder – they'd probably get it twisted." She took another bite. "The boss said ladders used to be longer. Mine's seven feet."

"In my day, they were eleven or twelve – I'd need help to shift it. How does your picking rate compare?"

"I beat the boys every day. If I don't get caught up in their fruit fights. Only thing I can't manage well is reaching the tractor pedals," she laughed.

"While it's lunch break, could we look at where you live?" Rose asked.

They wandered through the dappled shade of the pear trees, to a long, low wooden building. In the distance the family home sat comfortably on a rise.

"I want to stay around here. Who'd work in an office?" They ducked under a full line of washing and stepped into the workers' accommodation. In Coreen's yellow-painted room was a single bed with two coats thrown on top. Letters poked out from behind an odd-shaped mirror. A set of drawers. Enamel mug, plate, travelling alarm clock. No cooking or heating.

"Where do you eat? "

"There's a kitchen at the end with a fridge for your food, if the boys haven't got it full of beer, or someone gets hungry and takes your stuff. We get lunch in the orchard but make our own dinner. Some of them bike into town for fish and chips.

"Is there somewhere to wash?"

"There's nothing for girls. I even hate using the lavatory. It's disgusting. The boys expect me to clean it. Mrs McCauley lets me shower in the house. And watch television any time, as long as I mind the children when they go out."

A mutually agreeable arrangement?

"She got her husband to put a lock on my door. Not many places around here take on girls."

"You're making it easier for the next one. Orchardists tell each other if girls are worth taking on."

"Really? I never would have thought." Coreen turned to look at her. "What are you doing this for? Mrs McCauley did tell me."

What was she doing this for? Taking a leap into the unknown; seeing a slice of life off the farm; doing something her own way? "I love living in the country. Like you, I think. A group of us from Women's Division of Federated Farmers is trying to find out what young women like you need, if you're after a career on the land," she said. "If we know the obstacles – legal issues, pay, conditions, anything – we can help. I'm on a training board too. If you want to study the science of what you're doing, or the business side, or practical courses, we'll support you. What would you like to be doing in ten years' time?"

"Ten years! I can't imagine. Probably be married," Coreen laughed.

"You can build a career at the same time." Twenty years earlier, it wouldn't have occurred to her either.

※

By the spring, she and Barbara had visited fifteen girls. The phone bill made her eyes water, let alone the mileage on the car. But she could claim that. Her furthest trip was to a Te Anau girl, a musterer with one eye on the farmer's son and the other on her next mountain climb. Rose had chuckled at her story the whole way home.

After the girl's brother had been killed felling a tree – a tortuous tragic explanation – she'd inherited his dogs and spent hours training them. At the sheep dog trials she'd won every section she entered. The men let her enter because Patrick had been their mate and, after all, they were Patrick's dogs. And Patrick's truck, hers now, was the only roadworthy vehicle to get them to Young Farmers' Club.

She may as well join, the blokes had decided. Not as a real member. Obviously. You'd have to be a bloody idiot to think girls could join.

※

Rose found the Kelso girl rubbing down in the stables, muttering at the horse for getting so muddy. Pip smelled as if she slept there, a sour pixie-faced girl not hired for her personality. The only time she looked lively was talking about taming the wild out of new animals.

Her lean-to room off the stables had electricity: a single light bulb, a single plug. Her clothes spewed out of an old tea chest. A sack mat lay on the concrete floor beside the bed. What future did she have?

"Is your father a farmer?"

An abrupt nod. "Less said about him the better. Walked out on Mum and us. Back country, west of Garston. My brother's supposed to be running it now."

"How's that working out?"

"Dunno. None of us talk to each other." So this tiny draughty room was home. Rose blinked in surprise when the young woman reached over and grabbed every training pamphlet she had.

Most farm girls did whatever the farmer asked willingly. But the work was seasonal with no forward plan, little time off and no contract, the pay spasmodic. When farm finances got tough, even being known to the family since birth was no guarantee of a job.

Our own members don't keep hours, Rose thought; none of our husbands keep hours. You stop when the job's done or night falls. Some wives talked as if having a girl out in the old cottage, in conditions they would never accept themselves, gave them status.

It would take more than sympathy to achieve change.

※

Back home the family lined up to watch *Peyton Place* on television. Salacious rubbish, but Robert liked it. She had a report to write. Her last interview was a girl sacked for insisting on time off after sixteen twelve-hour summer days in a row. The weekly mailman was her only transport out.

There was probably another side to the story, but the young woman clearly needed help. Still, Rose paused. Since when had she become a moderator?

"Is that you, Barbara?"

"It's me," the voice croaked.

"You don't sound much better."

"Can't shake it off. I found two more girls, at the A&P show, but I've got an idea. I think we have enough information from girls now. What if we survey farmers themselves? We could raise awareness of employing girls and get a clearer idea of their attitudes. What about a postal survey?"

"Now that I'm teaching it's a great idea."

※

In a still-sleeping house the next morning, Rose put her hand on the doorknob. Aunt Marion's voice on the telephone had sounded as vulnerable as a wisp of cloud on a windy day.

Amidst the heavy smell of boy and a tousle of bedclothes, Adam twitched.

"Adam," she said gently. He turned over and opened his eyes.

"Sad news. It's Grandad." *My poor boy.* "I wish I didn't have to tell you this. He died last night. In his sleep."

Adam sat up, staring. "He can't have. He was there yesterday. After music."

She sat on the edge of the bed. "We've been lucky. Having him for so long." From the beginning it was Neil that Adam had crawled to for stories and songs. Adam was hardly at school when his grandfather had taught him how to skin a possum and line up a rabbit in the gun sights. There was always a glint in his eye when she dropped Adam at the house: "Guid to see yer, laddie. I saved yer my shortbread. Don't be telling Aunt Marion and you could get anither piece. Has that teacher taught yer an ounce o' anythin' today?"

Her last image of them was Adam up the ladder cleaning the spouting and Neil on the wooden bench below, waving instructions with his walking stick.

Tears rolled down her face. Rose had loved him from the start. Adam's head sank against her shoulder as she rocked him, his tears wetting her arm as they would again, to his embarrassment, at the funeral.

47

"Could you spare your Adam occasionally, Robert?" neighbour Murray asked as they finished mustering at the tailing yards. "I'll pay him the going rate."

Anything Adam earned, he saved for a motorbike. Not a Harley – fair go, Mum! – perhaps a BSA. Or a Suzuki.

At fifteen, Adam was not an early riser. Working for Murray meant early starts and a midday meal at the house. And ten minutes with a smoke on the back step.

Rose growled at the back of her throat at the smell of Adam's clothing after he'd been working at Murray's. But they also smelled when he had been out with his friend Lachlan.

"Have you been smoking, Adam?"

"Gee, Mum. Would I be that stupid?"

He was probably smoking.

On a bank overhanging the tracks, Adam and Lachlan waited, popping broom pods, jumping on and off the line, ear to the rails. Suddenly they tensed, then hid as the engine and wagons of the Roxburgh train clanked past, struggling up the incline towards the Round Hill tunnel.

Ready? Leap. In one movement, they were on the rear platform of the guard's van. Heart racing, Adam pulled Lachlan down after him, their backs curled against the lumbering metal. They clamped their mouths and eyes shut against the dense smoke in the tunnel as the train crept through, and breathed with relief on the other side.

Ten minutes later they were through the town, slowing up the far hill. "Ready," Adam hissed. "Jump." He threw himself into the bracken and rolled out of sight until his heart settled and the train was a distant hum. Under the fence they slithered to run low along the hawthorn hedge. Nonchalant now, they strutted into the store. Lachlan leaned on the counter and eyed the storekeeper. "Two packets of Capstan, thanks. For my father."

"Must be a worried man, your father."

"Eh?"

"When they double their cigarette order it's the meat price for most, or not enough rain." He pushed the packets across the counter, keeping his hand on top. "Sometimes it's family troubles. Sons mainly." He turned his hand over. Adam passed his money to Lachlan under the counter. Lachlan tipped their coins into the storekeeper's open palm, avoiding looking him in the eye.

They sauntered back to the river, releasing their nervous energy in whoops and yells and ack-ack fire at communist spies. Past the eel hole, they lay in the long grass to puff smoke at the clouds.

"It's nearly time," Adam said, urinating into the river. Ducking from bush to bush, they sheltered behind the decaying railway station and lit up again.

Every few minutes one of them crouched, an ear to the line. At last the distant rumble of the returning train made the track sing. The boys scrambled up the hill ready for the most hazardous leap – the train slowed less in this direction.

They left the train separately, Adam the last to land in the broom. He headed up the ridge into the trees. Deep in the pine needles, he hid the cigarettes.

"Had a good afternoon, Adam?" Rose asked.

"Not bad," Adam replied, and headed to his bedroom.

He's up to something, Rose thought. But she would not know of these escapades until a slip from the storekeeper long afterwards and Lillian's discovery in the pines.

※

When Bella left home, a fundamental shift occurred, the house more male than ever. One husband, two hungry sons, and Lilly. But Bella was here, her first weekend home. Eyes glistening, chestnut hair sharply cut, bags draped along her open arms as she climbed from the bus.

The kitchen table was covered with shopping. "And look – Gene Pitney's new EP."

"Put it on. Put it on," Lilly clapped.

"I'll show you the Mashed Potato." Bella hummed and wiggled. "It's the latest craze. Come on, Tom. On your feet."

Robert came in at the music. "Bella!" He swept her up in a quickstep around the kitchen.

"This one's for you," she said to Rose later, their backs to the coal range. Rose unwrapped the brown paper. A paisley blouse! "Oh Bella. You scamp. Spending money on me."

Bella was bursting with the pleasure of it, "I wanted to get you something from my very first pay and this – it's you."

"You mustn't spend all your money, especially on me. Promise me you'll save some, every payday."

"I promise. Now try it on."

Two nights passed in a flash.

Our children are peeling off, one by one, Rose thought, whole, or just parts of them at a time, each in their own style. Unpredictable and unknowable.

❧

"I'll be off to the accountant straight after the morning round," Robert said on Wednesday night, tying a knot in his pyjama cord. Snow had fallen, but they expected rain to melt it overnight. Yesterday she had to fit chains around the mud-laden tyres to get up the hill.

"We're supposed to go together."

"How can we, when you're working?"

"You can't go anyway – I have the car all day. Jeff's classes, remember?" Rose closed her book. "It's on the calendar. I've done the meals."

"I told you this would never work. You'll have to cancel."

"I'm not letting them down. Can't you work around us for a change?"

If he won't agree, I'll have to dig my toes in, thought Rose. This is not what I wanted.

Margaret, where are you when I need you?

48

"BLAST. THE PHONE'S DEAD," Rose said the next morning. "I hope the principal realises we can't get to school." Snow had been heavy all night, tapping on the bedroom window.

"No school today then," Rose caught Robert's fleeting smirk. No accountant either. The day would be a trial, so little space in an isolated house with one storm raging outside and another festering within.

Suddenly the light went off and the red glow of the heater faded. "Ach, no. Power's gone. Adam, could you please fill the other coal bucket?"

"Adam's with me," Robert cut in from the doorway. "Start loading the hay," he said to Adam. "Don't go near any broken wires."

"Robert, he could get a bucket befo ... " But the door shut.

A snow-laden branch of the wellingtonia had snapped the power lines. How could they report the break with no telephone? The tap dribbled into the empty kettle. She huffed. Why hadn't she filled containers the previous night? No electricity meant no pump and no water.

For now there was hot water, although an empty cylinder could burn out if Robert didn't refill it soon. Every cup of tea, every teaspoonful of hot food now depended on the coal range again, like the years before electricity when they'd been one hour from Dunedin but an epoch away in technology.

Outside, the wind blew snow into drifts, dangerous for sheep who could bury themselves in unexpected deep pockets. Robert took two shepherd's crooks from the laundry hook. "Adam, here, take your grandfather's."

"Shoulda stayed in bed," Adam muttered.

"Can I come?" Tom pleaded, watching them zip oilskins over their Swanndris.

His father looked Tom's slim ten-year-old body up and down. "Your gumboots are too short. Might end up fishing *you* out of a drift. Next year, lad." He patted him on the shoulder. Tom looked dejected. Adam did a silent "Ha, ha" jiggle behind his father's back.

"Tom," called Rose. "Are you up to stomping along the road through the snow?" His face lit up. "Take this note to the Wilsons, to call the power board. Stay in the middle where the snow's thin. No silly tricks looking for the deep parts at the edge."

"Oh, Mum." He rolled his eyes. But he'd try it anyway.

Late in the afternoon Robert brought a drum of rainwater from the shearing shed, the tractor and trailer wheels grinding snow into mud in the yard. After tea, they gathered, moth-like, around the kerosene lantern on the kitchen table in a warm shared glow. Adam and Robert slumped, dazed with weariness, slurping cups of Milo.

Without a newspaper Robert was restless. "Why don't you write to one of your daughters?" Rose suggested. He scowled, then changed his mind. He was on his fourth page to Frances, a librarian now in Christchurch, when Rose filled the hot water bottles.

"Murray Wilson gave me an idea," Tom said. "Snow sleds. We've got wood and sacking."

"Don't you go cutting up all that good timber," Robert warned.

"Oh Robert, let the boys have a go at it." Rose felt around in a high cupboard for candlesticks for the bedrooms.

What would it take to get their easy rapport back?

※

The first night was an adventure. On the second, the boys pushed through the hallway door, casting huge lumbering beasts across the ceiling with their candle-cast shadows, enhanced by roaring bass and shrill soprano werewolf howls.

"Lilly, Lilly, we're coming to get you."

"Get away."

"Roar!" Crash.

"Leave me alone." Blankets muffled her voice. Rose and Robert reached for the handle of the passage door simultaneously. Each gestured the other to go, shrugged and turned away, leaving the children to sort it out for themselves.

A deep sense of misery enfolded her. Three days of digging vegetables from the white mounds in the garden followed. Three days of meat rationing. How long would six month's supply of beef stay frozen without power? She mustn't open the freezer door; after last year's disaster, she couldn't bear the thought of burying more.

The wind died on the third day as Rose ripped June off the calendar.

Morning clouds over Mt Stuart still threatened snow, but by afternoon the snow had softened the sharpness of rocks and crags into benign forms, and drifts of rain were unveilling every distant shape.

On the fourth morning, a vehicle drove along the road. Lillian and Tom pressed their noses to the window. "The power board truck. About time."

She could hear another vehicle. Mail. A woman to talk to. Rose rushed through slush and rain as an arm squeezed bundles of mail and newspapers into the letterbox. Lillian ducked under her arm. "Newspapers please?" She grabbed the bundle and ran back inside.

"She's after a puppy in the Pets for Sale. How's the road further down?" Rose asked, opening her umbrella.

"The worst is this last mile from where the grader's stuck."

"Could I drive out?"

"It's a bog at the junction. You might make it tomorrow. But toss a shovel in the boot. And plenty of sacks." She roared off.

The linesman huddled in the garage, water dripping from his oilskin. "That's the power reconnected, Robert. I'd exercise my chainsaw on those if I were you," he said, pointing to sagging branches of the wellingtonia. "Next snowfall, power'll be off again. See you at Camera Club, if you make it." He touched his forehead in farewell, murmured "Mrs McLeod", and dashed through the rain.

※

"The worst's over," Robert said that night, burying his face in his hands. "I'm off to bed."

"I need to finish my annual report while it's quiet," Rose said.

She gathered the scattered mail. A postcard from Frances, Cathedral Square with pigeons. Loose pages from Bella flexing her new vocabulary: orthopaedic surgeons, obstetrics, paediatrics, sutures. Robert's photographs of Helen, in her white uniform, proudly holding her physiotherapy diploma. Except now that she had seen that women could be doctors, she wanted to be one.

Helen's eyes, like her own. But the blonde hair colour? Oh Helen, she sighed, what are you doing to yourself?

Refocusing, she flipped through the Women's Division branch annual reports in the foolscap record book. Nearly twenty years of catering at A&P shows since their first year, 1953: teamwork in tight spaces, rain or shine, serving hot soup and toast, fruit cake, saveloys and gallons of Mrs Satterthwaite's mutton curry with boiled potatoes. Women's Division speakers offered expertise in every aspect of housekeeping: flower arranging, cleaning products, preserving vegetables, sewing demonstrations.

And the dances. So many dances.

But look at this year. She wanted to show Robert. Beekeeping and farm forestry. Soil science. Accounting. Only one cooking demonstration all year. Have farmers' wives changed so much? Robert would have shown an interest once.

How cynical she'd been about gardening and baking competitions in the 1950s. And now, she'd won the most points for the year. Of course as leader she was obliged to enter. But winning the sewing? Wonders would never cease.

Nothing was recorded here about their regional efforts, all those welfare issues – submissions to Parliament, calling for a ban on smoking in restaurants, opportunities in rural areas for continuing education, more flexible school bus services, rural preschool education, country libraries. Action against the easing of the law on rape, where laws tended to shelter the rapist, not the victim.

A Woman's Place is Everywhere. Make Policy, Not Tea.

❦

The washing had to go out before the next storm. She rubbed shirt collars with Sunlight soap. Everything of Adam's smelt of cigarettes and stale beer. Disgusting. Sad. In her teenage years, there was Bible Class and study, orchard work, camping holidays and sport, all the while trying to ignore the approaching war. No time for rebellion.

And Robert? No chance to be a teenager at all.

Adam played rugby. She applauded the sport – but the after-match! Cars, motorbikes, alcohol, girls. More than anything, the distance home, the road accidents.

And the after-after-match: the arguments with his father that rocked the house, especially now that Adam matched his father's height. The sleeping in on Sunday mornings, the not coming to church. It was distressing, waiting through the heavy silences that followed for the moment to negotiate peace.

She bent to pick up his trousers from the floor. Robert was so strict with him. He expected Adam to learn by following, not by challenging how he did things. He recorded Adam's working hours: after school, weekends and holidays, paid farm wages according to government rates, just as his father had done for him.

How could she persuade Robert to give the boy more rope? Was he trying to protect Adam from the world he was growing up in: free love, drugs (not if she could help it), "Lucy in the Sky with Diamonds", rock music, long hair, flinging off every expectation of adult behaviour. Elvis and *It's now or never, my love can't wait*, John Lennon and Yoko Ono in bed together. All you need is love, yah yah yaha ya. No wonder Patricia Bartlett was gathering support for the Protection of Community Standards, despite increasing noise from mocking "modern" thinkers.

She turned the trouser legs inside out. Something fell to the floor. She picked it up, turned it over. Could this be … ? The packet felt toxic in her fingers. She leaned back against the laundry wall and slid it into her apron pocket.

Condom.

Sailors. American servicemen.

Condom.

She had never seen one before. She'd not seen one now. It burned a hole in her pocket. She stuffed the socks into the washing machine without taking out the bidibids.

Staring blankly through the kitchen window, she tried to think. Robert had to know. They had always told each other the truth – at least careful versions of it. But what is the truth? Is he ruining the girls of Balclutha after rugby every Saturday? Is there one girl? Has this come from a packet of twelve?

Is it even his?

Rose stretched to her full height and walked up the passage to his bedroom. Usually she knocked; today she flung the door open.

"Adam. Up. Get up right now."

He rolled over in a bundle of blankets and peered through the gloom at her with one eye. This was not like his mother, his face said. What was she on about?

"You're in deep trouble, my boy." Thrusting her hand forward, she confronted him with the small packet in her hand.

Adam groaned and rolled away, then with a sudden yelp, lunged at the packet. But she was too quick, too angry, too upset. She sprang back to the doorway.

"Get dressed. In the kitchen. Five minutes. Unless you want the whole family to know about this when they get back.

What was she doing? He could get on his motorbike and be off. Calm down, she told herself. There had to be a reasonable explanation.

※

Three days later, Rose and Adam sat on the kitchen floor marking the floorboarding ready for new lino. She marked. He nailed, roughly, inconsistently. She had hit in a few nails, perfectly, before this division of labour. Women could make choices – she was choosing to let him nail to make the point that women were never to be treated as the playthings of men. She wasn't about to remind him that she'd nailed apple cases all her childhood.

He'd had the long-overdue talk now. The one where Robert used every euphemism to describe physical changes. And babies. The one where she left the room about then. The one where Rose struggled not to interrupt when Robert spoke of women as gentle creatures to be honoured and held up as models of respectability and decency and were not to be touched intimately before marriage. The one where Robert warned him about the way women egged you on with their wily ways, dressing to leave nothing to the imagination, and then expected you to stop. And how the woman was in charge of how men behaved and he should follow their lead and if they had no boundaries they certainly weren't the marrying type.

Rose thought he had done quite well, until then.

"Hoi! Men have to control their own urges too. Don't blame it all … on the girls. Men pretend they're blameless by having dozens of deeply insulting words to describe women. Adam, be friends with lots of girls, but stay out of the dark corners, stay away from drink."

He sat, legs apart, head down, through the whole debacle. Now he peered up from under his dark eyebrows. "Can I go now?"

Robert and Rose looked at each other and shrugged. She remembered a psychologist on the radio telling parents that no matter what, never cut off communication. Never.

The three sat there silently, each in their own thoughts. Would it have been easier if she'd talked to him more, if Robert hadn't disciplined him so strongly?

Robert battled on as if Adam had already left. "Haven't we set him a good enough example? Too many sisters fussing over him, not enough discipline. He'll need to be a leader, not just on the farm, but in this whole community."

"He's far too young for such a burden," she said, hoping he wouldn't say more. Robert would have seen this future as a gift after the war – but Adam?

"Life throws us all sorts of appealing temptations," Rose said quietly, reaching her arm out to him. He shrugged her fingers off his shoulder. "Somewhere deep inside you know right from wrong. Keep listening to that voice."

She stood up, arms clutched tightly across her chest. The clock ticked. Beyond the fence, a cat was sharpening its claws on the trunk of the pear tree. Adam's eyes lifted as she turned to face him again. "Don't think forgiveness lets you off the hook. Having free will sounds as if you can do what you like, but it really means you have responsibility – otherwise face the consequences. And that, dear boy, is where we are right now."

His head hung down again. Was he suffering her words until he could leave, leave here and her and everything in his way? If only his father could see the young man in front of him, not just another knot in the generational rope of sons trained in their father's image.

At least it had cleared the air. By the time she had him hammering in nails fast and true, Rose believed him; the condom came from a visiting health nurse. All the boys carried them. Robert didn't think that improved anything; the woman should be stopped from promoting promiscuity.

Later Robert sat on the bed taking off his shoes.

"Takes me back to army days, that does."

"What does?"

"Frenchies. Used to hand them out by the dozen with the toothpaste. By Jove, some of the boys … "

"Rob!"

"They'd pick up any old crow that was hanging around."

"Robert. I don't want to hear it."

A shoe thudded to the floor. He shook his head as if to clear his mind. "No. You really don't want to hear and I don't want to tell you." He placed his shoes neatly at the bottom of the wardrobe.

Rose lay on her back. There was more than just teenage angst in Adam. He seemed to have an urge to push out, not just the boundaries of behaviour, but his whole world of reference. The opposite of his father, yet the image of him in many ways. Give him a year or so, he'd likely try mixed flatting.

※

Bella, if asked directly, would have readily given an opinion on mixed flatting, though not one based on any moral imperative. She licked Dennis's eyelashes delicately and rolled off. Secretiveness definitely enhanced their three weeks of sharing this mattress on the floor of his friend's flat. Knowing where to get the pill through nursing friends meant just one intensely embarrassing interview with a doctor, having to lie that her parents knew and approved, but then dozens of carefree days to follow. She could hardly bear to leave the bed, especially for eight o'clock lectures, which she had more or less abandoned. Somehow she would have to survive with only the memory of his skin on her fingertips for a whole week; he couldn't avoid a geology field trip to the Canterbury foothills. Time for that promised girl's trip home, her nursing friends kept reminding her.

A whole week. His downy leg extended from the tousled bedclothes.

His face glowed with satisfaction. A twitching smile curled at his mouth. Silently she lowered herself over him. Six inches away he snapped his eyes open and roared, grabbing her around the buttocks, tossing aside her draped blanket, rolled right, left and right over – to stop, lock eyes, lock tongues …

Mixed flatting? Perfect.

49

Despite the cold, Robert had no choice about cutting the wellingtonia branches today even if it was his birthday. Snow was forecast again.

Right now, the cattle needed urgent attention.

"What about rugby, Dad?" Adam asked, tossing a billiard ball from hand to hand.

"I haven't got time to take you to rugby. We're shifting the cattle. Feed's had it where they are. You can't waste a perfectly good afternoon chasing a ball around a paddock."

"But Dad!"

Rose came into the laundry with an armful of sheets. "What's going on?"

Adam hung his head. "He won't let me … "

"There are more important things than rugby."

"What time's your game?" Rose asked Adam.

"Two-thirty. In Balclutha." Forty-five minutes away.

"Not that he's going," Robert said.

"Robert. The team depends on everyone turning up."

"Got reserves haven't you? Have to have. People get injured."

"But I'm not injured."

"Adam, just disappear for a few minutes, will you?" Rose cut in. He slunk into the kitchen like a wounded dog.

Robert leaned against the wall, his head to one side, his exasperated, waiting pose. Rose dropped the sheets on top of the washing machine and faced him. "Can't you give him a bit of space?"

"He's got a whole farm of space."

She sighed. "He needs a bit of fun with people his own age."

"And I need him here."

"You have him most of the time."

"For goodness sake, Rose, he's got a lot to learn."

She took a deep breath. "Is it possible for you to shift the cattle on your own if I can arrange to get him to rugby?" She had no idea how.

Robert took his long oilskin off the hook. "Why do you always take the children's side? Can't you see my point of view for a change?"

Because you walk away and toss orders over your shoulder, she thought. "Because you usually find something more important to do than listen."

"You don't know what you're talking about."

Rose clamped her mouth shut. More would only inflame him. Robert pulled his boots on.

"Why don't you tell him?" she said. "If you just walk off, he'll think you can't be reasonable." And pent-up anger would remain.

Robert's boots dragged to the kitchen door. He leaned into the room. "Mum's sorting transport. Make sure you win." Shaking his head, he closed the kitchen door and rolled his eyes.

A stream of freezing air rushed in as he stepped outside.

50

Rose stared at the smudged chocolate cake recipe. In one definitive action, she closed the Aunt Daisy recipe book, jammed it into the drawer and took out her Alison Holst. It was time for a break from tradition.

She checked the unfamiliar recipe – *Fold the grated orange rind into the creamed mixture* – tucked the bowl into her left elbow and set to with the wooden spoon.

With the cake in the oven, she wiped a circle in the steamy window. July was never her favourite month. The pungent diesel smell of oilskins, the damp wool of Swanndris. Ice inside the sash windows. You could still see your breath in the hall at midday.

The kennel door flapped. Nothing else moved, not trees, not even insects.

Through the kitchen window came a metallic clanging as branches tumbled. A moment later the truck came into the yard, too fast. Only yesterday Robert had agreed to trust Adam with the keys.

"Mum!" Slam. "Mum!" Thumping boots, the rush of cold air. Suddenly Adam filled the door frame. "Call the ambulance. Dad's, Dad's cut – he's chopped through…" He clutched the side of his neck, his eyes huge. "There's all this blood. Quick, he's lying there." He pulled her towards the door.

He stopped. "Ring the ambulance first. Hurry."

Within moments of phoning she followed him out, flicking her coat from the peg. The ambulance would take forty minutes – they would have to meet it. So many questions: was he conscious? Dear God, please. Were his eyes … what did they ask?

Through the gate, they clambered over branches. Two whimpering dogs circled a pile of winter clothing. Her dependable, intractable Robert lay inert. The chainsaw was entangled with the ladder, the chain half off, red and lumpy.

Rose let out a half-formed pathetic cry. One step forward, she would be into something she had no experience of. An old fear battled with the immediate needs of Robert, and Adam too, looking to her.

Robert opened his eyes. He stared past her and shut them again. Blood covered one side of his face. His right ear was – missing. It was impossible to see where his face ended and his shirt began. Blood matted the hair above his ear, where the ear should be. His eyebrows streaked with crimson, eyelashes glumped together.

Adam turned away and retched into the long grass. Rose tried to focus on the parts she could recognise. "Robert! Wake up. Don't go to sleep. Listen to me. Wake up!"

Rose whipped off her apron, folded it into a pad and pressed it onto the wound. "Urgggh," struggled from Robert's throat. He stretched his legs out. She could smell it now …

※

The next thing Rose knew was Adam shaking her arm, exasperation in his voice. "I knew you'd faint on me. Get up."

She stared back, blinking.

"Just get up." He offered a hand.

Why could she never face blood without fainting? She rolled onto her hands and knees. "Back the car out and stop here."

Adam's mouth fell open. "The car? Me?"

The car was strictly out of bounds. At least until he was sixteen.

"Go on. I know you can. I'm not leaving him. Get clean towels from the bathroom first. Hurry." Adam ran towards the house.

She felt Robert's pulse. Moderately strong. But he wasn't responding to her voice. "Robert. Robert. Please – don't sleep. Don't make me slap you."

Ben and Mack looked at her with plaintive eyes, their shaggy heads turning in unison: Robert, Rose, Robert. Mack licked her face.

Rose sat back on her heels. The car crept smoothly towards them.

"Take off your shirt, Adam. We need the sleeves to tie this in place." Adam shivered, then leaped away to grovel in the glovebox. "This do?" A handful of binder twine. Much better.

They propped Robert up, his head swathed in towelling and twine. Adam hoisted him under the armpits. She took the weight of his legs.

Between them they bundled a groaning Robert into the back seat. Adam clambered in.

Not even adrenaline had alleviated the cold in her fingers. Back in the house she could hardly open the catch on the blanket trunk.

At the back door she stopped. Lilly was due home soon. She rang Ness. "We've had a bit of an accident. Robert's cut himself." Focus on the facts. "Quite badly. Could you keep her there till I call – and Tom after rugby? Overnight? Oh Ness, thank you. Yes, he'll be fine."

He had to be.

※

Halfway to Clarksville they met the ambulance. Rose stood back as two officers secured him to the stretcher.

Robert's eyes closed again. "Do you think he … ? It's not too bad is it?"

"We'll do our best, Missus. Are you following?"

Rose kept the ambulance in sight, her fingers tight on the steering wheel. Beside her, Adam tapped his leg. "See those skid marks? Jeffrey Curtis. Rolled last Saturday after rugby. They reckon there was blood all over … "

"Adam! I'm driving."

"Sorry."

At last the arches of the Balclutha bridge appeared. The bumps of the concrete joins echoed her heart: live-on, live-on, live-on, live-on.

※

An hour passed. Two. Rose sat outside the theatre. At first she had clung to Adam. Tears came. Then Adam slumped into a chair under the poster of happy children advertising the joys of the tetanus vaccine and flicked magazine pages back and forth, his hay-studded socks crossed at the ankles.

She tried to pray but the words tangled in her mind.

At last the surgeon appeared. Rose sprang up. "Mrs McLeod," he smiled, unthreading the tapes of his mask. "Your husband's stable, but we need to keep him here for now. He's a very, very lucky man. Forty-eight stitches in all," he said, drawing a finger down his jawline. "Yes, forty-eight. Half an inch lower, he would have hit the carotid artery."

He puffed out a breath. "Incredibly, nothing's broken. Keep him away from chainsaws for a while, eh?"

Rose felt the terror slide down her back. "Adam. Did you hear that? He's safe." Adam nodded slowly, lips twitching with a suppressed grin.

In the recovery room one side of Robert's face was embroidered with tidy lines of crosses. One eye crinkled into a smile and closed again in pain. He fumbled with her wedding ring. From somewhere in the mangled mess the doctor had found bits of an ear.

※

In the car they remembered other near misses Robert had survived: the D2 tractor sliding into the gully, a rockfall in the goldminer's shaft, that time a steer pinned him in the Manuka rail tunnel. And much longer ago, 1944, the Battle of Monte Cassino, when a shell killed the person beside him.

"The most amazing survival story," laughed Adam, "is living through hundreds of your scones."

"Nothing wrong with my scones."

"There is when they're two days old."

"Since when did any food last two days in our house?"

Then they had run out of talk. Fragments of carlight caught a mailbox, the eyes of a possum, the sign to the Glenore Cemetery. Through the Manuka Gorge, snowflakes fell on the windscreen. Finally, there was the turn-off. Manuka Hill Road, hard right and steep. Her spirits lifted with the familiar bends, tyre marks pressing into the thickening snow.

Ben leaped up as she opened the car door. She nuzzled his cold fur and rubbed him behind the ears. Mack joined him. "What are you two doing out at this time of night?" And then she remembered. The open kennel door.

She paused at the back door, suddenly exhausted. She readjusted the pile of blankets to feel for the light switch.

The smell hit her first. Something burning?

The kitchen was full of smoke. In the oven, the remains of a cake.

Happy Birthday, Robert.

51

IN TWENTY-THREE YEARS, this was the first time Rose had been in the double bed alone. Not counting six periods in the maternity ward, two weeks for Frances in 1948, eight nights for Lilly fifteen years later.

Robert's injured face kept bursting into her brain. Shaking, she clutched the woollen blankets, her wide-awake eyes scanning the room in search of something solid from the grey silhouettes: the Victorian dresser, the photo frames on the tallboy, Robert's dressing gown on the back of the door – anything to replace matted blood and rolling eyes.

About three am she wandered into the kitchen. Adam was pouring hot chocolate.

"Want one?" He held up a mug.

"Please."

His pyjamas hung off him, misbuttoned, untucked. She loved that crumpled male look, like his father years ago. His tousled dark hair parted over one eye just enough for him to see where the liquid sloshed into the mugs.

"You probably saved your father today. If you hadn't seen him, I wouldn't have noticed for hours. You know how he stays out, even when it's snowing."

"Yeah. No feeling for cold." Adam was stirring, stirring his mug.

"Are you all right?"

"I'm OK. Try to get some sleep, eh Mum?" He gave her a gentle thump on the shoulder on his way past.

Rose sipped her chocolate. What if Robert hadn't survived? The enormity of how greatly she depended on him, how they all did, overcame her. A reliable steady man. Honest. Stubborn. Quick to seek company but just as content with solitude. A man in tune with the phases of daylight and the seasons, who wore his understanding of the land as a second skin.

But the shouting, the battles to get him to consider the children's needs, that feeling of being squeezed from both sides. His refusal to give her financial autonomy.

But this was not the time to think of their disagreements.

She pulled her dressing gown around her legs. Right now, she'd forgive him anything. He'd been given back to her.

If he lived.

If not, how would she manage the farm?

She froze at the thought, mug in mid-air. Six children, eight hundred acres, two thousand sheep, three hundred cattle, two hundred goats. Could she ever understand the watering systems, crop rotation, fertiliser, soil chemistry, winter food supplies, cultivation, drenching, shearing, crutching, forestry pruning, flood management, mud?

Mud she knew about.

She shuffled across the floor, left her mug in the sink and stood still, massaging her cheeks. A flurry of loosened snow splashed against the glass. This winter had been long, but spring would eventually arrive with a vigour that always surprised her. Newborn lambs and calves, the hillsides fresh with promise as if stroked by a water-laden brush in a child's magic painting book.

And Robert would be there.

Calmer now, she slipped between the flannelette sheets, exploring the novelty of blankets and pillows to arrange as she wished. She traced his shape with her leg, longing for the warmth of him, body and soul.

❧

In the morning she woke with a start. Twenty past eight. Three children to get ready for church. Yesterday's events rushed in as she felt around the wooden floor for her slippers.

She stopped. Church was not where she needed to be today.

The bare facts of Robert's accident were enough for Aunt Marion. "Do what you must. Call me again after the hospital."

Car doors slammed in the yard. Lilly and Tom rushed into the kitchen, Lilly hugging her around the waist. "How's Daddy?"

"He's sore," Rose said to Lilly's upturned face, stroking her hair, "and looks a bit patched, but he shouldn't be in hospital long."

"Did he chop his ear off?" she asked.

"Not right off. The doctor's mended it. Just as well – the way you like things in pairs, you'd want the other one off to match." Satisfied with her mother's blurring of the truth, Lilly slipped away to her bedroom. Seconds later she poked her head back around the door. "Does that mean we aren't going to church?"

She nodded. "Don't get used to it. Get yourself a biscuit, Tom." The tins were already rattling.

On the back of the truck, Adam had left a space for Lilly amongst the stacked hay bales. He squeezed in beside her as they sped along the road, Ben on top of the bales, his fur horizontal, tongue dangling crazily as strands of saliva floated back over his shoulder.

"Which paddock, Tom?" she asked inside the cab against the rattle of the truck. The sooner they finished the sooner she could get to the hospital.

With the gleam of responsibility in his eye, Tom jerked his thumb towards the next ridge. "Mary's Hill," he said. Traces of yesterday's bales were scattered below the flax bushes.

They stopped at the gate. Tom went to open it. The Blue Mountains, fifty miles west, were usually purplish-grey, but today they were part of a corrugated white landscape. Towards the east the land fell away to the plain with no snow at all. Heavy grey stratus clouds layered the view towards the coast.

"Come on, Tom." Rose leaned out the truck door. "What's the problem?"

"Gate's stuck. It's too heavy."

She climbed down, planted her gumboots squarely and shouldered the gate. It swung open. Tom hooked the chain around the post.

"Ten in this paddock, Adam?" Rose called across the hay bales. Adam's head bounced up from behind the bales and nodded.

Sheep emerged from the gully. The children cut twine with their pocket knives and tossed slices of hay as the truck crawled along. Ten uncut bales over the fence to the cattle, and back over Mary's Hill, Adam and Lilly huddling together on the empty deck with Ben.

Rose leaned out of the cabin. "Any sheep down, Adam?"

Adam thumped on the cab roof. She stopped the truck. "There's one at the edge of the gully. Don't drive down, you'll get stuck."

Before she could answer he was lolloping down the slope, Ben at his heels.

Lilly squeezed into the cab with Tom, competing to cover the windscreen with steaming breath. Rose massaged her mittened fingers. No heater here.

Standing astride the cast sheep, Adam rolled her over, one arm around her neck, the other under her belly. She stood dizzily, unable to balance the weight of her own wet wool. Standing astride the ewe, Adam walked her to the hay.

"Another fat old mama with no sense of direction," he called cheekily into the truck window.

"Not so much of the 'fat', thanks," said Rose. "Get in behind."

"Woof," answered Adam to her command and clambered back on top.

Rose could never have lifted that sheep. Without Robert, only Adam was strong enough.

The truck creaked and groaned over the frozen tractor ruts up Mary's Hill. Mary, who had died four years before but had left twenty years earlier, remembered in a hill. Mary was an enigma; Rose could never fathom whether to treat her as a woman or a farmer.

Would one of her own girls have made a farmer? Too late now, the three eldest with city professions and city friends. There was still Lilly. But farmers were men. Who needed wives. You could define a farmer by what he didn't do. He didn't cook or bake or mend. Didn't bear children or dispense sticking plaster or midnight cough mixture. A farmer didn't ensure pet lambs were fed, the vegetable garden planted or the sheets smelled of fresh air and sunlight. A farmer could never be his own helper at short notice when the cattle broke out or the sheep needed shifting. How could a woman be a farmer and all this too? A farmer takes a wife. Hey ho the derry-o.

Except for a few stubborn, anti-social women like Mary, who had tried to be a farmer before the world was ready.

Now the world had changed.

What kind of mark would Rose leave on the world? A paddock or two, like her?

I should have made more effort to know her, thought Rose, sliding the truck key back under the paring cutters as they pulled up in the yard. Ben leaped down ahead of Adam. "We managed that pretty well without Dad, didn't we?" Rose said. There was no enthusiasm in their nodding faces.

The house was chilly. No hot food or well-stoked fire waiting as she always had for Robert.

The phone was ringing. "Mrs McLeod? It's the hospital."

288

52

SHE FINISHED HER TOAST amongst the wreckage of discarded breakfast, imagining Robert in his narrow bed trying to ignore the noises from the sluice room. If his head injury was still concerning the medical staff, the less the children knew the better.

Adam was on his way to school now with the others after loading the truck before dawn. She could manage the feeding out, slowly, clambering on and off the deck, even in this rain.

"Home's where I'm most needed for now, I'm sorry," she'd told the headmaster last night. Everything depended on her.

"Yoohoo." Robert's friend Keith was coming through the back door. "I heard about Robert. How are you managing?"

"Where do I begin?" She covered her face and turned away. No tears, please God. "He may have complications."

"Hey, hey, he'll be back," he said awkwardly from the far side of the room.

Rose wiped her face with the kitchen towel. "You hold yourself together for the children and then – sorry."

"Did he tell you he was worried about abortions in the cattle?" He shifted his weight from one leg to the other. "Can't afford to lose any animals." Keith put his hat back on. "Sorry I can't stay now. I have to take the family to the aunt's funeral in Dunedin. But I'll ring tonight."

※

Rain or no rain, Rose would inspect the cattle. The truck hummed down the gravel road towards Nugget Stream, wipers at full tilt. On the hill beyond, black-wet cattle huddled under the gum trees. Exactly what would an aborted calf look like? A slick, slimy, bloodied sack of wet hair, embryonic outsized hooves, gelatinous unformed limbs? Gulls would make short work of it.

Around the corner she skidded to a halt. Where was the road? A brown torrent of water was swirling into a small lake. Normally the stream ran through a culvert. Something was blocking it.

What am I supposed to do, Robert?

She lowered her head and bumped her forehead over and over onto the steering wheel, squeezing her eyes shut. She could go home, leave the aborting cows to their fate. Or call a neighbour, plead the helpless woman. Is that what Mary would have done?

After a moment, she sat straight again, drumming her gloved fingers on the steering wheel. She pulled the oilskin hood over her head and stepped cautiously into the water, poking Robert's shepherd's crook ahead of her. From where the road rose over the culvert, she could make out a pale mound.

A dead sheep was blocking the culvert.

Instantly she knew she hadn't the strength to pull it out. Robert would have waded in, heaved the sheep onto his back. She would need to head back for the tractor, Robert's thigh boots, a chain, a sack, a woolpack, something large enough to contain it. If it had been dead for a while, it could distintegrate.

Or she could wait till the water went down. She hugged her cold hands higher under her armpits.

No, she must get to the cows right away.

※

Cold grabbed her fingers as she fought against the current to work the wool pack under the sheep. At first nothing budged. She wedged her boots against clumps of reed roots for stability and lined herself up with the flow of the water, bending over the woolly mound. Her numbing fingers grappled to loop the chain beneath the sack, everything slimy and slipping away into the brown water, thick with mud with clumps of sodden roots and clay of collapsed banks. A chunk of wool came off the carcass in her fingers. She tossed it behind her, losing her footing to the force of the water. I can't do this, I can't. Her heart beat, her face was awash with tears and rain, her hair clinging, yet she lifted her head to search for something to help her move the animal – anything.

A bent waratah came away at her tugging. Wedging the metal fencing pole under the sheep, she heaved with all her strength. "Move, move, you stupid ewe, roll over," she shouted above the noise of the stream. A leg flopped up, the hoof waving as if to say goodbye, but she grabbed it, tied it into the sacking and fished out another leg. Then the head, looping and weaving sacking and chain, careful not to puncture the bloated stomach, remembering from years ago the foul smell as putrid innards squelched from a burst carcass.

Suddenly she lost her footing and slipped full length into the freezing water, which rushed through every layer of her clothing. For a moment she saw her body from above, hair and flesh and bone surrendered to the water, another inconsequential animal, alone. Then she struggled against the current. With a loud and long maniacal laugh, she staggered, heaving life back into her flesh, bones into battle.

PART FIVE

PART FIVE

53

Two hours later the stream flowed through the culvert. Rose drove towards the gum trees, exhausted but dry again. Shafts of light still chained threatening clouds to the earth, though the rain had stopped.

She had never wandered among cattle without Robert, and never without fear. In the truck, she circled in low gear, preparing herself to use the new first aid technique for fainters, clenching her fists at the first sign of blood to keep her blood pressure up.

"Sounds like those five have aborted. I'll be up first thing," the vet said later. "How's the patient?"

Rose gasped. She didn't know. "Comfortable and dry."

As soon as she put the phone down it rang again. "Mrs McLeod? Potae Shearing."

Shearing? Impossible. Unless they hired more men, or … "Can we shift to the school holidays?" She'd need Adam to fill the shed, and Tom who was just as competent.

At the back door after collecting the children from the school bus was a beef casserole and muffins and a hot shepherd's pie. Her heart lifted. She was no longer alone.

"Before you run off," Rose said, "let's work things out. Lilly, the jobs list please. If we get more done first thing, I could pick you up from school to visit your dad."

There was a tap and a whistle at the back door. Her friend Ness walked in and hugged her. "Joe found a dozen ewes on the road – don't look worried, they're in now. And he's mended the gap. Hey, Adam, isn't your mother looking more like a farmer every day? She's even got mud in her hair."

"Keep your kind remarks to yourself," Rose laughed. "I'm worried about the tree saplings leaning against the shearer's hut."

"Weather any good tomorrow?"

"Showers and cold."

"Leave it with me."

Robert lay diminished by the hospital bed. Thick padding covered his right ear, held by a bandage around his head. Rows of stitches were visible below. Above the bandage his hair splayed in all directions. "Ahh, there you are." He reached out a hand.

"Are you feeling better?" Rose pulled a chair close to the bed.

"I'm still getting dizzy. But you don't get a wink of sleep in here with nurses waking you for injections and tablets and your temperature," he said. "I'm mighty sick of these four walls and there's so much to be done at home."

The children disappeared to visit a school mate with a broken leg.

"Don't worry. We're managing the feeding out." She told him about the vet coming.

"Don't you go organising anything," Robert said. "Things can wait."

Why had he said "organising" so disparagingly?

"Your saplings are withering, Rob. You'll have nothing to plant soon." There could be a concession. "What if you drew a planting plan? We could at least mark it out." She burrowed in her bag for a writing pad.

"Make sure the vet doesn't stay all day," Robert said as he drew some curved lines. "He can charge like billy-o."

"We couldn't get the school holidays for shearing, but we did manage a weekend." She didn't tell him she'd employed an extra shed hand.

"The rate you're taking over I'll have to get out of here fast." He grabbed one of her Belgian biscuits and bit it in half.

"Taking over? Robert, I'm doing my best to keep things ticking along."

Robert suppressed a laugh. Rose jumped to her feet.

"I've waded into freezing flood water and dragged a sheep from a culvert with a tractor I've never driven." She could still feel the slimy wool. "I've inspected the back ends of thirty cows, which I did willingly enough, and you call it 'taking over'."

An orderly walked in with a dinner tray. She lifted the lid. Roast beef and vegetables.

"There's an hour's drive and an hour's cooking until I get your family a meal half as decent as that." She grabbed her notepad and walked to the door, bumping into a nurse. "Is he restless again? I'll get the doctor to check his medication."

How could she have been so unsympathetic? she asked herself, her foot heavy on the accelerator. She'd blown the whole episode out of proportion. So had he, unwilling to admit her contribution even from his sick bed. He deserved it.

"Be quiet children, I'm sick of your noise," she snapped to the back seat.

※

Ness had the knack of getting things done. Ten minutes of phone calls: five men and three women turned up. Rose had come with two spades, but Ness's husband had a speedy post hole digger. He wasn't useful just for rescuing cattle beasts from railway tunnels. She measured spaces according to Robert's sketch, allocating three varieties of trees to one hundred and fifty holes around the toe of the ridge.

The day became a winter picnic, as the laughing children watered the holes and each other from the mobile tank, lugging trees bigger than themselves, stamping them in, making sock puddles across the kitchen later as Rose stirred cocoa over a fresh fire. What pure gold friends.

She checked the calendar. Camera Club tonight. An apology. Church leaders meeting? A reluctant apology for herself. Dog dosing on Tuesday. What must she do for that?

The bank tomorrow. Postpone?

No. This time she'd go by herself.

※

"Just because I'm a woman doesn't mean I can't do 'men's things'," she exclaimed to Robert as they drove home across the Tokomairiro Plain.

"Well, some of them," he laughed.

Incorrigible man. "Look what women do in this community now. The old model's on the wane. Women *can* be farmers."

"So you're running the farm now?"

Rose changed gear for the hill. "Until the last three weeks, I didn't know I could push myself so far. I can manage better than I imagined."

Robert sat up like a frightened rabbit.

"With help," she continued, "and mistakes. I want some life of my own too, not necessarily with pupils who are just waiting for their sixteenth birthdays to leave school. I don't want to be a full-time farmer, Robert. I'd much rather be an extra pair of hands when you need me."

"Struck it lucky, didn't I? Marrying you."

"AND share the decision-making, finances and long-term planning, with both our names on the bank account. Really working together. I've got more to offer than 'woman's work'. You've just chosen to ignore it."

Silence.

She took a deep breath. "I kept the appointment at the bank."

"You did *what?*"

"Settle down. He suggested we restructure the loans. I didn't decide anything. We *decide* together."

"Exactly what are you on about?"

"Oh Robert. This farm will always be more yours than mine, but until we pass it on, it's ours. Our home, our good years. Our burdens, our debt."

He stared at her speechless.

※

Robert strode into the kitchen a week later in hat and coat and dropped a newspaper parcel onto the bench. "My turn to wear the apron tonight. Jack told me what to do with this fish and I reckon you deserve a night off." He paused. "Or you could do the potatoes. And carrots. Whatever you like. Leave the fish to me. What are you staring at, Adam? Go and dig the carrots for your mother."

Robert cooking? Was this symptomatic of a deeper injury? He seemed genuine. Dumbfounded, she peeled potatoes at the bench beside him, sneaking sideways glances while she heard every detail of Jack's instructions.

After Grace he sat back triumphantly. "Watch out for bones, Lilly. Right. Rose, everyone. I want all the family – at least the half present – to hear me say that your mother has been a pretty good farmer lately, so the neighbours keep telling me. No, Rose, my turn. It wasn't easy lying in that hospital bed ... ," they all roared with laughter, " ... knowing what you had to do, Adam, and you Tom. I was a bit grumpy with your mother getting carried away with the job ..."

"Grumpy? You were downright rude."

"She came into the hospital capable of saving the world with her I-can-do-anything face. Made me feel more useless than I was already."

Where was he going with this?

"No criticism, mind." He held up his palm to stop her objecting. "I've come to my senses. This mother of yours does a darn good job. She's capable of saving the world, well my world anyway. So." He faltered, reaching to put his arm around her. "So, your mother and I are going to do things differently. Together. That's it really. Tuck in."

❦

"Rose."

One of the Elders, Angus, was striding across the grass towards her after church.

"I was hoping to catch you. Easier in person."

What was he after?

"I wonder," he puffed, "if you would consider helping me with something." Interesting so far.

"If I can."

"The National Party's taking a fresh look at health, particularly rural health. Keep this under your hat." He looked at her directly.

"Of course," Rose said, puzzled.

"We're after a lay person for a new Board of Health. I'd like to put your name forward."

"Me?" Rose jerked back.

"Yes, you. You've done work with farmers and church people and women's groups. You have a broad perspective. You know how to talk to all types, and you listen."

"I don't know anything about health."

"How many children do you have again? Ever dealt with the elderly? Illnesses? Accidents?"

"Far too often." Travel complications and child minding, when Adam got adhesions after his operation. And Frances broke her arm. Helen's tonsils. Varicose veins. Meningitis. Chainsaw accidents. Fundraising for the Sudden Infant Death Syndrome research team.

"I think you could assess what's going on in any rural community pretty fast. You'd be a lay rural advocate. Interested?"

Interested? She could hardly contain her excitement.

"What would it involve?"

"Probably one meeting in Wellington a month. Funded of course. To be honest, it's still evolving."

A car door slammed. Raised voices. Tom ran from one back door to the other.

"I'd better go. I'm interested. Very interested. When can we talk again?"

"I'm back in Wellington tomorrow. We'll be in touch."

※

Rose unloaded the afternoon tea basket onto a full bale in the woolshed. Somewhere downstairs Tom was rattling his tin of stones, helping his father pen three hundred ewes. Robert's whistle pierced through the steady hum of the machines and Gene Pitney on the radio, *If I only had time, only time.*

The pony-tailed shearer joined in, holding the cutting handpiece as a microphone, *Dreams to pursue ... if I only had time ...they'd be mine.*

His mate slapped his arm and nodded towards Rose as they pushed through separate low swing gates into the pens. He held two fingers up. Two more sheep before smoko.

Stretched over the nearest ewe, he took hold of her front legs and turned her upside down against his legs, backed through the swing doors and slid across the floor to the machine.

The sheep relaxed. He razored off the short wool around her eyes. Avoiding her teats, he gathered the cut belly wool in one hand as he cut it and heaved it into the belly loft. His arm made long blade strokes up the back. The wool peeled onto the floor like a garment, white, thick. Maintaining the rhythm, he rolled her to the other side, kicking the unbroken fleece through mid-turn, long cutting strokes barely interrupted. He pulled the cord. The whirr of the machine dropped to a hum. Standing the naked sheep upright, he tapped her on the backside and sent her out through the chute.

Deftly the rousie tucked the leg wool under and folded the

abandoned fleece back on itself. He scooped it up and carried it to the skirting table.

Rose waited for her favourite moment.

Against the afternoon light, the airborne fleece expanded into ridges and curves, an enlarged echo of the animal, owning the air in one glorious arabesque – the shape full of movement and energy. On the skirting table it relaxed, flat, drooping over the edges, thick, finely crimped, warm and resilient.

They were behind on the pressing. The truck would be here soon for twenty-five bales. Rose took the bag needle and twine from the padded sacking tube on the door and began sewing the square end cap onto the full jute bale in the press, overlapping the corners as Robert had shown her, knotting and reknotting where the pressure would be when they released the press, strong looping stitches: end, bale, end, bale.

Adam opened the side of the metal frame and hefted the bale onto the barrow against his body. The load hid all but the hook as he manoeuvred four hundred pounds of wool through the door as easily as a sack of pine cones.

Suddenly Lillian appeared. "Can I do the number? Pleeease." Always, always, there'd be a child waiting to stencil the finished bale, rubbing black nugget through the number wheel. Then the farm brand.

Bale 21: Romney ewe fleece, Rose wrote in the book.

Adam swaggered back. "First day doing that, Mum," he said into her ear. She smiled to herself as she loaded fleeces into the empty bale. Such a different boy from last week. Hardly a boy. Taller than his father.

Adam climbed inside the press, tramping the wool as she added more.

The machines stopped.

"Tom?" Robert called. A boy emerged in the belly loft covered in wool. "Pretty full up there. I'll get you to load up a bellies bale later, but I need you taking a mob back to the paddock."

"Have a drink first, Robert," Rose insisted, dispensing mugs of cordial and tea.

※

Before they knew whether international buyers had outbid each other or turned their backs on their wool, lambing was imminent. Rose and

Robert spent a day in Dunedin, shopping, visiting the accountant. Together.

It was dark as they turned into the yard, bumping over ridges and lumps of winter mud.

Robert came into the kitchen the next morning. "No children around?"

She shook her head.

"Good. I found this on the road." He pulled a stiff mass of fur from under his coat.

"Cheetah. No!" Rose clasped her hands over her mouth and stared up at Robert. Poor Lilly. Her lovely kitten.

"What happened?" But she already knew. The thud under the car last night. "Are you going to tell her?"

"I was hoping you would."

The fridge hummed into the silence.

"We could NOT tell her. Leave her to think she just – disappeared," Robert said.

Silence. "That's hardly honest."

"If I make her disappear now, it will be." Robert held the kitten like a piece of wood and walked outside.

Is long-term unresolved misery better for a child than short-term shock and recovery? She would have argued with him before.

Compromise was impossible. She could live with Robert's choice.

※

A month later Robert pulled up under the plum tree and came down to the window with a spring in his step. Rose swung the window open. "Is Lilly around?" he asked.

"Lilly?" Rose shouted into the house. No answer. "She's probably with Tom and the Tonka trucks."

"Got a surprise." Robert went around the side of the house. Two minutes later he was pulling Lilly up the steps.

"Why do you ... ouch, Daddy, you're hurting."

Rose dropped the teatowel and followed.

"There's a puppy in the car."

With a wide smile Robert gestured her in.

Lilly lifted a white wire-haired terrier from a damp box. She looked up at her father. "Why is this puppy here?"

"He's yours," Robert said, crouching beside her. "All yours."

Sometimes, thought Rose, he is the most perfect man in the world.

❦

Bella screwed the teat onto the bottle and shook the pet lamb's milk mixture. "What's that tune you're humming?"

"It's a new hymn." Rose sang the words. "*Brother, sister, let me serve you, Let me be as Christ to you.* I want it at my funeral."

Bella gawped at her. "Mum."

"Don't look at me like that. Think of it as a memory test. I'll still be around for ages."

"It's not funny." Bella looked relieved. "Lilly. Tom," she shouted. "Milk's ready."

"I'll still be here long after you run the ward and have children of your own. You'll have to wait till I'm old and cranky," she curled her body into a shrinking version of herself, "and my teeth fall out."

Bella laughed. "That'll be easy."

"What's going on?" Robert grinned as he came in.

Rose poked her chin at him. "Nothing. And nothing comes of nothing." Cordelia again.

"Now that you're both here," Bella said, wiping the bottles, "I'm investigating going to Australia when I'm qualified. What do you think?"

54

THE PHONE RANG.

"Hi Mum."

"Helen. Helen?" Rose hadn't heard her voice since she had moved to a position in Auckland two months ago. Something must be wrong. Or exceptionally good news.

"I'm in Dunedin, rostered off for three days."

"Are we going to see you?" What was she doing coming south so soon? More money than sense.

"I thought we'd come out tonight."

Rose caught her breath. "Marvellous. Who's the 'we'?"

"Max. My – just a friend."

"Will you be here for dinner?" Rose flicked her mind over the number of chops in the fridge as she twisted her finger through the phone cord.

"No. A bit later."

Helen sounded flat. Tired. "Are you alright?"

"Fine. I'm fine. Are you both home tonight?"

❋

She pushed the carpet sweeper around the lounge, clattering along the tiles at the edge of the fireplace. Something didn't feel right. Had Helen lost her job? Perhaps she'd misread the tone and it was good news. No, she would have blurted it out.

Perhaps she'd decided to toss it in and go to university after all – or get engaged to this boy. Max?

We brought our daughters up to be independent, she thought, sweeping the same piece of carpet over and over. Their choices, their issues to deal with. If her way was not to be their way, so be it.

But Helen's voice had no edge of excitement, but a dullness, a covering up of something lurking beneath.

As soon as they heard the car, Rose, Tom and Lillian jumped up.

"Come on, Robert, pull your eyes away from the television. It's your daughter. Coming, Adam?" Seconds after the doors slammed, Helen was swallowed up in hugs.

"This is Max everyone. Mum, Lilly, Tom," she pointed. "And Adam down at the gate. Hi Adam." Tom hefted Helen's pigskin bag over his shoulder as they jostled through the dying light into the house.

Helen looked happy to be home, a little pale, a little quiet perhaps. Her fair hair was pinned in a new style, high at the back with loops of lazy curls. Max hung back, hands in pockets, stooped heavy frame, hair to his shoulders. A well-worn saggy hand-knitted jersey.

There was a familiarity between them, but anything more?

"Can I take Helen to see the puppy?" Lillian pleaded, arms wrapped around her sister's hips. "With the torch – then I'll go to bed."

Rose shrugged. "Off you go then. Straight to bed after, mind. She'll still be here in the morning." Adam and Tom cornered the boyfriend, a pharmacy student.

"You study chemicals, right? Do you know how to make explosions?" asked Tom.

"Or that stuff for chemical warfare? Like in Vietnam?"

"Enough you two." Rose interrupted. "He didn't come here for an inquisition."

❦

Rose gave Helen a hug as they waited for the kettle to boil. "So good to have you home." And on her own, now the other three were in bed.

"Nothing like it," Helen said into Rose's shoulder. There seemed to be a note of relief, heavy with something more. Helen didn't look at her directly but peeled away, stacking cups and saucers onto the tray.

"Take the sugar bowl for your father," Rose called after her as she buttered the gingerbread.

Robert was taking his usual tentative approach to any young man interested in his daughters. He opened the Wonderheat and stirred the fire with the poker. Max sat on the sofa next to Helen, ill-at-ease, head down. Mouthed words passed between them before Helen spoke.

"The thing is ... the thing is, we want you to know that, well, I'm pregnant."

Silence. Rose's mouth went dry. Silence filled the room, not a benign quietness but a seething mass of air building up into a vortex.

No sound no words no reactions.

"What did you say?" Rose stared at her.

"What did you say?" demanded Robert, his hands tightening on the rolled arms of his chair.

Helen repeated her words.

Rose drew in a gasp. "No, no, Helen, you can't be." She fought off a feeling of disgust. Her Helen. It couldn't be true. She turned away and stared into the fire.

"Are you sure?" she whispered.

"I've seen a doctor."

"You're the father?" Robert directed at the boy.

He nodded. "And I will stand by her."

"You'll get married."

"No," said Helen, struggling against the quiver in her voice. She looked from one parent to the other. "No, we've decided – we don't want to marry."

Robert leaned forward, his eyebrows knitted together. "But a baby needs a family. Of course you'll marry."

"Helen," Rose wailed, too numb for more words.

"Dad, that would be a good thing if we loved each other, but we don't, enough, we won't, we …"

Robert was on his feet. "If you don't love each other, why on earth are you in this position? Eh? Why?"

Rose reached for his arm. "Keep your voice down. Shhh. We don't want the little ones to hear." Robert hung his shaking head.

"So it's all your fault," he said, flinging himself around to face Max as he spat out the words.

"It's not only his fault, Dad." Helen said.

"I'm sorry. I never hurt her. It wasn't like that. This wasn't supposed to happen."

"This is exactly what is supposed to happen. Sex is for having babies. In families. To married people."

"Robert!"

"Didn't we teach you anything, my girl? Didn't we take you to church, teach you some restraint, some self-respect?"

"I thought you would understand." Helen shrank into the sofa.

"Enough." Rose felt the painful reality taking hold. "Let's all calm down. Sit down, Robert. I can't think straight. You'd better start with the facts. Did you know you were pregnant when you left?"

"My uniform was becoming tighter. And you don't get fat on the food in our flat." She sighed. "When I started feeling a bit seedy, I put that down to the building at first. I'm still not used to the air in Auckland Hospital."

"It's far too late for all that now. What are you going to do if ... ?"

"Robert, Robert, please stop pacing. Sit down."

Robert sat, his head heavy in one hand, eyes shut.

Silence again.

"Have you told anyone else?" Rose asked.

"Just my flatmates. Claire persuaded me, us, to tell you in person."

"That's one good thing. Don't tell anyone. The younger ones must never know. For their own protection." If the school community found out, she thought, they would be teased and humiliated. Tainted for good. "You're home as you told them, for a few days off." Rose sighed deeply. "Oh Helen, Helen." Tears welled up in her eyes.

Robert pushed his way past Rose's chair and left the room.

She followed him into their bedroom where he sat slumped on the bed in the dark. "Where did we go wrong?" he said quietly. "Where did we go so wrong?"

Rose fumbled through a drawer for a handkerchief.

"We must go back in." She patted his shoulder.

She glanced through the lounge doorway, looking at the backs of the two young people. Few words passed between them.

"Your parents are taking it pretty well."

"What?"

"Well no one's thrown anything or drained the whiskey bottle yet. If this was my family ... "

"Well it's not. Maybe you should tell yours on your own."

Robert walked slowly back into the room and seated himself in the far corner, arms folded against his chest. Helen jumped up and attempted to hug her mother, but Rose couldn't offer more than a stiff-armed grip and release. While love was indisputable, Helen had stepped across the divide.

"What I cannot understand," Rose began, dabbing at her nose, "is if you behave like this before you're married, you know there are ways to avoid pregnancy. Why … ?"

"Everyone thinks they can carry on exactly as they wish," Robert interrupted, " but once you lose your reputation it's nigh on impossible to get it back. The McLeods have always been a respectable family. Till now. I told you mixed flatting and that student health service handing out the pill willy-nilly would lead to this."

"But Dad. It's only the really bold girls who ask a doctor for the pill. Hardly any doctors will give it to unmarried couples."

"Quite right. You've no self-control, no discipline. You've got a lot to answer for, young man. What on earth do you think you were doing?"

"I didn't want this to happen, I am so, so, sorry." Helen's words were lost in an outpouring of tears at last, everyone waiting, and waiting, until she quietened into sobs. Vibrant, forthright Helen, diminished to a vulnerable, frightened child.

Beside her the young man squirmed. "Perhaps I should head back to Dunedin. Lectures in the morning."

"Go now," Helen cried out. "You brought me out here. That was all I asked."

He walked off with barely a farewell. Rose stared after him, unable to think of a parting comment.

"What was he here for if he's not going to marry you?" Rose asked.

"We were trying to be honest and face realities. Even if we don't want to be stuck with each other for the rest of our lives." She screwed the hanky around her fingers. "I needed him to bring me home. I wanted to tell you together, not have one of you meet me at the airport, tell one, then the other. And the kids would be around." She started crying again. "I hate doing this to you," she wailed through the tears, "and ruining the family's reputation."

Rose had regained her self-control, though her handkerchief stayed ready in her left hand. "Do you have any plan at all?"

"I went to see a doctor about an abortion."

"You what?" Rose and Robert said in unison.

"He wasn't exactly helpful," she cried, tears streaming down her face. "He said he wished girls would keep their legs together." Rose felt her mouth hang open.

"Don't be so crude." Robert thumped the arm of the chair.

"And you have to be twenty-one and call it something else." Helen covered her nose with her handkerchief and squeezed the words out between blows. "I couldn't do it. I'm giving the baby up for adoption."

Adoption? How *could* Helen give her baby away? Especially once she'd felt it kicking and stretching. Her grandchild. Their first grandchild.

Her hands began to tremble. Breathe, breathe. Don't think of your own loss, don't remember. She gripped the chair.

But what choices were there?

A heavy silence descended.

Opening her arms, Rose stepped forward. Helen rose to meet her embrace. Neither spoke as Rose began to absorb the worst news a mother could hear. She held Helen firmly, aware of the unison of their breathing, two lives containing a third, the beginnings of a life she would never be closer to than at this moment.

She felt exhausted, unable to listen or comprehend more.

"Enough for tonight. For all of us."

※

Robert bent over his diary. "Helen home with friend. Sad news." The ink of "friend" was lighter, the full stop loitered over. Nothing else to say. Rose rested her arm around his neck, her head against his. Then silently each undressed, a slow-motion routine. Remove, fold, drape on chair. From under the pillow, pyjamas. Nightdress. Light off. Lift the blankets in unison.

Rose stared into the darkness, rigid. Beside her Robert breathed in. Paused. Forced his breath out. She reached for his hand. Wordlessly they flung themselves together, clutching, her fingernails digging into his back, her tears wetting the hair of his chest. He rolled over her, kissing her fiercely, lips, breasts, neck, breasts. She grabbed him, urging him into her, gripping his buttocks, take me away, away, away, obliterate this evening, this horror, this shame.

It was over too soon, nothing had changed but Robert's breathing. In his arms she inhaled the familiar sweet almond scent of him. The only sure place in the world.

I wish for my daughters such a place, such a knowledge. Not for a night, or a month, but for all the knocks of life.

Dear God.

They rolled apart, tossed into a pretense of sleep. That boy would walk away from this, get on with his studies, barely a ripple in his life. But Helen?

One o'clock.

Helen, oh Helen. Are you lying awake staring into the darkness?

Two o'clock.

"Robert." He turned from his own wakefulness. "She could have the baby and we could bring it up."

"Pardon? We bring it up? A baby not our own?"

"Partly our own."

But already the idea was dissolving into the indelible memory of babies, and the relief of seven years baby-free since Lillian and her hysterectomy. She was over fifty, for heaven's sake.

"Ridiculous," Robert whispered. "No more babies."

Three o'clock.

If Helen kept the baby, what then? Give up work, for how many years. Five? Could we send money for food, a flat, everything for five years? Or longer?

A heavy strangling clutched her stomach. "Oh, God, why did this happen to us?"

Three twenty-five.

How would the National Mortgage react to sending monthly cheques to a pregnant daughter?

Three forty-five.

There's my Family Benefit. The other children would just have to miss out. *Family* Benefit.

Four o'clock.

Blast those chimes on that grandmother clock. Every single quarter hour.

She isn't the only girl to fall pregnant. What do they do? Somewhere in Dunedin there must be a home for single mothers. Or up north. I never, ever thought I would have to find out.

Do I know anyone who has been given this same news, and lain awake till sunrise?

Four-thirty.

Stop that clock!

Helen must come home to recuperate afterwards. To get back to normal and help her forget. A fresh start.

As soon as she can get on a plane.

But she's made her own bed. Till then she'll have to lie in it.

55

Rose stared past the bed lamp into the dark corners, struggling to shake off the deep malaise that she could usually outwit during the day. "Don't think about her," Robert said. They'd hardly talked about it in the months since. Like the war, some things were best buried. Helen's sparse letters, hidden from the children, gave her new address, her living situation of light duties at a private Auckland rest home. She could stay until the birth. But every thought about Helen remained raw, every aspect of the situation squeezed until the space where Helen lived in her heart was crumpled to a tight ball. What she could hardly bear was her own failure, her failure to be the parent Helen had come to find. "Focus on the others. It's only six more months," Robert had said. "Helen must forget about it as soon as she can. So do you."

Meanwhile, Frances was bringing Geoffrey home to meet them in the school holidays. Tom was packed for camp, Lilly itching to get her hands on his guitar for three days. Adam was quietly smug about the teacher's words on his latest essay: "Witty and fluid in style. A promising writer." Much more engaging than her notes for tomorrow's mission meeting in Balclutha.

Someone she knew must have struggled with images of a daughter's pregnancy growing. Her isolation. Her inevitable loss.

※

Lorraine and Rose waited in the car, weary after an all-day forum. Lorraine unfolded the newspaper against the windscreen in the passenger seat. Rose glanced across at the headlines. "Record year for adoptions." Her heart stopped. Below in smaller print: "Domestic Purposes Benefit set to pass."

Lorraine's hand began to shake. Rose looked at her face transfixed by the page. "What is it?"

"My daughter." Lorraine whispered. "That's about my daughter."

Rose could not hold back. "Mine too." Their eyes locked. Gwen tumbled into the back seat.

"Ahhh. That's better. I've been thinking about what that speaker said, about mission needs closer to home, rather than boxing up everything for the Pacific. There might be some local families who could do with a help along. It would be harder with people you see every day, wouldn't it? It's easier to send things overseas, don't you think?"

Rose revved the engine and pulled into the traffic.

56

She rose early to watch the mists lift beyond the harbour, peeking through gaps in the hotel curtains. Coming back to Wellington always gave her a sense of homecoming, but like its existence on a faultline, each visit brought a seismic shift of perspective.

Directly below, taxi drivers huddled together, rubbing their hands. A flock of pigeons rose over the street lights, lifted, turned, vanished over warehouse roofs. What a bonus. Travel for the Health Board and visit your best friend after a ten-year absence.

At lunch Rose put down her knife and fork. "I thought I knew Patricia well enough to suggest inviting a doctor, a woman doctor, to talk about … ," she shaped the word silently, "… contraception."

Margaret tucked into her coq au vin.

"And Patricia said, 'Surely that's a confidential matter between you and your doctor.' Where were we supposed to find out anything? All my doctor said was 'Be careful'. Then, oh, the diaphragms." She shuddered at the horror of that first fitting.

"Everything was so invasive," Margaret laughed, leaning lower over the table. "Except famously unreliable rubbers."

"Robert hated them. Reminded him of the army." They sniggered. "When it came down to it, self-restraint was the only thing you could utterly rely on."

"The contraceptive pill would have changed our lives."

Rose smoothed her serviette over her lap and focused on eating for a few minutes. "Do you remember me writing about getting rashes? And fainting a lot?" she said. "I read somewhere those first pills had twenty times the dose we needed. Twenty times!"

She looked at her watch. Fifteen minutes until the next session.

"There's a workshop on health and fertility this afternoon. Funny how easy it is to talk to people who don't know your personal history. I just want country people to get a better service."

"We're no different."

"Maybe not personally. Life falls apart in the country if you're not healthy, though. It can take two days to get to an appointment in town and back. Two days for two people away from work. Then there's childcare and animals. But mention fertility issues ... people are so inhibited."

The waitress collected the plates.

"In other ways, we're less inhibited. Everyone knows your economic ups and downs, even if we don't talk about them directly. Most townies know little – you pretend you can't even see each other."

"Territorial instinct," laughed Margaret. "It's all about choice, dear girl."

"My neighbours don't even knock, just yoohoo on the way in." Rose dropped a sugar cube into her coffee.

"So no talking about family planning."

Rose shook her head. "Sometimes I think we're improving. You know how Professor Geering stirred up everything, including homosexuality. There's a male couple in the township. You get used to them being a bit odd. People accept them. One of them's keen on classical music."

"They're probably hiding." Margaret suddenly became tense, her eyes flashing. "They risk being imprisoned, you know." After a moment, she said quietly, "Jim's agreed to be on the committee for Homosexual Law Reform."

Rose's mouth dropped.

"Most of our friends react like that." She patted Rose's hand. "Sorry, I don't mean ... we both have family members. You wouldn't believe the vitriol, the persecution."

In the silence Rose waited, giving Margaret time to steady herself. Should she ask who she meant? No need. She'd known all along. "Country people *have* to be accepting, Margaret. At some point, we have to rely on each other."

But were country people as accepting as she'd said? Perhaps only if they conformed. She couldn't ignore the similarities between Margaret's concerns and Helen's situation: the secrecy and the shame. Especially the shame.

It was time she told Margaret what she'd been hiding.

The taxi driver turned up the radio. "Better see if there's any news about those Frenchies – think they can blast their nuclear tests here cos we're so far from France. Our Navy's sending two frigates." He caught her eye in the mirror. "Got your colour TV yet, Missus, ready for the Royal Wedding? Princess Anne and ... what's his name?"

"Mark Phillips." He sped up past a trolley-bus. "Have you seen old Selwyn Toogood on the telly? *It's in the Bag?* Better than the radio. Think I'll have a go. Prob'ly get the booby prize." He chuckled and concentrated on the traffic.

"A social worker who deals with adoption," continued the news, "is concerned about the predicted drop in the number of babies available once the Domestic Purposes Benefit allows single mothers to keep their babies." Rose sat stock still. "In recent years there has been an equilibrium between the four thousand childless couples wanting to adopt and the same number of babies offered for adoption. Childless couples may have to look beyond New Zealand." The driver switched the radio off and turned into the taxi rank.

※

The Friendship descended over Silver Peaks towards Taieri Airport. More than twenty years ago she'd come home in a DC3, baby Frances inconsolable from the pressure in her ears. "Shhh. Shhh. We'll see Daddy soon. He'll be so happy to see you." His letters were full of missing them both. On the way north, the three-day train trek had been an adventure at first, the baby such an ice-breaker. But feeding a baby in public had thrown her. After the privacy of her cabin on the Lyttelton ferry and the semi-darkness of the overnight train, there had been nowhere private on the crowded bus to Tauranga, squashed next to a shipping engineer even if he turned the other way as she fed Frances under a shawl. Frances arrived unsettled, Rose exhausted.

The house at Otumoetai had been built by then, but what an unexpected gift from her parents, that flight home. Frances had stopped crying the moment they landed.

But Robert was not there.

For half an hour she had sat on her suitcase. Robert ran towards them looking sheepish. His first visit to the airport, thinking he knew the roads, seeing a plane land from the wrong direction in a car that had to be run in at twenty-five miles per hour. His hands slumped by his side. "Forgive me?"

"Of course. Let's go home." He'd wrapped his arms around them both as she had imagined he would.

※

Today, no baby – heavens, Frances was married – just her satchel in the overhead rack. Across the tarmac she could see Robert's hat. And his camera.

She smiled in a half-hearted pose. He let the camera hang and came towards her.

"How have you been?" she asked.

"Ticking along. And your meeting?"

"We won't know till the Budget."

How could she convey the exhilaration of discussing the health of the nation in a way that included country people as more than the invisible afterthought of policy making? Such a responsibility, and smugly she'd had to admit that medical experts had listened, attentive to every comment she'd made.

But how could she convey the feeling of revealing, unpeeling herself each time she left her family and her hills to see herself anew, wholly herself, not his wife or the children's mother; rediscovering the girl she'd once been, enriched and embellished by the imprint of how they'd all influenced her.

And the enduring affection she had for Wellington, the tidal pull and thrust – attraction, repulsion – echoing faintly between visits. Come back to me, stay, escape.

She took Robert's elbow. "It's been brilliant. And demanding – I've never had to read so much every night. Margaret sends her love. And my brothers." Robert lifted an eyebrow. "Wellington wind's not bad when you're looking at it from a hotel window. My very first hotel."

Ten years ago she would have seen his lack of understanding as a failing, a lack of empathy, that they were doomed if they didn't comprehend each other's every need, want and passion.

Now she accepted it. Why should he understand? How could he? He was her life, just not the whole of it.

57

Rose stirred the cocoa into the mixture, her left arm clutching the bowl on her hip. The traditional Edmonds chocolate cake recipe. Extra vanilla; he liked that.

She poured the mixture into the tin and set the oven timer.

Adam chugged his motorbike to the rise under the pear tree and beckoned: come, now. What was he after? She was still anxious about his safety, at seventeen, travelling country roads where no one expected a motorbike to rise over a ridge.

But he'd earned it, working this year before university. His employer had praised his speed at picking up new ideas and his empathy for animals.

"Hey, Mum. Come for a ride?"

Do I want to hold onto my boy, feel the air in my hair and put my life in his hands? "Just a minute. I'll get a jacket."

※

They cut across tracks and bumped around the edge of the swede paddock. Robert was planting another block of blue gums.

"Let me off here, Adam. I'll walk home." Today the air was so clear the Blue Mountains folded into layers of indigo. She could imagine precisely where the fruit trees snuggled into the Teviot Valley, and where the Clutha River plunged over the Roxburgh Dam and charged to the sea behind her. This was still her favourite spot, the twin peaks of the Remarkables in quiet command of the skyline a hundred kilometres away.

Under her feet, the rolling hills and green pastures Robert never wanted to leave.

Neither did she.

He waved. Still exhilarated by the ride, she moved quickly across the paddock, cheeks flushed, hair blown free.

"Do you mind that we've never built here?"

Robert cocked his hat and rubbed his right hand around his neck.

Fragments of gum clung to his wide-brimmed hat and poked from his shirt. "Ideal site all right. No. Doesn't stop us from coming. Might not be a house for us, but the shelter will be ready for the next generation. These trees will be worth a bob or two eventually."

Rose ran her hand down the side of his face. "That doctor did such a good job with the stitching." She kissed him on the cheek. "Cake's in the oven. Can't let it burn," she laughed. Glancing back, she waved and walked on, swinging her skirt, knowing he would still be watching.

58

ROSE LAY IN BED warming her feet on the hot water bottle. Her whole body felt cold after the phone call from Sydney. Bella's engagement was off.

She had sounded more relieved than distressed, but so far away. Rose had liked Gavin, once they understood his strange colloquialisms. She'd even become used to the idea of Bella marrying an Australian. Should she go over? She couldn't have while they were "living together", not that those words needed to be spoken aloud. This generation was in such a rush.

Yet this straitjacket of morality was so constraining. We lock our shames in dark corners, she thought, so concerned with walking the path of respectability, forgetting forgiveness and turning the other cheek and seventy times seven.

Perhaps it wasn't such a bad thing that couples were knocking holes in old conventions, finding incompatibility before it was too late.

※

Six months later, Adam sat astride his motorbike, visor up. Most of his belongings were already at Lincoln University after their January visit, but the saddlebags bulged with music tapes, packages of baking and food from Aunt Marion. At least that was what she hoped they were full of. She squeezed one jar of blackcurrant jam in each side.

Robert had agreed that Adam needed a broader understanding of soil and crops, animal breeding and business management. And here they were. First son off to university. Robert said his goodbyes and turned away, leading the dog towards the kennel.

Rose wrapped her arms around her boy with a deep sense of imminent loss. "It's good to know you're heading towards what you really want to do, isn't it?" she said.

Adam's eyes stared at her. His helmet strap under his chin moved in a swallow. "Actually, Mum, if you genuinely want to know – I wanted to be a journalist." He held her gaze for a moment. Then lifting his fingers in a wave, he looked over his shoulder towards his father, revved the engine, tooted and left the farm behind.

Rose stood still. Surely he didn't mean it. Could he? Why didn't I ask him before? She stroked her hands down her apron. The elastic cord binding her to her eldest son stretched into an unending thinness as the roar faded into the distance.

Does Robert have any idea?

She walked slowly into the empty kitchen. The echoes of their arguments bounced off the silent walls, intersecting, shedding every memory of meaning. To tell Robert would be devastating. Or had he guessed?

To not tell him would be dishonest. Or considerate, perhaps, marking time.

If Adam is to become a journalist, he will find a way.

Perhaps it's a passing phase.

Was he telling the truth? Or firing a poisoned arrow at her heart?

Something in the air had lightened, a pressure lifted. Adam was taking a step along his own independent path. What was I expecting? It's time.

❦

"I feel quite shaken," Ness said as Rose dropped her at her gate. "We mustn't let this lie. See you on Sunday."

Rose pulled out along the gravel road. What a mixed afternoon. Top points for baby knitting, classic sponge and her chrysanthemums. But the pleasure had been swept aside by the speaker's message. Danna Glendinning, from the Waikato, brought a warning. "Is your stake in your own land safe?"

Women of the land must think of their roles as equals, not husbands first, children second, themselves a distant third if they mattered at all, Danna had said. Farmers' wives must go to lawyers and accountants with their husbands and understand their full economic situation. This was not about disparaging men but encouraging women to become actively involved.

And if they didn't? In two recent cases, the court had decided that the wife had no legal right to stay on the farm after the death of her husband. She had no money to buy a house elsewhere and no right to sell the farm to recover any, despite working there all her married life.

A farmer's wife could be forced from her home, her friends and her community, with nothing. What an awakening.

Rose pulled into the garage and sat thinking. When she'd feared for Robert's life, she'd worried about the children's future, not her own. Robert accepted her at appointments with the accountant now, but she still thought in terms of being helpful to him and to the children's future, not as an equal partner. An inherited farm was so different from Frances and Geoffrey having joint ownership of their first city home.

Husbands should have been at the meeting. The Matrimonial Property Bill was overdue, but theirs too. Meanwhile, Lilly was bringing Patrick home for the weekend.

※

Lilly and Patrick. There was more going on than a romantic stroll. They walked hip to hip. Was that the slow opening of the spare room door in the night? How could she catch Lilly alone?

"I'm taking Patrick to the cattle yards with me," Robert called through the kitchen window. "Lilly can catch up when she's out of the shower."

This time she must be bold.

"Lilly."

"Mmmm?" She lay on the floor with her nose in an Asterisk book, her wet hair dangling in front of the heater.

"Oh dear, this is hard for me."

Lilly sat up. "What is?"

Rose perched on the edge of the sofa. "You and Patrick are pretty close. Am I right?"

Lilly pursed her lips and nodded, a startled look in her eyes. "You're not trying to break us up? Just because he's Catholic."

"No, no, no. We like him."

Do it, she told herself. "I just wanted to be sure you had … thought about protection."

"Protection?"

She swallowed. "I think it would be a good idea if you were on the pill." There. She'd said it.

Lilly stared at her.

"I've seen what can happen. Look, just make sure you don't have any babies until you are ready."

Lilly hung her head and blushed. "Mum. It's OK." Rose tried to read her expression.

"We went to a doctor together."

Rose flung herself back on the sofa and laughed. "Well, that's a relief." She bounced up. "Cup of tea?"

59

"I THINK WE SHOULD EXPAND the survey," Rose said to Barbara in Dunedin, shuffling papers. "These replies are surprisingly supportive of female farm workers but imagine the results if we covered the whole country."

"This is astounding." Barbara looked through the pages of Rose's report. "Most farmers have volunteered advantages. What about whether they'd support their own daughters into a farming career?"

"That's the biggest surprise – most of them say yes. But will they in reality?"

Barbara was silent for a moment. "Expensive, going nationwide. Good timing, though. Dominion Council's coming up, Federated Farmers conference after that."

After lunch back home, Rose settled on a more personal agenda. Someone had proposed her for Rural Woman of the Year. Thank heavens she had gone to Toastmistress. The topic? "Women's role in the country – the next ten years."

The phone rang.

"It's Ness. I couldn't wait to hear about the Southern Cross."

"The royal lunch?"

"Did you meet her?"

"The Queen? No," laughed Rose. "They were far across a crowded room."

"Did she speak?"

"Her limit is three speeches a day apparently. The mayor spoke – seems we're a commonwealth of volunteers, just like us."

And they served wine. Rose and Robert had reached for their glasses at the same instant, sipping the sweet taste of summer, a taste Rose couldn't decide if she liked. "Don't drink it all," whispered the woman beside her. "It's for the toasts." She felt more naive than she had for years.

"How's the speech going?" Ness asked.

"Just starting."

"You'll knock their socks off."

Women's role in the country? Now field days for women were flourishing. Women ran finances. They hired someone to cook, to free them for tractor work or milking cows. The whole notion of partnership had changed. Fewer children, more working in tandem.

The speech grew on the page, full of the opportunities country life offered. Be realistic, she told herself. This is no picnic. Confront the hours alone with small children and later once they've gone. The distances. The dangers. The farmer who lay injured under his tractor for six hours, the lack of activities for teenagers who fill the void with slalom driving, tanked with Dutch courage.

You don't set out for personal satisfactions when you're working for a community but that's the result. Friends made along the way. A most satisfying life, the more so when it's been a struggle.

She wouldn't mention her decision to resign from much of it. Something else was calling for her total attention.

The pages filled with stories, saluting the vision of creative women – and men too – respecting the land, feeling rain on their faces and sun on their backs. Finding love in the hay paddocks.

❧

"A new photo?" Rose pulled her chair closer to Robert's pile of mail.

"Look at this – Adam's Chamberlain tractor. Twice the size of mine. Dual wheels. The cultivator must be forty foot wide."

"Not a tree for miles," Rose mused, leaning on her elbows. "He's found the landscape he was after."

Rose turned the photograph over to read his enthusiastic caption.

"He's not coming back, is he?" Robert said quietly.

❧

Rose took her by the arm, loosely so that Aunt Marion might think she was directing her own momentum towards the front door where the sun streamed into the hallway.

"Are we going to the library?" Aunt Marion asked.

"Much better than that. I want you to help me with the gardening."

"Shall I drive?"

"Not today. We'll just walk." Aunt Marion suddenly sped up, her physical vigour intact. Rose hooked the familiar round cane basket over her arm. Aunt Marion tried to shake it off.

"Can you hold these?" Rose put the secateurs into her right hand. Her fingers closed around them. Rose pushed a protective glove onto her left hand. "See all the deadheads on this rose bush?" She gave Aunt Marion's wrist a gentle pull. "Cut them off and put them in your basket. Just like last year."

Aunt Marion stared at Rose, her blank eyes gazing past her, the secateurs adrift in a royal wave.

Rose tried again, moving Aunt Marion closer to the bush. But she pulled away, shaking the glove off, frightened, and sank into the cane chair. "I'll make girdle scones for Neil," she said, shutting her eyes.

Rose slumped down on the front door step, her head in her hands. Aunt Marion, the last parent alive, was no longer able to put her clothes on correctly and was just as likely to take them off again. People were right. She couldn't continue caring for her, up several times in the night with her wanderings. Rose wanted to keep her here till the end, but it was becoming too hard.

She peered down the dark and silent passage. Light streamed in from open bedroom doorways, filtered through swaying branches of the silver birch trees, dancing and floating like ghosts.

How empty this house is without the children.

There is another conversation I must have. Soon.

60

Rose watched as Helen changed her daughter's nappy on the lounge floor. A happy child. Intelligent eyes.

Three days to enjoy Josie, her first grandchild.

Not her first grandchild.

"Up you come. Sleepybyes." Helen carried the waving child into the bedroom.

It was time. There was no one else here.

"Cup of tea, Mum?"

"Come and sit down. Here." Rose patted the sofa.

Helen moved slowly towards her. "Sounds serious. Are you all right?"

Rose took her hand and looked down, tears coming to her eyes.

"What is it? Mum, what is it?"

Rose looked up, chewing the corner of her lip. "I've waited too long. Far too long."

Helen looked puzzled.

"A few years ago you came to me in a very difficult situation. We were ... I was shocked. Scared for you." A lump came to her throat. Words struggled to find shape. "All I did was turn my back." She covered her face with her handkerchief. "I regretted it far too late. Oh Helen, I am very, very sorry."

Helen remained silent, her face pale and sagging.

"I've watched you pick yourself up. Look where you are now, with Simon and Josie. But I gave you no support."

"You couldn't," Helen whispered.

Rose put up a hand to stop her interrupting. "In effect, I disowned you over critical months." She looked down, shaking her head. "You should never have had to face that alone. That brave decision. That terrible decision."

Helen took her hand and breathed more rapidly. "I made myself forget. I've pushed it so far back. The only way."

"Today – it's such a short time later in the large scheme of things.

With the Domestic Purposes Benefit now, I can see how young women can manage." Rose pulled her hand away and wrapped her arms around her own body. "We were so blind. So tied up in our own restrictions. I've wanted to say this for a long time."

Helen's face was streaked with tears. "It was the blackest, loneliest time of my life."

She pulled her mother into her arms where they held each other, each in a different part of the memory. Each with a loss that forgetting would never erase.

"I know he's with a good family," Helen said quietly into her ear. "He'll be loved and looked after, much better than I could have done. I understand what you did. If there's anything left to forgive, you're forgiven."

A car pulled into the garage.

Simon came through the front door into Josie's room.

"Mummy. Look at me." Josie swayed, a long red sash looped around her neck, the gold-tassled ends to her knees.

"What's this?" asked Helen, turning the folds over to read the letters. "Rural Woman of the Year. It's your sash, Mum. That's precious, Josie, we'll take it off gently."

"Leave her. She may deserve it one day more than I did," Rose said quietly.

EPILOGUE

Rose sits on the verandah admiring the garden. Rhododendrons elbow each other around the perimeter in a show of apricot and cerise. Full buds cover the camellia Robert bought last winter after Aunt Marion died. The dogwoods, azaleas and forsythia are aquiver with small birds. Her lilies have multiplied into confident clumps.

If she were speaking the truth (and she values truth, though not too honest a truth to hurt oneself on the barbs of it) she would admit that moving to a small house a mile down the road for six months was not just to get Robert off the property. It was for her, too, a buffer against creeping sadness, regret and (admit it) grief; such a paradox, that a city Women's Division of Federated Farmers branch waits to welcome her.

One thing is certain: she will not stay to share a house with a new daughter-in-law for three years. Or two years. Not even one. If.

How could she not be here for the first freesias scenting the spring air, the blossom of her orchard trees, or the tui singing from the kowhai over the woodshed? And the mists lifting from the hills, lambs tripping over their own lanky legs on warm evenings.

She wraps her fingers through the handle of the teacup. Somewhere behind the feathery maples, where weightless leaves lift and nod, are the looping wires of the elegant old fence, Alice's fence, still keeping sheep from chomping through the hebes and the michaelmas daisies.

Far off a farm bike roars up a hillside. Stops. A farmer commands his dog to muster the stragglers from the opposite face. They run the wrong way. This she knows from fragments of sound, word and tone.

And that dinner will need to wait another hour.

She sees herself again, sitting here thirty, no, forty years ago, on this step. Full of optimism and energy. Love had caught her up and whisked her into this unknown place, set her life on an uncertain course. No expectation of wealth or fame. Just a happy life. And the land had tossed and tugged at her heart, drawn her into itself.

Now she must push it away. Disentangle. Help Robert disentangle. Every journey begins with a single desire. And a singular pain.

The land lives on.

It is no longer her turn.

Tom bounds up the back steps and calls through the empty house.

"Out here," she replies. So much depends on Tom's decision. Is the family to be lost to this land or rooted more deeply by the next generation?

His frame fills the doorway in a heartbeat, hands pressed into the sides of the door frame, lunging his body forward. He can't keep still for a moment. He turns his back to the sun and stands in front of her, his mouth shaping and reshaping something significant. Robert appears, shirt sleeves rolled up, looking pleased with the world.

"It's settled," Tom announces. "Julia's agreed about the farm. We'll move in before hay-making."

ACKNOWLEDGEMENTS

Over the years of this book's preparation, my family has shared many personal stories that I have woven into the texture of the narrative. Janet, Ailsa, Ian, Bruce and Isabel, I owe you more than I can say. Thanks to Ian Baumgart for setting me right about details of trams in wartime amongst many things, and Margaret Robb for her tales of life in wartime Wellington.

Thank you to my daughters for their responses to early drafts and especially Rachel for her detailed feedback, which assisted me towards a sharper perspective.

Georgina McDonald wrote *Grand Hills for Sheep* many years ago. After reading it at seventeen, I learned it was about my ancestors, Scots farming families finding their place in Otago. Her silent voice kept telling to me to write about rural life too.

In the writing world, thanks to Tania Roxborogh for giving me the push to get started and to Diane Brown, tutor extraordinaire, for wrestling with my early writing.

I appreciate being awarded a Society of Authors manuscript assessment at an early stage and the feedback of Rae McGregor. I am especially grateful to Geoff Walker, editor, for his professional guidance.

All my writing group friends have offered me support and critical contributions: Ann Horner, Gweneth Williams, Laura Lewis, Kura Carpenter, Sinead Holmes, Trish Saunders, Beverly Martens, Rachel Stedman, Philippa Jamieson, Kimberley Beale and especially Jane Woodham.

Particular thanks to Gay Buckingham who has gone the extra mile, reading the penultimate text and nudging me towards the truth.

Thank you to all the unsung heroes, the women of the land who can now call themselves farmers, who demonstrate adaptability, expertise and quiet resilience. New Zealand depends on you.

And special thanks to my husband Tony who has lived it all vicariously.

REFERENCES

In the making of this book I have referred to many sources:

Diaries 1948-1980, Colin McCorkindale; Family tape recordings and letters; *Stepping Stones*, Jean McCorkindale and Ian Baumgart; *Standing in the Sunshine*, Sandra Coney; *As the Earth Turns Silver*, Alison Wong; *The Weekly News Those were the Days 1940s, 50s, 60s*; *The Outlook*, magazine of the Presbyterian Church of New Zealand; Minutes and Annual Reports of the Women's Division of Federated Farmers, Hocken Library; *Wellington's Hellenic Mile: the Greek shops of Twentieth Century Wellington*, Zisis Bruce Blades; www.paperspast.natlib.govt.nz; *Te Ara Encyclopedia of New Zealand* www.teara.govt.nz; https://en.wikipedia.org/wiki/New_Zealand; *Cracks in the Glass Ceiling, New Zealand Women 1975-2004*, Joyce Herd; *60s Chicks in the 90s*, Jane Tolerton; *Creating a New Zealand Prayer Book*, Brian Carrell; *New Zealand Country Women*, Michelle Moir; *The Way We Were: Wellington*, Valerie Davies; *The WEL history: the Women's Electoral Lobby in New Zealand 1975-2002*; YouTube recordings of Professor L. Geering from 1967; *Tomorrow's God*, Lloyd Geering; *Otago Daily Times*, 1967 issues, Hocken Library; *The Evening Star*, 1945 issues, Hocken Library; *Hot October*, Lauris Edmond; *On Active Service*, H. R. Mackenzie, 25th Battalion, 2nd NZEF, June 1996; *The Soldier Tourist*, Gunner N. H. (Joe) Brewer.

THE AUTHOR

Christine Carrell lives in Dunedin, New Zealand, with her husband, but often spends time in the hills around Arrowtown. She has travelled widely and lived in the UK, Canada and the Cook Islands. When not writing she enjoys choir singing, the visual arts and spending time with her daughters and their families. She began her working life as a radiographer but has worked mainly in education.